Lives Intertwined

I shiver at the thought I constantly try to push from mind, that Weldon *will* be executed. I promised Jack that if that happened it wouldn't haunt me forever, and the closer the date comes the more I realize I might not be able to keep that promise. In the beginning I linked his survival to mine, and now his demise might also mean mine. I cannot let this happen. . . .

Southern
Exposure

ANNE REED ROOTH

HarperPaperbacks
A Division of HarperCollinsPublishers

HarperPaperbacks
A Division of HarperCollins*Publishers*
10 East 53rd Street, New York, NY 10022–5299

This is a work of fiction. The characters, incidents, and
dialogues are products of the author's imagination
and are not to be construed as real. Any resemblance to actual
events or persons, living or dead, is entirely coincidental.

ISBN 0-06-101364-1

Cover illustration © 1999 by Edwin Herder

First HarperPaperbacks printing: August 1999

Printed in the United States of America

Visit HarperPaperbacks on the World Wide Web at
http://www.harpercollins.com

❖ 10 9 8 7 6 5 4 3 2 1

To my agent, Jane Dystel.
She knows how to hang in there.

Acknowledgments

The many lawyers and district attorneys who helped me with the legal aspects of this book are too numerous to name, but they know who they are and I'm grateful to them. I'd especially like to thank the superintendent of the Mississippi State Penitentiary at Parchman and the various officers who allowed me access to the facilities there, including death row and the inmates. I'll never forget the experience. My special thanks to Miriam Goderich at Jane Dystel Literary Management for her suggestions on making the manuscript better and to my editor, Jessica Lichtenstein, for guiding me through the waters to publication.

Oh what a tangled web we weave
when first we practice to deceive!

Sir Walter Scott

prologue

THE DEATH STAGE IS SET, GURNEY WITH ITS STRAPS ready, snaking intravenous lines cleared, automatic hypodermic syringes poised. The one-man act is about to begin. The green-walled execution chamber glows eerily, separated from the viewing area by two-way glass, and lends the impression of an aquarium.

A uniformed prison guard enters the small, square room. Before he can close the insulated metal door, moans and stressful protests intrude from far down the hall, death row. Members of the audience glance uneasily at each other, imaginations working. Tension marks their expressions. Perspiration dampens clothing. The tiered observation room is stuffy, smelling of sweat, stale tobacco, and cleaning fluids. The victim's family is present. They have long memories, haggard faces permanently etched by grief, but eyes lit with hopeful expectation that the final revenge will deliver a modicum of satisfaction, ease throbbing hearts.

The condemned has no family present. Two prosecutors from the D.A.'s office, along with members of the attorney general's staff, try to conceal expressions of triumph. Heavy with burden, the defense lawyers huddle close. Several police officers and a sheriff are there because their presence is required by law. Superintendent of the Mississippi State Penitentiary. The prison attorney. Representatives from the governor's staff. Two reporters. A novelist. All here to witness the grim exhibition that has been delayed by numerous appeals for six years.

All heads return to the chamber as the prisoner is led in by two gleaming black guards. He is trying to hold on to some last shred of dignity but losing it fast. His hands and feet are manacled, his eyes wild with fear, his face already ghostly. A clergyman follows, lips moving in rhythm with his slow pace. The prisoner is quickly strapped onto the table, bonds around arms, legs, stomach, and chest holding him in place. A trained staff member establishes an intravenous line into the condemned man's vein and attaches a cardiac monitor to his chest. The warden, along with a doctor who will pronounce the instant of death, are in the anteroom. A telephone awaits that last call from the governor. It does not ring. Hands on the clock point straight up.

The guards, staff member, and preacher back out of the chamber, slam the door, and seal it. Alone now, the prisoner opens his mouth, but the cries of agony and despair cannot be heard. The warden has already issued the execution order. The technician's finger moves slowly to make contact with the button that will activate into the intravenous line a series of chemicals. First, five grams of sodium Pentothal to cause unconsciousness, then 50 cc's, a lethal dose, of pancuronium bromide to paralyze muscles, and finally another 50 cc's of potassium chloride to stop the heart. In his final terror-stricken seconds of life, the prisoner strains against his bonds, turns toward the audience, and hollers one last word. *"Leona!"*

Suddenly his face turns into hers, and she becomes the condemned. She wakes up screaming. The clock is ticking.

1

THE LETTER MIXED WITH JUNK MAIL CATCHES MY attention. Postmarked Parchman, the envelope is rumpled, the pencil print smudged, and postage is due. I don't know anyone in the Mississippi State Penitentiary and never expect to since I'm not a criminal lawyer. However, the sender's name in the upper left-hand corner does ring a vague bell.

I glance at my secretary, who is watching me fan through the afternoon delivery. She suddenly busies herself at the typewriter, maybe trying to fix it. This is a bad drawback to a one-room, storefront type of office. She's disappointed at the lack of checks in particular and my ability as a rainmaker in general. Fellow southerners would say, "She has a mouth on her,"—their euphemism for smart ass. That's one of the reasons I hired her. Another is because she's deserving, was unable to secure office work elsewhere in town, and is saving to go to law school.

A third reason I hired her is that lawyers are supposed to have secretaries. Lawyers are supposed to have many things. Clients. Money. I don't have many of the first or much of my own of the second. Maybe it's because I really haven't put my heart into being a lawyer. I've written a few wills, closed two estates, handled two divorce cases, and sued several people. I won two cases and lost four. I've been in practice only a year and a half, if that's an excuse.

After I returned with a load of baggage, emotional and very, very real, from an extended stay in Europe, I entered law school with a twofold purpose: I wanted a way to earn my own living, however meager, and my father, a card-carrying member of the landed gentry in the rich Mississippi Delta country, thought I needed to redeem myself in the eyes of everyone. Other people's opinions have always been important to my parents, Lily and Byars, the Binghams, with a capital The. I had not only disappointed my father, I had horrified him. I knew better than to look to my mother for an ally, as she always deferred to him.

Feeling ancient and shouldering more personal responsibilities than other fresh-faced, eager students, I barely scraped through Ole Miss. "Leona Bingham, you're smart but don't apply yourself" was the professor babble I heard often enough, which incorrectly labeled me as lazy. It took me three times to pass the Mississippi bar exam. Some don't call that redeeming yourself, but I had fallen into a state of ennui from which I still haven't fully emerged.

I tap the envelope on the desk. "Tarsha, who is Robert Weldon?"

"You don't know?" Her perfect skin has the sheen of a melting Hershey bar, and her dreadlocks sway gracefully when she moves her head.

"If I did, would I ask?" Like Tarsha, I try to keep my tongue poised for a snappy rejoinder. Clever lines can mask a lot of feelings, I've learned.

She picks up a pencil and examines the point. "He's on death row. Has been for about six years. It's been awhile since the state has executed anybody, especially a white man, but after all kinds of state and federal appeals and rejections and lifted stays, Robert Weldon's execution date's been set for next month. It's election year, and the governor's plank is to come down hard on crime. He's a strong advocate of the death penalty and bucking for the black vote, so to show how fair he is, the governor is determined to execute a token white."

"Robert Weldon was convicted of?"

"Murdering April Brown, a black girl right here in Grenola, some years back, stabbed her to death. If it had been vice versa the case would have made more waves."

Her statement is right. The Deep South now turns a politically correct face to the world, but unfortunately the line in "Dixie," "Old times there are not forgotten," sums up our true racial attitude. Sometimes I think living here is like taking a step back in time.

"What's the scoop on Weldon's background?"

"I think he was about thirty-five at the time, poor, blue-collar worker. Hadn't lived in Grenola all his life. Guess you were still off in France at the time, or you'd have heard about it." Discarding the pencil, she taps a few typewriter keys, then looks at me. "Why are you curious about him?"

I hold up the envelope. "He wrote me a letter."

Her onyx eyes widen. "Wonder why?"

"Maybe he's looking for a pen pal." I slit open the letter, wondering why, too. How would a death row inmate know my name?

I read the letter, stick it back in the envelope, think about it, take it out again, and reread it, more slowly this time. I feel Tarsha's eyes boring into me and look up.

"Well?" she asks, a portrait of curiosity.

"Says he's currently without representation, fired his last set of lawyers. Claims he's innocent."

Tarsha looks incredulous, then amused. "And wants you to represent him?" She titters. "About the only way you could get him out is to stage a prison break."

"You do have a gift for words." I try not to take her statement so much as an insult to me but as it relates to Robert Weldon's own impossible situation. Weldon has to be bottom-fishing for a lawyer. I can't help him. Wouldn't know where to start, even if I considered such an undertaking, which I wouldn't. He is probably already doomed, but if I took up the gauntlet, his fate would surely be sealed. Anyway, we are all dying; Robert Weldon just knows when.

I take one last look at his letter, a smidge titillated by a sentence. He has tried to grab me by suggesting that I read I Corinthians 15:51–55 in the Bible. He is probably a religious nut who has found God while behind bars and facing his Maker. Robert Weldon doesn't have much time. I will write and decline so he can get on with his last-ditch search for a new lawyer. The state cannot execute a man who does not have legal representation. If Weldon can't find a lawyer, a deputy state public defender will be appointed.

I glance at the bookcases lining one wall. "Do we have a Bible by chance?" I want to look up the sentence, then forget about Robert Weldon.

"A Bible? We don't even have enough law books."

We don't have enough of anything in the office except my parents' old discarded furniture. A leather couch that sounds like old men farting when sat upon. Two faded wingback chairs that were once navy blue. Two scarred desks with cigarette burns in the leather tops. No plants, no pictures on the walls. Lily and Byars offered to set me up in a snazzy space, but I refused, wanting to arrange my own nest. I just haven't gotten around to it.

"I wonder what happened to J. Clyde Perkins? He represented Robert Weldon at first," Tarsha muses.

"J. Clyde Perkins represented Weldon?" I'm stunned. This man is the modern-age Clarence Darrow in the South, with fees to match his reputation. He heads the biggest law firm in Memphis, four floors of genuine rainmakers. I always heard there were no rich men on death row. "How could Robert Weldon afford such a lawyer?"

"Pro bono work, obviously."

I am still stunned. "Free? I never heard of J. Clyde Perkins working for free."

Tarsha shrugs. "Maybe he got an attack of humanity. Regardless of what they say about lawyers, some do have a conscience."

"J. Clyde Perkins doesn't lose cases. If he couldn't keep Weldon off death row, the evidence against him must have been strong. Either that or the prosecutor . . ." I stop in mid-sentence. The district attorney at the time of Weldon's conviction had to have been Jack Flannery, now the attorney general.

Tarsha finishes my sentence. "Was very clever and very effective. That case put the county D.A. on the state map." Her eyebrows lift. "Speaking of Jack Flannery—Junior, not Senior—you have a game at the club?"

I look down at my tennis warm-ups I'd worn to the office. "Yep, we do." We play several times a week and have since we've been able to hold tennis racquets. Jack was my first boyfriend, my love from grammar school through college. Then I dealt him a blow, for which I'm profoundly sorry. My parents gave me a trip to Europe for a graduation present which lasted longer than everyone expected. Jack waited years for my return, then finally married a girl from Texas. She died of cancer three years ago, leaving him with a young daughter and another bruise on his heart. He followed in his father's footsteps and became district attorney of Sunflower County. We've recently taken up where we left off, but the intervening years have exercised their toll on our relationship. It's still a good one, but not intimate like in our college days. Though Jack would never push, he gives every indication he wants to sleep with me again and progress from there. I'm ready for sex but not commitment, and one without the other would only lead Jack in the wrong direction. The past still has its deep hook in me.

I push back from my desk, rolling halfway across the room in my swivel chair. I clamp my tennis shoes to the floor to stop myself. "I'm heading to the club. See you in the morning."

"Yeah, bright and early so I can get a head start on all these bills." She pats the stack.

I cringe at the thought of our bank balance. "Well, we're about due for a call from Mrs. Pearson." This elderly lady constantly changes her will at any imagined slight from her son and daughter-in-law. Having her for a client is the equivalent of owning a small annuity.

"Tarsha, the mail's already gone out for the day, so type a letter for me to Robert Weldon and I'll send it first thing in the morning."

"Saying?" Her voice rises an octave, and her face registers a mixture of disbelief and shock that I might even consider taking Weldon's case.

"Saying I have to decline due to other commitments and I wish him luck . . . so forth and so on." I grab my shoulder-strap bag and leave.

I look toward the round bell tower that crowns the columned yellow brick courthouse. The chimes from the four clocks housed there echo through the center of town. Jack is probably already on his way to the club.

I pause a moment, studying the town. Robert Weldon has seen what I see, walked down the very same street, shopped in the same stores that I do, and I am free while he's locked behind bars, grasping for representation. But why had he chosen *me*? Maybe he hadn't. Maybe he'd written the same letter to a dozen lawyers to see who would respond. I toss the subject from my mind.

I hurry along the sidewalk of Main Street. Byars has been a major force behind the planning commission which allowed Grenola to retain its dignity with its original brick-fronted stores. Fast-food joints, discount houses, the small mall, and car dealerships have been relegated to the township's outskirts. I pass the quaint and musty old bookstore, the beauty salon where gossip is exchanged, the bank, and the two-story building where most lawyers and doctors have their offices. People have already flocked to the soda fountain in the drugstore and occupy ice-cream parlor chairs around small tables. I once rode my pony straight into the drugstore and ordered a cone at the counter. In those days I was full of "piss and vinegar," according to Byars, a man openly proud of his offspring, though I suspected he was always secretly disappointed I wasn't a son. He has Charles, my cousin and his nephew, to make up the deficit now that I've fallen from favor.

The Inn, all three stories of it, stands at the end of the town square. A scalloped puffy green awning tops the black front door, and privet hedges shaped into topiary triangles grow in large planter boxes. As kids Jack and I ran through the lobby and rode the elevator up and down as many times as possible before we got caught. I held the record with twenty trips. I remember those times with a sense of wistfulness. I

was a competitor back then, long before the radio
talk show personality advised listeners to "go out and
seize the day."

Jerking me back to reality, Mary Jessica Bond, a
fiftyish society maven who years ago inherited a fine
plantation to which Byars holds the mortgage, tod-
dles out of The Inn and into my path. She squints as
the sun hits her. Cocktail time has come early for her.
If rumors are accurate, I can't fault her for belting a
few.

"Well, Leona, I was just on my way to your
office . . . 'bout some business. Maybe you've heard."
Her eyes flick over my outfit with a hint of disdain,
but she quickly checks her reaction. She can't say I
overdress.

I stop. "What's up, Mary Jessica?"

"After all these years Albert and I have split up.
He's gotten involved with this . . . a younger woman
from Natchez." She says this quickly to have the preamble out of the way. "Now here comes the rub."
Her mouth tightens. "He thinks he's entitled to half
my land because he's worked it and improved it, and
I intend to fight him tooth and toenail. There's no
way in hell any judge in this town will award *him*
what's mine."

Albert's originally from Kentucky and still considered an outsider in the community, so she's probably
right in the long run. However, the court battle will
likely be protracted, being a field day for opposing
counsels who fatten their wallets off other people's
bitterness. I'd suggest an equitable settlement, but
Mary Jessica wouldn't buy it. Although this smacks of

a push from Byars in my direction, somebody has to do the job and I need the money. "Who's representing Albert?"

"Davis Howard from Pitts, Moody, and Morris in Jackson." Instinctively Mary Jessica draws her purse closer to her body. "What's your retainer fee, Leona?"

I take a deep breath. "Ten thousand dollars."

Her eyebrows arch. She glances toward the office building across the street. "Ten thousand? That's what the Buchanan firm here charges." She appears primed to say more, like lawyers' fees should be commensurate to their abilities, then visibly relaxes, obviously considering her case a slam dunk anyone could handle. "Fair enough."

"Why don't you come to my office tomorrow and we'll get the ball rolling?" While Robert Weldon is desperate for my representation, Mary Jessica barely deigns to allow me the privilege.

"I'll come after lunch. I don't like to be out and about too early."

The case doesn't appeal to me, but the fee does. I cross the street built over Indian Bayou, the lazy body of water dividing the town. A deep-shadowed carpet of greenery borders the water, and cattails grow in abundance around the banks. Shawled with gray moss, giant ancient cypress trees spring from the middle of the murky water and cypress knees jut up like gnarled old fingers.

I climb into my blue Ford Bronco and head toward the country club, driving down Percy Street, where the oak trees meet in the middle to form an emerald tunnel. A few more cases like Mary Jessica's and I might be able to swing a small place here. Though the architecture of the houses is different, I like the sense of continuity, of heritage, of quiet dignity about them. Most of the residents' parents and grandparents lived in the homes before them. I could easily imagine someone's ancestor languishing on one of the verandas with a mint julep.

On the outskirts of town, I pull into the winding driveway leading to the country club. Mimosa trees, whose blooms look like spiky Christmas ornaments, and tall magnolias dot the sweeping lawn. The clubhouse is a long, dark brick structure fronted by white columns and green shutters on the windows. I stop in the parking lot filled with Cadillacs dusty from gravel plantation roads. A statue of a jockey in bright racing silks stands guard over the area. I've often thought of lashing a bridle from my Ford Bronco to the metal ring in his hand.

I check my image in the mirror. The sun has streaked my wheat-colored hair, which is frizzy and about as manageable as a Brillo pad. I apply lipstick and grin to make sure I haven't colored my teeth. I've inherited Lily's clear skin and eyes green as clover. No one calls me beautiful, but Jack uses the term *striking*. That's good enough for me.

I pass through the club foyer toward the locker rooms. All the Mary Sues and Barbara Anns and Baby Janes of Grenola are playing cards in private rooms and sipping daiquiris. They smile and wave. I do the same and keep walking. They wouldn't dare slight me, Byars Bingham's daughter, to my face. But wait until I'm out of sight. Their heads will almost collide, and their tongues will waggle with delight about Leona Bingham and her past. They'll speculate how Jack could be governor or attorney general one day, if he had the right wife, one with no skeletons in her closet for the press to rattle. I'd have to agree. I broke his heart. I can't sully his reputation, though I sense he'd risk a career for marriage.

I peel the blue warm-up off my white regulation tennis dress, throw it in a locker, and grab my racquet. Heading to the courts in back, I cram on a hat and add dark glasses. The May sun is strong, promising a blistering summer. The *whap-whap* of a ball against the backboard is loud. Jack is warming up. He has a powerful serve, but I can beat him when a case he's prosecuting has cost him his concentration. All in all, we're pretty evenly matched.

I prop my foot on a chair by the umbrella table to tie a loose shoestring and watch Jack for a second. He's tall and lanky, and now that he's older, his shoulders are slightly stooped. A wedge of sandy hair that he constantly rakes back hangs across his forehead. He's gentle, comfortable to be around, and his sense of humor is unexpected by those who don't know him. In court he gives the impression of a simple country fellow, an Honest Abe, an Atticus Finch, who's struggling with the law, lacking in ability and bumbling through the case. I've almost laughed aloud at this performance he's designed to bloody the opposition. His ability takes my breath away.

I straighten and call, "Jack, you're wearing yourself out. I'll kill you."

"What, Gussie? No ruffles today?"

I touch my skirt. "Plain Jane."

"You? Never." He moves to the net. "Which side you want to start?"

"We'll spin. I don't want you saying I took advantage." We go through this ritual every time we play.

We take our places, and Jack serves. He aces me. "I hate you for that," I yell.

He laughs. "You'll get over it."

"Not in your lifetime." I crouch, ready to move, eyes on the ball.

Jack runs me all over the court today. For some reason I can't get a grip on the game. I bash the ball into the net so hard I knock off my sunglasses. I'm sweating and tired. I'd die before I'd call a halt to the match. I hold out for three sets. He beats me three-zip.

I half expect him to leap over the net like a triumphant John McEnroe or Boris Becker. He saunters off the court. "You kind of lost it today."

"You're a wizard at observation." I catch up with him. "You can buy me a drink for that."

We sit at an umbrella table. A waitress in a crisp blue uniform with a ruffled white apron takes orders, a Tom Collins for me and a tall lemonade for Jack since he's returning to his office. I fan myself with my hat until our order arrives. I savor that first cool sip.

He lays a hand on my arm. "Dad's coming in from Jackson this weekend. How 'bout dinner one night while he's here? I'll barbecue."

"Sure." I remove the cherry from my drink and place it on a napkin. "Speaking of your dad, he prosecuted Robert Weldon, right?" I don't know why I bring up the subject. Robert Weldon is like a pebble in my shoe.

Jack sips his drink. I notice the white rim around his tan finger where he's recently removed his wedding ring, ready to move forward with life. "Yeah, he did. Why do you ask?"

I squint up at the sun. For some reason I don't want to face Jack. "I got a letter from him today. He asked me to represent him." Without looking, I know two vertical lines have appeared between Jack's eyes as they always do when he's taken aback. I'm waiting for his reaction, but he doesn't answer right away. Jack has a tendency to analyze his words before speaking, so much so that I sometimes think he's been struck dumb. Maybe that's a good trait. I know I rattle off answers much too quickly and often regret them later.

"That would be a tremendous responsibility," he finally says.

Good answer, I think. Jack is much too kind to knock my ability by asking, "Why you?" or say that I'd have to stage a prison break to free Weldon. "Yes, it would. That's why I wouldn't do it. One of the reasons." I look at him. "Why do you think he picked me out of the hat?"

Jack rakes his hair back with his fingers. "Got me. He's from Grenola, but doesn't have any family. Maybe he wrote to several lawyers here. Want me to ask around this afternoon?"

I nod, wondering why I care. I don't mention the quote from the Bible that I intend to look up later.

"I know one thing. It takes a team of lawyers to research and mount any last-ditch appeals for a death row inmate. Virtually impossible without a staff to work on all the motions and miles of paperwork." He stares at me in case I have ideas.

"I know you must have gone to Weldon's trial. What kind of impression of him did you get?" The sun or the Tom Collins is making me dizzy. I decide not to drink any more.

"Oh, I was there. The courtroom was packed. Everybody wanted to see J. Clyde Perkins in action. Weldon didn't take the stand, but I've heard him talk. He's not an educated person, but he's intelligent, fairly well-spoken. Nice enough looking man." He stops and scratches his chin. "Funny thing, I remember that struck me. He looked so . . . so sincere. Naive almost. I don't suppose he looks like that now." Jacks sits up straight. "I do remember his eyes, the way he looked at someone. You can't be around him and not be affected by those eyes . . . penetrating, sort of hypnotic."

I pull the stem off the cherry and chew it. "What was his motive for killing that girl, April Brown?"

"She was pregnant. The prosecution—uh, Dad contended she threatened Weldon with exposure, demanded money. April's mother testified that her daughter was seeing a white man. She didn't know who, but said April told her that she was going to meet the man and he was going to pay for getting her pregnant."

"What led to Weldon's arrest in the case?"

"A policeman passing by picked him up close to

the murder scene, out by Four Mile Lake. Weldon had blood all over himself and was running down the road with the murder weapon, going for help, he said. Claimed he was walking home and heard this moaning, then saw this woman down in this little ravine. Said he looked out at the woods around the lake and saw a man running away, a white man, he thought. Weldon said the woman wasn't dead yet and that he climbed down to try to help. He said he didn't know her, had never seen her before. He pulled the knife out. Obviously they found his fingerprints on the handle, *only* his. The policeman that stopped, a witness for the defense in the trial later on, corroborated Weldon's statement by testifying he saw a man running through the woods, too, a few minutes earlier, but thought he was black. Hard to tell with the shadows in the woods."

I perk up, ready to punch holes in a story. "The knife handle had to be bloody, so when Weldon pulled it out, he could have smeared any other prints, or the killer could have worn gloves."

Jack grins. "Spoken like a true defense lawyer. Just what J. Clyde Perkins argued."

"And the policeman testifying he saw someone run away, too. Wasn't that enough to prove reasonable doubt?"

"It would have been in most circumstances. You should have seen J. Clyde Perkins gloat on the way back to the defense table after the officer testified on Weldon's behalf."

I was caught up in the trial, eager for more. "So then?"

Jack checks his watch and looks anxious to return to his office. "On cross-examination, Dad established that the officer, Ray Bell Crosby, and Robert Weldon were friends, fishing buddies. He didn't hammer but carefully and patiently, almost ad nauseum, had the officer go over and over his statement about seeing the man running away in the woods. Dad kept pinning him down, asking if he'd ever been out to that spot before and what he was doing out there. The officer testified that he was eating a late lunch he'd packed, as he often did there, the scenery being so nice and all. J. Clyde Perkins got nervous and agitated, figuring something was up."

Now I could almost feel it coming. "And I guess it was, huh?"

"Yep. Dad destroyed the officer's testimony and J. Clyde Perkins's case by putting this woman on the stand who discredited the officer about as badly as Mark Fuhrman was in the Simpson trial. Said she and the officer—a married man, incidentally—met out there often for a 'little afternoon delight,' if you call that having lunch. This brought the house down, and the judge banged his gavel like a sledgehammer." Jack checks his watch again. "I remember this vividly. After the courtroom was quiet, the woman looked at the jury and said, "I drove to that spot in my car, got out, and got in with Ray Bell. Now, I don't know how he could claim he saw anybody running in the woods when he was horizontal in the backseat of his car with me on top of him until we finished and left in our separate cars."

I suppose the testimony was humorous to some,

but I feel an inexplicable letdown. It never ceases to amaze me how a twist of one's testimony can shape another's destiny. "How many inmates are on death row at Parchman?"

Jack seems restless, tired of these questions. "Forty some odd. Many more blacks than whites. The last execution was a few years back." He sighs. "I guess Robert Weldon will be next, short of a miracle. One thing for sure, a lawyer never wants to give one of those guys false hopes." His eyes lock on mine. "There's always the few last-ditch motions and appeals, but there's not much legally that I can see that would actually help Weldon."

"I've passed by Parchman a million times on the way to Memphis. I guess you've been there . . . to death row."

Jack stands. "Yes, only they call it Maximum Security or MSU thirty-two C, not death row." He stares long and hard at me. "I don't think I slept a wink for nights after I saw it." He breaks eye contact and glances toward the clubhouse. "I have to get going."

I rise, mulling over what he said. Going to Parchman had to be a chilling, frightening experience. A job for the tough, not the meek.

He hesitates before leaving. "What are you doing tonight?"

I hate to dim the anticipatory glow is his eyes. "Going to the Big House for dinner." My term for my childhood home.

"Say hello to Lily and Byars. I'll call you before you go." His lips brush mine.

Jack heads for the locker rooms to shower and change. I skirt around the clubhouse to my Bronco and arrive at the school just as the bell rings. Yellow buses line the side street. An older honor student lowers the flag down the pole on the playground. I watch the children spill out of the three-story brick edifice where I attended grammar school. My son is building memories as I did. I can still almost smell the chalk and erasers, the lunches growing ripe in the lockers.

My eight-year-old bursts through the front door, his backpack strapped on and bulging with books. Red and yellow splotches of ketchup and mustard have turned his T-shirt into a Jackson Pollock painting. His blond hair glistens in the sun. He's a wiry little kid with a bucked-tooth grin that's going to cost me at the orthodontist. I marvel that I could have played a part in creating anything so special. I named him Byars, after my father, gave him my maiden name, Bingham, and call him Bingo.

"Hey, Bingo."

"Hi, Mom."

He hauls himself into the backseat. He usually sits up front with me. I turn around. His top lip is slightly puffy and maybe the red blotches aren't ketchup. I face forward and turn the ignition.

We cruise along, not speaking. He's usually full of conversation. I don't invade his privacy, figuring he'll eventually level. We have an open relationship. "So, how was school today?" That question seems an innocuous enough.

"Okay," he says.

I watch him in the rearview mirror. He has long, thick eyelashes that I would kill to have. His cowlick sprouts up like a plant on the back of his head. He stares out the window. It breaks my heart to see him troubled. I'd like to solve all his problems, but know that's not possible and not to his benefit, even if I could.

He leans forward and braces his arms on the back of my seat. "Mike Kelly called me that word again."

I feel an arrow in my heart. "Bastard, huh?" I contend that airing words disarms their potency.

"Yeah."

"And what did you say?"

"I said it wasn't a bad word because it was in the dictionary and he ought to look it up."

The first time this happened, I had Bingo find the definition in Webster's. He learned that the word defined a child born of two parents who were not married. Nothing more, nothing less. He felt better about it after that. "Then what happened?"

"I didn't hit him right off like I did before. You said not to, that I wouldn't be a wuss if I just walked away."

"But you did finally hit him?"

"Well, yeah, I had to. Kit Flannery heard what he said and walked over and bopped him across the head with her book. He drew back and was gonna hit her. I hit him first, then he hit me back and called me a frog, said everybody born in France is one. Kit started crying and went and told the teacher. Miss Woods fussed at her for hitting Mike, but she made Mike stay after school. Every day this week. He has to

write, 'I will not call people names' a hundred times
each day.'"

Bingo chuckles, and I can see in the mirror those
two big front teeth and that goofy grin I love. He's
okay for now, but I'm saddened to think that my
indiscretions will again be visited on my son. I try to
concentrate on something other than the past, but
Paris and Jean-Paul Patel take center stage.

Both the city and the man are intertwined, but
their images are slowly growing murky. Still, I have
on occasion vivid flashes of memory. We were introduced at a small cocktail party hosted by a French
couple I met aboard ship as we crossed the Atlantic.
Their apartment overlooked the Seine with a startling
view of Notre Dame. On their balcony Jean-Paul and
I toasted with champagne to "beginnings."

Charismatic, mercurial, the dark, curly-haired man
with twinkling sapphire eyes and a melodious voice
shut Jack Flannery from my mind as if he'd never
existed. I didn't realize I had thrown my soul to the
wind. Jean-Paul amused me, made me laugh, bought
me roses, put magic in my life, I thought. During my
tour of Europe he joined me in several capitals, and I
returned to Paris to be near him, taking a small
apartment with trust funds left to me by my grandmother.

We fought. We made up. We had nothing yet
everything in common. He loved America and often
visited relatives in New Orleans whose ancestors had
settled there before the Louisiana Purchase. He lived
in the back apartment of his aristocratic parents'
home on the fashionable Avenue Foch with week-

ends spent at their Bordeaux wine country château. I thought it strange, but tried to overlook the fact that he never introduced me to his family. In the end, I realized that although I came from what was considered a well-to-do family in Grenola, my background counted for naught in haute Parisian circles. The crushing blow came the day the doctor confirmed I was pregnant.

Before I broke the news to Jean-Paul, he arrived at my apartment that final day to disclose that his engagement to a titled woman was to be announced in Paris society. Their parents expected the marriage, and he could not disappoint the families or defy custom, as he and his betrothed had been committed since their teenage years. He was pained by the situation, but heartened that he and I could continue our relationship, following an old French custom to have a mistress, the true but unmarriageable love in the shadows.

Brokenhearted and unable to accept the role, I refused to see him again, but my curiosity demanded a glimpse of his intended, Michelle Armand. I staked out her address, and as she emerged from a palatial Avenue Montaigne residence, entering a chauffeured limousine, I followed her to the Ritz, where she joined a group of ladies in the bar. She was everything I painfully imagined, willowy, straight honey-colored hair, flawless skin, dressed in a haute couture suit that probably cost three thousand, gold jewelry, a buttery leather Gucci bag, legs like long stems, feet in alligator pumps with stiletto metal heels. Worst of all was the carefree attitude she displayed. Her friends were carbon copies. I felt as if the whole world were a tuxedo and I were a pair of brown shoes.

Amid cries and pleas from my horrified family to have an abortion and keep secret my indiscretions, I once more stood my ground. After months of agony and all alone in a Paris hospital, I gave birth to Bingo. With the exception of whispered calls from Lily, there were no cards, no flowers, no baby gifts, but my gift of Bingo was enough.

Reluctant to return home, we remained in Paris until my funds dissipated and I was left with little choice but to do what was best for my two-year-old. I figured we could survive the unpleasantness we were sure to encounter in more familiar surroundings.

We faced Grenola, but I was not the same as when I left. After floundering for a time, we moved to Oxford, Mississippi, for three years, where Bingo flourished in day care and I struggled through Ole Miss law school.

"Mom, do we have to go to the Big House tonight?" Bingo brings back reality.

"Lily and Byars like to see you." This is partially true, though they eye Bingo suspiciously when they think no one is watching, looking for flaws or traits they might find unacceptable.

He groans. "I have lots of homework."

"Then you'd better get started right after your snack."

Skirting around town, I head home down the deserted back way. We bump down a gravel road that winds through woods so dense the sunlight is diffused in odd angles. Taking this shortcut, I always feel that

I've slipped completely away from civilization. I love the forest and know it like the back of my hand. Byars taught me to shoot and hunt and fish and ride in this secluded area. I hope he'll do the same with Bingo. He needs a man to teach him things I can't.

Around a curve in the road the meandering bayou comes into view, its lazy waters host to cypress trees that grow towering from the muddy depths below. To the left, cotton fields stretch as far as I can see. The wealthy reside on surrounding plantations with such exalted names as Woodburn, Forkland, Deerfield, and Holly Ridge. The Bingham family's original ten-thousand-acre plantation, Fox Run, has grown with the absorption of other farmlands. Courtesy of Byars, my home is on recently annexed land. The place stood vacant for years, so I don't feel as if I'm a charity case.

I speed across the road that divides the bayou and enter the grounds surrounding the house, a row of weeping-willow trees lining the circular gravel driveway. The isolated two-story wooden Victorian, topped on one end with a turret and fronted by a wide porch—called the gallery in olden days—is my refuge from the world. Hydrangeas the color of bubble gum fill the flower beds. They need water. I position a hose on the plants and give Bingo a look. He's squirted me before when my back was turned.

Bingo's dog, a collie he named Mister Marvel, runs up, wagging his tail and panting. Bingo falls to his knees and hugs him, smoothing his pet's ears back against his skull. Mister Marvel shivers with delight and licks Bingo's hands.

We climb the steps to the gallery. White rocking chairs are lined up like soldiers at attention. A swing suspended by chains from the ceiling moves with the breeze. Bingo and I painted the floor a shiny gray when we first moved. I've added fern hanging baskets, and the overall effect is inviting.

I unlock the door, and we dash through the house to the sunny yellow kitchen. Mister Marvel collapses on the floor, limpid eyes on his master. Bingo sits in one of the captain's chairs at the round maple table. I pour a glass of orange Kool-Aid, his favorite, and add a saucer of chocolate chip cookies. He's talking non-stop about school and homework as he shrugs off the backpack like some insect shedding its skin.

"I'm going upstairs to shower and dress. You do the same after you've finished your homework and then we'll go. Okay?"

"Okay." He feeds Mister Marvel half a cookie.

I walk through the dining area into the living room. The house came furnished, not much to my liking, but I personalized it by painting the dining room table, chairs, and breakfront a Chinese red. I covered the couch and big, puffy chairs in the living room with a bright flowered chintz material. Lily and Byars, of course, offered to buy new furniture, but I preferred to turn what was already there into something special and put their discards to use.

I plunder through the bookcases that flank the brick fireplace, but can't find my Bible from Sunday school days among the books of my youth. It's probably boxed in the attic at the Big House, where Lily stores everything she doesn't use. She and Byars will certainly have a Bible on their shelves. I wonder what it's a testament to that I don't.

I tramp up the stairs, testing for creaks now that I've added an old Oriental runner looted from Lily's attic. I plan to plunder that musty, spidery place again soon for a desk for Bingo's room so he doesn't have to study at the kitchen table.

In my bedroom, I shuck off the tennis dress and shoes. Suddenly I hear a noise, a tapping sound. I'm glad it's not nighttime. Hurrying to the window, I brush aside the white organdy curtains, raise the window, and peer outside. The trellis, entwined with morning glories and reaching the guest room window, has broken free from the side of the house. Another project.

I shower, work on my hair with a curling iron, and dress in fresh stone-washed jeans and a white shirt with black embroidery around the collar and cuffs. The old pipes tell me water is running in Bingo's bathroom, and I smile. I never have to nag him about washing up or punctuality. He's a self-starter. I touch up my makeup, add gold loop earrings, and urge my feet into black cowboy boots. The phone rings. I plop on the canopy bed where I spent every night of my childhood and answer. It's Jack. I can always depend on his word, unlike another from my past.

"Leona, I've talked to several lawyers here at the courthouse, and none of them received a letter from Robert Weldon."

I trace the pattern in the soft blue-and-white quilt. "So, I guess he probably did single me out."

"Can't blame him for that. I do, too."

He warms my heart. I wish he made my blood rush. Maybe in time. "Thanks, Jack." I think about the letter. Why me?

"Leona, you're surely not even considering . . . just remember what I told you about going to Parchman's MSU." He pauses. "It'll do something to you."

"I'd just like to know why Robert Weldon picked me."

"Let it go, Leona. Parchman is full of desperate people waiting to die, and they'll grasp at anything to survive. I know a lawyer who had a client on death row who'd lost all his appeals. He went to see the execution. Gas chamber back then. He had to have psychological counseling for years . . . never was the same again."

I don't want to hear this. I check my watch. "Jack, I'm about to be late. Talk to you tomorrow, okay?"

Bingo and I meet in the kitchen. He's slicked down his damp hair and dressed in khaki shorts and a tan T-shirt. We feed Mister Marvel and drive the three miles to the Big House.

On either side of the driveway gray stone pilasters embedded with plaques announce the entry to Fox Run. We cruise down the long road bordered by giant magnolia trees. I never have a real sense of coming home. Everything is a stage set and the characters play their parts. The two-story columned house is Tara revisited. Fingers of ivy clutch the walls, and multicolored zinnias grow in curving flower beds. The entire scene looks as if it has been freshly varnished.

Byars and cousin Charles, along with his three

teenagers, brandish mallets on the croquet court by the side of the house. Byars looks like the typical Big Daddy in knife-pleat white pants and white shirt, a red ascot around his neck, and a plantation straw hat on his head. As always, Charles is his mirror image. Bingo likes the cousins, two boys and a girl, and wants to join them in a game.

I cut the engine, wave at the group, then head to the front door as Bingo scampers toward the court. Julius, the family butler, opens the door before I can. He's been with Lily and Byars since they married. His hair is white now, and his skin glistens like an oil slick.

"Evening, Miss Leona."

"Howdy, Julius." I hug him with affection, then glance up the winding staircase. Lily is fluttering down the steps, making her entrance. Her pink-and-green flowered dress ripples as she descends. A lace handkerchief is always tucked into her sleeve. Anyone can see that she was startlingly beautiful as a young woman. In an effort to sustain her youth, she wears her hair too long and applies too much makeup for a woman her age, which cancels the desired effect. Most consider her a bit fey, but I sense something sad about her, as if she hadn't received from life what she expected, that, like me, she's snagged somewhere in the past and unable to shake free. I've always wished for a close relationship with her.

She smiles. I have inherited her dimples. "Leona, I'm so glad to see you. Where's Bingo?"

"Outside playing. Good dress, Lily."

Estelle, cousin Charles's wife, comments from the

living room, "Yes, isn't it beautiful? We found it on our last shopping trip to Memphis." She walks into the entry hall, and we stand on the black-and-white-checked marble floor like pieces on a chessboard.

"Estelle, you don't look too shabby yourself. Great, actually." She's model thin with porcelain skin and raven-dark hair. The red dress is becoming. She would blossom if it wasn't for Charles. In my book, anyone who puts up with him is a saint. I've noticed bruises on her arms on occasion and hate to think what they might mean. If I knew for sure that he mistreats her, I'd tackle him with both fists. For certain I'd tattle to Byars, hitting him where it hurts most.

Lily gestures with her hand. "Let's all go out on the back terrace and have drinks. Lord have mercy, it'll be too hot out there before long." She turns and heads toward the open French doors at the end of the hall, high heels clicking on the floor.

"I'll be right there. I'll have a vodka and soda. Wedge of lime if we have it. I want to look up something in the den." I glance at Estelle. "We still have a Bible in the bookcases?" She now knows the house better than I.

"You going religious on us, Leona?" She has a good smile and white teeth to match.

"It's about time, don't you think?" I chuckle. "No, I just want to look up a quote I heard today."

"The old family Bible's where it always was." She follows Lily to the terrace.

The grandfather clock in the entry bongs the wrong time, as usual. Wonderful smells drift from the kitchen. Roast and apple pie. The food, down-home kind, is so incongruous to the royal surroundings. The living and dining rooms are formal—Oriental rugs over parquet floors, Queen Anne furniture, brocade draperies, carved mantelpieces—but the den is a man's room, Byars's room. Green leather wingback chairs flanking the fireplace. Knotty pine walls. Bookcases crammed full. A two-seater couch upholstered in a tartan plaid. A partner's desk. A stuffed deer head. Glass display cases with racks of guns. As a child, I loved this room best. I still do. It smells of cigars and long-extinguished fires in the fireplace.

I spot the gold leather book on the shelf. I ease onto the couch and open the Bible, glancing at the family tree on the first page, heavy on Byars's side, thin on Lily's. Like me, she's an only child. Her parents died young, left her a hefty inheritance, I was told. I know she has her own money. I page through until I find I Corinthians, then the verse, "Behold, I show you a mystery."

I reread it, trying to understand the meaning. I'm not sure what to make of it. What is Robert Weldon trying to convey? Puzzled, I rise and return the Bible to its place. I stare a moment at the framed needlepoint sampler my grandmother has stitched in bold gold letters, A QUEST IS AS IMPORTANT AS AN ACCOMPLISHMENT.

I retreat to the back terrace. Drinks in hand, Byars and Charles have joined Lily and Estelle, all seated on a grouping of black wrought-iron furniture padded with gray cushions. I peck Byars on the cheek, speak to Charles, and sit next to a glass table where my drink waits. The children are laughing on the croquet court. The sound of mallets hitting wooden balls is loud.

I sip my drink, thinking about the quote from the Bible and its meaning. Byars snags me with his piercing cornflower-blue eyes. His skin is tan and full of lines from the sun. Now that he's removed his hat, his shock of white hair is in slight disarray. He's a big man, and I was formed in his formidable shadow. He can make people tremble.

"You look like you've seen a ghost, Leona. Is that the thousand-yard stare I've heard soldiers get?" Byars lifts his glass of bourbon and swigs. "You with us?"

I shake off my thoughts. "Present and accounted for."

"Maybe it's lawyer fatigue instead of battle fatigue," Charles adds. He always wraps his sarcasm in a smile, hoping no one but the recipient will notice the barb.

I look at him, purposely searching his face. Prick. "Charles! You must not have gotten your vaccination. You're foaming at the mouth."

"Oh, hush up, you two," Estelle says with a nervous little laugh.

Lily abruptly changes the subject to some funeral she attended and the food they served. Byars lights a cigar as big as a weiner. Charles follows suit. I watch him emulate my father with distaste. He has Byars's good features, but destroys them with a perpetual frown he can't hide. No matter how hard he tries, he will never be the man Byars is. Charles was a bully growing up, but never showed that side to Byars. His father, Byars's brother, was not as successful nor as popular as Byars. After Charles's father died, Byars filled in the gap. Charles would like to be Byars's only heir, but here I am, messing up the line of succession.

Byars nonchalantly checks the end of his cigar. "Did you by any chance talk to Mary Jessica about her case today?"

"I did." I change to the subject that occupies my mind. "Charles, do you believe in the death penalty?"

"What do you mean?" He looks at me like I've gone mad. "You're not talking about Mary Jessica, are you?"

"Hardly. Do you believe in the death penalty? It's not a trick question. I just want your opinion. What about you, Byars? While Charles is forming his opinion, tell me yours." I gulp my drink. It goes down like a cold wire, and I'm ready for another.

Byars hawks out a doughnut of a smoke ring. "Well, yes, I'm for it. If someone takes another's life, they should have to pay with their own life."

Charles nods. "An eye for an eye. It deters crime."

I'm quick with a reply. "That's not what statistics say. There are close to two thousand inmates on death row in this country." I sling out this fact, not knowing if it's exactly true. Jack said there were about forty on death row at Parchman, so I multiplied that number by the number of prisons I guess there are in the United States. It sounds authentic. "Lily, what about you? How do you feel about capital punishment?"

Her eyes dart around, land on Byars, then move to me. "I would have to worry about someone who might be innocent." Count on Lily never to answer a direct question.

"Estelle?"

She looks at Charles before she answers. He doesn't like her to disagree with him. "I don't think anyone has the right to kill another person."

After those profound statements, Byars and Charles launch into the merits of capital punishment. I fix another drink at the pushcart bar and interrupt the conversation. "I guess you all remember the big murder case here J. Clyde Perkins tried."

"Robert Weldon," Byars says. "He killed that black girl."

Everyone jumps into the conversation with their version of the trial, except Lily. She dabs her forehead with the handkerchief and watches me. She knows me well enough to suspect I didn't bring up the subject for nothing.

I interrupt again. "I got a letter from Robert Weldon today. He wants me to represent him." This stops all conversation. Cold.

"You?" Charles finally asks, as stupefied as if I'd told him I was being crowned queen of England.

Byars worries on the subject before speaking, then sloughs it off. "Well, that might be a noble pursuit for some, but you have to think of yourself, guard against damaging yourself. I mean, surely you aren't thinking of such a thing. Bottom line, it's a lost cause. You don't need that. Besides, you'll be too occupied with Mary Jessica's case."

"You wouldn't want to get mixed up in something that . . . that dreadful, I know," Estelle adds. "Of course not." She smiles, confident of my prudence.

Lily looks directly at me. "What if that boy's innocent, though? Like everybody else, I went to the trial. He looked innocent to me."

Byars and Charles appear to want to laugh at her statement, but of course don't. It was naive of Lily, but I wonder if for once she is taking a stand, in her way, for me, thinking that I want the case. Maybe she thinks it's a chance for me to build a reputation as a lawyer. Of course, she doesn't understand all the legal ramifications of mounting last-minute appeals like Jack. He said it would take a team of lawyers.

Charles turns to me with his best smile. "And what about you, Lee? We haven't heard your opinion. Do *you* believe in the death penalty?"

I don't like to be called the diminutive of my name, or the intimacy it implies, and he knows it. I fake thinking over my answer, then face Charles with an earnest expression. "No, Charles, I guess I don't believe in the death penalty, or I would have gotten an abortion."

"Oh, my goodness!" Lily quickly knots her handkerchief under her sleeve and rises. "I'll call the children and let's all go in to dinner and not talk about this subject anymore. Somebody will represent that young man."

Yes, someone would. But he wants me. The quote from the Bible ripples through my mind. What is Robert Weldon trying to tell me? I might just drive up to Parchman tomorrow and find out, then tell him in person that I can't represent him. A letter will take time to reach him, and his days are precious. I remember Jack's words on the horrors of the penitentiary, the desperate people waiting to die, and feel a chill.

2

TOSSING AND TURNING, I RECALL JACK'S STATEMENT about his sleepless nights after a visit to Parchman's death row. I can't sleep and I haven't even been there. The trellis slapping the side of the house hasn't helped matters. When the first rays of the sun crack around the curtains, I bolt to the bathroom, throw water on my face, brush my teeth, and don my comfortable old terry cloth robe. On the way downstairs I consider checking on Bingo, but don't want to chance waking him. At this hour he's snoozing soundly, Mister Marvel at the foot of his bed.

With coffee brewing, I decide to make pancakes from scratch, a treat usually reserved for Sunday. I'm a better than average cook, nothing gourmet, but I produce simple food with no trouble. Sipping orange juice, I grab the griddle from the cabinet—and upset one of the clay flower pots on my windowsill. I clean up the dirt and ruined blooms, realizing I'm nervous.

I stopped smoking when I was pregnant, but keep a pack around as a reminder of how strong I am.

I rummage in the drawer, find the cigarettes, and light one with a kitchen match. The first drag hits me like a Mack truck. Pouring a mug of coffee to complement the vice, I settle at the table with an ashtray. Checking my watch, I decide to call Tarsha, an early riser.

I take another jolt off the cigarette. I feel dizzy. "Tarsha . . ."

"Anything happened?"

"No, I'm just up early. Mary Jessica Bond is coming to the office this afternoon. Wants me to handle her divorce. Ten thou retainer."

"Yes!"

I picture her raising a fist in the air. "My reaction exactly."

"Just like you predicted, Mrs. Pearson called after you left and wants to change her will again."

"Can do." I hesitate. "Listen, don't bother about writing Robert Weldon. After I drop Bingo at school I'm going to drive to Parchman and see him in person. He wrote that he'd put my name on his visitors' list, just in case." Parchman is about forty miles north of Grenola, so I can drive there in thirty minutes, tops. With no experience, I can't gauge how long it will actually take to pass penitentiary protocol before I see Weldon, but I should be back in my office before noon.

"Leona, surely you're not even thinking of taking on his case." Her tone is incredulous.

I puff on the cigarette, then crush it in the ashtray.

"No, of course not, but I just thought it would be . . ."—I search for a word—"kinder to go in person and not waste any of his time by writing a letter." Plus, I have things to ask him. "I'll see you around noon. Hold down the fort."

I whip batter, fry bacon, and set the table. Mister Marvel bounds into the kitchen and skids to a stop on the tile floor. In rumpled blue pajamas, Bingo is right behind him, his cowlick at attention. He rubs sleep from his eyes. "Yum. Yumo. Pancakes and it's not even Sunday." He plops down at the table and spots the ashtray. "Mom! You didn't smoke this cigarette!"

"Don't be fresh, kid." I smile and pour him milk. I open a can of dog food for Mister Marvel, fill his water bowl, and the three of us eat.

I leave Bingo with his chore of clearing dishes and go upstairs to dress. I decide not to shower since I did before dinner last night and know I'll want to after Parchman. Two in one day is overkill.

Standing before my closet, I mull over what to wear. I cringe when I recall a movie about a female FBI agent going to see an inmate. She is advised to keep to the middle of the hall lined with cells so that none of the convicts can reach out and touch her. She does as she's told, but is jeered at and spat on by maniacal prisoners, then hit with excrement and other unmentionable body fluids. My pulse accelerates and I'm suddenly ambivalent about going to Parchman.

As I apply makeup and tackle my hair, I light another cigarette, then remember other movies and television shows where lawyers in nice enough prison visiting rooms speak with their clients, but are separated by a thick glass partition reinforced with mesh wiring. Surely Parchman will be similar, and I won't be thrown within reach of violent murderers and rapists in a Bedlam-type setting.

I select a navy blue pantsuit to camouflage my legs and a white high-necked blouse that will be ringed with makeup by day's end. I try to sink into my clothes like a turtle into her shell. Slipping on navy low-heeled shoes, I take my matching shoulder-strap bag off a closet rack and study my image in the mirror on the door. Pure business, certainly not feminine enough to attract unwanted attention from sex-starved convicts with nothing to lose.

I stuff my rarely used monogrammed briefcase with yellow legal pads to appear the busy lawyer, and take a deep fortifying breath. I'm ready. Parchman, here I come.

I lock the front door while Bingo fills Mister Marvel's plastic bowl with water. He places it in the shade of the trees, and we pile into the Bronco, driving quickly to town. I drop Bingo at school with a promise to pick him up at the end of the day, then head to the intersection of highways 49 and 82 on the outskirts of Grenola.

I drive north, smoking another cigarette. To my left the levee snakes along the Mississippi River. As if flattened with a hot iron, the level land on either side of the highway stretches as far as the eye can see. The rich, sandy loam is grayish and planted with straight, long rows of blinding white cotton. The deep green, shiny leaves on the stalks have a neon quality. An army of red tractors manned by black men wearing bandannas to keep sweat from their eyes moves through a vast soybean field. I think of Robert Weldon and how he's locked away, never to glimpse such a scene.

I pass through rural towns, Sunflower, Drew, Ruleville, where pickup trucks are the obvious choice of transportation. Small convenience stores, service stations, and dilapidated shotgun houses blight these desolate places passed over by prosperity. I speed up, anxious to reach my destination and have my curiosity satisfied. I wonder what Jack and members of my family would think if they knew my destination.

As I drive, I recall some facts on Parchman I learned during the sleepless night from my book on the State of Mississippi Penal System. Housing close to six thousand inmates, it's a working farm approximately seventeen thousand acres large, made up of thirty different camps or units. The separate HIV camp has 180 infected prisoners. The MSU, particularly Unit 32C, are the high-risk areas, and Unit 17 is home to the gas chamber and lethal-injection room. Colored clothing denotes prisoner classification, green and white horizontal striped pants for trusties, or low-risk convicts, black and white for medium security, red and white for maximum security, and red jumpsuits for those condemned to die. Death row inmates, the only ones allowed televisions and radios in their cells, do not work, and labor by other inmates is voluntary—either that or they remain locked in six-by-nine cells all day.

Suddenly a yellow road sign jolts me back to reality, and my eyes hold on the words STATE PENITENTIARY—5 MILES. Instinctively my foot lifts off the accelerator. A sense of unease grabs me, as if I've been warned of an approaching danger or hazardous restricted zone. I have a choice. I can wheel around on the highway and go home. On the other hand, I will never understand the message behind the quote from the Bible and why Robert Weldon picked me.

My foot connects with the accelerator, and I roll down the window for a breath of fresh air. The day is a scorcher, hot and sticky, like suffocating under a blanket in an overheated room. Dust devils, resembling little tornadoes, swirl across the dry fields. I round a bend, and the prison looms to the left of the highway. An arch with the words MISSISSIPPI PENITENTIARY spans the entrance. Watched over by a rifle-toting guard on a horse, a gang of inmates wearing green-and-white-striped pants, trustie garb, chop weeds and pick up litter along the highway. I wonder about their chances of escape, if they could possibly make it to the Bronco without being shot, commandeer it, and drive away in a rain of bullets with me as their captive. This is not a comforting thought.

I turn off the highway and stop at the guardhouse just past the arch, not knowing what to expect. Maybe they have visiting hours like a hospital and will turn me away. A uniformed guard with a pistol on his hip steps out and leans into the window. "Hep you?"

"Ah, yes," I say, trying to maintain a firm voice. "I'm a lawyer, here to see a Robert Weldon. He's on . . ." I almost say death row but remember that Jack said it's called MSU. "He's in MSU, thirty-two C." I don't want the guard to think I'm some rookie.

The guard reaches for a clipboard from another guard in the gatehouse. Sweat discolors the armpits of his shirt. "Name, please, ma'am."

"Leona Bingham."

"Client's name's Robert Weldon you said."

"No." I lean out of the window. "He's not my client. I'm just here to see him." I wonder if that makes a difference. Maybe I should have lied. "My name's on his visitor's list," I say with some authority.

The guard walks to the back of the Bronco. I look over the seat. He's writing down my tag number. Balls of perspiration roll down my back. Maybe I should tell him I've changed my mind. I face forward and he's back at the window. I grasp the steering wheel harder to stop my hands from shaking. The engine is running. I could roar around the guard-house and disappear down the highway.

"Any guns?"

"What?"

"Do you have any guns in your possession?"

"No."

"Cameras or tape recorders?"

"No."

"You have any liquor?"

The question momentarily amuses me. Does he think I'm here to party? "No."

The guard inside hands him a card, and he places my prison pass on the dash by the windshield. "Just go on down this main road till you come to the third street, take a left, and drive to the back of that building." He points.

I look toward the red brick building. "That's the MSU?"

"No, ma'am, that's the administration building. You'll have to see the prison attorney first."

I don't know why and am afraid to ask. I ease down the road, looking from side to side. Shaded by trees, a Visitor's Center sits to my right; there's a long, narrow brick house to the left, possibly the superintendent's residence. White frame homes with trusties tending flower beds are on either side of the narrow road. The place reminds me of a southern rural town, not a prison setting. I guess the guards and their families live in those places. I wonder if these people have children and how they could raise them in the shadow of a prison.

As instructed, I turn left. A number of small buildings line the road. The brick administration building is dead ahead. I brake and notice three gleaming black trusties sweeping the front steps. I'll have to walk right past them to reach the front door. This makes me uneasy. I don't see any guards with rifles. What am I doing here? That old saw about curiosity killing the cat may well be true in my case.

I turn off the ignition, make sure to take my car keys, and stride quickly toward the entrance, clutching my briefcase and shoulder-strap bag. Focusing straight ahead, I try to project the illusion of authority.

As I mount the stairs, one of the inmates makes

eye contact. He smiles, revealing gold teeth. "Morning, ma'am."

I am paralyzed, but try to summon a pinch of bravado. "Morning. How's it going?" What a question I've asked. I increase my pace, nervous I might trip on the steps and fall. I envision the convicts flinging themselves on top of me.

"Fine. Could be better, could be worse." He chuckles.

I reach the landing and put the front door between us. The humidity has kinked my hair and melted my makeup. I'm a wreck and haven't yet arrived at the MSU, where really dangerous inmates are under lock and key. I check my watch. Bingo's recess period has begun and he's on the playground. Tarsha is typing in the office. Jack is at the courthouse. Lily is probably having a Coke on the back terrace. Byars and Charles are riding around the plantation, checking out the cotton. Estelle is at some meeting or shopping. I wish I were with any one of them. I wish I were anywhere but here.

I follow the arrow to the prison attorney's office. His name is not painted on the door. The position is probably a transient one, lawyers moving on and up to better things before the paint can dry. I knock.

An older, bald man in a white short-sleeved shirt opens the door. He's probably moving down the ladder. "I'm Leona Bingham. I'm a lawyer here to see Robert Weldon. My name's on his visitor's list."

He sticks out a beefy hand. "John Dobbs." We shake and he ushers me inside. His face reminds me of a basset hound, his eyes sad from sights they've seen.

The office is cramped and sparsely furnished with haphazardly stacked ledgers and government-issue metal and wood furniture. He gestures to a chair and rests his ample bottom on the edge of the desk. On the walls are pictures of the current governor of Mississippi, Robert Danforth, and the attorney general, Jack Flannery Sr. I cringe under the A.G.'s stare, a man I've known since childhood. He would not approve of my visiting a man he'd successfully prosecuted.

John Dobbs presents a clipboard with a pen. "This is a waiver for you to sign. Standard procedure—that you won't sue the state of Mississippi if you are in any way injured while on this property, and in case of a prison break or riot that you, if taken hostage, will not expect any specific measures to be employed solely on your behalf."

I read over the wording carefully and with mounting horror. What would become of Bingo if something happened to me? His father doesn't know he exists and wouldn't take responsibility for him if he did. I fumble with the pen, hesitant to sign. I struggle to soothe my ragged emotions. I've come this far and am almost proud of myself for it. Lawyers are in and out of here every day and nothing happens. Am I a wuss, as Bingo calls cowards? I scribble my name and hand the clipboard back to John Dobbs, Esquire.

"I'll call MSU and tell them you're here." He picks up the phone, gives instruction, hangs up, and focuses on me. "A lawyer's visit with an inmate is usually limited to an hour, but when an execution date has been set we relax the rules, so you can take as long as you want to, can come and go near 'bout any-time. It'll get frantic around here on toward the end, and my phone will be ringing off the hook, what with the warden calling, the attorney general, his staff, the governor, his staff, the press, and of course you."

"Whoa." I put force behind the word and shake my head. "I'm not representing Robert Weldon. I just came to visit."

"May I ask why?" His face sags even more. He's disappointed in me.

"Why I'm not representing him or why I came to visit?"

"Actually, both."

"I'm tied up with other things at the present." Mary Jessica's divorce will keep me hopping while her retainer keeps me afloat. "Robert Weldon wrote me and asked if I'd represent him. I thought it would be kinder to come in person to tell him that I can't rather than send a letter. I realize his time is limited." I hope I redeemed myself in his eyes.

"I see." He stands. "They'll be expecting you at MSU. Go back to the main road and follow the arrows, and they'll point you to the MSU. You'll then go into section thirty-two C." He sticks out his hand again. "Nice meeting you. And be sure to lock your car doors when you get out there."

I leave with a weird letdown feeling. The trusties are gone and I check the backseat floor before start-ing the engine. I return to the main road, taking a left at the arrow sign, moving deeper and deeper into the bowels of the penitentiary.

The dirt road ends at a red-brick two-story building surrounded by two tall chain-link fences topped with razor wire that glistens in the sun. MSU prisoners in orange-and-white pants horse around in the exercise yard. Bulletproof-glass watchtowers manned by armed sharpshooters are stationed at all four corners of this high-risk unit. They mean business here.

I close the car door, lock it, and walk on hard gravel toward the gate. I glance up at the watchtower. A bucket tied to a rope comes down with a jerk. The guard puts a bullhorn to his mouth. "Put your car keys in it." I do as I'm told, and the bucket rises. "Proceed," the guard calls down.

A buzzer sounds, then hums, and the first gate jerks and clangs back about two feet. I enter the area, and the gate closes behind me and locks with a quick click. I'm trapped in a secure area between the first and second gates. The second gate slides open, and I walk through and realize that I am in the exercise yard where the MSU prisoners are loose. They all turn to stare, ten of them I count, all violent and dangerous or they wouldn't be incarcerated here. The gate closes behind me, and my heart beats wildly. Sweat forms under my arms. Any one of those prisoners could rush and attack me. I hear catcalls and have the urge to run. Looking up quickly at the guard towers, I take some comfort that the rifles are trained on the convicts. The main door of the unit opens, and a guard with a bull neck and bulging biceps steps out to greet me. "Sergeant Samuels. Sorry, but I have to frisk you."

I almost groan. What next? How many more hurdles? "Right here?" I glance up at the guards, then at the open windows along the tiers. I hear loud noises, people talking, sobbing, ranting and raving, cursing. Soon faces will appear to watch him fondle me.

"Just spread your legs, please." He reaches for my briefcase and purse, runs his hand around in them, feeling the contents. He touches my ankles, goes to my knees, waist, and makes a quick pass under my arms while I look at the sky. He's professional and the frisk is over quickly. "Come with me."

I follow him around the side of the building. He selects a key from the ring and unlocks a door. "This is the visiting room. Go right on in, ma'am."

The room is large and divided by a waist-high brick wall topped with thick metal grating that runs to the ceiling. Metal chairs furnish the section for lawyers and visitors. Plastic chairs are provided on the inmates' side. Small rectangular slits are cut into the metal screens before each chair, a conversation hole. A counter reaches the length of the wall, a place for papers and arms to rest. Ashtrays are supplied. The floors are concrete, the lighting, a harsh overhead fluorescent. A unit air conditioner, cut into the outside wall, groans and labors to cool the windowless area. The place is rancid with the stink of cigarettes, sweat, and fear of desperate people who've received bad news here.

"Take a seat, please, and I'll go get Robert Weldon. I'll just lock this door where we came in. Weldon will come in through that door." He nods at the one on the inmates' side.

All alone in the room now, I sit facing the slit in the screen, my bag and briefcase by the chair. I have tried to picture Robert Weldon, but can't get a firm image. Jack said Weldon was not an educated person but intelligent, fairly well spoken. Mostly Jack remembered the eyes, penetrating, almost hypnotic. Jack is afraid I'll get sucked in by a desperate convict who'll grasp at anything to survive. I light a cigarette as the knots in my stomach tighten.

I jump as the lock on the inmates' side resounds in the empty room. The door eases open slowly; the guard moves in and stands aside. Robert Weldon appears in the doorway. His eyes seek me out and lock onto me. He wears a red prison jumpsuit, his hands cuffed behind him, legs in shackles, feet in cheap rubber flip-flops. He's medium height, slender, but muscled from obvious workouts.

The guard leads Weldon to the chair directly in front of me, sits him down, and unlocks the cuffs but not the leg irons. Weldon flexes his wrists. His dovish gray eyes never leave mine. His dark hair is damp, combed back, and exaggerates a prominent widow's peak. A few premature gray strands highlight his temples. His skin is smooth, unblemished, probably once a good olive shade but now fading to a pasty color. He gives me a hint of a smile, only a hint like Mona Lisa's, but I catch a glimpse of extraordinarily white, even teeth. I wonder if he's blessed or if the state provides dentistry on death row. That seems incongruous.

The guard speaks over his shoulder. "I'll be right out there in the hall." The dead bolt clicks into place on the other side of the door, and we are alone.

Robert Weldon's eyes eat into me, measuring, weighing. Calculating? Somehow his presence seems to have rearranged the molecules in the air, altering the atmosphere from being as it should. I am deeply affected by him. He is not as I expected. Even handcuffed, he manages to convey a sense of dignity. My reaction to him scares me. I have to keep my head. My voice seems to have deserted me.

"Thank you for coming." His voice is soft with the honey of a southern drawl.

Words still fail me. I drag on my cigarette for something to occupy me, then wonder if I should offer him one. Maybe they're considered a weapon of sorts and not allowed. I reach into my purse and offer him the pack.

"Thank you, I have some." He takes a pack from the only pocket in his jumpsuit. "I do need a light, though."

I pass my cheap plastic lighter through the slit, wondering where he gets cigarettes. Does someone send them? Does he buy them in prison, or are smokes issued to inmates? He lights his cigarette, hands the lighter back. I study it for an instant. He's touched it. His fingerprints are there, as they were on the knife that killed April Brown. I drop it into my purse.

Cigarette in hand, he rakes back his damp hair. "I was lucky today since I have a visitor. We don't get a shower every day, although we do get one hour of exercise every day. Ten of us at a time are allowed to go out."

"Mr. Weldon . . . Robert, I looked up the quote in the Bible. 'Behold, I show you a mystery.' The words brought me here. What do they mean? What were you trying to tell me?"

He takes a pair of gold wire-framed glasses from his pocket and adjusts them on his nose. They lend him the air of a young professor. "What it says. There's a mystery that's never been solved." He drags on the cigarette. "A murderer is loose in your town, in Grenola. He's out there and he thinks he's free, gotten away with it. All these years he's thought that. And if I'm . . . gone next month, he'll be right. No one will look any further. But as long as I'm alive, there's still a threat to him, even though I've been convicted and locked up." He takes another drag, and smoke lingers before his face. "I'm still a threat if"—he points the cigarette like a finger—"if someone looks for April Brown's killer in another direction . . . not at me."

I clear my throat. "Robert, you're talking to the wrong person. I, ah, I'm not a very good lawyer."

"I've had good lawyers before. Look, look where I am." He leans forward, arms on the counter, his mouth close to the slit. "I never thought this could happen to a person . . . not in this country. Whenever I heard someone was convicted of a crime, executed even, I always thought they must be guilty. Now I know better. It sure can happen. I begged Mr. Perkins to let me take the stand. I thought the jurors would see . . . see that I was innocent. Know it when they heard me talk, tell my side. He advised against me taking the stand, said he knew what was right."

I lift my hand. "Wait a minute. Run that by me again. You mean, you actually requested to testify and Perkins refused to allow it?"

"Exactly. What did I know? I went along with what he said. I was so stunned, so shocked by the verdict that I couldn't think straight. Then I had another set of lawyers after Perkins quit, and they told me to listen to them. They filed all kinds of motions and appeals. Got me a stay finally and I was starting to believe in them. The stay got lifted. Those lawyers quit, and the state appointed me some more lawyers. They started doing the same things, over and over again. Flooding the courts with paperwork.

"Frivolous, I believe, is the word that was used. Frivolous appeals. Rejection after rejection. Mississippi Court of Criminal Appeals, State Supreme Court, Fifth Circuit Court, U.S. Supreme Court. One lawyer even went to the governor begging for clemency. And now I've come down to it. The time is here, and I still can't believe it. I'm only allowed five appeals, and three have been used."

He crushes out his cigarette, then stares at me, those eyes holding my attention. "This all started with April Brown, and it should end with her. Once I was arrested, no one looked any further for her murderer. All the legal stuff started rolling, lawyers trying to defend me, trying to save me once I was convicted, and the most critical point just got drowned out— finding the real guilty person. I've been thinking, and I can see it all now. I should have had lawyers who were willing to go at this from another angle. Start with April Brown, investigate the past, everything about the case. The killer is in there somewhere and can be found out. That's the only thing that's going to save me now."

"All that in forty-five days?"

"It's enough time."

"And after six years?

"I know about cold trails, but it's all there somewhere . . . the killer's there."

"Plus, filing motions and appeals, only two left, with fresh angles to buy some time in case you get down to the wire and the murderer hasn't been found by your execution date? Robert, I have no staff to help me, only a secretary who wants to go to law school. This is impossible for me to handle. A more capable lawyer with a large staff is what you need."

"Even if I'm executed . . . even after I'm dead, I'd still want people to know I didn't murder April Brown. I want the mystery of who did it solved."

"What you're asking . . . I mean, you'd need a detective and a lawyer rolled into one. A relentless one at that. I'm certainly not a detective." I look him straight in the eye. "I told you I'm not even a good lawyer. No staff. And relentless isn't a word I'd use to describe myself. This is an undertaking I'm absolutely not prepared for, not under any circumstances. I'm sorry, Robert. I'd like to help if I could. Please understand that for your own sake, for your own best interests, you need a team of skilled attorneys with a staff to fight for you."

He continues to stare at me without a change of expression. I light another cigarette. He doesn't. Maybe he has to ration himself. I offer one of mine. He declines. "Robert, I understand your message behind the quote 'Behold, I show you a mystery' now, but there's something I still can't figure."

"What's that?"

"Did you by mistake think I am some high-powered, talented lawyer?" I pause. "Tell me, why did you pick me?"

For the first time he averts his eyes from mine. The question has some impact on him. I'm on edge, waiting for the answer. He's composing his words.

"I don't want to hurt anyone, I just want out of here. I'm innocent, Leona." He looks at me. "Okay if I call you that?"

I nod. "Go on."

"Let's just say, for instance, that if during the course of investigating my case and trying to find April Brown's killer, some information was uncovered that could hurt certain people but could help me in the long run . . . well, I need to be sure that the information would be used in the right way—to help me, not hurt others."

This is a puzzle if I've ever heard one. "What information?"

"I was just saying for instance . . . hypo- . . . hypo- . . ." He grasps for the word.

I help him. "Hypothetically." Jack said Weldon was uneducated. I think he's been studying while in prison.

"That's it. Speaking hypothetically, *if* I knew and *if* I told anyone, nobody would believe me. Ravings of a condemned man, they'd say. It wouldn't help me."

He's evading my question. He knows what information but isn't going to tell. "You're saying someone else has to find out this information, someone believable, and use it in a proper way, right?"

"Right. I'm also saying this information may never be found out by someone investigating my case or doesn't have to be used even if it is found out. All I need is for April Brown's killer to be fingered, and I'm a free man."

"You still haven't answered my question. Why me?"

He hesitates, then turns those hypnotic eyes back on me. "I think you are the best person to handle this information. If you find it, you'll know why."

His statement packs a punch. Now he has me. If I don't take the case, I'll never know what he's talking about, and it will plague me forever. On the other hand, should I take the case, I still may not discover this mysterious information or be able to find April Brown's killer or be successful with any new motions or appeals to save him. That will plague me forever.

I stare at Robert Weldon and have a sudden hunch about the information of which he speaks so vaguely and who might be involved. That is why he chose me. What do I do if I find this person has been responsible for something untoward? *What do I do?* What am I thinking? Am I going to take the case?

"Robert, I don't know anything about you. Start at the beginning . . . your background, the arrest, and through to the trial and your conviction." His face lights up, and I remember Jack said you never want to give a condemned man false hope.

"Does this mean you'll take the case?"

My breath hitches. I don't know the answer to his question. "Tell me about yourself."

He rests his arms on the counter. "I'm forty-one. Born in the hill country in east Mississippi, near Starkville. Poor country, not like the Delta. My dad left town before I was born. My mom worked at the sawmill, kept books. She died when I was just a kid. I was passed around from relative to relative. Ones I was living with at the time got laid off from the mill when the economy turned bad. Money was tight, and I dropped out of high school, got a job as a mechanic to help out. I liked working on cars, was good at it. After a few years I decided I'd move on to the Delta where money was more plentiful. Got a job at a garage in Grenola. Walter's Cars. Walter Boyd owns it."

"I know him. Go on."

"I saved some money, made some friends . . ."

"Who were they?" He gives me names. "Go ahead."

"I had a pretty good life. Put a down payment on a nice little house out by Four Mile Lake." He tells me where he lived, describes his house. "That's where it all happened—April Brown's murder—out close to the lake. I got off early that day, was walking home to work on my car. It had thrown a rod. That's when I saw her down the hill. I didn't know her, had never seen her before." He pulls a cigarette from his pocket, and I give him my lighter. He returns it and takes a drag, deep in thought. "I've got my high school equivalency since I've been in prison, took some college correspondence courses and I've read a lot—about law, psychology, criminology, things that interested me and related to my case. Well, the way April Brown was killed, stabbed to death. I've read that stabbing and strangulation are personal-type crimes, not ways a stranger is going to choose to kill somebody. April Brown was out there to meet somebody she knew."

"April Brown was pregnant, right?"

He nods. "The autopsy showed she was. She didn't

look it." He pauses, then continues. "I was walking along, and all of a sudden I hear this moaning. I look around, trying to decide where it was coming from, and I get a quick glimpse, a real quick one, of a man running through the woods. White man, I thought. I could have missed him if I'd looked in another direction first. Then I hear kind of a cry, and I look down the edge of the road to this ravine and see a woman stabbed and bleeding. I hurried down there, stumbled and fell once, to try to help her. Red bubbles were coming out her mouth. I just pulled out the knife without thinking, panicked. I told her to hold on, that I was going for help. I got back up the ravine and ran down the road a ways toward town, didn't even realize I had the knife in my hand. Then I see Ray Bell Crosby cruising down the road in his police car, and I flag him down and tell him what's happened. I know him real well. We fished together sometimes. Well, he said he thought he'd seen a black man running through the woods. It could have been. It's real shadowy in there, but I know I saw somebody. Anyways, Ray Bell and I drive back to where the woman is and go down there. She's gone by then . . . dead. He calls it in to the chief on the radio, and we wait there. It was awful to look at her. I could tell, though, that she had been a good-looking woman.

"Pretty soon the chief's there with some more officers, and then the coroner comes with some people. I tell the chief what I saw, and he takes me back to the station with him. It's in the same building as the jail, you know. He says we need to talk. I already know I was at the wrong place at the wrong time . . . out there on that road."

"Did he read you your rights?"

"Yes, and that's when I started to get scared. Before long he says I'm under arrest and locks me up. I haven't been out from behind bars since that day, and nobody has ever looked further than me for April Brown's killer."

"I know a little about the trial." Jack's words stick in my mind, how the police officer's corroboration of seeing a fleeing man was quashed by a witness called to the stand by Jack Flannery Sr. I'm burning to have my next question answered. "How did you get J. Clyde Perkins to represent you?" During our conversation I made a mental note of the fact that he wanted to testify and J. Clyde Perkins wouldn't allow it. This could be grounds for a fresh appeal, maybe, if it hasn't already been used.

"He just appeared and said he was going to handle my case. Said I had nothing to worry about."

I wonder how many people have heard that from lawyers. "Did he talk about money with you? Payment for services?"

"I'd heard of him before, of course, and told him I didn't see how I could pay him. He waved his hand and said, 'Don't worry about it.' I was shocked he'd do that for me. I mean, who was I?"

I am still surprised that J. Clyde Perkins would work pro bono on such a low-profile case. His reputation is not that of a soft-hearted person who offers his services for free, especially without benefit of publicity. Something doesn't fit here.

"Leona, I don't have any money. I lost my house, couldn't keep up the payments, of course. But if I get out of here, I'll work and pay you off one day, if you'll take my case." He hesitates. "If I don't get out . . . well, you'll be left holding the bag. So, I realize it's a gamble on your part, but that doesn't change the fact that I'm innocent."

I remember the maxim of American justice: Better that a hundred men go free than one innocent man be punished. I think about the sampler my grandmother cross-stitched: A QUEST IS AS IMPORTANT AS AN ACCOMPLISHMENT. Maybe this quest is for me. Chill bumps rise on my arms. Based on nothing but instinct, I believe Robert Weldon is innocent and was wrongly convicted.

After my sojourn in Paris I lost all confidence in myself, all faith in my ability to excel. Despite that, I'm tempted to take a shot here, since he's willing to bet the ultimate on me. His case would occupy my every waking moment. I would have to kiss Mary Jessica and her fat retainer good-bye. I'm torn in all directions.

He watches me as I vacillate. Waiting for my answer, he doesn't appear desperate or ready to beg as Jack predicted. I try to think logically and clearly about the decision that will undoubtedly impact my life. If I don't step up to the challenge, I will forever blame myself for cowardice. I take a deep breath and plunge. "Robert, all I can promise is to do the best I can." Now that I've committed, a well of excitement bubbles inside me. I feel strangely alive, reckless, frightened to hold a man's life in my hands, but strangely alive.

"That's all I can ask," he answers with that vague smile.

I inquire about the lawyers who represented him after Perkins and what motions and appeals they filed in his behalf. I have to get going, yet I hate to leave this man in this hellhole. What do they feed him? I'd like to take him home with me, let him shower all he wants, give him a beer, cook him a good meal. He senses our time is up and his face turns sad.

He stands when I do. "Robert, I'll be back soon and give you a report."

"Thank you, Leona." He punches a buzzer by the door, and the guard comes in to handcuff him. His eyes linger on me.

Bye, I mouth.

After he leaves, I go to the door on my side of the room and remember that it's locked. I knock, and a different guard unlocks the door. Outside the building I pass through the two security zones, and my car keys are lowered in a bucket.

Sitting in the stifling heat of my Bronco, I worry about my decision and then try to recapture that feeling of aliveness, the sense of purpose I experienced when I said I'd take the case. I realize I have to set my feelings aside and put Weldon first. I must vibrate with determination, hum with conviction if I'm to succeed, and I must start this instant. An idea strikes me, and I turn on the ignition, drive back to John Dobbs's office.

I enter the building and rap on his door. He doesn't have far to walk, so he answers quickly, surprised to see me.

"Mr. Dobbs, I wanted to let you know that I'll be taking on Robert Weldon's case after all."

He brightens. "Well, I'm glad to hear it. I'll put you on record as his official lawyer. You can file the agreement between you and him with me when you have it ready. It goes in state records at the Capitol."

Neophyte that I am, I have to ask some questions. "Do I have to come here every time I visit Robert Weldon?"

"No, you can go directly to MSU. You and he can meet in the law library in that unit now that you're his lawyer. We allow fifteen prisoners in there at once. Some of those on MSU research their own cases." He hesitates. "You don't have to be afraid. Their leg chains are hooked to an iron loop secured in the floor."

That information is comforting. I check my watch. From now on I'll do that a lot, I suspect. I'm now running on a fast treadmill to beat a deadly time limit. "Mr. Dobbs, could I use your telephone? I'll reverse the charges." He nods.

Tarsha answers and accepts the charges. "Tarsha, I'm still at Parchman." I turn my back on Mr. Dobbs. "I've decided to take on Robert Weldon's case."

Her silence is deafening, but finally she speaks. "You must be on some serious hallucinogens."

I ignore her comment. "This case is going to take all my time, so I can't handle Mary Jessica Bond's divorce. Call her and cancel the appointment this afternoon and explain that I'm too occupied with another case to do hers justice and that I recommend the Buchanan firm."

"Oh, man, I already had half of that retainer money spent. Robert Weldon doesn't have any dough. You can't afford pro bono work."

That's true, but I can't afford not to take his case. "His execution date is set. I'm talking only weeks here. We'll get by."

"Leona, taking on Weldon's case is about more than just money. It's going to raise some racial issues here in Grenola. The black community is not going to be happy with you."

I hadn't considered that. Many people won't be happy with me, least of all April Brown's family. "So long as you're with me. Tarsha, we're going to have to work hard and long. I'm going to need your help."

"I'm sure the legal experience will be good for me. You forgot to say that."

"You with me?"

"I'm here."

I realize I can't charge a call to John Dobbs's line, and I can't make the next call collect. "Tarsha, I need to visit with J. Clyde Perkins about Weldon's case. Call his office in Memphis for me and ask if I can come in this afternoon. Say it's an emergency. I'm halfway to Memphis now, so I could get that out of the way." J. Clyde Perkins could be in court or in Calcutta. I glance at the telephone and give her the prison attorney's number. "I'll wait here for your call. If I don't hear from you in five minutes, I'll know you've gotten me in to see him and I'll head to Memphis."

"The Man himself, huh?"

"Yeah. Listen, I need some more favors, okay? Go to the courthouse and get the trial transcripts of the *State of Mississippi* versus *Robert Weldon*. Call Jack Flannery and tell him I can't play tennis today and I'll talk to him later." I dread that. "I'll need some help with Bingo. Could you call Lily or Estelle . . . ?"

"I can take care of him for you."

"I do appreciate the offer, Tarsha. That'll work great. An extra key to my house is in my desk. Pick up Bingo at school, tell him I'm tied up, get some takeout for dinner, Kentucky Fried, whatever. I'll pay you back. I'll be home around dinnertime, and we can eat and go over the transcripts tonight."

"And feed the dog. Surely that's in my job description." She disconnects.

Someone knocks on the door. Dobbs answers, then tells the man to wait outside, that he's busy now. "A reporter from the *Clarion-Ledger* in Jackson." The prison attorney and I chat. I don't really listen. My thoughts crowd my brain. Robert Weldon had not asked any personal questions. I'd want to know the background of a lawyer I was counting on to save me from the death chamber. He obviously already knows something about me. He chose me to represent him, stated I was the best person to handle some information that might come to light. Who told him? I check my watch. Time is up and the phone didn't ring. Now that my path has tangled with Robert Weldon's, I don't know where it will lead, but Memphis is the first stop.

3

I LEAVE PARCHMAN BEHIND, STILL SHAKEN BY MY close proximity to convicts in the MSU. Being within spitting distance of such violent men takes an emotional toll. But overriding that experience is the shock of my impetuous decision to take on Robert Weldon's case. I fear I have stepped off a precipice into an abyss, pulling him with me. Only a legal parachute will save us. I take a deep breath.

All the way to Memphis I review my knowledge of appeals and motions. Claiming ineffective counsel is the most common and standard appeal. I rehash the appeals Robert Weldon's previous lawyers had used. The attorneys representing Robert Weldon after J. Clyde Perkins declined to continue had not claimed that Weldon received ineffective counsel, obviously afraid of the high-powered Perkins or too respectful of his reputation. Instead their appeals claimed that Weldon had not received a fair trial, the second most common claim. After rejections from the various courts, those lawyers quit and a third set of state-appointed attorneys took up the gauntlet, turned around, and appealed that Robert Weldon had ineffective counsel from the second set, but not J. Clyde Perkins. It seems that no one is willing to challenge or possibly incur the wrath of the mighty J. Clyde Perkins.

On the outskirts of Memphis, I look up J. Clyde Perkins's address in a phone book while a service station attendant fills my gas tank. Driving into the city, I park at an underground facility and walk to the tree-lined mall just off Main Street where cars are no longer allowed. Perkins's office, all four floors of it, is in an old, elegant building that has been restored to its former grandeur. The view of the Mississippi River is awesome.

Entering his plushly carpeted, spacious reception area, I feel as if I've stepped into an English country manor home. The pastoral scenes on the walls are dimly lighted by ceiling fixtures not much larger than pinpricks. Couches and chairs in muted colors are puffy enough to get lost in, the end tables shining with beeswax. He has more cut flowers in crystal vases than I have in my yard. I try to picture Tarsha and myself in such a setting. Although this is the Deep South, I expect to hear clipped, proper British accents.

The receptionist reminds me of a Norman Rockwell librarian with a bun at the nape of her neck and glasses perched on the end of her nose. She glances up from her appointment book. "Yes, ma'am?"

I'm wrong about the accents. "I'm here to see Mr. Perkins about the Robert Weldon case . . ."

Before I can introduce myself, she says, "Oh, you must be L. Bingham."

I almost laugh. Leave it to Tarsha. All the big-timers have initials. F. Lee Bailey. J. Edgar Hoover. J. Clyde Perkins. And now L. Bingham.

"I'll ring Mr. Perkins's personal secretary, and she'll be right out. Won't you have a seat?"

"Thanks, but I've been sitting awhile. I'll just stand." I peer down the long halls going off in several directions like spokes on a bicycle wheel. I wonder how much the people in the offices along these corridors make. I suddenly feel intimidated by these surroundings. I'm in way over my head. My name does not strike chords. Perkins would never have seen me on such short notice had the Robert Weldon case not been mentioned.

"Mrs. Bingham?"

I turn and have to look up at a towering woman, six feet if she's an inch, her shiny blond hair in a neat page boy. Her gray tailored suit is unisex. She stares at me as if I'm not what she expected, not up to standards. Granted, I've been through the penitentiary part of the day, now hot and wrinkled from driving, but I started out passable.

"Yes. Here to see Mr. Perkins about the Robert Weldon case."

Her expression is pinched. She hesitates, looks down the hall as if she doesn't know where to lead me, then comes to a decision. "Well, please follow me."

She takes the hall in long, athletic strides, with me

at her side like a dog on heel. J. Clyde Perkins's office is a corner one, naturally, his name in gold raised letters on the door. Unlike the transitory prison attorneys, J. Clyde Perkins is here to stay.

She taps on the door, then opens it without a bidding to enter. "Mr. Perkins, L. Bingham." She stands aside so that I can enter.

I pop around the door frame. Mr. Perkins is seated behind a massive mahogany desk. He looks up and stands, obviously taken aback by my presence. He blinks like he's clearing his eyes to see better. It dawns on me now that they clearly expected a male version of L. Bingham. "Mr. Perkins, Leona Bingham." I stride over, hand extended and give him a hearty shake. He's short and overweight, shaped like a pear in his blue seersucker suit, a red bow tie under layers of chins. Black strands of hair are wrapped around his head to help hide his baldness. His eyes are sharp as an eagle's and warn that he's not one with whom to tangle.

"You're here to see me about the Robert Weldon case?" His stare pierces right through me. I haven't done anything and I feel guilty. I can imagine his effect on a witness on the stand.

"Yes, sir, I'm representing him," I say with as much command as I can muster. I am determined not to wilt.

His eyes dart to his personal secretary. She leaves, but some message has passed between them. He whirls around the desk, surprisingly light on his feet for a heavy man, and sits. He gestures to one of the high-backed leather chairs before his desk. "Please."

The Mississippi River is framed in the window. Barges and tugboats glide through the murky waters. I hear a toot from a paddle-wheel boat of yesteryear that is filled with passengers leaning over the rails.

He rests his elbows on the desk, steepling his sausage-like fingers. His nails shine from a recent manicure. "What firm are you with, Miz Bingham?" His question is couched with friendly indifference.

I station my briefcase across my lap. "I have my own firm in Grenola." I glance at his diplomas, awards, and pictures with various dignitaries on the paneled walls. His leather-bound books in the floor-to-ceiling shelves rival any library's collection.

"Do you have a card?"

I've never had any business cards printed, but make a mental note to do so. "Not with me."

"How many associates in your firm?"

"Well, actually, there's just myself. I'm it." I smile, hoping to convey that I'm enough.

He remains expressionless, a poker face I can't read. "And how did you happen to come about representing Robert Weldon?"

I'd like to ask the same question of him. "He wrote me a letter, asking me to represent him. I've just come from seeing him at Parchman." I want to fidget, smoke, do something, but force myself to remain still. "You do much pro bono work, Mr. Perkins?"

His gaze is steady on me. "Not much."

"I understand Robert Weldon's case was pro bono."

He doesn't answer, and the silence between us lengthens. I feel the need to jump in with some conversation, but before I can, he does. "Just what is it you're here about, Miz Bingham?"

"I thought if I had the benefit of copies of your briefs and trial notes it would help me with my appeals. I was thinking on the way up here that the U.S. Supreme Court outlawed the death penalty in 1972 and those very same justices reinstated the death penalty in 1976. Judges change their minds, and some of those judges in the Mississippi Supreme Court, the federal district court, the Fifth Circuit, and the U.S. Supreme Court, where appeals for Robert Weldon were denied, are no longer on the bench, so I feel I have a good shot with new appeals and even with some that were already used by Weldon's former lawyers." *And in the meantime try to find the real murderer.* But I don't say that.

"What basis for appeals do you have in mind?" His tone is suddenly wary.

"As you know better than I, Mr. Perkins, there are various kinds I can use. I just have to pick the best one." I don't want to rile him by mentioning ineffectual counsel because I need his briefs and records to help me. I read that the lawyers for William Bonin, "The Freeway Killer" who was executed in California, were so desperate to save him they went so far as to seek a new trial based on their own self-declared incompetence. No chance of J. Clyde Perkins making such a move.

In a preamble to what he's about to deliver, he clears his throat to grab my full attention. "Miz Bingham, you don't have a chance in hell to save Robert Weldon. I couldn't. That case was doomed from the start, and I never should have taken it on. It's been a thorn in my side ever since. My advice to you is to go back to Grenola and forget about Robert Weldon. You'd be doing yourself a favor."

"I wouldn't be doing *him* much of one, though."

He frowns. "He's had all the favors he needs. Robert Weldon is guilty, and he's going to be executed. My files aren't available to you and wouldn't do you any good anyway."

I am tempted to say, "Well, fuck you very much."

"Mr. Perkins, why didn't you let Robert Weldon take the stand at his trial? He said he wanted to and you advised against it."

Perkins swells with rage, eyes glinting hard. "Young lady, that is a lie. He never wanted to take the stand. And if he had, he would have tangled himself up more than he already did. Robert Weldon is a congenital liar. There were things he didn't tell me and some that he did were lies, and I got caught with my pants down because of it. Even though Weldon's guilty, I could have gotten him off if he'd told me the truth so I could have been prepared. Jack Flannery, Mississippi's esteemed attorney general, prosecuted Weldon, as I'm sure you know. He made his reputation off me and that case because of those lies. Now, one last thing. If you're considering using ineffectual counsel as an appeal, my advice to you is don't even think about it. I promise you, you'll be very, very sorry if you do." He stands abruptly, dismissing me. "Good afternoon, Miz Bingham."

I feel like a prize fighter to whom a knockout blow has been delivered. He wouldn't have answered my questions about Robert Weldon's lies even if he'd given me time to ask. I quickly gather my purse and briefcase and leave without a word. I can hear my heartbeat in my ears. I make it to the reception area without stumbling and sense that everyone I pass has labeled me a fool. I want to fall through the floor, through the earth, and come out somewhere in China.

In the blinding sun and staggering heat I move like a robot to the parking area and light a cigarette before starting the engine. Weldon struck a nerve with the reason he chose me, that I might uncover sensitive information and would understand best how to handle it without hurting anyone. Has Robert Weldon conned me, as Jack warned is the wont of desperate men on death row? Did Weldon actually lie, or was J. Clyde Perkins fried simply because he lost the case? Of the two, which is the more believable, a reputable lawyer or a man convicted of murder and sentenced to death by twelve jurors?

I'm agitated, upset, my emotions in tatters. I reach the city limits, getting lost only once on the newly constructed freeways. Highway 49 will take me straight to Grenola, but loops by Parchman first. I can easily drop by the prison and tell Robert Weldon the deal is off and to find someone else. End of subject. End of a complication to my life. I'll just fill my pocketbook with Mary Jessica's retainer.

As I drive, I try to concentrate on something other than Robert Weldon's case, but my mind won't leave it alone. If I don't handle the case, another lawyer could stumble across the information and use it to harm, where, according to Weldon, I would employ

it to help. Why did Weldon's previous lawyers not
uncover this information? Is there really any information? Surely Weldon wouldn't play so casually with
his own life.

The road sign ahead announcing Parchman forces
me to a decision. Do I detour by the prison or keep
going? As in Paris, have I been so gullible once again?
I felt so alive for a short spell, off on my quest to try to
save Robert Weldon. I'm on the verge of tears, my
emotions in an uproar. Somehow in my mind my
revival and Weldon's survival are interlocked.

I drive right by the entrance then look at the penitentiary as it disappears in the rearview mirror. There
has always been something in life that set me apart
from the crowd, an only child, the most daring of the
group, an unwed mother, an emotional dropout, the
only one in my class to take the bar three times, and
now the champion of a convicted murderer.

Jack always comments that I drive like I stole the
car. I do just that and make it home in record time.
Tarsha's blue Honda is parked in my driveway. On
the water in our rowboat with Mister Marvel, Bingo
fishes. I wave at him. The bayou is shallow and Bingo
can swim, but I worry about water moccasins even
though I've warned him to be on the lookout at all
times.

Inside, Tarsha sits at the kitchen table with the
trial transcripts stacked precariously high. A bucket
of fried chicken and several smaller takeout cartons
litter the counter. She's still in her usual secretary
attire, a white cotton cable-knit over a flared ankle-
length navy skirt and a necklace as large as a tire

chain. She carries an autographed picture of Whoopi Goldberg in her purse and imitates the smile often. She'll sway juries one day.

"Well, if it ain't the financially challenged pro bono defense attorney in person."

"Somebody's got to do it."

"Give me a rich client anytime."

"It's been a long day, and I couldn't have gotten through it without your help. I'm dying to tell you about it, but I need to go to the bathroom first and get out of these clothes." I pour a drink of water from the pitcher in the refrigerator, gulp it, then touch the cold glass to my forehead. "Be right back."

I use the bathroom, put on jeans, a denim shirt, my run-over loafers designated for yard work, and join Tarsha in the kitchen. She fingers one of the trial transcripts.

"It must have been something, going into death row at Parchman. I would have been scared. Yea, though I walk through the valley of the shadow of death, I *will* fear evil. Thy rod and thy staff don't mean beans when a convict is leering."

I search the kitchen drawer and grab a cigarette. "I see you attended Sunday school regularly."

"So let's hear it."

I light the cigarette, much to her surprise, and relay the events of the day, everything from the Bible quote to the reason I believe Weldon chose me to my encounter with Perkins.

Glancing at me, she asks, "That's incredible. So you actually think this—this sensitive information Weldon says you might uncover that could hurt somebody has to do with Jack Flannery Senior?"

"He was the district attorney who prosecuted Weldon. Weldon must have friends here in Grenola who've told him I'm close with Jack Flannery, and Weldon suspects I'd never harm the family where others might." I lift my shoulders and display my palms. "It's my best guess." I hope my best guess is wrong. I open the refrigerator. "I'm keyed up from the day. Let's have a glass of wine."

"As long as the vintage is right," she says with that toothy grin.

"Aren't we the little connoisseur." I pour two stems full.

"I'm learning. Gotta know those things when I get away from the cotton patch." She takes a sip. "And you and J. Clyde didn't hit it off."

The cold wine soothes my parched throat. "He's a perfect shit, but I can't say I wouldn't want him as a lawyer if I were in a jam. He's plenty shrewd. It bothers me that he said Robert lied. To me, Weldon was so believable, especially about wanting to take the stand. It's Weldon's word against Perkins's. That'll be our first appeal, ineffectual counsel. Right." I am talking more to myself than to Tarsha. "A claim has to clear through four courts before it's extinguished, the Mississippi Supreme Court, the federal district court, the Fifth Circuit, and the U.S. Supreme. If I could just get Weldon a stay, we could buy some time, but a stay would probably be issued by a federal judge. No claim can be raised in federal court until it's been presented and denied in state court." The information the computer in my mind has pulled up from law school surprises me. "We'll start on it tomorrow. Tonight we'll go through as many of the trial transcripts as we can. You game? Can you stay and help me?"

Tarsha nods, and I see in her eyes something I haven't seen before. My newfound zeal surprises and pleases her. "I want to make a list of all the people I need to talk to. Jack Flannery Senior I see Saturday night." The attorney general's office battles death-penalty appeals, and as a result Jack Flannery Sr. and I will be in direct conflict, both adversaries determined to win. Somebody has to represent Robert Weldon, and nothing personal should be involved. Besides, I may be in a position to keep the A.G.'s reputation intact. "I'll want to talk to people associated with Robert Weldon, witnesses at the trial, jurors, April Brown's family and friends. I need to know everything about her."

Her faces suddenly clouds. "And that's where you'll run into a buzz saw—her family. They're not going to be too keen about somebody who's trying to free the man who was convicted of murdering her. See, like I said on the phone to you, you aren't going to be too popular with the black community 'cause they finally think they got some justice. White man kills a black girl and he's going to pay for it, not like in the old days. Same thing happened back then, he'd get off. Not nowadays, though, now that some progress has been made." She averts her eyes from mine. "But here you come trying to . . . it's gonna stir up some problems. Even my momma told me today that I ought to quit my job when I told her you were taking on the case. My boyfriend, too."

This gives me pause. "I never thought about the position I'd put you into with this."

"Hey!" She holds up her hand. "They don't understand. I do. Don't sweat. Besides, I need the job. Listen, your mother called several times today, and Jack Flannery called twice late this afternoon, wanting to know where you were. I called him like you asked and just said you couldn't play tennis, didn't say where you were. Maybe you'd better buzz 'em."

"Yeah. Will do." I hope the case won't damage my relationship with Jack. If not a heated, passionate affair as with Jean-Paul, this alliance gives me a sense of balance, of contentment, and security I don't want to lose.

"By the way, old lady Pearson called and changed her mind about redoing her will. Guess her kids must have been nice to her today."

I glance out the kitchen window when I hear a car pull into my driveway. Lily always seems too fragile to maneuver such a big car. I view her as the lens of a camera covered with gauze would capture her, a wispy image, an ethereal presence shimmering throughout my life. "It's Lily." I go to the front door.

Lily pulls the lace handkerchief from the sleeve of her green voile dress and pats the tiny perspiration beads above her lips. No matter how hot the weather, her makeup and hair are always perfect, just as if she's been wrapped in cellophane. "You've been gone all day. I called. I think I know where you were." Her anxious green eyes flit from one place to another.

"Come on back to the kitchen. Have a glass of wine."

Her high heels click across the floor. In the kitchen, Lily looks at Tarsha as if she should be serving the table, not sitting at it, then tries to cover her reaction. Sadly, ideas planted at birth are usually etched for life. I was a freethinker and rebellious enough to be impervious to such archaic views.

"Why, hello, Tarsha. It's nice to see you."

"And you, ma'am."

I may as well air my position. "Lily, if you thought I've been to Parchman to see Robert Weldon, you were right." I pour her a glass of wine while she surveys our dinner encased in cardboard.

"I thought as much from the way you talked last night at dinner." She takes a sip but doesn't sit at the table. "What did you think of him?"

"He's a nice-looking man, smart, well-spoken. Been studying since he's been in prison. He seemed sincere." I don't disclose the reason he chose me or mention the Bible quote, but tell her about seeing J. Clyde Perkins. "Hell, I think Robert Weldon's innocent, and I'm going to represent him and try to find who did murder April Brown." I wait for the criticism. Unlike Byars's beef with me for taking on such a case in lieu of Mary Jessica's, Lily's objections will be wrapped in cotton but nevertheless apparent. They see me as a "society" lawyer who represents moneyed, respectable citizens, one who doesn't dirty her hands with the unsavory or strain her pockets for the financially depressed.

A little smile of satisfaction graces her lips. "Good for you, Leona."

This giant step in opposition to Byars throws me a

curve. I want to hug her. "Thanks." I pour myself
another glass of wine. "All I can promise is to do my
best. Talk about ineffectual counsel—Weldon needs
a lawyer with a staff. Tarsha and I will just have to
manage it on our own." I don't look at Tarsha. She
knows how monumental the task is.

Lily sits at the table with Tarsha. I want to hug her
even more. "Leona, tell me about J. Clyde Perkins.
What all did he say to you?" She runs a manicured
nail up and down the frosted wineglass, making
squiggly patterns.

Leaning against the counter, I light a cigarette,
and Lily does not comment on the old habit I've
revived. "He was very brief and to the point. He
thinks I'm a fool to take this on and threatened that
I'd be sorry if I used the appeal of ineffectual counsel. He said Robert Weldon is a liar."

Lily stares into her wineglass. "And you believed
him? Robert Weldon, I mean, not Perkins."

I look at Lily, the gentle curve of her neck, the tiny
blue veins beneath her skin, the delicate body that
seems as if it could be whisked away with a strong
wind. "I believed him, but if he lied, I'll find out." I
tap my finger on the trial transcripts. I already knew
from Jack that the officer who picked up Weldon at
the crime scene and later corroborated his statements
about seeing a man fleeing had been discredited by
another witness who was in the backseat of his police
car at Four Mile Lake. That had not proved Weldon
was lying about seeing a man in the woods, but had
obviously impacted the case, leaving Weldon with an
unsubstantiated claim, one that might have created

reasonable doubt about his guilt had the officer's testimony not been refuted. There had to be other damaging testimony. "Lily, you said you went to the trial."

She waves her handkerchief. "Well, who didn't? Just about everybody in town went. Not every day, I couldn't take it, but Estelle and I went some. Byars and Charles, too."

"Do you remember offhand any witnesses contradicting any of Robert Weldon's statements, something that in J. Clyde Perkins's words caught him with his pants down?"

Lily presses her handkerchief to her temple as if to push out a recollection. "Something about a car, not the police car that brought out all the laughs, which I incidentally didn't think was funny a bit. The policeman's wife was sitting right there, embarrassed to death, hearing that brazen woman say she was on his backseat with him." Lily's cheeks flush as if she was as embarrassed by the testimony as the officer's wife. "There was something else . . . about Robert Weldon's car . . . Oh, pooh, somebody could have fixed that car. I didn't think the mechanic knew what he was talking about. Another man testified Robert Weldon knew about cars. Then there was the missing coat."

Whatever Lily is vaguely recalling I can find in the transcripts, but my curiosity is piqued. Before beginning work, I should visit the crime scene to get a feel of the area, have it placed firmly in my mind. "Tarsha, you must know exactly where the murder took place. Probably everybody in town does."

Tarsha rolls her eyes. "Grenola's only tourist attraction? Sure, I know."

"I want to take a ride over there after we eat, and then we'll tackle the transcripts." I'll call Jack before I start to work.

Lily checks her diamond-studded watch. "I'd better be going. Byars will be wondering where I am this time of day so near supper time." She rises and rinses out her wineglass at the sink. "Do you want me to tell him about your new case or do you want to?" She keeps her back to me.

"Suit yourself. This case is going to monopolize all my time, so I can't handle Mary Jessica's divorce." I open the bucket of fried chicken, thinking we should eat and get started before dark.

She worries on that statement, then sighs. "You have to do what you have to do."

I walk Lily to the front porch and motion for Bingo to come in from the bayou. She turns to me, touching her hair like the southern belle she is. "Byars won't be very pleased, you know."

"He won't be the only one." The list is growing.

"He'll think it's waste of time and effort on your part. Don't let it discourage you, Leona. You know Byars. He's just the way he is, always thinking how something will look to everybody. His mother was just the same, and he learned it at her knee." Lily gazes across the bayou. "I wonder how he'd think it would look if you got that young man off. Now, wouldn't that be something?"

Bingo and Mister Marvel dash around the car. "Mom, Mom, I caught a catfish, but I let him go."

Lily pats Bingo on the head and twists toward the car to keep Mister Marvel from jumping on her and soiling her dress with his muddy paws. After Lily drives away, Bingo hoses down Mister Marvel while giving me a running commentary of the day's events. Mister Marvel shakes himself dry, and we go in to eat.

Tarsha and I pile chicken, beans, potato salad, and cole slaw on the plates. The three of us gather around the dining room table with Mister Marvel crouched by Bingo's chair. "Where am I going to do my homework? The kitchen table is all messy." Bingo has a milk mustache that makes me laugh.

"What's wrong with here at the dining room table?" I bite into a drumstick.

"I can't see in here at night. It's too dark."

Tarsha clucks her tongue. "We'll get you an oil lamp to study by like Abraham Lincoln. Maybe you'll turn out as well."

"Fun-nee," Bingo says, drawing out the word. "Mom, you said we'd get a desk for my room from Gran's house."

"We will when I get to it. Tarsha and I'll move our stuff in here. The dining room table gives us more room to work. Let's eat up. We're going on a little ride as soon as we're finished. We can take the brownies with us in the car."

"Where?" Bingo pushes his beans back and forth like he's counting on an abacus.

"Just a place I need to see for my work."

"Do I have to go? I want to stay here and watch TV."

Sometimes Bingo amazes me with his adult-like behavior, but today he's childishly cantankerous. "You can't stay by yourself. We won't be long."

"Mom . . . yes, I can. I'm not going."

"Bingo, enough. Finish up," I snap, on edge from the day.

We polish off the meal, pack up the remains, and drive into Grenola. Eating brownies, Bingo and Mister Marvel scuffle in the backseat, oblivious to the conversation in the front.

Even though it's getting late, the sun is still out, days growing longer as summer approaches. Tarsha eyes the stores in the strip mall on the outskirts of town. "Right there's Walter's Cars. It's where Weldon worked. You turn left on that road right on up there, and it'll take us to the spot by Four Mile Lake. I guess you know the other side of the lake is where all the fishing boats and bait shops are. A few beer joints. The side where April Brown was"—she glances at the backseat—"where we're going is pretty isolated. A good spot to meet somebody if you don't want to be seen."

The road is part dirt and part gravel and winds through a grove of pecan and oak trees. Through the thicket I can see the curve of Four Mile Lake. The lake is wide but named for its length. Cypress trees grow along the borders, casting deep shadows on the water. A few fishermen paddle their rowboats away from the wooden docks, their lines dragging behind them. A whooping crane takes flight, afraid of the intruders.

Tarsha points. "See that clump of trees and bushes over there on the bluff? That's where the policeman was parked." She snickers. "His version of lover's lane. Hot stuff happenin'. Can't see a car there from the road."

Bingo moves to the window, his antennae up and

catching signals. "What's so funny? What about a policeman?"

I reach back and ruffle his hair. "Nothing's funny. It's about a case of mine."

"What case?" He mashes his nose and cheeks against the glass to distort his features, something he's seen a comedian do.

"What if you freeze like that?" Tarsha makes a face at him.

He ignores her. "What case?"

I explain, "A man I represent has been convicted of something he says he didn't do, and I'm trying to help prove him innocent." I hope this is the end of his interest, but he's a curious sort.

"What did they think he did?"

Tarsha whips around and puts her chin on the back of the seat, locking eyes with Bingo. "Murdered somebody, okay?"

"Jeez." He slams back against his seat, keeping clear of her.

The road narrows, curves, and gradually turns into a slight incline with a grassy ravine below. A lone tree stands like a sentinel. "Right here," Tarsha says. "This is the place. Right down there."

I stop the car, get out, telling Bingo to keep Tarsha company, and edge down the slope where Robert Weldon encountered April Brown. The loose dirt almost causes me to slip. I stand in the exact spot and look up toward the road. I can see only the hood of my car. I glance around in all directions, at the woods and the lake glistening beyond them. Except for the screech of a bird and the wind rustling through the trees, the place is eerily quiet. I can imagine April Brown lying there, moaning, her life's blood draining from her. She met someone by the lone tree on the road, not here, and was pushed or fell after she was stabbed to this spot.

Deep in thought, I climb the incline and stamp dust off my shoes. Robert Weldon was walking home from work to fix his car when he found April Brown. Something is out of sync here. I get in the car and start the engine. Bingo and Mister Marvel are wrestling. "Tarsha, you know Apple Orchard Road?"

"Yeah. This road hooks on around to it, but there's a cutoff back down the way we came that'll take you there. Why?"

I wheel around in the road. "Weldon told me where his house was. I want to go by it."

I retrace our tracks, take the cutoff, and turn onto Apple Orchard Road. Houses are situated at odd intervals along the winding lane, some near the road on small plots, many set back in trees on larger acreage. All are frame structures with mailboxes in front. Most yards are carefully tended, but a few are overgrown with weeds, blighting the otherwise pleasant working-class neighborhood. I slow in front of the address Weldon gave me. The small white house is contrasted by freshly painted black shutters. The screened front porch has a ceiling fan and rattan furniture. The front steps need repair and the free-standing garage lists slightly to the left. I wonder how it looked when it belonged to Robert Weldon. I wonder why he took the long way home by Four Mile Lake when he could have taken the cutoff and gotten there quicker.

I cruise down Apple Orchard until it meets Four Mile Lake Road, take that road to the cutoff, and go back to Apple Orchard. "This is what I call going around in circles," Tarsha comments. "Guess you have a reason, huh?"

I tell her what's on my mind and let her chew on it until we hit the edge of town. Walter's Cars is still open. On an impulse I pull into the parking area. "Back in a flash."

I catch Walter Boyd locking the back door for the night. He's tall and thin, but his beer belly makes him look as if he swallowed a watermelon. Tufts of black hair poke out of his ears. He's totally bald, and his shiny head could light his way on a dark night. He's honest and charges fair prices. Who would know whether a car really needed an overhaul or a new transmission, but if Walter says so, it does.

"Well, hey, Leona. Whatcha need?" His hands are gnarled, grease caked under his fingernails. Tools litter the oil-streaked concrete floors. An old Dodge is suspended on the pneumatic lift. Tires are piled high against the wall.

"Walter, good to see you. I'm representing Robert Weldon." I watch closely for his reaction.

He smiles, and the crinkles etched on his temples fan upward. "Well, I'll be danged. You?"

I nod. "He worked for you, I understand."

Walter takes a greasy rag from his pocket, almost mops his brow with it, then throws it on a can. "Best mechanic I ever seen. Could take a car apart and put 'er back together quicker'n anybody. Shame about him. You seen him?"

"Today, at Parchman." It seems longer ago.

"How's he look?"

"Okay. He looks okay. Doing pretty well, given the circumstances."

Walter shakes his head. "I'll never forget that day it happened, never if I live to be a hunnert and two. No, sir."

"Tell me about it."

"Well, he was wanting to get off early. Never asked for any time off, so I was glad to let him go, he being such a good worker and all. Weldon said his car needed fixing, thrown a rod. He walked to work that morning. Bright and early, too. Always the first one here, 'sides me, of course. Anyhow, he says to me he had to go somewhere that night and needed his car. So I says, why, sure, Robert, go on ahead and get it fixed. I'm figuring he had him a date with that Louella Waters he was going with, pretty uptown, she is. He left here 'bout one-thirty. I was a fixing to close up later that afternoon when I heard they done arrested him for murder. Like to have floored me, it did. I never believed Robert could murder nobody. No, sir, not Robert Weldon."

I'm feeling better all the time. I still don't know why Robert Weldon took the long way home that day, but maybe he can answer that to my satisfaction. I realize how desperate I am to believe him. "Why did Robert take the long way home that day when he could have turned off on Apple Orchard and gotten there sooner?" I think how fate plays a hand. "He wouldn't have stumbled on April Brown if he hadn't gone that way."

"Said to the cops he swung by Four Mile to pick up a jacket he'd left hanging on a tree branch the night before while he was waiting on Louella Waters to row over from the other side to pick him up and take him back to the action side of the lake where all them cafés are. I testified for him, you know. Like to scared the shi—shucks outta me up there in front of everbody, but I told 'em what a good mechanic he was. Never made no mistakes. No, sir, none. Well, that D.A. made a fool outta me."

"How so?" My good feeling is evaporating, and I brace for a blow.

"Well, Robert told the cops his car had thrown a rod and he was walking home to fix it. He's got tools and all out there. A day or two after he was arrested, the cops went out to his house with a warrant and took a mechanic with them. Some guy works over at the Chevrolet place on the highway. Robert's car started right up. See, wasn't nothing wrong with it. That's what the D.A. springs at the trial. Plus, the cops searched and couldn't find that coat Robert said he left."

My breath catches in my throat. This will all be in the trial transcripts. Suddenly I'm afraid of other discrepancies Tarsha and I will find tonight. Though Perkins warned me that Weldon was a congenital liar, I chose to believe my new client.

"That there fancy lawyer of Robert's was hollering, 'Objection, objection' near about every breath he took. I thought he was gonna have him a heart attack right there on the spot." He shakes his head. "I sure hope you can do better for Robert than that man did.

No matter what, I still don't think he killed that gal, but that D.A. made things look mighty bad for him at the trial, mighty bad. I just hope you can find the sumbitch that did kill her so they'll let Robert go."

He doesn't hope as much as I do, if somebody besides Weldon did kill her. "I appreciate your help, Walter. I may come back to talk to you again. Hold a good thought for Robert." I try to act cheerful, to project a confidence I don't feel.

Back in the car, I light a cigarette and, heavy with worry, tell Tarsha what I've learned. I'm anxious to dig into the transcripts. "I pray we don't find any more inconsistencies."

Tarsha turns to me, a crease between her eyes. "You know what? If J. Clyde Perkins said he got caught with his pants down, I think this case is gonna jump out and bite *you* on the ass."

4

I JOG AROUND THE BAYOU, KEEPING AN EYE ON THE house where Bingo sleeps and another on where I step. Water moccasins sometimes laze around the muddy banks. A ghostly mist hovers over the water, and the howls of wild dogs in the forest pierce the early morning air. I feel as if I'm all alone in some godforsaken place.

The noise from the trellis woke me at five o'clock from fitful dreams of Robert Weldon. I calculated that I'd been in bed little more than four hours. I feel awful, throat parched, eyes grainy, head busting. I'm depending on the exercise to revive me.

Breaking into a run, I dwell on my phone call to Jack last night, our stilted conversation punctuated by long silences. He understood how I might have some empathy for Robert Weldon after seeing him, but felt taking on the case was a grievous mistake. "Odds are, he'll be executed and you'll never get over it, never be the same person again. I've seen it happen before. Why buy failure? Let some hard-skinned attorney who's used to losing death-penalty appeals handle his case. It's routine to those guys." I appreciate his concern, but that does little for my situation, this nagging sense that compels me to continue. The case has eaten into me like a hungry termite into wood, and I can't tell Jack why.

Exhausted rather than invigorated, I return to the house. Catching my sweaty image reflected in the kitchen window, I mash down my spiked hair and blot my face with a paper towel. I gulp cold water.

In preparation for my return I had set the coffee process in motion. The percolator groans, over-worked from last night. The kitchen smells like a stale pool hall. Opening the window, I empty ashtrays into the wastebasket, rinse coffee mugs, and stare at the mess Tarsha and I made.

I drag the yellow legal pad over and study my notes from the trial transcripts. I already knew about the perfectly running car that, according to Weldon, had thrown a rod, and the missing coat, but what I didn't know rocked me. The murder weapon was a butcher knife with a seven-inch blade, a common type sold in a set of four. A search of Weldon's house produced such a set, but one was missing. Weldon, according to police reports, claimed he'd never owned such a set of knives.

Trying to neutralize the incriminating evidence, Perkins implored the jury members to go home and check out their knives. His words in the transcripts: "See if you have a full set of knives. I know I don't. I looked. Things get misplaced or lost. A missing knife from Weldon's kitchen is of no significance. But the point here is that Robert Weldon didn't even own that set of knives. Has the prosecution shown you any proof that he did? Believe me, they've been looking. Have you seen any sales slips? Any clerk that remembered Robert Weldon purchasing those knives?"

He spun a scenario for the jurors, trying to raise reasonable doubt. Talk gets around in a small town fast, he reminded them. The murderer knew Weldon had been arrested for something he didn't do, knew Weldon claimed that his car had thrown a rod, knew his reason for being at the crime scene, to retrieve his coat. What a perfect cover, then, for the killer. Let Weldon take the blame. He was in the wrong place at the wrong time. The real murderer quickly removes any evidence that substantiates Weldon's statements. The killer, someone with a knowledge of simple mechanics, repaired Weldon's car, removed Weldon's coat, planted that common set of knives, minus one, in Weldon's kitchen. Then he's home free.

It's apparent from the transcripts that Perkins performed masterfully, given the circumstances. I feel like a sleaze for claiming ineffectual counsel, but lawyers are allowed to travel certain legal corridors, however shabby. I want to believe Perkins's scenario. I have to believe, despite the evidence. Twelve jurors didn't.

Flannery's pitch was more convincing. "Robert Weldon aspired to marry Louella Waters, a girl from a family who owned a farm-equipment dealership. A step up financially and socially for Weldon. There's your motive," he declared. "Just what do you think would have happened to Robert Weldon's relationship with Louella Waters if it had become known he'd impregnated April Brown? And, opportunity. April Brown didn't live anywhere near the crime scene. What was she doing out there, then? Her mother testified she went to meet the white man she'd been seeing and was going to make him pay for getting her pregnant. She was there to meet Robert Weldon, and he kept that rendezvous. There was no other reason for him to be at that exact place at that exact time."

I drink coffee, smoke a cigarette, and consider eating. My stomach is knotted. I make a plan for the day. From now on every minute counts. I can spare enough cash for Tarsha to buy a fax machine, a must for the office now. Once I draft the appeals, they can be faxed to the court's clerk and the ruling can be faxed back to me, saving precious time. Death-penalty appeals generally take time to work through the courts, but once an execution date has been set, the courts' opinions are handed down with lightning speed. The Buchanan law library is more extensive, to say the least, than mine, and I called a member of the firm last night for a favor. While I work in their library during the morning, Tarsha will gather information I need. Later in the day I will begin my investigation and talk to those who top my list.

A knock at my front door startles me. Engrossed with plans, I didn't hear a car. I hurry to the living room and peep through the curtains. The sun has risen, and Byars is on my front porch, khaki shirt and pants freshly pressed, boots shined to a mirror finish. He exudes Old World elegance, but on occasion contradicts his countenance. I've seen him hoist a bottle of bourbon and swig like a boorish longshoreman. I have seen him cry like a child over the death of his hunting dog.

"Good morning," he greets me as I open the door.

"So far," I answer.

"I was on the way to pick up Charles. Thought I'd stop in. Got some coffee going?"

"Sure. Come on back to the kitchen." Byars and Charles put in long days. They're up when the hands, as the field workers are called, begin work, and oversee the plantations until noon. After lunch they take naps, unlike the hands, and resume patrolling the gravel roads through the land, stopping to chat and confer with the foremen until sundown.

I pour Byars a mug of strong black coffee. "You're up early." He glances at the piles of trial transcripts.

"I have lots to do," I answer, my eyes tracing his Roman nose. His presence always seems to fill a room.

"So I hear." He tastes the coffee. "I also hear you're not taking Mary Jessica's case."

"My time is limited. I can't do both and do justice to either one." I may not be able to do justice to the one.

"Bingo not up yet?"

I shake my head, knowing Byars is raring to tear into me. Those intense blue eyes are fixed on me like lasers ready to burn through skin. I decide to open the subject. "I've been up most of the night going through the transcripts. I think I have a pretty good feel for the case now." Lightning may strike me at any moment. "To start, I'm going to claim ineffectual counsel against J. Clyde Perkins. Robert Weldon wanted to take the stand, and Perkins wouldn't let him. I just may get lucky and find a sympathetic judge along the way." Three of Weldon's five appeals had been exhausted. One of the last two must strike home or he is out. The thought shakes me to the core.

Byars takes a ragged breath. "Why are you doing this? You think you're a better lawyer than J. Clyde Perkins?"

I interrupt. "No—"

He interrupts. "I'm not finished. You won't get anywhere with the courts, for chrissakes, and will just publicly call attention to yourself and to failure. Believe me, this case is about as futile as trying to push the cork back in a champagne bottle. And for what? All the time and effort you'll put out and not a dime in return for it. You need to think of your repu-tation and your shallow pocketbook you so adamantly refuse to let others help fill. Representing these . . . these kind of people will get you nowhere. I can't imagine what you're thinking."

I can and wish he'd be proud I've bounced back to life. "Byars, I believe Robert Weldon to be inno-cent."

His face turns to the consistency of granite. "Oh, you do, do you? You have some mystic power that sees beyond what twelve jurors saw and heard. Now you're just going to get everybody in town all riled up and talking about you, especially the black contingent. I'm saying all this for your own good, Leona. You don't want to be the topic of conversation here again, the object of ridicule. I hate to see you get hurt." He lets out a rush of air. "Leona, drop this case right now before it gets any further. Some hard-nosed lawyer will take it on and roll with the punches when it's over."

"But he'll waste time with all the legal aspects and won't look for the real killer." I put some heat in my words.

His face flushes, veins in his forehead distended. "That's what you intend to do?"

"Yes, Byars, that's what I intend to do."

He slaps his hand on the table. "This is more than ridiculous now. It's dangerous, even. Just for a minute, say Weldon isn't the killer and you go out trying to find out who is, poking around. You think the killer is going to just sit still?"

I think about what Byars just said and admit the prospect scares me, but if any concrete evidence is uncovered, it becomes a police matter. I don't antici-pate facing a murderer alone.

"Leona, You've always been pretty good at acting without thinking."

He can make me feel like I've sprouted horns and stuck him with my pitchfork. "I guess I know what you're referring to now . . ."

Ignoring the break, Byars continues, "Never *considering* the consequences to yourself or others."

"You're off the subject now."

"Maybe so, but while I'm off of it I might as well say what I think. And I think you've never forgiven

me for . . . about . . . about Paris, my attitude, my disapproval, just like any father would have toward an
unmarried pregnant daughter. You hold it against me
and want to hurt me."

My temper is rising. "Byars, holding a grudge
takes too much energy. You're damn well entitled to
your opinion as well as I am mine, but you're not
entitled to control people. And that's the key word
here, control. If you think I took this case to hurt or
embarrass you, you're way off base. Why, for once,
can't you just be proud of me? 'My daughter's fight-
ing for the underdog, isn't that something?' No, you
have to twist it around. This case has to do with me,
not you. You don't need to attach some strange motivation to it." I think of Lily's words, but won't reveal
their origin. "I wonder what you'd think if I prove an
innocent man has been wrongly convicted. How
would that look to everybody in Grenola? I would be
the topic of conversation again, but with a positive
twist this time."

"Hi, Grandpa." Bingo comes to the table, Mister
Marvel behind him.

We both look at Bingo. I wonder how much he's
heard. Byars ruffles Bingo's hair and asks when he
wants to play croquet again. Bingo asks if Byars will
take him horseback riding. Byars agrees to take him
soon. I'd be grateful for that extra time to work without having to deal with Bingo, and I'm pleased that
Byars will spend time with Bingo. My son needs a
male presence in his life. I think of Jack and how
good he'd be with Bingo. I'd be good for Kit Flannery, too. She needs a mom. When I returned from

Paris, I was on the outside looking in, envious of Jack, his wife, Rebecca, their perfect life with their child, all that I had missed out on. Then their world was snatched from them.

I walk Byars to the door while Bingo eats cereal. "I just hope you'll reconsider and drop this case." He focuses on the bayou like he's in a trance. "Damn it all to hell. I just can't see you up there at Parchman penitentiary on death row talking to some convict."

I'm sorry we've tangled. I don't like discord, but we've danced this dance before and at a more dizzying pace in the past. "Byars, this is something I have to do. To me, Robert Weldon is a human being, not a case."

"It's like this Weldon has cast some spell over you." He stalks down the steps, then turns back. "Think about this, now. What if you persevere and get this Weldon off and then find out he was guilty all along? What then?" He continues to the car and I watch him drive away.

I think of the horror of the scenario Byars raised. I'd read of just such a case. I've heard the best criminal lawyers never ask clients if they are guilty. They don't want to know. I couldn't represent Robert Weldon if I thought he was actually guilty. Going back inside, I feel beleaguered, but try to rise above it.

Bingo and I dress, and I drop him at school early, under a rain of protests. Classes won't begin until eight, but the library is open and I expound on the benefits of extra study time. The playground is supervised, and I figure he'll linger there rather than crack a book, especially if Kit Flannery is around.

I arrive at the law offices of Craddock, Watts, and Buchanan, located in a two-story office building a block from my place. Their space can't compare to J. Clyde Perkins's, but it's upscale for Grenola and a sight better than my cubbyhole. Dressed in a gray cotton suit and carrying a briefcase—stuffed for real this time—I pass the secretary's muster and plant myself at the long walnut conference table in their law library, ready to work. I'd give my right arm for a paralegal to help with research.

After surrounding myself with enough books to build a brick wall, I discover some interesting statistics and avenues to travel in case my appeal of ineffectual counsel is rejected. One is to claim Weldon's previous lawyers did not adequately investigate his claim of innocence. That is certainly a valid appeal. Another is, if a witness committed perjury. I have to throw that out unless I discover it to be so, an unlikely event but not entirely impossible. Nothing to bank on, though.

Another appeal strikes me, one that has not been tried to date, a claim that lethal injection is cruel and unusual punishment. In 1984 a law passed the Mississippi legislature decreeing that those convicted before that time were to be executed in the gas chamber, but those convicted after that date were to die by lethal injection. Appeals in every state had claimed that the gas chamber was obsolete and cruel and unusual punishment. Most states adopted lethal injection as a means of execution, as it was considered quick and painless.

A quick computer search adds fuel to the thought.

I'm excited by the information and how I might turn it into a legal tangle, buying some time. Contrary to claims, lethal injection is not always quick, clean, and painless. Of the thirty-eight states that have the death penalty, thirty-two use lethal injection. All but seven of the fifty-six people executed last year in the United States died by lethal injection.

In the 1985 execution of Stephen Morin in Texas, technicians took more than forty minutes to find a suitable vein. In another Texas execution in 1989, the IV came out of the condemned man's arm, spurting chemicals onto the floor. James Autry was strapped to a stretcher in a Texas prison with the IV dripping for ten minutes before his death while witnesses said he thrashed about complaining of severe pain. When John Wayne Gacy was put to death in Illinois in 1994, the chemical intended to stop his breathing clogged in the line, causing the execution to take eighteen minutes.

I lean back in the leather chair, wishing for a cigarette, wishing for a computer. I will have to buy one, even if I have to use an installment plan. Tarsha will be ecstatic. I feel a stir of excitement.

At eleven, I drop into my friend's office, thank him for his help, and ask for more when needed. We have a cup of coffee, discuss the case as much as confidentiality allows. He is surprised that I've taken it, as I'm not a criminal lawyer. I tell him that I plan to outwork everybody to compensate for inexperience. He smiles and nods, but his expression is one of extreme doubt.

I make fast tracks to my office. Tarsha has the fax

machine assembled, and I admire it like a child with a new toy. I tell her we'll get a computer.

"Joy to the world. We are in business." Her smile is wide and warm. She's called the two sets of lawyers from Jackson who represented Weldon after Perkins. Unlike Perkins, they have agreed to send copies of their briefs, motions, and documents from appeals, anything to help save Robert Weldon's life.

"That's good news." I sit at my desk and remove the paperwork from my briefcase. "So, you have some background information on April Brown we didn't get from the trial transcripts?"

She taps her fingernails on the table. Today she's wearing shiny black nail polish. "Yeah, I poked around in my neighborhood. Talked to several people who knew her. She didn't have any close friends, thought she was above most folks. April Brown was a fox, good figure, graduated from high school and went to work in a beauty parlor. She had ambition, saving up to head to California to be a model or a movie star. Thought a white man might be her ticket outta here."

I perk up. "So, was there more than one white man in her life?"

"Nah, just this one, so they said, but she never said who he was. Told people he was gonna take her to California. April Brown's brother, Babaloo Brown, owns what used to be called a juke joint over near the lake. He lives in the back of it. Both of them, April and Babaloo, came a long way from where they started. Mr. Brown's dead, but he was a sharecropper, and Mrs. Maudie Brown, their mother, as you know from the transcripts, cleaned houses and took in ironing."

I light a cigarette, feeling my stomach rumble. "I want to talk to the brother. Mrs. Brown is already on my short list."

Tarsha eyebrows lift to inverted V's. "You'd better not be planning on going to Babaloo's place by yourself. Uh-uh. It's rough. Bunch of guys hopped up on no telling what and in you walk? Never been there myself, but I hear things, like it's where you go to score. Little white powder in cellophane packages, I reckon."

"I can't imagine that Mr. Babaloo Brown would be happy to walk in here and talk to me. I'll have to go to him and to Mrs. Brown."

"Girl, they aren't gonna be happy to talk to you anywhere and may not."

"I have to try." And my approach must be diplomatic. "After lunch I'm going to talk with the chief of police, then try to see Mrs. Maudie Brown and after that the officer, Ray Bell Crosby, who picked Weldon up at the lake. If I have enough time, I'll try to contact Louella Waters." Without the resources, I can't even hire an investigator most law firms have on retainer, just waiting in the wings for an assignment. What I wouldn't give for some help in that department.

"You got appointments?"

"I'm not going to make appointments with anyone I plan to talk to. The surprise element. Makes conversation more spontaneous."

"You read that in a paperback detective novel?"

The phone rings, and Tarsha picks up the receiver. "Law offices of L. Bingham and Associates." Tarsha winks. "Tomorrow? We're fairly well booked. Just let me check the schedule to see what I can work out." She pages through a blank legal pad, holding it close to the receiver for sound effects. "Maybe around eleven-thirty I could squeeze you in. Fine. See you then." She hangs up and wheels around in her chair.

"Well, who was that? You're sure free with my time."

"The president." She rolls her eyes. "That was a reporter from the *Clarion-Ledger* in Jackson. Gary Marshall. Wants to interview you about the Robert Weldon case."

"How could he know?" I remember the reporter waiting to see the prison attorney, John Dobbs, and tell Tarsha how this likely happened. "Suits me. Might as well garner some publicity for Weldon's cause. Who knows what might happen?" I hand Tarsha the lawyer-client agreement that the prison attorney requested. "I drafted this last night. Let's fax it to Parchman so John Dobbs can have Weldon sign it, then file with the state."

I grab a yellow pad, and as I begin the first draft of my appeal, the front door opens. Lily and Estelle enter, bustling around as if they've never seen my office digs.

"Morning," they say almost in unison.

"Morning," I parrot. Lily looks with approval at my gray outfit. I guess anything beats warm-ups in a law office. They are geared up for a luncheon in someone's garden. Estelle is so thin in her yellow linen sheath that she could walk with two champagne flutes resting on her pelvic bones.

"Leona has an interview with a reporter from the *Clarion-Ledger*," Tarsha tells them.

Lily seems startled at first, then pleased. Her smile is so sweet, so genuine. I know she's probably taken some guff from Byars. Both Estelle and Lily have to walk on eggshells around their husbands. "Why, that's wonderful, Leona. Right here in this office." She pulls her prop, the handkerchief, from her cuff.

Estelle hooks her purse strap over her arm. "Actually, that's something we wanted to talk to you about . . . this office. Now, don't get me wrong, Leona, but I know how stubborn you can be. It would give us something to do." She looks at Lily for support. "I have so many nice things in storage that I don't use, brass lamps, end tables, and there's everything in Lily's attic—an Oriental rug, a breakfront, some prints for the walls—and I have a big plant in a brass urn you could have. We could get Julius to help and a few hands off the field and a truck."

The desire to do something for me burns in their eyes, an appeal to assure me of their allegiance. And this place begs for help. I'm too busy now to do anything about it. Lily's attic is like a warehouse, where any of us can feel free to pick and choose. Why not afford them the pleasure? It's something small I can give them in return. "I'd appreciate your help fixing this place up. Do what you like. I'll like whatever you do."

Estelle whips a tape measure from her purse and has Lily hold the other end. "Don't let us bother you, now. We won't get in the way." An idea strikes her, and she drops the tape measure. It whips back into its cover like it's alive, and Lily jumps away. "Lily, let's not go to that party today. Let's just go home and change clothes and get started fixing up this place." She turns to Tarsha and me. "Y'all have that interview tomorrow, and the office ought to look nice. What if he takes pictures?"

"That's a perfectly good idea," Lily says. "I didn't really want to go anyhow."

They head for the door as if racing to see who can exit first. Hand on the brass knob, Estelle looks over her shoulder. "Leona, I know you're going to be awful busy, and if you need some help with Bingo, I'd be glad to oblige."

"Appreciate it," I answer. I will need help with Bingo, and he enjoys his cousins.

"Instant decor," Tarsha remarks after they've gone. "'Bout time this place got spiffed up. Something to look at besides drab." She plunders in the desk drawer and pulls out a brown paper grease-strained sack. "I brought two sandwiches for lunch today. Want one? Tuna or egg salad?"

"Or ptomaine. That drawer's not exactly a refrigerator. I'll take the egg salad. I'll go to the drugstore and get us Cokes to go with them. Be right back." I push away from my desk.

The sidewalk is scorching and reflects the heat. We'll have a record summer. I smell ozone in the air, a prelude to a thunderstorm. I picture Robert Weldon in the treeless, dusty exercise yard for his hour out of his cell. What a pitiful event to look forward to as the day's highlight. Would he be free by summer to sit in the shade and fish in the cool lake? Would he be dead and buried in some pauper's field? I shiver at the thought that his survival is up to me.

The ceiling fans' lazy blades whirl in the drugstore, barely stirring the air. I stand at the old marble counter and order two Cokes to go from probably the last soda jerk on earth. He even wears an old-fashioned white cap like those I remember from my youth. I pick two straws from the dispenser and hear my name, the diminutive. I know who it is before I turn.

"Hey, Charles."

"Taking a break?" He always looks as if he knows something I don't. I halfway expect to see canary feathers at the corners of his mouth.

"That's the good part about being my own boss. I just stop when I want to." I take the Cokes and pay.

He leans on the counter, invading my space. "You should stop it all together, this case. Byars is really upset about it. Hardly said a word all morning."

"Charles, this case is my problem and nobody else's. I just wish everybody would stay out of my face about it." I twist the top of the paper sack after I put in the drinks.

"If you continue to pursue this, you're going to wish you hadn't."

I stare at him. He has a cocky way about him. Unlike Byars, Charles confuses macho with manly. "What is that, some kind of threat? What difference does it make to you what kind of case I take?" I notice the soda jerk listening and turn my back.

He puts on his sunglasses. "I just hate to see you make a fool out of yourself."

"I'll try not to disappoint you," I answer.

"You're hardheaded, Lee."

"Thanks, Charles. I don't often get compliments from you. Now let me give you one, more than one, actually. You're one of the best-looking men I've ever seen. Your wife is spectacular. Your children are great. You've got the world by the tail. And there's enough room for both of us here. So, why don't you relax and enjoy what you've got and quit pushing me, okay?"

I can't see his eyes behind the sunglasses, but I sense they've turned harder than usual. "See you, Lee," he says, and strolls toward the front door.

I head back to the office, upset by the encounter. I want to get along with Charles, but we have no history of accord and may never. We simply have no affinity for each other. I find it sad that we can't be like brother and sister.

Tarsha and I have a quick lunch, discuss plans, and I leave for the police station. I pass the columned yellow brick courthouse built on a square of land in the center of town. The magnolia trees on the green lawn are filled with white, velvety blossoms. I wave at several people coming down the courthouse steps and cross the street to the police station adjacent to the jail. The iron bars remind me of Robert Weldon. I can imagine him incarcerated there six years ago, peering out at the people who walked free down the streets of Grenola. I wonder if the evidence from the case is still preserved at the station.

I enter the small front room of the police station, where a young officer in a blue uniform mans the front desk. A radio crackles in the background. Crime is almost nonexistent in Grenola, except for a few drunken drivers, speeders, and petty thefts. I can imagine what a furor the murder caused and how anxious the officers were to solve it. Maybe too anxious.

The officer looks at me with recognition I can't return, though I think I've seen him. "Why, it's Miz Leona Bingham."

"Last time I looked. How are you?"

"Near 'bout starvin'. It's lunchtime, you know, and I was a fixing to go over to the café. Fried catfish plate lunch today. What can I do for you?" He smiles.

"Chief Lewis in? I need to see him."

"He is. Right on back there in his office." He motions with his head.

I walk back and tap on the slightly ajar door. This is no scene from a movie with phones ringing and tough detectives hustling back and forth. The chief has held this position for as long as I can remember. He was once the football coach. "Did I hear right?" He calls out. "Leona Bingham? Come on in."

I push open the door. "It's me."

The chief still has a military crew cut, but his hair is gray now and he's grown gaunt over the years. He stands and offers his liver-spotted hand. We shake and I sit in the wooden arm chair by his square, scuffed desk. "Well, danged if you didn't turn out right pretty. I've known you since you was a mite, you know."

I laugh. "You had to run me out of The Inn lobby. Elevator offense."

"You and Jack Flannery both." He picks up a

half-smoked cigar and chews on the stub. "Now he's the D.A. and you're a lawyer. And I hear you two are back together again. Go figure. So, what's up?"

"I'm representing Robert Weldon."

His eyes narrow almost imperceptibly. "Zat so? Now, how come you to take on a case like that?"

"His execution date has been set." I rummage in my purse and light a cigarette. "He wrote and asked if I'd represent him. I went up to Parchman to see him and decided I'd take the case."

"What'd he say to make you decide to take it?"

"He claims he's innocent."

A smile cracks across his wizened face. "Never saw one who didn't."

My next statement will be an affront to the man who arrested Weldon and charged him with murder. "I happen to believe him."

He rocks back in his swivel chair. "Well, I reckon it's your right to, but you're wrong. Sure as I'm sittin' here, Weldon killed April Brown. I did not arrest the wrong man. No, sir, not me. He even claimed he didn't know her, never saw her before that day, but I know better."

My heart cranks up a notch. "How do you know that?" What more can come to my attention? This wasn't in the trial transcripts.

"I been dealing with human nature all my life— boys out on the playing field, folks brought in here. I've heard it all, every kind of excuse, and I just know when somebody's lying." He taps his chest with a fist. "Right here in my heart. I know it. I couldn't prove Weldon knew April Brown. Lord knows I tried, but I know he did. Flannery Senior knew it, too. We had enough to convict Weldon, so it didn't matter in the long run. That fancy man Perkins gave Mr. Flannery a run for his money, he did, but our homeboy came out on top." His eyes lock onto mine. "Too bad our homegirl won't, though. Leona, you're gonna lose your client. Governor Robert Danforth is gonna have him an execution to prove he's hard on crime. Texas and Louisiana and Florida, all of 'em been executing convicts like they was flies, and Mississippi hasn't executed anybody in a few years. Well, that's gonna change. Robert Danforth's gonna change it.

"Know something. It was before your time, but when I was a kid, they had the electric chair. Had portable ones they brought around in trailers to the jails. Brought one right here one time and electrocuted a fellow. I was around the corner at the American Legion Hall at a dance, and we knew this man was gonna be electrocuted. Sure enough, the lights dimmed and flickered and went off for a second while they were pouring the volts to him. Gave us all the creeps. I heard some god-awful stories about electrocutions. This one guy just wouldn't die. They just kept hitting him with the volts till flames and sparks came out of his eyes and ears. I heard his eyeballs finally popped out. So they invented the gas chamber to make killing more humane, and now they got lethal injection to make it even more so."

My lunch is in my throat. I wouldn't normally be so affected by the conversation if I wasn't so personally touched by the possibility of my client's execution. "I've read about some cases involving lethal injection, and they don't sound like that method is so humane."

"About as humane as killing can get, I reckon."

Just because Chief Lewis felt in his heart that Robert Weldon knew April Brown didn't make it so. I think it is wishful thinking on his part, his conscience telling him that he nailed the right man. April Brown was pregnant by a white man that no one ever saw her with or heard her speak his name. He is the man I have to find. He's not just any man, but a man with much to lose, a man willing to go to any lengths to keep from being exposed in this community as the father of April Brown's baby.

"Is Ray Bell Crosby still on the force?"

"Nah, he's retired now. Got him a little farm over near the levee on Cypress Road. Raises soybean crops. Nice little lake stocked with catfish. Did pretty good for an old redneck feller. I'm glad of it. I like him personally. He was a good officer. Real smart."

"He was Robert's friend, right?"

"Oh, yeah, they was fishing buddies. He did what he could to help Robert, saying how he thought he saw somebody running from the scene like Robert said, but ole Ray got clobbered on the stand." His cheeks redden, and he looks at a spot on the wall. "Guess you know all about that testimony of that gal he was with. Sybil, her name was. Sybil Cooper, a manicurist. Raising her skirts for just about anybody, I heard. I was surprised Ray Bell's wife stuck with him after that, but she did. I guess she just didn't have nowhere else to go. Sybil moved on after that . . . to Jackson, I think." He looks at his cigar, comes to a decision, and lights it, enjoys the puff enough to close his eyes for a second. "So, you'll be appealing Weldon's conviction. What grounds you using?"

"Ineffectual counsel. Weldon wanted to testify, and J. Clyde Perkins wouldn't let him." I check for a reaction, but Chief Lewis hoards his emotions.

"You think the outcome woulda been different had he testified, then?"

"I don't know, but he didn't get the chance he should have. Maybe a judge will see it that way." I stub out my cigarette in an ashtray shaped like a horseshoe.

Chief Lewis shrugs. "Maybe a federal judge, but you don't have a chance in Mississippi courts, in my opinion. Jack Flannery has plenty of influence there, and Governor Danforth is up for reelection and needs the black vote." He laces his hands together. "Yes, sir, that Flannery's one sharp dude, he is. I say he'll be the next governor after Robert Danforth. Now you're gonna be bucking Mr. Flannery." He shakes his head as if my task is clearly impossible.

I glance out the window, hoping to appear casual. "The Weldon case sure made Mr. Flannery's reputation. J. Clyde Perkins and his big guns don't lose many cases."

The chief grunts. "Perkins just hadn't come up against Flannery before. Never could understand how come Mr. Perkins took Weldon's case, for free, too. I thought it was strange. Just walked in here big as you please next day after I arrested Weldon and said he wanted to see him, was gonna represent him.

Flannery like to have flipped when he heard who Weldon's counsel was. I think he made up his mind right then and there that he was gonna beat Perkins."

I wanted to ask about Weldon's demeanor after he had been arrested but wouldn't get a fair evaluation since Chief Lewis was convinced he killed April Brown. Ray Bell Crosby could likely give a better description. I won't get anywhere with Chief Lewis concerning Jack Flannery either, as he's obviously in awe of the man. "Do you still have the evidence you collected back then?"

He looks toward his row of green file cabinets. "Well, I reckon so. The evidence list is in there, and I guess the actual stuff is in the back storage room where we keep things. You want to see?" He pushes away from his desk and moves to the file cabinets, as agile as a young man.

He pulls out a binder book, his lips moving as he reads. "It's all listed here. We can go back to the storage room. Come on and we'll see what we got."

I follow Chief Lewis down the hall to a room he unlocks. The dank area is lined with metal shelves stacked with numbered cardboard boxes. The chief squints, looking from box to box. "Here. Here we go. Right here." He seems proud to have found the box. He removes it, places it on a long metal table, lifts off the lid, and peers inside. "Take a look."

April Brown's clothes and belongings are wrapped in plastic bags. Blood, now rust-colored, stains her pink-flowered blouse, and the fabric is slashed from the stab wound. I can picture the fury behind the one who wielded the knife. Robert Weldon's blue denim shirt is neatly folded, but splashes of blood are clearly visible. I pick up the plastic bag containing the knife and turn it over in my hand. I have never touched a murder weapon before. An eerie sensation grips me and slithers down through my bones. This simple kitchen utensil ended a person's life.

I fan through the crime-scene photographs. Even in death April Brown was a beautiful light-skinned woman. Her arms and hands are graceful, her legs shapely. She could have easily been the model she had hoped to become.

I stare at Robert Weldon's pictures after he was arrested. He looked much younger than he does now. He has lived a hard six years. I glance back at his folded shirt beneath the plastic. Would there be so much blood on the shirt if he had stabbed her and run away, as the chief and D.A. contended? Was it there because he leaned too close and pulled out the knife, as he claimed? I have read about experts who are able to re-create crime scenes through the position of blood splatters.

A thought strikes me, and I can't be sure if it is outlandish or sound. Six years ago when Robert Weldon was convicted, DNA analysis was in its infancy, but today's technology is a different story. So many ideas collide in my mind that I don't know where to begin, but I do know that I have to push forward in several directions and fast.

5

I TRAVEL DOWN A DUSTY GRAVEL ROAD THAT LEADS to a small farm where April Brown's father share-cropped. Although the sun is shining, raindrops blur the windshield's dusty surface. The wipers will only smear the glass more. I hunch over the steering wheel to see better and keep out of a ditch.

The cotton stalks are high on either side of the road, and the foliage is lush, though the crops need a heavy rain. Unfortunately, in the Mississippi Delta the capriciousness of the weather determines a farmer's profit or loss. I bear right, down a narrow lane to the Browns' house, a typical shotgun shack. Adjacent to the house is a garden with beans and tomatoes growing on poles. Watermelons, squash, corn, turnip greens, and onions thrive in the rich soil. A coop houses chickens, and a pen holds four fat pigs. Sharecroppers sustain themselves through hard times with what they can produce.

The two chinaberry trees offer scant shade to the

small yard, where grass grows in uneven clumps. A mangy yellow dog sleeps by the front steps. The front porch is screened, and a few pieces of green metal yard furniture are arranged in the cramped space. I can understand April Brown's ambitions to escape the hardscrabble life and that she figured her looks, her only asset, were the ticket to travel.

The dog opens one eye as I climb the stairs. I hope he catches Mister Marvel's scent on me and instinctively knows that I am kind to animals. I knock on the screen door and glance at the toolshed at the side of the house, not wanting to appear anxious to anyone on the inside who may be peering through the curtains. I don't hear a sound. No television, no radio, no footsteps rushing toward the front door. Rain patters on my head, running down my forehead. I wipe the drops away with my sleeve.

I knock again, unobtrusively test the screen door, and find it locked from the inside. Someone must be home, unless they left from the back door. Eyeing the dog, I mosey around the house as if I belonged and check the back screen door.

I return to the front and try again, rattling the door this time. The dog growls low in his throat and gets to his feet. With each bark he jumps straight up in the air, paws working, his version of running in place. I talk to him, but the barking grows louder, more fierce. I judge the distance to the Bronco and decide I can't cover it without a chase and possibly a bite on the leg if I'm not swift enough. I can't stand here forever, and just as I'm about to chance a race with the agitated canine, the front door creaks open.

"Shut up, Spike. What's going on out here? Me, I was taking my nap."

The dog quiets at the sound of the wizened old black woman's voice. Her hair is a white skullcap of tight coils. Her wrinkled mouth looks as if it's been closed by a drawstring. Vertical lines etched on her forehead give the impression of dark war paint. A flowered cotton housedress hangs on her scrawny frame, pink terry-cloth slides on her feet.

"Mrs. Brown?"

"Yas'um."

"I'm Leona Bingham, and I'd like to talk to you about your daughter, April." I figure this approach is better than stating I'm Robert Weldon's lawyer and risk getting shut out before I begin.

"She's dead. Kilt by a white man long time ago. Robert Weldon." Her eyes are alert now and burning with fury. "He gon' die now and burn in Hell, where he oughta be." Her mouth moves as if chewing something. "Why you want to talk about April?" Suspicion has sneaked into her voice. Her teeth are yellow as old ivory piano keys.

I wipe my face on my sleeve again. "Could I come in? It's wet out here."

"Yas'um, I reckon." She shuffles to the door and unlocks it. Her hands are rough, fingers gnarled from doing other people's work. I feel sorry for her. I wonder how she survives now that she's unable to clean and wash and iron. I hope her son, Babaloo, contributes to her welfare. "We can sit in here in my parlor," she says in a raspy voice.

I follow Maudie Brown into what she calls her

parlor. The walls are papered with pages from an old Sears and Roebuck catalog, now yellowed with age. From childhood I remember the same wall covering in a house on our plantation where I sneaked to from the Big House to play with the black children who lived there.

Maudie Brown has unusually nice but worn furniture, probably hand-me-downs from old employers. Crocheted antimacassars cover the arms of the chairs and couch. The shades on the twin iron pedestal lamps are discolored where bulbs have touched the fabric. Framed pictures of April Brown line the mantel over the small brick fireplace in a shrine to the dead daughter. There are no photographs of the son, Babaloo, but one of an old man in what was probably his best Sunday suit. The husband, I guess. A corner whatnot stand displays an array of figurines, ballerinas, dogs, cats, and a giraffe, prizes that may have been won at a county fair. The door to the kitchen is open. An old four-legged stove is wedged between two metal cabinets, a chrome dinette set upholstered in red plastic in the center of the room.

"Ma'am, please have a seat." Maudie Brown settles her thin frame onto a chair and looks lost in it. The veins on her spindly legs are distended. "There ain't nothing more to say about April, so why have you come here?"

Now that I'm inside, I feel I should explain my position. "I'm Robert Weldon's lawyer, Mrs. Brown. I know you'd like to see the man who killed April punished. So would I, but what if Robert Weldon isn't the one?"

She is startled. "How come you say that?"

"Well, there've been many cases where the wrong man has been convicted."

She nods. "Guess so, but not this time. Robert Weldon, he done it. Mr. Jack, he said so."

"Mr. Jack Flannery wanted to win the case. I know you must have talked to him a lot before the trial and rehearsed what you were going to say." This is common practice for both sides to coach their witnesses and not unethical. "On the witness stand, did you tell everything you knew, or were there things that you knew that Mr. Jack didn't ask you about? Things he might not have wanted to come out in the trial."

Her eyes snap as she thinks over my questions. She's quiet so long I decide she's not going to answer. Then she finally speaks with reluctance. "Mr. Jack say just tell truth and I be fine. He say answer the questions I's asked, but don't tell no more than that, 'specially to the other side. You're the other side, but I guess it don't make no difference now what I say. Nobody gonna save that guilty man. Not now."

"But if he's not guilty, your daughter's killer is still loose." Her expression shows I've planted a small seed of doubt, and I continue. "So there were some things that you and Mr. Jack knew that he didn't ask you about and the other side didn't know to ask you about?"

Maudie Brown glances down at her slides, moving her feet around like her toes are playing piano. "I reckon."

"What?"

"Well, April, she never talked much about herself and what she was a-doing." She shakes her head. "Sakes alive, I knowed that going out with a white man was trouble before it happened. She say he was gonna take her to California, but first he had to get rid of his woman. I thought she meant his wife."

"And Robert Weldon didn't have a wife," I quickly add, leaning forward with a twinge of excitement.

"Yas'um, that's right. Mr. Flannery, he quizzed me over and over, askin' me if I was sure April didn't say 'wife.' I say no, she say 'woman,' which I took to be his wife 'cause after she say that, I say, 'He's white and he's married, too,' but April, she don't say nothing after that."

"In other words, she didn't correct you when you said wife."

"That's right."

I recall nothing in the trial transcript about this. "So, Mr. Flannery didn't ask you about this at the trial."

"No. He say we just leave that alone 'cause it was too confusing."

I relax, able to see his point. No proof of anything. "And you had no idea what this man's name was or anything else about him?"

"Not till later, then I know he was Robert Weldon. Like I say, April didn't talk much. She hide things."

"Was she close to your son, Babaloo? Maybe she talked to him about this man."

"Babaloo. Now, what kind of name is that? He calls hisself that, but he's named Bob. Bob Brown, like his daddy. Ain't none of my children ever gone to church like Mr. Brown and me." Sadness crosses her face. "Shame. I raised them right. April come to no good and Bob will, too. If she talked to him about that man, he ain't said."

"Tell me about that last day when April went to meet the man." I know her testimony from the transcripts, but figure something new might slip off her tongue.

Maudie Brown looks out the window, frowning, trying to bring back that awful day. "April was mad 'cause she's pregnant. Was mad ever since she found out. Said this man was gonna give her some money so she can have it taken care of, else she gonna make trouble for him. He was gonna meet her down by Four Mile and give it to her; then when everything was over they was going to California. She didn't go to work the day before. All day just sittin' in her room, waiting till time to go the next day. Wouldn't eat, wouldn't talk. Then the day she was to meet him, she dress and leave for work. Didn't never come back, po' girl stabbed by that Robert Weldon out there by the lake. Wasn't nobody else there but him, and he was there at exactly the right time. He done it. Can't be nobody else."

It's hard not to agree with her last statement. He was there at the right time—to fetch a coat that wasn't there. Never asked for time off from work until that day, but Weldon wanted to repair a car that didn't need it. He wouldn't have wanted his girlfriend, Louella Waters, to know about April Brown, if he was involved with her. Although I can rationalize, the facts still make me queasy.

I'm getting nowhere, blazing no new trails with fresh evidence, and time is moving right along. Plus, I'm raising everyone's ire by taking on the case. Maybe I should call a halt, but if I do, I'll never know the secret Robert Weldon says I might uncover, information that only I could best handle. Maybe there is no secret. Maybe Robert Weldon is only a con who has conned me.

I rise. "I appreciate your time, Mrs. Brown, and I'm sorry to bring up painful memories, but Robert Weldon claims he's innocent, that he's the wrong man. I'm just trying to find out if that's so. I'd hate to see the wrong man put to death for murdering your daughter while a guilty man goes free. I'm searching for the truth, is all." I picture Weldon's face behind bars at Parchman, hear his solemn claims of innocence.

"He ain't the wrong man."

"Maybe not. I hope I haven't bothered you too much."

She rises and hobbles with me to the front door. "Spike, stay," she says, then looks at me with rheumy eyes. "You jus' doing your job. Don't make no difference."

I steer clear of Spike and am relieved to reach the confines of the Bronco. The rain has stopped, and the humidity rivals a steam bath. I turn the air conditioner to full blast. Depressed, I drive toward town. These mood swings drain me dry. At least I didn't ride an emotional roller coaster in my past state of inertia.

Ray Bell Crosby, who was sympathetic to Weldon and testified on his behalf, is high on my list of people to interview. I need a boost. From the chief's description I know exactly where Crosby lives. I decide to see if he's home; if not, the drive will do me good.

I skirt around town and take a rural gravel road that winds through a thick stand of oaks and over an old rickety iron bridge. The waters of the Sunflower River are rust-colored. Two young boys who live in shacks along the banks are skinny-dipping. People here call these dwellers river rats or crackers, lower on the scale than rednecks. The Delta has some caste system.

I reach the levee, where cattle graze on the grassy slopes, and follow the dusty road past a small man-made lake. Ray Bell Crosby's name is painted in red on the mailbox. I drive down a road bordered on either side by a white fence. His house, a rock and rough plank structure, could pass for a rich man's weekend lake retreat. The front porch runs the length of the house and sports a glider and redwood furniture padded with brown vinyl cushions. I'm thirsty and need to use the bathroom. I hope some-one's home and in a receptive mood.

Just as I kill the engine, a man steps out on the porch and flicks on the ceiling fans. He looks toward the Bronco. If that's Ray Bell Crosby, he's not the beer-bellied Bubba type I expected. Dark-haired, he's downright handsome, good physique with buns like a running back. He's wearing faded jeans, a denim shirt with the sleeves rolled up, a cowboy belt with a silver buckle as big as a tin can top, and alligator boots.

"Howdy," I say, getting out, trying to be folksy.

"Howdy to you," he answers, this Marlboro Man caressing me with his eyes. He walks right up to me.

"The name's Ray Bell. Ray Bell Crosby. What can I do you for?"

His smile is dazzling, blinding out here in the hot sun, and full of mischief. Though Chief Lewis praised his ability as an officer, I have to remember he's a Lothario whose testimony was contradicted in court by a woman named Sybil Cooper. "I'm Leona Bingham. I'm representing Robert Weldon. I'd like to talk to you, if you have a minute or two." I watch for a reaction, but he keeps his smile going.

"A lady lawyer, huh? Well, how is Robert? I guess you've seen him." His southern drawl is slow and pleasant.

I nod. "He's okay, under the circumstances, holding up."

"Come on and sit on the porch, where it's cooler. I got plenty of time. Ordinarily I'd be working out on the lake, but my trot lines are all set out for the evening."

I walk up the steps, feeling his eyes bore into me from behind. "Nice place you have here."

"It's okay, nothing compared to the Bingham place, but I like it. Guess you're part of that clan. I know Charles. He your brother?"

"Cousin."

"Oh, you're Byars Bingham's daughter. Yeah."

I can see the recognition clicking. The unwed mother. The wild one of the distinguished family. I pause before taking a seat. "Say, could I have a drink of water and use your bathroom? I hate to ask right off like this, but I'm in need of both."

"Why, sure. My wife, Wilma Ruth, went over to

the neighbors down the road with a cake she baked them, but she made a big pitcher of lemonade before she left. Maybe you'd rather have an ice-cold beer. I believe I would."

"A beer sounds great."

He shows me into his house and points at the bathroom down the hall. The bookcases lining the knotty pine walls are filled with detective novels. I smile to myself. He's a frustrated shamus no longer on the force and unable to ply his trade.

After using his facilities, I glance around on the way back to the porch. The place has an overall feel of masculinity—the rock fireplace, the polished wood floors, the braided rug, the mounted deer heads, gun racks, and comfortable leather upholstered furniture. Where is his wife's touch? Maybe she has no say in such matters.

He's lounging in the glider with two longnecks in each hand. I accept one and sit in the nearest red-wood chair, taking a swig. "This was my dad's house. I grew up here," he says, as if anticipating my thoughts. "Momma died when I was eight, so just the two of us lived here until he died. He was the sheriff of Sunflower County for years. We were hunting and fishing buddies. I miss him. Never changed a thing after he was gone." He sips his beer, then stretches out his long legs, hooking one over the other.

"I understand you and Robert were fishing buddies, too." I light a cigarette after setting my beer on the floor.

"Yep, we fished together some. Never really got to know him real well, but I liked him."

I decide to cut right to the heart of the matter. "Do you think he's innocent?"

Ray Bell exhales and looks out over the lake, squinting from the glare. "I did at the time. Haven't thought about it in a while, but . . . yes, I guess I still do, even though the case against him was pretty strong, the facts and all." He takes another slug of beer, stares at the label, and dislodges a piece with a fingernail. "I guess you know about my testimony at the trial." I nod, and he avoids my eyes. "Pretty embarrassing thing in front of everybody. I might have been in the backseat of my car, but I did see somebody running through the woods, like Robert said he did. 'Course, after the D.A. put Sybil Cooper on the stand, nobody put much stock in what I'd said."

I lean forward, feeling a rush again. "You testified you thought the man was black. Robert thought he was white."

"He could have been white—shadows and all in the woods. He also could have nothing to do with the killing, just somebody out there in the woods." He shrugs. "I don't know."

I take a drag off my cigarette and stare at Ray Bell through the smoke. "I wonder how Jack Flannery happened to get on to Sybil Cooper. How'd he know she was out there with you? I assume you didn't tell anybody. Why would she?"

"Sybil was a talker. Guess she told some girl-friends about us and it got around. This is a small town. I should have known better than to get mixed up with her. I just made a mistake, is all. And all of Grenola heard about it in court. That was the worst day of my life." He shakes his head, as if trying to rid himself of the memory. "I never talked to her again after that. She moved on off."

Ray Bell is good-looking and Sybil Cooper probably bragged in the wrong place about their liaisons, word reached Jack Flannery, and he subpoenaed her. I can empathize with Ray Bell. I committed one indiscretion, and all Grenola knows about it also.

Ray Bell makes eye contact. "After Sybil got back in her car, I started on down the road in my car and saw Robert running along. He was half crying, half hysterical. Just panicked. If Robert just hadn't of pulled out the knife and starting running down the road with it, things would have gone better for him. I believed everything he said that day. He's either the best actor I ever seen or innocent. 'Course, the chief didn't see it that way—or none of the other officers, for that matter. I don't know. I just don't know and probably never will." He works on the label more, ripping it one way, then the other. "Guess you'll be appealing right away. What are you planning to use?"

"Ineffectual counsel."

Ray Bell looks startled. "Against J. Clyde Perkins? Man, that takes balls, if you'll pardon my saying so." He smiles, and I detect admiration in his eyes.

"Robert says he wanted to take the stand and Perkins wouldn't let him."

"Don't you think that's good advice in most murder cases?"

I hate to tell him I'm not a criminal lawyer and have no experience in such matters, that I only know what I've read. "It might have made a difference. I went to see Perkins, and he said I'd be sorry if I used that appeal." I glance at the horses in Ray Bell's pasture, wishing I could afford one for Bingo.

"He threatened you?"

"I guess you could call it that. What can he do to me?"

"I don't know. He's got clout in legal circles, and he's a tough booger. I wouldn't like to tangle with him."

I don't relish the thought. "I have some other appeals in mind if that doesn't sail, but time is so short and I'm trying to do two things at once—detective work, come up with some new evidence, and legal work. I don't know if I'll get anywhere on either count. I don't even know if I'm asking the right questions. I don't know if I'm talking to the right people . . . just the principals in the case." That beat feeling is descending on me again.

"You don't have an investigator working for your firm?" He looks amazed.

"No, and I'm the firm, except for my secretary, Tarsha, who wants to be a lawyer. She's out right now trying to talk to the jurors on the case, see if they had any unauthorized contact with anyone during the trial. Maybe someone got to them." The jury was composed of seven whites and five blacks. I wonder about the racial mix. "I'm just trying to cover every angle I can." Thinking about my own naivete has already worn a trench in my mind. "I talked to Chief Lewis and saw the evidence he collected back then— the knife, Robert's shirt . . . covered with blood. I've heard that forensic experts can practically re-create a crime scene from blood splatters."

"They can throw some light on it now. Didn't used to be able to," Ray Bell answers quickly. "The state has a good forensics lab in Jackson."

"I'd like to get them to take a look at Robert's shirt. I wonder how I go about doing that."

"I could probably help you out there. I know some guys in the forensics lab. I don't think this will do you much good, though. I know a little about the subject. When a person is stabbed by another person facing the victim, the blood tends to go back, not forward, so it doesn't get on the killer. Robert said he leaned down and pulled out the knife. In that case the blood would have spurted forward, as the shirt showed. However, it could be argued that they tussled before she died or that Robert pulled the knife out to get rid of the weapon. So I don't think examination of his shirt would be of any value."

If he's right, this leaves me with one less avenue to travel. I still cling to an earlier idea about a DNA expert, but it's far-fetched and probably not feasible. I decide not to mention it. Put it on hold for a last-ditch effort.

Ray Bell swats at a large horsefly and rests his forearms on his legs. "How'd you come to represent Robert?"

I tell him about the letter and the visit to Parchman.

Ray Bell is deep in thought, chewing the side of his lip. He stops and focuses on me. "You know, I'm not without experience in terms of investigation. Had training in Jackson before I went to work here. I had other offers. Sure, Grenola's a small town, but I didn't want to leave home." He pauses. "I'm not very busy these days. I could help you out with the investigation, relieve some of your burden so you could concentrate on the legal aspects. I've got an antenna for this type of thing. Ask the chief, he'll tell you." He grins, eager to jump on my bandwagon. "What do you say?" He pauses. "Maybe you'd like to check with Chief Lewis before committing."

I've made so many rash decisions that I hesitate to leap on the offer without knowing more about the man, but I need help. I like Ray Bell Crosby. Chief Lewis said he did, too, and praised his ability as an officer. "I can't pay you anything." Both Perkins and I have heard that line before from our mutual client.

"No big deal. If we can prove Robert's innocent, that's payment enough. Shake." He extends his hand and I take it.

I now face a decision. Other than Tarsha, I've told no one about my conversation with Weldon and why he chose me as a lawyer. I should tell Ray Bell now that he's on my team. I vacillate, wondering if I'm making a mistake, but I can't keep secrets from my investigator. I clear my throat and repeat Weldon's words verbatim, then add my take that this somehow involves Jack Flannery and Weldon chose me because of my link to the former D.A.'s son.

Ray Bell stares at my mouth as if he's reading the words rather than hearing them. He looks puzzled, eyes snapping, trying to sort out the situation. "Maybe Flannery is the kind of guy who'll do anything to win."

His inflection implies he doesn't think highly of

Flannery. "I've known him all my life. I'd hate to think he'd do anything improper to get a guilty verdict."

"This was much more than getting a verdict in his favor. Flannery became A.G. because of the case . . . beating Perkins. Folks say he's ambitious. The case was his first step on the path to the governor's mansion. He saw an opportunity and grabbed it." He frowns. "I think I'd better help Tarsha check out the jurors. I need to dig around in Flannery's background. Certainly April Brown's, too. I could start tomorrow. What time can I meet you at your office? I'll go from there."

"Early. Seven o'clock."

"You're a real go-getter."

If he only knew my background. "Well, we're short on time, or rather, Robert is." The thought of such an awesome deadline boggles my mind. Everything I do besides eating and sleeping will have to be aimed toward helping Weldon. My personal life will be on hold, unfair as that is to the principals, especially Bingo. Jack, too. I check my watch. "I'm not near finished for the day. Lots more ground to cover." At lunch Tarsha and I planned to drop by Babaloo Brown's place tonight, taking her boyfriend, Tyrone, with us. I'd like to have Ray Bell along, safety in numbers, but he starts tomorrow, and considering the pay scale, I don't want to push for overtime. I can update him if I discover anything of value.

I thank him for his offer of assistance, and he walks me to the car. I head home, grateful to have someone on my side, someone with some expertise in investigation. As I drive, I think about what a DNA expert might be able to conclude if presented with the right evidence—if that evidence is still available.

Tarsha picked up Bingo after school, and I join them on the gallery. At the table, Bingo has a pencil poised over a tablet, Tarsha behind him, riding herd over his homework. "I made three A's today," he tells her.

"Yeah, little buddy, but you have five subjects. You should have made five A's," she argues as he leaps up and runs to hug me.

"Mom, Mom," he almost shouts. "I need a break."

I laugh at his term. "Well, take one." I pat Mister Marvel as he bounds up the stairs and tries to lick my hand.

Tarsha and I watch the two race toward the bayou; then she turns to me. "You should see the office. It's taking shape. Your mother and Estelle have been in and out of there all day with their lackeys hauling in furniture." She picks up a cookie off Bingo's plate and samples it. "I talked to three jurors so far and got no place. Had a time just running down those three. *Only* nine more to track. Jeez." She makes a face. "This could take forever. Forever we don't have."

I review my day, finishing with Ray Bell Crosby. "We've got ourselves an investigator."

"Yeah. So, now we have a dream team. More like a nightmare, if you ask me," she comments. "Ray Bell Crosby, some old ex-policeman cracker who was out screwing on the job."

I feel a little smug. "He just might surprise you."

"How much you paying him?"

"Nada. He's going to work for free."

"Yeah, and my momma always says you get what you pay for."

I let that pass. "We all set for tonight?"

She nods. "Tyrone doesn't want to go, but says he will because we can't go to Babaloo's alone. You meet Tyrone and me at the Texaco station 'bout eight, and we'll go together." She snatches her purse off the swing and almost gallops to her car.

I go inside, plop down at the kitchen table, and dial Estelle. "Tarsha says the office is looking great. Can't thank you enough."

"Lily and I are having a good time doing it. It'll be ready for your interview with that reporter tomorrow. You'll be real proud of it. Y'all will have a nice place to work now. I was just fixing to call you. Have you seen the evening paper?"

Our local edition, the *Enterprise-Tocsin*. "No, why?"

"There's an article in there that says you're Robert Weldon's new attorney and a review of the case. Word on the Grenola jungle drums travels fast."

I hope publicity will be beneficial to Weldon's case, jog some memories, and compel someone with knowledge to come forward. "Estelle, I need a favor."

"Shoot."

"Could you keep Bingo for me tonight?"

"Why, sure. You have a date with Jack?"

Don't I wish. The company would be welcome. I reveal my plans and listen to silence on the other end. Finally she says, "Leona, white folks don't go to those places. I think you're making a big mistake, liable to get into some trouble out there. Byars would have a stroke if he knew where you are going."

"So don't tell him." I explain that I have to talk to Babaloo Brown and this is the only way.

"You just be careful, you hear? I'll come over and get Bingo, and he can eat supper with us. Why don't you just let him stay the night? We'll take him to school in the morning."

"That sounds good, and thanks, Estelle." The time will allow me the chance to concentrate on the appeal without interruption after I return from Babaloo's.

The trellis has robbed enough of my sleep and I intend to fix it now. I locate the ladder in the garage and call to Bingo to help. He's always anxious to lend a hand and feels grown-up when I ask a favor. I stuff nails in my pocket and hook the hammer through my belt.

"This thing is rotten," he says as we haul the ladder around the house.

He's right. I hope the rungs will hold while I nail the trellis back in place. "I'm going to tell the yardman to haul it away when he comes to mow the grass."

We lean the ladder against the house, and with Bingo steadying it, I begin my precarious climb, careful to test each rung as I ascend. Leaning sideways, I hammer the nails into the trellis as I go.

I check the trellis to make sure it's secure and quickly make my way to the ground. Bingo's cheeks are flushed from the strain. "Okay, pal, let's haul it back to the garage. Aunt Estelle is going to pick you up, and you can have dinner and spend the night with them."

"Yippee!" he shouts.

I'd rather like it better if he wasn't so enthusiastic about leaving me, but I'm glad of his independence. "Better get your things packed while I take a shower and change."

We dash into the house and part company. After a quick shower, I towel dry, put on stone-washed jeans, a blue jersey pullover I've been saving for some occasion yet to come, and boots. I retouch my makeup and allow my hair to curl and frizz on its own. Rummaging in a drawer for a bottle of spray perfume, I touch the velvet box. I open it carefully and find the cherished debate medal nestled inside, the only prize I ever won. I stare at the word WINNER engraved in script and remember how triumphant and proud I felt on stage in the high school auditorium. Against all odds, I had set my sights on that medal, spending countless hours researching, memorizing, and organizing my material. Hard work, tenacity, and a little luck had paid off that time. Lily, Byars, and Charles sat in the front row, Jack Flannery Sr., an astonished frown on his face, just behind them. Tears streamed down Lily's cheeks, and Byars had to turn away to hide his emotions. I know he read it somewhere, but he said that the more worthy the opponent, the sweeter the victory. The worthy opponent I whipped that night was Jack Flannery Jr. If he had to be whipped, he was pleased that I was the one doing the whipping.

I hear a car and go down to the front porch, where Bingo is already waiting with his backpack stuffed to capacity. In anticipation of the evening, he's put on a fresh cotton shirt and a pair of khakis, slicked down his cowlick. He glances at the car, then back at me with a hint of worry. "What are you going to do? You'll be by yourself," he says as Estelle mounts the steps.

He may be happy to go, but at least he's thinking of me. "I've got work to do. I'll be busy and won't miss you one bit." I give him a loony smile, imitating one of his. "Mister Marvel will keep me company."

"The kids are sure looking forward to this." Estelle tries to ruffle Bingo's hair, but he dodges her, trying to keep his locks in place. "Fried chicken and a fresh peach cobbler for dessert, then y'all can watch a movie. We've rented three from the video store."

"Yea!" Bingo exclaims. He hugs me, runs to the car to deposit his backpack, then pats Mister Marvel good-bye and climbs into the passenger seat.

"I declare, I'm worried about you tonight, Leona . . . out at such a place."

"I'll be okay." Fine lines fan from the corners of Estelle's eyes. She's usually immaculate, but her makeup is smudged, her slacks and blouse wrinkled. She and Lily have worked all day purely for my benefit. With sadness I envision how Estelle will look as an old woman. "I can't wait to see the office tomorrow. Again, I really appreciate what you and Lily did."

Her eyes sparkle, and the fatigue is overcome with enthusiasm. "It was good fun. I'm so excited about your interview tomorrow. Leona, this could bring you lots more clients . . . from all around the state. And think of the money you might make. Leona, it's a good start. A reputation builder."

Money and more clients are not uppermost in my mind at the present, but Robert Weldon's salvation is. And if I lose my case, what reputation that interview might build is shot to hell publicly. I remind myself that my client has far more to lose than I.

"I was saying to Lily that I wish I could be independent . . . do something satisfying on my own. 'Course, my family and home keep me busy, but you know what I mean." Estelle glances toward the bayou, a longing in her eyes.

"You've got lots of talent, Estelle. A flair. You ought to open up a decorating shop here; then people wouldn't have to go to Memphis to buy." Where did I get my license to advise others how to make the most out of life? I've dragged through the last few years like a slug. I catch myself in mid-thought. I've vowed to put self-flagellation behind. What I did in the past has nothing to do with what I can do in the future.

"You think so?" A shadow crosses her face, and the enthusiasm fades. "Charles probably wouldn't like the idea."

"Do it anyway." I'm playing devil's advocate. "Quit tiptoeing around him."

"Oh, Leona, you hush, now." She fans away a fat mosquito buzzing by her ear. "Speaking of Charles . . . well, I told him Bingo was coming for supper and spending the night, and he asked what you were doing. I just hated to lie. I told him about you going out to that juke joint to talk to Babaloo Brown." Her face flushes slightly. "I told him not to tell Byars, though."

"Estelle, I'm old enough not to be scared of my daddy, and you've been married long enough not to be scared to your husband."

"I'm not scared of him. I just don't like to cause trouble. I'd better go. Bingo is hot in the car and supper's waiting." She hurries down the steps.

I wave as they drive off and go inside. Lighting a cigarette, I settle at the kitchen table to call Jack. As I'm about to hang up, he answers, out of breath. "Are you that out of shape?"

"Leona, hi." He sounds glad to hear my voice. "Dad got here this afternoon, and we were in the backyard playing badminton with Kit. Looking forward to tomorrow night. Seems like I haven't seen you in such a long time."

"I know. To me, too." I drag on my cigarette, thinking about his father and the confrontation tomorrow night. I miss Jack but couldn't afford the time at this point to spend an evening with him if Jack Senior wasn't there. This is a sad commentary on the status of our relationship, but time has never counted as it does now. "I guess you mentioned that I've taken Robert Weldon's case."

"The subject came up. It's in the evening paper. See it?"

"No, but I've heard about it. I'm doing an interview in the morning with a reporter from the *Clarion-Ledger*. What did Mr. Jack say about me taking the case?"

"He was pretty surprised, to say the least."

"Did he say he's scared of me, that I am a formidable adversary?" I try to make light of the situation, although going up against the attorney general makes me shake. Added to the fact that I'm suspicious of what he might have done to win the verdict that led to high office. What will I do if I find that is so? Whatever it takes to save my client.

"Not in those words," he answers, ever the diplomat. "Say, what are you doing tonight? I could drive out for a drink."

I tell him. He is shocked and doesn't think I should go. We tangle a bit, and I reiterate that I must speak to Babaloo Brown and this is the only way. He knows it's useless to try to stop me from doing my job. We sign off on a coolly pleasant note. I regret the way this case is affecting my life, maybe costing a relationship I once so carelessly wasted and now have within my grasp. I sigh and push personal troubles aside for now.

My lunch will not carry me through the evening, and I decide to eat before I go. I slap together a ham sandwich with a thick slice of tomato and globs of mayo, grab a package of potato chips, and save some calories with a diet soda. I take my dinner to the gallery and hear crickets chirp and frogs croak around the bayou. I enjoy listening, but they're lonely sounds and make me feel that way. Robert Weldon would give anything to trade places with me, to be an audience to that chorus, to drink in the view across the bayou. I take a bite and wonder what he had for dinner.

The phone interrupts my thoughts, and I fly inside, afraid it's Tarsha and her boyfriend canceling. Am I brave enough to go alone? Maybe Charles has leaked my plans to Byars and he's fuming. I pick up the receiver ready to do battle.

"Hello."

No one answers. "Hello," I say again. This is no wrong number or they would speak or hang up. "Hello. Who is this?" I can feel a menacing presence on the other end, coming right through the line to reach out to me.

The line goes dead. I replace the receiver. Was someone calling to check if I'm home? An uneasy sensation descends over me. If someone is trying to scare me, they've succeeded. Is this just a warm-up for what is to come?

6

THE MOON IS A SLIVER OF PEWTER AGAINST THE dark sky. Superstitious since childhood, I'm glad there's no full one over Grenola tonight. Crank calls are common, but I've attached an ominous meaning to the one I received. I try to toss off the notion as a touch of paranoia.

At eight on the dot I pull under the Texaco station's overhang, where harsh lights illuminate the area like a stage set. My windshield is crusted with bugs. There must be more insects in the Mississippi Delta than in the Amazon basin.

Tarsha and Tyrone are nowhere in sight. I'm not buying gas, but I tip the attendant a dollar to squeegee my windshield. While he's in the process, Tarsha and Tyrone wheel off the highway and park by the side of the building.

Swaggering toward me, Tarsha is more festooned than dressed. With her shiny neon red pants and bomber's jacket covered with multicolored buttons and badges she almost glows in the dark. Moving like a head full of pendulums, her dreadlocks are capped with large red beads. Red cowboy boots complete her outfit. I've never met Tyrone, but know he's a hard-working electrician who's built a thriving business. He's the color of coffee with too much cream and blessed with the athletic sleekness of a greyhound. In a blue-and-white-striped short-sleeved sports shirt and navy khakis, he pales beside Tarsha's fiery image.

"This is Tyrone," she introduces him, placing the emphasis on the first syllable. "Tyrone, my boss. Lazy Leona I used to call her."

"I never knew that," I say, smarting a little from the comment.

"It was behind your back. Now she's a slave driver."

"How you, ma'am?" He offers his hand, and I feel the calluses. "Want me to drive? I know the way."

"And you can sit in the back of the bus," Tarsha says to me with a mischievous gleam in her eye.

Tyrone drives as carefully as if the police are following. "We oughtn't to be goin' to this place tonight. I hear it can get real rough."

"Just be cool. We'll be okay." Tarsha puts on an oversized pair of sunglasses with red frames.

"You won't attract much attention," I tell her. "Just blend right in with the walls." Although she's voiced misgivings about going, I think she's secretly excited.

Tyrone slows on the edge of town, which has recently become racially mixed. "Now, there's a nice little house. See the For Sale sign? Wonder how much they're askin'?" He catches Tarsha's eye.

Tarsha gives the cottage a cursory glance. "Yeah, it's a sweet place. Nice hedges and flowers."

I feel a wedge of pity for Tyrone. Tarsha's sights are set on places other than Grenola. In a way, she's like April Brown, ambitious, anxious to move on to higher ground. Only Tarsha is going to do it with her mind, not her body. Tyrone is so enamored that he doesn't see it coming—like me with Jean-Paul, I have to admit. I never saw it coming until I was hit between the eyes.

We head down the action side of Four Mile Lake, passing small cafés and bait shops with neon beer signs in the windows, dusty pickups in the gravel parking lots. Babaloo's place is secluded at the far end of the lake, a cinder-block structure with no windows in front and dim lights by the entrance.

The parking lot is crowded, and the building seems to vibrate from the music inside. Several men stand by a Cadillac sedan, smoking, cursing, passing around a pint of whiskey jacketed in a brown paper sack. They stop and stare as we pass. The three of us exchange uneasy glances and enter the darkened, noisy place. It takes a minute for my eyes to adjust. As I suspected, I am the only white person here. The jukebox continues to pump out its throbbing, pulsating music, but the conversational level drops to near zero. Everyone around the red-and-white-checked oilcloth-covered tables and those in the wooden booths lining the walls turn with hostile eyes to study the trio that has just invaded their territory. My heart hammers. I shouldn't be here, but try to remember my mission.

A tall, thin woman in a green dress that reaches her ankles swings around the bar and slowly walks toward us. "Look at her hair," Tarsha says under her breath. "She could scare people with that wild style."

I shush her. "Don't make things worse."

Tyrone supports my advice. "Yeah, your mouth can be too big sometimes. I ain't in no fightin' mood."

The woman stops a few steps away. Her skin glistens, and her high cheekbones give her a haughty look. "Yes? Can I do somethin' for you?" She has an exotic, musky scent.

I am poised to ask for Babaloo Brown when Tyrone says, "Could we get a booth and order somethin' to eat and drink?"

His approach is better. If we settle down like regular patrons and spend money, the tension might lessen. The hostess nods and leads us to a back booth near the bar and the swinging kitchen door. All eyes follow as we're seated. The woman deals menus like playing cards.

"Is Babaloo Brown here tonight?" I don't want to make this trip again.

"Yes. He's in the back, but he's busy right now."

I clutch my menu like it might escape. "Could you ask him to join us when he's free? I need to talk to him about something."

She looks at me without blinking. "I'll ask. A waitress will take your orders." She saunters away and disappears behind the swinging doors.

Tarsha taps her nails on the table. "Don't drink anything unless it's out of a can or a bottle."

"The food must be okay. Everyone else's eatin' it."
Tyrone studies the menu.

"Probably so," Tarsha comments. "Cooking kills
all the germs."

A skinny waitress who looks no more than fifteen
arrives with a pad and pencil. Her white blouse and
black skirt hang on her, probably hand-me-downs
from a meatier predecessor. She's no advertisement
for the food. We order beers, platters of ribs and chit-
terlings, fries, and slaw. The ham sandwich I ate at
home sits like a brick in my stomach.

She's back quickly with ice-cold beers, and I light
a cigarette, trying to relax. A few customers resume
drinking and eating, but most still watch us with suspicion. Two couples venture out onto the small dance
floor. Babaloo Brown is coining money if his place is
this packed every night. If he isn't selling drugs, as
Tarsha hinted, I have to admire his enterprise.

The waitress serves platters piled high with fried
goodies. Tyrone spears a bite with his fork and chews
with a growing smile. "Man, I love these chitlins." I
follow suit and try to think of something other than
the origin of the food. Fried hog intestines are not
high on my list, but I admit they are delicious. We dig
in, so engrossed with cleaning the plates that the man
by our table goes unnoticed for a moment.

"You wanted to see me," he says in a deep, melodious voice that could rival any stage actor.

The three of us look up in unison at Babaloo
Brown. He's as big as a pro-linebacker, completely
bald and wears one gold earring to match a gold front
tooth. In place of a toothpick a nail hangs from the

side of his mouth. His bizarre attire includes a bright, flowing orange satin artist's smock, baggy harem-type black pants, and sandals. His coal-black eyes are hard and mean.

I tap the grease off my lips with a paper napkin. "Yes, I'm—"

"I know who you are," he interrupts. "Lawyer for Robert Weldon, out botherin' my momma today." He chews on the nail. "We finally get some satisfaction, some justice here, and you out tryin' to turn it around in your favor." He turns and glances around the room. "Now, wonder what'd happen here if I just stopped the music and threw you to the crowd, tell all these folks here what you tryin' to do. They ain't gon' be happy 'bout it. Not one bit." He glares at Tarsha, then Tyrone. "And what you two doin' out wid this white lawyer woman?"

I shiver at the bad turn in the situation. As I gather my wits, Charles pushes through the front door and heads toward us. I can't believe it. Things will really get out of hand now. I expect Byars to follow any moment.

"Hey, Bobo." Charles gives Babaloo a friendly punch on the shoulder.

Babaloo's smile widens so broadly, I think his lips will crack and the nail will fall. His anger melts at the sight of Charles. "Charlie, my man, how you doin'?" They shake hands.

Charles turns to me. "I see you've met my cousin, Bobo. Lee Bingham."

"Leona," I say, unable to keep my mouth shut.

Babaloo looks puzzled, eyebrows lifted. "Your

cousin? This lawyer's your cousin? Mr. Byars's daughter? I didn't know what her name was. Momma didn't say when I went by today to drop off some money for her."

"Bobo and I go way back," Charles explains. "Why don't we pull up a chair and join them, Bobo? Have a drink. I'm buying."

"On the house." Babaloo pulls two chairs to our booth and they sit.

Those two go way back, Charles said. Way back to what and where? I'm sweating and hope it's not obvious. Holding my hands in my lap to stop the shakes, I introduce Tarsha and Tyrone. Both manage a stingy smile, then grab their beers and down them.

Babaloo snaps his fingers at the waitress. "Beers all around." He turns back, assessing me. Charles has tamed him momentarily, but I still detect the remnants of hostility just beneath the surface. What is the connection between Charles and this man? I need to say something, try to explain my position.

Charles lays the groundwork. "Bobo, you're a smart guy. People bow and scrape to you, call you mister. Now, you gotta understand and not take this the wrong way. If my cousin here wasn't representing Weldon, it would be someone else doing it."

I see an opening after Charles has massaged Babaloo's ego. "By law, nobody can be executed without being represented by a lawyer."

"Uh-huh," he mutters, moving the nail to the other side of his mouth with his tongue.

I light a cigarette. "Now, I know you want justice for April's murder, some satisfaction that at least her killer pays for what was done, although it won't bring her back."

"You got that right."

"That's all I want, too. To see that justice is done. Let's just take a 'for instance.' For instance, what if nobody had been caught after April was murdered, nobody arrested? You know that happens with many crimes. You and your mother would be on fire with anger that the killer got away with it, wouldn't you? April's dead, but he's still free."

He nods, eyes ablaze with curiosity at where I'm leading. I have everyone else's rapt attention.

"Wouldn't you feel the same way if they convicted the wrong man and the murderer was still free?"

He nods again.

"What if that's the case here? Robert Weldon's the wrong man and your sister's killer is still free, not going to pay for what he did."

"It ain't the case here," he almost snarls.

"How do you know that for sure?"

"How do you know it ain't?"

"I don't, but I'm trying to find out. And I need all the help I can get. The other lawyers never properly investigated Robert Weldon's claims of innocence, but I am."

"Along with tryin' to save his ass."

"I can't save his ass if he's guilty. I may not even be able to save it if he's innocent. When he's executed, it's over. Case closed. Nobody's looking any further. And if he didn't do it, the killer's home free. You want that? I don't think so. If I could just uncover some evidence that points away from Robert Weldon and to someone else, I might find out who murdered your sister. If I can't, maybe Weldon did actually do it. They've already nailed him, and he'll pay." I take a drag and exhale a cloud of smoke. I don't know if I'm striking home or talking in circles.

"Weldon claims he saw a man running through the woods that day, a white man. Ray Bell Crosby said he saw a man running through the woods, too. Thought he was a black man, maybe." I lift my hand as Babaloo starts to interrupt. "I know Ray Bell's testimony was discredited by the woman he was with, but I talked to him today and he still says that even though he was in the backseat of his car, he *saw* that man. I believe that man was out there. Maybe he had nothing to do with your sister's murder. But maybe he was the killer, not Robert Weldon. Ray Bell thinks Weldon's innocent, so much so that he's going to work as my investigator."

"That's news," Charles comments with a sly smile. "Good-looking guy. Real stud. Better watch it, pretty single woman like you."

I don't like the comments or the interruption. I had a rhythm going with Babaloo. Before I can pick up the cadence again, the lady in green approaches and tells Babaloo he's wanted on the phone, further breaking the spell.

After he leaves, I ask Charles what prompted him to come here and about his connection to Babaloo. "We were just sittin' down to supper, and Bingo wondered what you were doing. I got to thinking about you out here, what you might get into on your own, and decided to come on out." He grabs a rib and gnaws on the meaty bone.

I can see him, irritated, inconvenienced, throwing down his napkin at the dinner table and stomping out to rescue his errant cousin. On the other hand, maybe he does actually care about my welfare. My heart softens several degrees until I remember his comments about Ray Bell and how I'd better watch myself.

He blots his lips with a napkin. "As for our connection . . . well, you know how there's always a kid in every group that's an entrepreneur right from the start. The first one who sets up a lemonade stand or sells something, mows lawns or runs errands for pocket change. That was Bob Brown, always out hustling. He was a scrawny little thing, though you wouldn't think it to see him now. His daddy bought him a secondhand bicycle one Christmas to help him get around faster. He'd go out and sell lemonade to the field hands for a penny." He swigs beer and spears a chitterling with a fork.

"Some redneck teenagers, three brothers, stole his bike. He knew who they were and had the nerve enough to go out to their shack to get it back. They jumped him, took him out in the woods, strung him up to a tree limb, and were gonna beat him with a bullwhip. Byars and I were out hunting and got separated. 'Bout that time I wandered up through the thicket and saw what was happening. I was just a kid, too, and all I had was a BB gun, but I aimed it at 'em and told 'em to turn the boy loose. They laughed and said my gun wouldn't hurt 'em. I said I could put out an eye with it, if they wanted to be blind to go ahead. They said I couldn't even hit 'em from that distance;

then Byars walked up with his shotgun and said he sure as hell could, though, and would blow a hole through 'em if they ever bothered the boy again.

"They scattered like ants, and the kid got his bike back. Next day he was out on one of Byars's plantations selling lemonade to the hands. Gave Byars and me one free." Charles smiles at the remembrance. "After that Bobo always chewed on a nail to make folks think he was tough. Tough as nails. Over the years he got tough for real. He's not one to mess with."

Thinking about the incident, I realize there are many experiences Charles and Byars have shared that I know nothing about. Theirs is a strong bond, one I shouldn't question or envy.

Babaloo returns to the table, hooks the chair around backward with his foot, straddles the seat with his arms over the backrest. "'Scuse the interruption." He drains his beer, slams the empty bottle down, locking eyes with me. "So?"

"So, if you know anything that might shed some light on the situation, something that might not have come out . . . anything about the man April was seeing"—I lean on the words—"I'd appreciate your help."

"It's been too long. Over six years. I'll give you a for instance. Just sayin'—mind you, I ain't sayin' I in any way think it's true—but just sayin' if Weldon ain't it, the killer, you ain't gon' catch who is now. And just say you found out somethin', somethin' as you said would point to somebody 'sides Weldon. What's gon' happen? It's too late to prosecute somebody else."

"No." I lean into his face. "No, it's not too late.

There's no statute of limitations on murder. In other words, someone can be prosecuted no matter what length of time has passed since the crime. There's a case where a man was convicted of murder forty years after he committed the crime."

"Uh-huh." Babaloo stares at me. "No offense here, but I got to tell you right off that I don't trust white folks. Ain't ever had no reason to." His eyes slide to Charles. "'Cept him and Mr. Byars. Them I trust."

Charles motions toward me with his head. "You can trust what she says, Bobo. I guarantee it."

Without a word Babaloo continues to appraise me.

Keep going, I tell myself. "Didn't April ever confide in you about the man she was seeing? You never know where some little piece of information might lead." I hear the pleading in my voice. I'm not to proud to beg.

Babaloo looks across the room, moving the nail from one side of his mouth to the other. "April was real mad and upset when she found out she's pregnant, but she never talked about that man 'cept to say he was gonna take her to California. She kept everythin' to herself. Always did, even as a little girl. When she say she's goin' to California, I tol' her nobody ever leaves Grenola, and if'n they do, they don't come back. Be sad not to ever see her again she goes to California." He sighs. "I won't ever see her again now." With a look of hesitancy, Babaloo reaches under the mandarin-type collar of his smock and fingers a gold chain heretofore concealed. Beneath the material, something hangs on that chain. "Tell you what. I'll talk to my momma. Maybe we might recollect somethin', come up with somethin' might help."

My antennae rises, and I feel a rush of excitement. He knows some tidbit he might grudgingly give up after he discusses it with Mrs. Brown. My eyes seek out his and beseech him to tell me now. Time is so short. He breaks contact and stands. Nothing is forthcoming now. I'm crestfallen that he won't part with whatever piece of information he has, but cling to the hope that this encounter has been productive, that he'll get back to me before it's too late.

The waitress presents the check, and as I reach for it Babaloo tears it in half. "On the house." He glances at all of us, lingering on Charles. "See you." He rises and ambles through the crowd.

Tarsha picks up a folded card on the table. "Look, they have live music on Saturday night. Maybe we can come back."

"Like hell," Tyrone answers, sliding out of the booth.

Pausing outside the door, I turn to Charles. "Thanks for coming." I put feeling into the statement.

"Try to stay out of jams, missy." He saunters toward his car.

Tarsha glances at me as we head to my car. "Thought you and Charles disliked each other."

"Maybe we're trying to get over it." I stop in my tracks, horrified. "Look!" I point at my car door.

"Oh, my God," Tarsha bellows.

Tyrone moves in for a closer look. "Who would do such a thing?"

Someone with a sharp object has scratched BITCH in large capital letters on my door. I'm overcome with fury. I kick the door with the toe of my boot. "Damn. Damn." I look for Charles, but he's driven away.

"'Least they didn't slash the tires." Tyrone grabs the keys from his pocket. "Let's get out of here."

On the way back to town I'm so mad I can't talk. I'll have to take the Bronco to Walter's to have the door painted. I'll have to rent a car. Bucks thrown out the window. My insurance deductible is a thousand. Tarsha turns slowly in the front seat to face me. The whites of her eyes stand out in the dark.

"You think this was some random vandalism, or was it directed at you?"

A worm of worry crawls around inside me. "Hard to say." I center on that strange phone call and tell them about it. Tarsha is now as concerned as I am.

At the Texaco station I thank Tarsha and Tyrone and say good night as they charge toward their car. I drive away with a sense of impending dread, but struggle to expel the mood with the hope that I made headway with Babaloo. I'm positive there is something he and his mother haven't told. If he doesn't come forward, I'll drag it out of him any way I can.

Reaching my house, I realize I've forgotten to turn on the porch lights. The dark Victorian suddenly lurks like a scary, haunted place, the windows' square eyes watching me. I curse myself for being so careless. Afraid to get out, I remain plastered to the seat. I could drive to the Big House for the night or to Charles and Estelle's, but my law books and papers are inside and an entire night's work will go unfinished.

Suddenly, like a rocket from nowhere, a body

launches into the passenger door, and I jerk toward the window, screaming at the face with fangs. My heart pounds a dangerous staccato beat. Peering inside, Mister Marvel claws the glass. My fright takes a moment to subside. I'm sure irreparable damage has been done to my vital organ. I open the door, and he slobbers all over me. Petting him, I dash to the front door.

Flooding the house with lights, I make sure all doors are locked before I go upstairs. Comfortable in my old terry-cloth robe, I throw cold water on my face and return to the kitchen. After giving Mister Marvel extra treats, I pour a tall glass of milk and settle down to work.

The phone sends a zigzag of apprehension through my system. Mister Marvel's ears perk. Letting it ring again, I pray someone is on the line. On the third ring I pick up with a low, hoarse hello to throw an unwanted caller off guard. I might have even sounded like a man.

"Leona, are you sick?"

"Oh, hi, Jack." I'm relieved. "No, just swallowed wrong. What's up?"

"Just wanted to see if you got home okay."

"I did, but the Bronco didn't." I'm mad again. "Some asshole scratched the word bitch on my door with a sharp pointed object like an ice pick or a nail—" I stop, remembering the nail Babaloo chews. Could he have done it? Was the show of friendship toward Charles a front?

"That's awful."

"Just calls for a paint job. No biggie." Making light

of it doesn't diminish my feelings. Was it random or was I a target? The word *bitch* connotes a woman, so the culprit knew the car belonged to a female.

"Was the trip worth it? Find out anything useful?"

"Maybe, I don't know. I have the feeling Babaloo Brown knows something he hasn't told." Jack will likely relay this to his father, a man I must now consider an enemy, but this pinch of information might rattle him.

"Leona, I wish you'd stop spinning your wheels on this case and let somebody else take it. I just don't want to see you hurt."

I don't want to see me hurt, either, and I don't want to argue. "I committed to Robert Weldon, and I'm going at it with all stops out. And I'd better get cracking right now. Night, Jack. See you at dinner tomorrow."

"Leona," he says before I hang up. "There's just one thing I'd like to ask you, and I won't bring this up again because I know there's no stopping you when you set your mind on something."

"What?"

"If Weldon is executed, are you going to blame yourself?"

"No." Truth is, I don't know.

"Okay, I'm glad to hear that."

Although I don't want to think Weldon might actually be executed, I can't help it. Dwelling on this aspect is counterproductive, I know. The way to save him is to put everything I have into the case and not clutter my mind with what-ifs.

"Leona, we need to carve out some time alone."

"Jack, I want to, but you know how pushed for time I am."

"I have a life and cases, too, but I can still find time for you," he snaps uncharacteristically. "At this point I still can."

He lets the impact linger, a veiled threat that his future plans may not include me. I blindly threw away a chance with him for Jean-Paul. Am I risking it again for Robert Weldon? Jack should understand the pressure I'm under.

"Jack, let's say good night before this conversation goes wrong."

"Fine, Leona. Good night."

I light a cigarette and pace the kitchen like a caged animal. My personal life is a mess, my professional one even more disturbed. Suddenly I'm staggered by a thought that pops unbidden into my mind. April Brown's murderer is a white man with much to lose if he was exposed as the father of her unborn child. If Charles knew Babaloo from way back, maybe he also knew his sister as well—from more recent times. Charles appeared at Babaloo's on the pretext of seeing to my best interests, but was it his hidden agenda to find out what transpired between Babaloo and me? Is he afraid of what information Babaloo might possess? And Byars is adamant that I drop the case. Does he suspect Charles is involved and is trying to protect him? Is this the information Weldon claimed I might stumble across? Charles had the opportunity to scratch bitch on my car. I want to scream. I want to shake these mind-boggling thoughts from my head.

Drinking cold water, I settle into a modicum of sanity. Surely my overworked brain is only playing tricks, reacting to too much input like an overloaded computer.

I grab my pen and yellow pads, determined to put everything behind but the business at hand. I concentrate harder than I ever have. With my head clear, I feel as if I've whiffed a jolt of oxygen. One thought after another blossoms. My grip on the appeal grows, and I pen concise paragraphs, hitting important points, making real progress.

Unaware of time, I work far into the night, referring to my books often, finding much needed ammunition to fire at the courts. I break for a cigarette, feeling my eyes grow scratchy. Yawning, I look at the clock and can't believe it's four in the morning, three hours until I'm due at the office. I want to keep going, but know I've come to the end of the trail for now.

I drag upstairs, set my temperamental alarm clock, and fall across the bed. Closing my eyes, I'm afraid to sleep for fear the clock won't wake me. Maybe just resting will rejuvenate me. I try to relax, but my muscles twitch with spasms. Ignoring them, I roll into a fetal position and hope for the best.

Babaloo comes into the room and drives nails into my skull with a hammer. The pain is piercing. My brain is exploding. I leap up to ward off the blows. The alarm clock is screaming its warning. Slamming the OFF button, I shake my head and grope my way to the shower.

My image in the mirror looks faded, like someone has tried to erase my features. My eyes are dull holes, my mouth a crack, my hair a fright wig. Remembering the interview, I apply more makeup than usual, tame my hair, and dress in a royal blue pantsuit with a matching blouse. I feel like a flower that has been force-fed with fertilizer to bloom. I look better than I feel.

I feed Mister Marvel while choking down a bowl of cereal with sliced bananas for strength. Stuffing my briefcase, I refill the dog's water bowl on the front porch and lock the door. Mister Marvel whines at being left alone all day. "Bingo will be here to play with you this afternoon," I tell him, and he wags his tail as if he understands.

Driving to town, I take deep breaths, sucking in oxygen like a dying patient. I take the Bronco to Walter's Cars, and the mechanic shakes his head at the damage, asking if I think the vandalism has something to do with the case, a warning maybe. "It's probably just somebody's opinion of me," I answer, trying to laugh off my real concern. Walter says the paint job will take three days to complete, taking into consideration the sanding, primer, a first coat of paint allowed to dry before the second is applied, then time for the final layer to dry. He does brighten my day with a loaner, a Buick from the last decade.

I park in my usual spot, and when I reach my office door Ray Bell is waiting. The Marlboro Man is dressed in freshly pressed jeans, a cotton plaid shirt, and boots, different clothes from yesterday but he sports the same megawatt smile. The creases the sun has etched in his face only add to his overall appeal. Country charm oozes from him like sap.

"Morning, boss lady," he greets me, as if we've been meeting here for years. I notice his big masculine watch and the gold wedding band.

"Leona will do," I answer, unlocking the door.

"Great office you got here." He glances around, surveying my space.

He's right. The transformation is startling. I'm amazed at what a few well-designed touches can add. The old furniture creates a certain shabby elegance, as if planned that way. Pieces that had already been here, the beige leather couch that farts when sat upon and the two faded navy wingback chairs, are bedecked with carefully draped, colorful afghans and needlepoint pillows scattered carelessly. Nothing too sissy or feminine, just straightforward. The two scarred desks, now separated by an Oriental screen made of rice paper, have been polished with dark wax to conceal the flaws. A beige rug with a Grecian key design partially covers the wood floors, and hunting prints line the walls. Three tall plants in brass urns especially appeal to me. Up yours, J. Clyde Perkins, in your fancy digs.

"I find it comfortable here, easy surroundings to work in," I say casually, setting my briefcase by my chair. "Have a seat, Ray Bell." I motion to one of the wingbacks, not wanting him to plop on the couch. "I went out to Babaloo Brown's place last night to talk to him."

"Did you?" Ray Bell looks surprised, possibly even a little hurt that I didn't ask him along. Maybe I'm wrong. I don't know him well enough to read him. "By yourself?"

"Not on your life." I tell him about the evening, including the phone call and car damage, leaving aside my suspicions of Charles.

"Jeez!" Frowning, he moves to the edge of the seat, resting his forearms on his thighs. "Still, it could be a break if Brown actually has something he might be willing to tell you. Might turn out that you're a better investigator than I am and don't need me."

"Oh, I need your help, all right."

He seems pleased to be wanted. "The thing about your car bothers me. Could be a coincidence, random, but I think we have to take everything as serious, even a threat to lay off the case. That article in the town paper last night spread the news around that you're handling Weldon's appeal. You've been digging around, talking to people. Word gets out."

I pull out a cigarette and light it. "Yeah, that scares me some, but it also gives me some hope. If someone's trying to scare me off the case, it means I'm digging in the right direction. Someone's getting nervous, and if someone's getting nervous, it only proves to me that Weldon is innocent." I pray Charles isn't the guilty one, that my unfounded suspicions are absurd. My family would be shattered.

"You're going to have to prove that to somebody besides yourself, and it could get rough, if somebody with a lot to lose is getting edgy. You sure you want to really pursue this?"

"I can't stop now that I've stepped into it." Just how far have I stepped and into what?

"Okay, I'll do all I can while you handle the legal end of things."

Tarsha charges into the office, dressed in her best black suit and white blouse, a single strand of fake pearls around her neck, the perfect secretary for a successful lawyer, ready for a reporter. "You must be the new man." She inspects Ray Bell with growing approval.

"And you must be Tarsha." He stands and offers his hand. "Ray Bell Crosby."

Tarsha actually bats her eyelashes, a coquettish reflex that Ray Bell seems to inspire. I wonder if I've done the same. "It's going to be a pleasure to have a real investigator around here."

"If you'll give me the juror list, I'll get started." He glances at me. "As I said yesterday, I'll dig around in Jack Flannery's background, see what I can come up with. You know, maybe I ought to go talk to Babaloo Brown, see if I can pull something out of him."

Babaloo said he had no reason to trust white people, and an investigator might prevent him from confiding in me. "Just let him be for the time being. I think I've baited him enough that he'll come forward, if he has anything to tell." I tell Ray Bell about the upcoming interview with the reporter from Jackson.

"Win this case, and you'll make a name for yourself." He puts enthusiasm into his words, like he's proud to be an associate. Success rubs off. He could be bucking to set up his own agency. More power to him.

I unload my briefcase and spread my work across my desk while Tarsha and Ray Bell confer over the juror list. He leans close to her. When he's ready to leave, he pauses by my desk. I can smell his faint cologne, something masculine like wood chips and cinnamon. "When are you going back to Parchman to see Weldon?"

I align my pencils and pads. "As soon as I file the appeal. I want to tell him about it."

"I'd like to go up there with you, okay? I'd like to see him, let him know I'm trying to help."

I smile. "Sure, why not?" I wouldn't mind company in Parchman.

He chews the inside of his cheek. "I thought about this all night. If Robert knows anything that might help us—you know what he said, the reason he chose you—well, I think we have to press him to tell us what he's talking about."

"We'll try." The puzzle was more than convoluted.

He departs, and Tarsha settles at her desk. The screen now separates us as if we have two offices. "What a hunk," she says. "I need an aerosol spray to get rid of the testosterone in the room."

"I hear you." I check my watch. "I'm going over to Craddock, Watts, and Buchanan. I'll be back in plenty of time to meet the reporter. There's one more person I'd like to talk to, Louella Waters, Robert Weldon's old girlfriend. I figure she'd be more likely to open up to a woman than an investigator. Besides, she and Ray Bell both testified at the same trial. Try to get an address for me. She might be married now, so you'll have to check it out."

"Long day ahead of you, then dinner with none other than the attorney general of the state of Mississippi, the man who fights death-penalty appeals. That ought to be an evening to remember." She gives me a limp wave. "See you when the reporter comes for the interview." She makes brackets with her fingers. "The *Clarion-Ledger* headlines: Grenola Lawyer Takes Up Where J. Clyde Perkins Failed."

"Don't bet your salary on me saying that."

"You better watch what you say. All eyes in the state of Mississippi and beyond will read what you say. And misconstrue it."

7

WITH THREE HOURS OF SOLID WORK UNDER MY BELT,
I head back to my office, lugging my heavy briefcase.
The humidity is oppressive. The few people sauntering down the sidewalk seem wilted, but when I pass,
they find enough energy to perk up and eye me with
unconcealed interest. I wonder if the incident with
my car has spread or if the article in last night's local
paper has aroused their curiosity. The *Clarion-Ledger*
will supply additional fodder when it hits the stands.
I hope the article will catch the eye and mind of some
sympathetic appellate court judge.

Nodding at Tarsha, I collapse in my desk chair.
I'm wired from too much caffeine and nicotine. Lack
of sleep doesn't help, either. If I'm going to get
through this, I must set priorities. An addled mind
will do no good for Weldon.

"Leona?" Tarsha comes around the screen and

stands by my desk, her face serious. "There's something I have to say to you."

"What?" I ask, immediately on edge.

She folds her arms across her chest. "You know, when I first came to work here, I really appreciated you hiring me when no one else would. But I resented how you just blew off what you had, how I would have liked to have all you did, how easy it came, and how I would have taken advantage of it. I always liked you personally, but I didn't much admire you. Now . . . well, you're hitting on all fours, and I'm real proud of you, Leona. Bucking the tide isn't going to be easy for you, but I'm glad to be aboard." She hesitates, almost embarrassed. "That's what I wanted to say." She turns and ducks around the screen.

She's touched me, though she doesn't understand the reason for my past lethargy. A lump rises in my throat. "Thanks, Tarsha."

"Welcome, Leona."

"You forgot the first part."

"What?"

"Lazy Leona."

"I'll never live that down. Wish I hadn't told you."

The screen now blocks my view, but I hear the front door open. "Good morning, sir."

"Gary Marshall from the *Clarion-Ledger*."

She ushers the reporter to my space, and I stand and introduce myself. Gary Marshall is a short, rotund man with a full reddish beard and a ponytail. In beat-up Nikes he looks fresh out of journalism school. His baggy khakis are wrinkled from the ride from the capital. He wears a knotted leather bracelet around his wrist, and coffee stains his white turtleneck.

"I do coffee. Would you care for some?" Tarsha inquires. I wasn't aware any was available, but Estelle and Lily probably provided a Mr. Coffee along with the decor.

"I think I've already had enough," Gary Marshall says with an easy smile and rubs the spots before taking a small recorder from his satchel, the kind I carried my books in to grammar school. "Mind if I record our interview?"

"Not at all." With little time to prepare, I remember Tarsha's warning that my words will be read throughout the state and maybe misconstrued.

He glances around. "You're a one-person firm, no associates?"

I'm slightly embarrassed not to have a mouthful of sir names to recite. Bingham, Slingham, Flingham, and Flungham. I try to keep a sense of humor. "That's right."

With a note of astonishment he digests that fact. "So, this is sort of a David and Goliath situation. Just you against the courts."

"I guess you could call it that."

"I'm just trying to get a handle for my article, a slant. Makes for better copy." He crosses his legs and with his fingers tries to pinch a crease into his pants. "You know, before the last execution in the state there were lawyers stationed at the governor's office, two at the supreme court clerk's in Jackson, one in Washington, and several on death row at Parchman. A big team working for the condemned. Weldon won't have that going for him."

I wince at the thought of Weldon being short-changed. Have I damaged him by taking the case? I have somehow linked Weldon's survival with my own. Have I been blindly selfish? Even if he had a battery of lawyers, none could care about him as I do. Is that enough?

He flips the record button, states the date, location, and my name. "Robert Weldon was represented pro bono by J. Clyde Perkins's firm in his murder trial, with Mr. Perkins himself as first chair. Now, in some death-penalty cases favorable decisions can be handed down at the last minute because the condemned man has had mediocre, even poor legal representation, but Robert Weldon's case is different. J. Clyde Perkins is considered to have one of the sharpest legal minds in the country. Weldon's subsequent lawyers, though court-appointed, had impeccable credentials, so it seems there's nothing left for Weldon except gangplank appeals, I believe they are called. Desperate motions, in other words. What's your take on that?"

He's done his homework. I'm nervous now that I've read a multitude of death cases where lawyers fresh to a case convinced judges to listen to issues different from the ones the original, less qualified lawyers presented, and gained a stay of execution, even a new trial, but Gary Marshall is correct. Weldon was, in reality, provided with good counsel. I toy with a cigarette, then light it. I must be careful not to set myself up for a libel suit. I've already secured a place on Mr. Perkins's bad side. "No doubt Mr. Perkins has a fine legal mind and a good reputation, but Robert Weldon told me that he wanted to testify at his trial and Mr. Perkins refused to let him. I think Robert Weldon was deprived of his rights, and therefore I'm using ineffectual counsel as an appeal."

"And you think the trial might have had a different outcome had Weldon testified?"

"It might have. He might have been able to convince the jury of his innocence. He didn't get the chance to testify and he was convicted, so we'll never know."

"Mr. Perkins has never before done a pro bono case personally. Have any idea how he chose to get his feet wet with Robert Weldon?"

"I've asked myself the same question." I'm still puzzled by it. I wonder if I'll ever know the answer to why Perkins just appeared at the Grenola jail to represent Weldon. There are so many facets to this case that I don't understand.

"How did you come to represent Robert Weldon?"

"He wrote to me, asking me to represent him. I went to Parchman to see him and decided to take the case. I believe he's innocent, as he claims."

"Then were you acquainted with Weldon in the past?"

"No, but he's from Grenola, where the crime took place." I drag on my cigarette, hiding behind a cloud of smoke. "I think he wanted someone on the scene so that the crime could be investigated more thoroughly than it was in the past. My investigator, Ray Bell Crosby, a former police officer, is looking into several angles as we speak. We have every intention of proving that Robert Weldon is innocent."

"In researching the case, did you find Mr. Perkins cooperative?"

"No."

"What about the other lawyers who represented Weldon after Perkins?"

"Very cooperative. They've agreed to turn over all their material to me."

Marshall caresses his beard. "This case has another twist. Jack Flannery was the district attorney at the time of Weldon's trial and prosecuted him. Winning a verdict against J. Clyde Perkins put the feather of the attorney general's office in his cap, so to speak."

I crush out my cigarette. "It was certainly a victory for Mr. Flannery. He is a very able man." I intend to find out just how able.

"So, you're acquainted with Mr. Flannery?"

"Known him all my life. His son, the present district attorney, and I have been close friends since childhood."

"Won't that make for an uncomfortable situation? The attorney general's office battles death appeals, so you're in direct conflict."

"It's our jobs, nothing personal." *Ha*, I want to add.

"There's talk around the capital that Jack Flannery is gunning for Governor Robert Danforth's job. Don't you agree that his chances would certainly be hurt if Weldon's conviction is overturned?"

"I would imagine that prosecuting an innocent man who was subsequently incarcerated for six years would damage someone's reputation."

"Don't you concede that Robert Weldon's best interests would be served by a lawyer with a large staff, more resources at their fingertips?"

"I certainly could use more help, but Robert Weldon couldn't have anyone who will fight harder for him than I will, anyone more determined to see him set free. I think that compensates to some degree."

"What about the victim's family, the Browns? Have you spoken them?"

"I have."

"And what was their reaction to a lawyer who's trying to save the man convicted of murdering a family member? Were they cooperative? Hostile?"

"April Brown's brother and her mother were both very fair to me. Certainly they want to see the person who's guilty of murdering April punished. Despite his conviction, that person is not Robert Weldon." I suddenly wonder why I keep referring to the killer as a person rather than as a man. A thought invades my mind. Could the murderer have been a woman? A woman who was jealous of April Brown? A woman who thought she was losing her man to April Brown?

"Let's talk about your background for a second. How many cases like Weldon's have you handled?"

I have been mesmerized during the conversation by Marshall's facial features, the reddish hair around the thick pinkish-purple lips, and can't dispel the vulgar notion that I'm looking at talking private parts. "I think you do your homework, Mr. Marshall and know the answer to that. I've handled zero criminal cases. Like that old saying, 'There's always a first time for everything.' You know . . ." I pause, gathering my thoughts.

"Even a rookie lawyer fresh out of law school could take on a battery of high-powered lawyers, all of them following the same procedures and operating according to the same laws, and if that neophyte knows that he is right, he stands a good chance of winning. I believe I will prevail in this case." The quote will look good in print, and my bravado might convince others I'm for real.

"Let's add a personal note. Tell me a little about yourself."

"A real little. Let's just leave it that I'm a single mother with an eight-year-old son."

We discuss the death penalty at length and my opposition to it. I lay some groundwork for the future by stating my belief that execution by lethal injection is just as cruel and inhuman as hanging, a firing squad, the electric chair, and the gas chamber. He turns off the recorder and loads it in the satchel as he stands. "Well, thanks much, Miz Bingham, and good luck."

After he leaves, Tarsha whips around the screen, pointing at the partition. "I think I liked it better when this thing wasn't between us. I heard, though. You did good."

"Tell me that thirty days from now and I'll believe it."

"The mail's come, and we have two stacks of material from Robert Weldon's appellate lawyers. I checked on Louella Waters. Last name's Fletcher now. Married a man who took over her daddy's farm-equipment business. Says she'll talk to you anytime this afternoon, but don't come around lunch 'cause her husband comes home to eat and he wouldn't want her mixed up in this. She lives at Twenty-nine Adair Street."

My stomach tells me it's time to eat. I check my watch. "I think I'll grab a sandwich at The Inn. Want to go?"

"Brought my own."

"I'll go through those files after I see the Fletcher woman. Ray Bell should be checking in later on. Maybe I'll give Babaloo a call. I know he was on the verge of telling me something last night."

The door opens and Lily floats in, admiring the final results of her efforts. "It all works. Darn if it doesn't, yessiree. Like it, Leona?" She lifts Bingo's backpack in the air.

"I sure do. It's great. What are you doing with Bingo's stuff?"

"Well, he didn't want to drag all his clothes he took to Estelle's to school with him, and she asked me to drop this by since I was coming in anyway. I couldn't find your car. I drove by where you always park, and it wasn't there." In her flowing flowered dress she looks a touch bewildered, like she's lost her way to a tea party.

Tarsha and I exchange glances. "It got scratched in a parking lot, and I'm having it fixed. Walter loaned me a car." Not exactly a lie and will save Lily from worry. I take the backpack and drop it by my desk.

"Maybe we could have a bite at The Inn if you're not busy, and you can tell me about the interview." Lily whips a handkerchief from her sleeve and blots her forehead. If not acquainted with her habits, I'd say she was in distress.

I grab my purse. "That's where I was headed. Let's go."

I try to hurry along the block to The Inn, but Lily ambles, pausing to window-shop, and forces me to slow my pace and hold my patience. When we finally reach the front door I hold it open for her, and we settle at a table for two in the peach-colored dining room just off the lobby. Each table has a rose in a crystal vase. The owner picks them from her garden every morning, trying to upgrade the shabby elegance of the place. The wonderful old paneling shines from the glow of the brass sconces. Everyone eats at The Inn despite the nasty joke that if you order a sandwich and a roach doesn't run out of it, don't eat it because the bug's still in there.

The lunch crowd spills in, and we nod and wave at the ones we know, which is a majority of the customers. They stare at me much the same as the people in Babaloo's joint. It seems that I'm a spectacle in either world. The lawyers from the Buchanan firm whisper among themselves, snatching glances when they think I'm not looking. My skin burns. I hope I haven't turned red.

Lily and I order club sandwiches and iced tea, then she asks about the interview. "I think it went well," I answer, lighting a cigarette. There's no ashtray and I figure we're in a no-smoking zone.

Lily toys with the salt and pepper shakers. "I hope you didn't say anything to rile Mr. Perkins, stir up a hornet's nest. You sure don't want to be slapped with a libel suit. That would never do. You have to be careful about that man. He's a powerhouse."

"Such a powerhouse that he lost Robert Weldon's case."

"Yes, well, that's certainly true, but I just wish there was some way you could leave him out of it. Try some other appeal that wouldn't involve him. There's no telling what he might do to harm you in the legal circles. He has tremendous influence with judges, and their respect for him might make you lose your appeal."

With a disgusted look the waitress plops an ashtray in front of me. I flick my ash in it. "Lily, don't sweat it. Do something to me? My reputation is damage-proof at this point."

"Well, it won't be forever. Especially if you get Robert Weldon off. Do you really think you can do it, deep down?"

"I hate to think otherwise." I ponder what she said about Perkins having influence with judges. I may be naive, but I believe the judicial system to be fair and open-minded.

"What does Jack think?"

"About my taking the case?"

Lily nods. "You and his daddy will be in direct conflict. I just hope it won't cause problems between you and Jack. He's the nicest man." Her eyes rake me over, trying to gauge if I agree.

"That he is." Lily would like to see me married to Jack, enveloped in a solid family relationship. I can't blame her. I'd wish the same for Bingo and some nice girl. Jack Senior once held hope that his son and I would marry, a great coup this link to the Bingham family. Not anymore. Not after Paris. And now I've topped that off by becoming his legal adversary.

I face the door when out of the corner of my eye I see Byars and Charles enter. Byars strides purposefully toward our table, Charles on his heels.

"What the hell happened to your car?" Byars questions in an irritated tone.

I wonder how he knows. Charles doesn't and couldn't have told him. I try to look puzzled.

"It's just sitting out in Walter's parking lot for all the world to see," Byars continues. "'Bitch' scratched on the door."

"Lord sakes." Lily looks stricken. "What happened? Why didn't you tell me?" All three stare at me.

I shrug and drag on my cigarette. "No big deal. Just random vandalism." I'm tempted to say, "Shit happens," but decide against it.

"Where did it happen?" Charles quizzes me, not knowing he's stepped into it now.

"Last night outside of Babaloo Brown's place on the lake." I glance at Charles.

He pales. He obviously hasn't told Byars about our rendezvous at the juke joint, though he could have made himself a hero in Byars's eyes for rescuing me. I look away from Charles, afraid my suspicions will filter through my expression.

Byars's face flushes with anger. "What is God's name were you doing at a place like that?"

I crush out my cigarette, eyes on the ashtray. "Investigating my case. I have to talk to the victim's relatives."

"And you think it was just a random act of vandalism?" Byars is incredulous at my apparent stupidity.

Before the discussion can escalate into a heated argument, Tarsha bounds through the front door and rushes to the table, eyes wide with alarm. I am immediately on guard.

"You better come back to the office. I called the police chief. He's on the way."

I quickly glance at my family members before returning to Tarsha. "What's happened?"

"Protesters out front with placards. All black, jeering about how you're trying to undo justice."

We hustle to the front door, leaving a group of curious diners in our wake. From the sidewalk in front of The Inn we have an unobstructed view of the commotion around my office. It's not a full-blown mob scene by any standards, but enough hecklers marching in circles to disrupt the peace and order of the town. They're chanting, "Execute Robert Weldon. Execute Robert Weldon." I read some of the placards hoisted by angry fists: JUSTICE FOR BLACKS. STABBED HER IN THE CHEST. STICK HIM IN THE ARM. APRIL'S DEAD.

The shopkeepers along the street are drawn as if by magnets to their show windows, some venturing timidly to the sidewalk. I glance behind me at the faces in The Inn's windows.

Byars's hands are clinched into fists. "We've never had anything like this happen before," he mutters, shaking his head. "Got the whole town talking. What's next?" He won't meet my eyes. I can feel his deep sense of embarrassment, how he's cut to the quick. Lily looks as if she might crumple to the ground. I'm sorry to cause them such anguish. Again, as Byars predicted, I'm the center of attention, the target of gossip.

I look back at the crowd at the window from the Buchanan law firm. I could easily get one of them to handle Robert's case pro bono and wash my hands of the subject. And if that lawyer lost the case and Weldon was executed, I would always think I might have saved him had I not been so spineless.

As Chief Lewis and his deputy pull up to the curb in a black-and-white, I feel obligated to approach the situation. Tarsha follows, bravely holding her head high. The closer I get, the more my legs tremble. I feel a spasm in my stomach. Chief Lewis raises his hands in the air and motions for the group to retreat. "Enough of this. Disperse now or I'll have to arrest you for disturbing the peace. Now, I mean it." The deputy touches his pistol as Chief Lewis threatens them again.

People from the courthouse spill out onto the lawn, watching the fracas. I spot Jack making his way through the crowd, a worried furrow between his eyes. Ray Bell Crosby rounds the corner and moves in to assist Chief Lewis and the deputy. "Get on about your business! This is not it!" he shouts to the crowd.

The angry momentum of the protesters is fading, the wind sucked out of them. Some shuffle away, others mumble to themselves. I slip around the crowd to the front of my office. One protester moves up close and spits on the sidewalk, purposely missing my shoes by inches.

"Hey," I call out to them, lifting my arms. "Hey, I'm just doing my job. I want justice as much as the next guy."

"Yeah," the spitter snarls, "and you gonna be sorry."

Ray Bell moves between us. "Go on, get away from here." He turns to me. "I heard this was about to happen while I was in their part of town talking to one of the jurors. Got here as soon as I could." Ray Bell gives the chief a two-fingered salute as he pushes toward us. "Howdy, Chief."

Chief Lewis nods and acknowledges him by touching his hat. "Ray Bell. Leona, you okay?"

"Wonderful." I roll my eyes.

Ray Bell explains to Chief Lewis that he's helping with the case. My family and Jack arrive in time to hear the bit of news. All but Charles, who already knows, seem stunned not only that I have an investigator but by my choice of one. I want to recite the old adage that beggars can't be choosers, but I can't insult Ray Bell. Even if I could afford a fee, I just might have chosen Ray Bell over others anyway. He seems more than up to the job.

Jack lays a hand on my shoulder and squeezes. "Leona, you're shaking. Maybe you'd better go inside and sit down. I'm sorry about this happening. It'll blow over. They're only a few rabble-rousers flexing their muscles. Don't let it get you down."

I am already down. How much further can I go? Tarsha's boyfriend, Tyrone, has arrived on the scene, looking grave, and they go inside to talk. I'm sure she'll be uneasy about going back to her neighborhood at the end of the day.

Byars steps up to bat. "Leona, I want you to give serious consideration to dropping this case now. The situation can't get anything but worse. You're in way over your head."

My gaze drifts toward Lily, who seems to be wrestling with some inner conflict. Frowning, Charles glances around as if he's found himself in alien territory. Suddenly, in my mind's eye, I see Robert Weldon behind bars, alone, with no one to champion his cause but some lawyer who will carry out his perfunctory duties until his client is executed. "I need some time by myself, okay?"

"We'll still see you tonight, won't we?" Jack's question is threaded with uneasiness.

"Sure." I edge toward my door, where Ray Bell is standing, and he lifts his shoulders as if to ask: Where do we go from here? "Keep at it and call me later at home," I whisper to him and duck inside.

Tarsha and Tyrone are deep in conversation. I know he's hassling her to quit, but she'll stand fast. Grabbing Bingo's backpack, my briefcase, and the stack of material from Weldon's previous lawyers, I check through the window to make sure everyone's gone before I leave. "Tarsha, talk to you later."

I juggle my load to the car and toss it into the backseat. Lighting a much needed cigarette, I inhale with gut-wrenching pleasure and head to Louella Fletcher's on Adair Street. Call me reckless. Call me crazy. There is something inside that demands I continue. I simply cannot suppress the urgent command. I take deep, fortifying breaths and finally relax to a degree.

Louella Fletcher's residence is a boxy old structure patterned in Jefferson Davis–style architecture,

the front porch wrapped with gingerbread wood-
work. It projects the feeling of quiet gentility from
another time. The dark green shutters are freshly
painted, and the shrubbery surrounding the house
looks as if trimmed with manicure scissors. I push
through a black iron entry gate fashioned with arrow-
like finials into the yard. The leaded windows on
either side of the front door are shielded by bunched
sheer material, but one is pulled back slightly, and
someone on the other side is taking a peep. Louella
Fletcher is awaiting my arrival.

She opens the front door as I step onto the porch
and glances up and down the street. She's wearing a
simple green shift and white sandals. "Leona?"

I nod. I don't recall having seen her, but people in
Grenola know the Binghams, if not personally, then
by reputation. "Thanks for seeing me on such short
notice."

She invites me inside. Louella Fletcher probably
was once the petite baby-doll type in high school,
likely a cheerleader with that round, pleasant face
framed with chocolate-colored curls and limpid
brown eyes that remind me of Mister Marvel's. And,
like so many of those cute apple-cheeked girls of yesteryear, Louella has turned plump. I could picture
her with Robert Weldon, though.

"Would you like something to drink? Tea, a Coke?"

A club sandwich, since I missed mine at The Inn.
A hamburger with trimmings. Peanut butter sandwich, anything to stave off hunger. The smell of a
heavy lunch she and her husband consumed earlier
lingers in the air. Most southerners have their big

meal at midday and eat light at night. "Tea would be fine." I sit on the couch in a living room filled with Victorian furniture while she fetches drinks. This was her family's home, and I envision Weldon visiting here, probably uncomfortable among the brocades and satins. He took a giant step up from his humble environment.

"Here we go." Louella hands me a tall, frosty glass of tea and a paper napkin. She settles on a burgundy overstuffed chair facing me, assing around on the cushion to get comfortable. "How is Robert? I take it you've seen him."

"Holding up well, given the circumstances." I sip the tea. It's sweetened with orange and pineapple juice, tasty. "He looks fine, matured from the earlier pictures I've seen of him."

Louella leans forward. "Please don't tell anybody you talked to me. My husband wouldn't like anything about Robert coming back into our lives. My daddy like to have died when I had to testify in the trial. You know how people in Grenola talk. I guess I've lived it down now, being mixed up with a convicted killer."

I can sympathize with her. "Tell me about Robert. You knew him better than anyone."

Her eyes fix on an amateurish floral painting on the wall, colors way too harsh, straight out of the tube. I wonder if she's the artist. "He was a kind man, very gentle. Didn't have much education, but he was always trying to learn, especially the use of proper English. I went to Delta State, and he was always telling me to correct him when he made a grammatical error. It was always like he was trying to live up to some image he had, if you know what I mean. We first met in the library. I was looking for some novels to read, and he was checking out books on subjects he would have learned in high school had he not dropped out. We got to talking, and he asked me out. Things went from there."

"What did your folks think about him?" I know the mentality of the class system in a small town.

"They didn't like that he was a mechanic, and that stopped them right there. They never bothered to look further into the man himself. My folks and I had lots of fights about it. They were determined that we wouldn't get married, and I was just as determined that we would and that I'd prove them wrong about him." Her eyes flash, revealing the old fire that once burned.

"Robert knew about their disapproval? Your fights with your parents?"

She balls her napkin into a knot. "He couldn't help but know. He was witness to some of them."

"You testified that the night before April Brown's murder, you and Robert were to meet at a restaurant out by Four Mile Lake. You got to the restaurant, waited, then he called and said his car wouldn't start. You then rowed across Four Mile Lake to pick Robert up because it was quicker than driving around to the other side to get him, and the two of you rowed back to the restaurant."

"That's right."

"And Robert claimed in a statement that while he was waiting for you to row across the lake, he was hot and hung his jacket on a tree branch. You testified that you didn't see that jacket hanging there; nor did he mention that evening that he'd forgotten his jacket."

She shrugs. "Well, that's just the way we were when we were together—you know, oblivious to everything but each other."

"That jacket was very important, though. It was the reason he was at the murder scene the next day, the reason for him not going directly home but taking the long way in order to pick up his jacket. It's too bad that you didn't see the jacket that night so that he could have gotten it then and wouldn't have been at the murder scene the next day. The jacket . . . the jacket that wasn't there, as it turned out." Was there ever a jacket? Robert is hiding information that could hurt someone. Louella? I play with a scenario. Maybe Robert Weldon had been fooling around with April Brown before he met Louella Fletcher. Louella finds out or Robert even confesses. Mrs. Brown said that her daughter was going to meet the white man who had impregnated her, make him pay. Robert tells Louella that April is threatening him, that he is going to meet April and try to straighten out the situation. Louella is petrified that everyone in town, especially her parents, will find out. Her parents would have been proven right about Robert. She would be the laughingstock of Grenola, both she and Robert ruined in town. No, Louella doesn't want that, so she beats Robert to the scene and silences April Brown forever. Robert arrives upon the carnage and suspects what has happened, but can't know for sure. He has to think of an excuse for being on the scene and comes up with the idea of the lost jacket. He knows he's innocent and figures he won't even be arrested, certainly not convicted. But what about the car not working? I can't play that into the scheme logically. I break back to reality. "Louella, I don't recall your being asked this question. Where were you on the afternoon of April Brown's murder?"

She stiffens like I've slapped her. The round, innocent eyes narrow. "What are you saying?"

"I'm not saying anything, just asking a simple question. Where were you the afternoon April Brown was killed?"

"Right here with my parents." She is indignant.

"They're both dead now, right?"

She leaps up, face flushed, veins distended and throbbing in her forehead. "I know about lawyers like you. You'll grasp at anything to get your client off, including trying to implicate an innocent person. I should never have let you come over here. I don't care if you are a high and mighty Bingham. Get out of my house right now."

The outburst sets me reeling. "Hey, listen—"

Her face is contorted into an ugly mask. "No, you listen. I'm gonna tell my husband about this, and if you ever call me again or come back or try to involve me in any way, you'll be sorry. He's mean. He'll beat the shit out of you or worse. And if he doesn't, I will." She points to the door. "You'd better get out while you can."

I should leave quietly, but I can't resist a jab. "You do have a temper to contend with. Bet it's gotten you into lots of trouble in the past."

I make it through the door just as she slams it behind me. I expect to hear glass breaking. After today's events, an ugly demonstration and a nasty confrontation, I'll certainly be refreshed, relaxed, on my toes, ready to meet the attorney general tonight.

As I start the engine I glance at the house. Louella Fletcher is on my list. I'm certainly on hers. I'll have Ray Bell check out her background.

Lighting a cigarette, I drive to the school. I feel guilty that I've hardly given Bingo a thought in almost twenty-four hours. He deserves more attention, but I'll concentrate on him as I always have in the past when this tough gig is over. He won't recognize the strange car, so I get out and lean against the fender.

He spots me, smiles, and lopes to the car, shoe-strings untied and flopping. "We get a new car?" He crawls in on the driver's side and scoots over to the passenger side.

"Not likely. Our car's in the shop. This is a loaner." I drive away, and we chat about the night at Estelle's house, what a good time he had. I tell him that we're going to the Flannerys' for dinner and have to hide my smile when he blushes. He's sweet on Kit Flannery but would never admit it.

"Why do I have to go to a girl's house for dinner? She'll tell everybody I'm her boyfriend."

"We're going because Jack is *my* boyfriend."

Bingo has a gleam in his eye. "Are you going to marry him?"

"He hasn't asked."

"If he does, we'll have to live with him and Kit. Then she'd be my sister."

"That might not be so bad."

Bingo thinks about that one all the way home. I give it a thought or two myself. It would be best for Bingo, but would it for me?

Bingo wrestles with Mister Marvel, refills his bowl, and we unload the car. I stack my files on the dining room table, give Bingo a snack of cookies and milk before he starts his homework, and go upstairs. I look up Babaloo's number and call. I recognize the woman's voice from last night, and over background noises from the bar she informs me that he's unavailable. I leave my name and number and decide to forget life for a few minutes by soaking in a hot bath.

Just as I've settled among the foam and bubbles, the phone rings. I would let it go, but I'm afraid it's Babaloo. I grab a towel and drip to my bedside table. Ray Bell is checking in, slightly downcast that he has nothing to report. My visit to Louella Fletcher boosts his morale considerably. Damn, I like that man's voice, the energy he puts into it.

I debate about getting back into the tub, but decide I've had enough and dress for the evening. Checking for spots or spills, I slip into green silk slacks, a matching blouse, and low-heel multicolored shoes that blend with everything. I keep economy in mind when buying footwear. Feeling the need of fortification for the evening, I hurry downstairs to mix a bourbon and branch to accompany me while I fix my face.

Seated at my dresser, I sip the drink and apply more makeup than usual, especially around the eyes. I don't overdo, but I want to impress Jack Senior.

Beauty and brains, a lethal combination, Mr. Attorney General. Beware of me. I take a closer look in the magnifying glass and decide I wouldn't scare anybody but myself.

Adding a gold choker and earrings Lily and Byars gave me one Christmas, I belt the bourbon and load a green leather purse with stuff from my old tote bag. I'm ready for the evening. Let the show begin.

Bingo has already fed Mister Marvel and is waiting in the kitchen, shined from head to toe in Sunday school clothes. We both have impressions to make. "You look pretty spiffy. I like you in long pants and a white shirt. Very grown-up," I tell him.

He shrugs off the compliment, and we head to town, not saying much on the way. I'm planning my conversation with the A.G., and Bingo seems lost in thoughts of his own. Sometimes he's moody and I feel I can't reach him.

We pull up in front of Jack's house, a place where I might have lived had circumstances been different. A replica of New Orleans–style residences, the home is hugged by a balcony edged with black wrought iron, faces sideways, and overlooks a courtyard centered with a bubbling fountain. Jack's and Kit's voices rise from the patio where Jack and I played as kids. Jack's mother died when he was a teenager, and he and his father lived on here until Jack married. Mr. Jack, as I've always called him, gave Jack and his bride the house as a wedding present and took an apartment. Now that he's the attorney general and lives in Jackson, he stays with Jack when he visits his old hometown. Memories linger for all of us in this place.

Bingo remarks on how neat the house is. I know he's comparing it to our ramshackle place. Jack and Kit open the wrought iron gate with welcome written all over their faces. Jack gives me a hug and a kiss on the cheek, and the gesture doesn't go unnoticed by the two youngsters. "How 'bout a daiquiri? I've just made a pitcher." Jack looks casual and relaxed in freshly pressed khakis, a tan polo shirt, and loafers with no socks. Kit, by contrast, has dressed in a starched pink pinafore and tied back her ginger curls with a big pink bow. Freckles pepper her upturned nose. She's a tomboy in a little coquette's clothing.

"I've just had a bourbon. Better stick with it."

Kit gestures with her hand. "Come on back to the den, Bingo. I've got my Sega Saturn hooked up."

Bingo is thrilled and obviously surprised that a girl owns the system he wants for Christmas. They disappear through the open French doors, and I settle on the patio furniture while Jack mixes at the bar cart. My vantage point affords a view of Rebecca's portrait over the living room mantel. My eyes trace her patrician features, the ginger curls Kit has inherited. Was their relationship as perfect as I have imagined? Was their sex steamy and uninhibited as I've pictured? I stop myself from wondering such things.

I sample the guacamole dip with a homemade cheese biscuit. The tinkle of the fountain is pleasant, and I feel removed from the rigors of the day. I know it won't last, but wish it would.

Jack hands me a drink, but doesn't let go of the glass when I try to take it. "I miss you," he says, then releases his grip.

"You, too," I answer, meaning it.

He rakes back a lock of hair. "As I said on the phone, it's not my fault."

"I know." I break eye contact and sip the bourbon. When the case is over, maybe he and I can go away for a long weekend, rekindle old passions, if that's possible. Sometimes I feel my soul is drained, never to be revived.

Mr. Jack bursts through the French doors, and I almost expect a blare of trumpets, though he wears a blue cotton warm-up instead of a crown and robe. His entrance charges the air for an instant. He is not unaware of his effect on people. His face is fine-boned, his nose hawkish, his hair graying, and his eyes, the color of washed-out jeans, are fixed unnervingly on me. He's tall and radiates energy. Electrified is the word I'd use to describe him. As a child I was afraid of him. Nothing has changed, I suddenly realize. No one, with the possible exception of Byars, could intimidate this man.

"Well, hello, Leona." A smile begins on his lips but not in his eyes. "How're your folks?" I can almost smell the magnolias in his speech and see the governor's mansion reflected in his eyes.

"They're well, thanks." I sip my drink for something to do and because I need it.

He scrutinizes me as if I've done something wrong. "Give them my best." He hustles to the cart and pours a daiquiri, sips from the stem glass. "Excellent, Jack. Very tart."

The table under the umbrella is set for dinner, and Jack pokes a long tong at the glowing charcoal briquettes in the grill. A platter with thick T-bones are waiting to be cooked. Nona, the maid who helped raise Kit, will bring the salad and baked potatoes. Later she'll present a peach cobbler and homemade ice cream. I know the routine for company well, and it doesn't vary much. It's always good, though.

Mr. Jack takes a chair facing me, sets his drink on a glass-topped table. "So, I understand you've taken on the Robert Weldon case. Word is, you're already having some problems with it—nasty demonstration on the sidewalk, I understand."

"True on all counts, but not insurmountable problems." I light a cigarette to cope with my unease. Jack looks up from tending the steaks, and his expression shows he's primed to support me if this formidable man makes it necessary. Jack is strong enough not to be overshadowed by his father.

Mr. Jack steeples his fingers. "I must say, you have more gumption than most. The majority of attorneys have never handled death-penalty cases, don't have the expertise, time, or resources to take on such a cause. You know it takes at least two hundred and fifty man hours to handle such appeals, reading thousands of pages of court transcripts, interviewing witnesses who were unknown to or maybe ignored by the police, and then having those witnesses not pan out. Certainly dropping all other cases that would bring in revenue. All that adds up to probably twenty-five thousand in attorney fees, maybe six thousand for an investigator, and that's the low-ball figure. Most lawyers just can't afford that kind of altruism, especially a one-lawyer shop. Yes, you do have spunk, I'd say. You're undertaking one of the most momentous cases you can ever handle, in an area of the most complex litigation that exists, and do the virtually impossible for no money. My hat's off to you."

As the old adage goes, he's damning me with faint praise. What he says is scary, but I don't reply and allow the silence to lengthen.

Mr. Jack frowns slightly. "I always had problems with each and every case. You see, what prosecutors fear most is convicting an innocent man." He hesitates. "Most people believe that a jury convicts a person accused of a crime. Not so. It's *not* what the jury thinks, it's what the prosecutor or the defense lawyer has *made* them think. It all boils down to who does the best job with the evidence they have to present."

I chew on that, convinced that Babaloo has something to disclose. Maybe Mr. Jack knows what it is and suppressed the information. "Sometimes all the evidence doesn't come out in trial." I don't want to sound antagonistic, but fear I might have.

He sizes me up, his expression reinforcing his earlier insinuations that I'm out of my league. "That's possible, but there certainly was enough to convict Robert Weldon. He was guilty." If he has anything to hide, he covers it well.

"I'm sure you already know it, but I've just found a court ruling in a case known as *Daubert* where the Fifth Circuit court in New Orleans lifted the ban in use of the lie-detector results as evidence. The ruling applies only to federal courts in Texas, Louisiana, and Mississippi. Robert Weldon didn't have benefit of a lie-detector test." I think about Louella·Fletcher. If

Weldon is covering for someone, that might show in the test.

The crease that Jack has inherited forms between his father's eyes. "And he won't have benefit of it now—not six years after the fact. My office will fight that tooth and toenail."

I know he means it. In pushing for a test I would likely waste time which could be better spent in another direction. "I've been talking with some of the witnesses—Mrs. Brown, her son, Babaloo, Louella Fletcher—"

"Ray Bell Crosby, too, I understand," he interrupts.

"Yes, he's my investigator. Robert feels that his claims of innocence were never properly investigated by his previous lawyers."

"I take it you're leaning more on the investigative aspects of the case rather than the legal end."

"Both, actually." I drag on my cigarette. "You know this town as well as I. Better even. Any white man here who got a black woman pregnant would have a powerful motive to keep her from exposing him, just as any woman whose husband or boyfriend was mixed up with April Brown would have a strong motive to kill their rival." I hesitate. "Robert claims he never laid eyes on April Brown until he saw her in that ravine."

Mr. Jack purses his lips and stares at me. "He claimed a lot of things." He samples his daiquiri, takes his time returning the glass to the table. "So, according to you, the whole town is now under suspicion . . . just forget all the evidence against Robert Weldon."

"Well, I practically got thrown out of Louella Fletcher's house today because I asked her where she was the afternoon April Brown was killed." Am I trying too hard to force a woman into the slot of murderer because I'm afraid Charles fits?

"Yes, well, I can understand her reaction. No one likes to have someone tear scabs off wounds that still probably haven't healed. And if you're thinking a woman might have killed April Brown, then I suggest you talk to the medical examiner." He gives me a look of a professor talking to a dull student.

Jack intervenes. "Let's stop all the shop talk and enjoy the evening."

Not anxious to let go, Mr. Jack continues. "I'll grant you, there is an air of mystery about the case, something that still baffles me."

I perk up, anxious to hear what he has to say.

"I don't deny I'm glad it happened, but why did J. Clyde Perkins suddenly appear at the Grenola jail to take on the case? And pro bono? Now, that is a puzzlement to me and always will be. I'd surely like to know the answer."

He is not alone.

8

THE SHELTER OF MY GALLERY OFFERS SCANT RELIEF
from the humidity. The ceiling fan barely stirs air
seemingly heavy and thick enough a knife could cut
it. I've dressed accordingly, white shorts and halter
top, but rivulets of sweat roll down my body until I
feel like a melting candle, soon to be reduced to a
blob. Ordinarily I'd work inside under more comfortable conditions, but Bingo is out of school for the
day. I'm forced to keep an eye on my bored offspring
until Estelle comes to relieve me so that I can visit the
medical examiner.

Stuck to the white wicker chair, I move my bottom from side to side and glance toward the bayou.
Bingo paddles the rowboat back and forth while Mister Marvel leans over the side, peering into the murky
water as if he's navigating. A flock of birds flies over,
and Bingo points his finger like a gun and pretends to
shoot. Mister Marvel suddenly cocks his head, trying

to understand. The frantic pace at which I work contrasts so severely to the backdrop of such placid scenery that I feel off balance at times.

Taking a sip of iced tea, I shift to trial transcripts, tedious reading that blurs my vision and challenges my mind. The Buchanan firm has allowed me to take out books from their library, and the volumes, places marked with yellow strips of paper, are stacked on the glass-topped wicker table next to the edition of the *Clarion-Ledger*.

I'm pleased with the article, although as with most news stories there are inaccuracies. The reporter quotes me as saying that I'm trying to uncover new evidence in order to gain a stay of execution for Robert Weldon and possibly a new trial, that my investigator, Ray Bell Crosby, and I expect to have witnesses heretofore not heard from to come forward. Ray Bell and I *are* trying to uncover new evidence to exonerate Weldon, not put him through the ordeal of another trial. And the only witness I have hopes of coming forward is Babaloo Brown. J. Clyde Perkins's name is bantered around, curiosity raised as to why he took the case pro bono, along with my claim that he was of ineffectual counsel and uncooperative in my attempt to save Robert Weldon from execution. I'm uneasy about that section and winced at the statement that the state-appointed lawyers did not adequately investigate their client's claims of innocence. It is true, but they have been cooperative enough to send their files and I didn't want them publicly bashed.

The article also touches on Jack Flannery Sr. and

how the Weldon case was a springboard to the attorney general's office. The reporter adds his flavor by speculating that Robert Weldon, if exonerated, has grounds for a lawsuit against the state of Mississippi for wrongful incarceration. He cites cases in other states where such judgments mounted into millions of dollars.

I wish the reporter had kept his opinion to himself. Every judge in the state likely reads the *Clarion-Ledger* or will be made aware of the article, and it could cloud their judgment when the appeal comes before one of them. What is one man's life compared to the millions it might cost the state if he's set free? To say nothing of the damage to the esteemed attorney general's reputation.

I jump when the phone rings. A creepy feeling now grabs me every time someone calls. I have answered three calls when no one on the other end speaks. As with my car, I don't like to think about the calls or what they could mean. At least the demonstration in town was a straightforward attack. Steeling myself, I let the phone ring a few times before I go inside to answer.

A stranger introduces herself as Karen Rice, a member of the Mississippi Appellate Project, and I listen with growing wonder as she explains in a clipped and precise Northern accent the reason for the call. Shock is a mild word to describe my reaction. I simply cannot believe what has happened, all due to the *Clarion-Ledger* article. It's done some good after all. We talk, then make plans. Hanging up, I go outside and stare at the cloudless sapphire sky. I want to shout, "It's not just me against the world now. The calvary is coming."

The need to tell somebody is overpowering. I hurry back inside and call Tarsha. Her mother informs me with barely disguised hostility that she and Tyrone have gone somewhere. I ask Tarsha's mother to have her return my call, not at all sure the message will be relayed. I call Babaloo again and leave a message with his sultry-voiced lady bartender. I'm sure that message will be relayed, but maybe not returned. The clock is ticking, and I need any scrap of information that might help. My constant companion is the fact that minutes, hours, and days are slipping away with little or no progress to show for my efforts. Maybe the exciting phone call will change that.

I return to the gallery and check my watch. Ray Bell should arrive soon to bring me up to date. I can spill the good news to him. With a smile, I wonder what Mr. Jack will think of the new development. At dinner he had watched me calmly, like a cat poised to pounce on a defenseless mouse when the time was right. I believe it's in my favor that he considers me no competition to him and his powerful battery of lawyers, and that my chances of prevailing are not even slim but nonexistent.

I press the iced tea glass to my forehead and see Ray Bell's pickup round the bayou, a cloud of dust in the wake. He circles into my driveway and stops. A woman, his wife, I presume, rides in the cab with him. He gets out, stomps dust off his boots, and bolts up the gallery steps, his megawatt smile beaming.

"Hey, Leona. Hot out today. I don't reckon we're gonna get that rain everybody was looking for."

"Guess not." When he's around, it's hard to look anywhere else but at him. I must appear as if I've just stepped from a sweat box, hair frizzed, face red and shining, clothes damp and clinging, while he seems unaffected by the heat, short-sleeved blue shirt starched crisp and jeans with a knife-edge crease. "Want some iced tea? Wouldn't your wife like to join us? It's bound to be cooler here than in the truck." I catch a glimpse of her taking measure of me and wish I had on more clothes, here on the gallery with her husband.

"Wilma Ruth's fine, listening to some program on the radio. She knows we have private stuff to talk about, and I left the air conditioning running." He plops into a wicker chair and stretches out his long legs, crossing one ankle over the other. "Guess I will have a little tea." His eyes give me the once-over.

Bursting to tell the news, I pour tea in the extra glass I brought out for Bingo and hand it to him. "Guess what? I just had an offer of help with Weldon's case from a group called the Mississippi Appellate Project."

"What's that?"

"It's a publicly funded organization in Jackson that assists lawyers for death row inmates," I explain, hearing the enthusiasm in my voice. "They've got a whole team to help."

He sits up straight. "That's terrific."

"I think so. The bad news is that they're tied up with another death-penalty case until after next week and I need to file before the week is over."

"Can't you wait for them?"

I shake a cigarette from the pack and light it. "No. There's no time to spare. I'm going to file the appeal next week, and while it's working its way through the courts, the group can help me with a second motion if the first doesn't fly." I pray the first appeal will catch the attention of a sympathetic judge and a second won't be necessary. I think of the newspaper article again, wondering about its effect.

He gulps the tea. "What basis of appeal do you intend to make if the ineffectual counsel doesn't work?"

"A first of its kind, that lethal injection is cruel and inhumane, same as the rest of the methods of execution. It's kind of a catch twenty-two, but it could spark some new legislation." I drag off my cigarette. "Have you found out anything to help us?"

Ray Bell sighs and shakes his head. "Not much. I've finished talking with all the jurors and alternates, and no one had any unauthorized contact with any outsiders. Certainly if any one of them had been offered a bribe or taken one or some such, they wouldn't admit it, but they seemed honest, nothing to hide. They all believe they did a good job and put away the guilty party.

"Now, about this Louella Fletcher's background that you asked me to check into . . ." He smiles at the thought of something. "Well, to quote an acquaintance of hers, 'She has such a complex that when Santa says ho, ho ho, Louella thinks he's laughing at her.' I didn't hear much good about her, hot-tempered, quarrels with neighbors over the least little thing, like one neighbor's dog that pooped in her yard. She took the dog stuff and smeared it all over their windows, threw it all over their porch when she knew they were having a party. Another neighbor's tree branches were hanging over her fence, and she got a chain saw and hacked off several big limbs—just butchered the tree. And the domestic violence . . . on several occasions neighbors called Chief Lewis to the Fletchers' house, said it sounded like someone was getting killed over there. First time Chief Lewis went over, he was expecting to find the husband beating up the wife. Turned out Louella and her husband were battering each other about equally."

I think about this, enlarging my suspicions. "Before I angered her, I could picture Louella and Weldon together. Now I can't see Weldon at one time mixed up with such a potentially volatile woman."

Ray Bell rattles the ice in the glass. "People say Louella wasn't that way back then, was a nice simple girl until Weldon was sentenced to death. It changed her personality completely. But the husband, Ronnie, was always in some scrape. Always had some get-rich scheme that failed. Then he took after Louella and her daddy's money. She fell for the first guy who came along after Weldon was gone. Guess she was just soured on life."

A murder, I'm beginning to realize, has a ripple effect. Many more people other than the perpetrator, the victim, and their families are touched by the tragedy. My thought is broken by the sound of Bingo's voice.

"Mom, isn't it time for Aunt Estelle to come get me?" He lopes up the steps with Mister Marvel on his heels and stares pointedly at Ray Bell.

"Hi there, big guy." Ray Bell holds out his hand. Bingo accomplishes the shake as I've taught him, firm grasp, meet the person's eyes.

"Bingo, this is Mr. Crosby, and he's working with me. He's an investigator. He used to be a policeman."

Bingo is clearly impressed with Ray Bell's résumé. He's watched enough television to recite all the gumshoes' names from the present to the past ten years of reruns. "You must have lots of equipment, like those listening devices that are about the size of a pen where you can hear what somebody's saying miles away. You ever shoot anybody?"

Ray Bell chuckles. "Well, no, but I shot at somebody once and missed."

Bingo wipes sweat off his forehead with his arm. "Don't you train at those shooting ranges where the targets look like men?"

"I did."

"How come you missed, then?"

Ray Bell is having a hard time concealing his amusement. "Actually, the shot I fired was just a warning. I wasn't aiming to hit the man."

This seems to satisfy Bingo that Ray Bell is competent. "Then you might have to shoot somebody in this new case you're working on and really hit 'em this time?"

Ray Bell exchanges a glance with me. "I sure hope not, Bingo. Say, you look like a pretty strong fellow. You like to ride horses?"

Bingo's face lights with pleasure. "Sure do. I get to ride sometimes at my grandpa's, but not too much." He looks at Ray Bell expectantly, as I do.

"I've got some horses and ponies out on my place. Maybe your mom will let you come ride with me."

The offer fills me with appreciation. I guess I'm always trolling for a male presence in Bingo's life. "Sure you can. Now, go get ready for Aunt Estelle."

He dashes off, and I tell Ray Bell that I'm going to see Dr. Hull, who performed the autopsy on April Brown, explaining that Mr. Jack smugly suggested that I should check with the medical examiner if I thought it was possible that a woman may have committed the murder. I catch a hint in Ray Bell's expression that he thinks I should have asked him to go instead.

"Since the attorney general made that suggestion, I'm sure he already knows the medical examiner will say it isn't possible that a woman murdered April Brown."

"I figure that, too. He isn't making suggestions on ways to help my case, I know, but I still want to talk to Dr. Hull about a few things."

Ray Bell clasps his hands together, twirling his thumbs. "So how did the evening go with Mr. Flannery?"

I fix on his pickup, wondering about his wife. "Okay. There's no question Mr. Jack is confident that he and his machine will crush any efforts to save Weldon. He views me as harmless legally."

His eyes search out mine. "How does he view you personally now?"

"I sense a hostility toward me, but he covers it well. He'd like me out of his son's life." It hurts that Mr. Jack judges me so harshly. "I take it you haven't come up with anything on him."

"No. Maybe I haven't come up with anything because there's nothing there. He's ambitious, powerful, and most folks have nothing but the best to say about him. Most likely our next governor if he can unseat Robert Danforth. Danforth's popular, though, and to get his job Flannery will have to come up with something to turn the public tide."

"Like some scandal?"

"Possibly. I'll keep working on Flannery's background, but I'm starting to think he's clean as a whistle and it's a dead end, a waste of time we don't have."

"Mr. Jack admitted he felt there was an air of mystery about Weldon's case."

Ray Bell perks up. "Yeah?"

"He's puzzled like I am about J. Clyde Perkins taking on the case, especially pro bono. Maybe you could sniff around that subject, see what you can find out."

"I could make a trip up to Memphis, maybe strike up a conversation with somebody in his office, poke around some."

Maybe he's good at a little "breaking and entering," could peek at the files. I want to suggest it, but some shred of character prevents it. "I like that. I just feel there's something strange about it. Perkins himself taking on such a low-profile case. Something doesn't jibe there. And I thought Weldon chose me as a lawyer because of my relationship to the Flannery family. Maybe I was wrong." If not my connection to the Flannerys, then why had Weldon singled me out to represent him? Charles pops into my head again.

"We'll try to get it out of him when we go to Parchman." Ray Bell's voice takes on an urgent tone. "Make him see he's absolutely got to tell us everything if he wants to cheat that needle next month."

I shiver at the thought I constantly try to push from mind, that Weldon *will* be executed. I promised Jack that if that happened, it wouldn't haunt me forever, but the closer the date comes, the more I realize I might not be able to keep that promise. In the beginning I linked his survival to mine, and now his demise might also mean mine. I cannot let this happen.

Ray Bell interrupts my morbid thoughts. "No word from Babaloo, I take it."

"No, but I still have the feeling he'll call with something." I don't know where these beliefs originate, why I think I'm graced with some special antennae.

"You sure I shouldn't go see Babaloo myself?"

"I just think it would scare him off—" The phone breaks my cadence. "I'll be right back."

Passing through the dining room, I eye the bills stacked on the table with a rise of nausea. Money is short and I'm spending countless hours on a case without pay, as Mr. Jack so masterfully pointed out. Byars calls me financially irresponsible, and deep down I guess he's right. I should think of Bingo's future and concentrate on making money to save. Bingo's books and school supplies are scattered on the kitchen table. The kid needs a desk I can't afford to buy. I have to make time to snatch one from Lily's attic.

I grab the receiver from the wall phone, again hoping it's not the caller who won't speak. It's Estelle, and she's upset. "What's wrong?"

"I had a terrible fight with Charles about my openin' up a decoratin' shop. He says you're the root of it, eggin' me on. Like he thinks I couldn't come up with an idea of my own. He was shoutin' at me, rantin' and ravin' that I ought to be satisfied with my life and stay at home and look after my own house . . ."

Someone besides Louella Fletcher also has a bad temper. "He ought to be proud of you."

"Leona, I hate to let you down, but now I've got one of my migraines and have to go to bed. I just can't keep Bingo. I'm so sorry."

"It's okay. I'm sorry about Charles being such an asshole. You *are* still going to open that shop, aren't you?"

A crazy little laugh escapes Estelle. "You *are* eggin' me on."

"Damn right. Get some rest."

I dial Lily. I can't very well take Bingo with me to the medical examiner's office to hear his gory report. I let the phone ring, and finally Julius answers. Lily and Byars are out for the afternoon.

I return to the gallery, and Ray Bell notices my expression. "Anything wrong? Another of those fake calls?"

"No, Charles's wife was going to keep Bingo while I went to see Dr. Hull, but she's got one of her migraines." I think Charles is the source of her headaches, not some actual condition. "Bingo can sit in the waiting room while we talk."

"Hey, that can't be much fun for a young fellow on a nice afternoon. I won't be able to accomplish much today, so let Wilma Ruth and me take him home with us. We'll ride horses."

"I can't impose on you."

"No imposition. A pleasure. We never had any kids, so we enjoy them any chance we get. All the neighbor kids congregate at our house." He rises. "Come on out to the truck and meet Wilma Ruth."

Wilma Ruth rolls down the window, and a cold blast from inside the truck hits me. "How do you do, Mrs. Bingham?" she greets me after Ray Bell introduces us.

"Please just call me Leona."

She seems embarrassed by an offer of familiarity from the high and mighty Bingham clan. She makes me want to explain that I'm the lowliest of the group. Wilma Ruth has been overexposed to the sun, crinkles around her eyes and crisscrosses etched on her cheeks. My quick take is that she's a prime example of the good country woman so common to the South, one who grows a garden, shells peas on her front porch, and cans and preserves food for winter consumption. She has a sweet smile and a kind of goodness that shines through her. I suddenly think less of Ray Bell for cheating on her and causing her public humiliation. But sex has toppled crowns and heads of state, so a man like Ray Bell is certainly not exempt.

"Ray Bell told me about those folks demonstratin' out in front of your office and about your car gettin' scratched up and those weird phone calls. Such a shame and you just tryin' to keep an innocent man from bein' executed."

It pleases me to hear someone say Weldon is innocent. "Thanks."

Ray Bell explains that they will keep Bingo while I visit Dr. Hull, and Wilma Ruth seems eager. "We'll be glad to have him stay for supper, too, if it would help you some," she offers.

I've spoken with Jack earlier, and he practically demanded that I have dinner with him at the club. I can't reject this unusual command performance, and my mind needs some down time. He suggested we drop Bingo and Kit at the movies, something we often do, while we have a quiet dinner. "I appreciate that, but I'm dropping him and a friend at the movies while I have dinner with someone."

Aware of my relationship with Jack, Ray Bell shoots me a knowing glance. "Want me to drop him off somewhere, or will you pick him up?"

"I'll pick him up around dinnertime. He and his friend eat hot dogs and junk at the movies."

Bingo appears on the gallery, and I call him to the truck, introduce him to Wilma Ruth, and explain the situation. He's clearly thrilled with the plan and scampers into the truck cab as Wilma Ruth moves over to make a place for him. I wave good-bye and return to work.

After a couple of hard hours at the books, I go inside to bathe and dress. Tarsha returns my call, and I relay the news about the Mississippi Appellate Project and their offer of help.

"Something like Alan Dershowitz's group. Bunch of unshaven radical shysters, I imagine, but who's complaining?"

"You should fit right in," I tell her.

We discuss the case, and I ask about the climate in her neighborhood, if she's had any flak since the demonstration.

"Oh, there's still some rumbling, some unrest. I don't discount more trouble cropping up. Some of those demonstrators can be pretty militant." Tyrone and her mother are the only ones razzing her for now, and she can handle them, she informs me. I don't doubt it.

I'd rather wear slacks and a comfortable shirt, but have to dress for dinner. Standards at the club must be upheld. A navy blue silk dress and fake pearls complete the picture of the perfect young Grenola matron. I dab on makeup and tame my hair into an windblown style with mousse and a glob of gel that's past its prime, according to the date on the tube. I ease into my killer-heeled navy pumps and fill a matching bag with necessities from my tote.

Downstairs, I open a can of dog food for Mister Marvel, careful not to get grease on my dress, and place his bowl on the gallery, then lock the door. He sniffs at the lump, and I chide him about being particular. "We can't have steak every night, doggie boy. You're a lucky pet and don't know it." I laugh when he barks at me like a recalcitrant child.

The paint on my Bronco door is shiny, but doesn't quite match the original factory color. Walter is a good mechanic, but doesn't have the eye of an artist.

Still, I'm glad to have the old buggy back home. It gets me where I'm going.

I'm a little late and put a heavy foot to the accelerator, making it to town in record time. Surrounded by a well-kept lawn, Dr. Hull's office is a freestanding colonial-style brick building a block from the middle of Grenola. He's a general practitioner and doubles as the medical examiner, since Sunflower County has little need for or the funds to pay a full-time one. As with most people in Grenola, he's been our family doctor since I was a child, and I still feel a stab of fear and apprehension upon entering his office. I picture him, as I did as a kid, in a white coat with a syringe concealed in the hand behind his back, ready to give me a shot when I'm not looking. The thought stops me in my tracks and draws me to attention. How do prisoners on death row feel, knowing without a doubt that a lethal injection is awaiting them just down the hall?

His secretary and nurse have left for the day, and I glance around his empty waiting room, where straight chairs line the walls and green vinyl tiles cover the floor. The walnut-veneer table holds stacks of dated magazines. My nose is assaulted by medicinal smells, and I have the urge to hold my breath as I call to him.

"I'm back here, Leona," he answers from down the hall.

I enter his small, cluttered office, and he looks up from his old desk. Dr. Hull is bald except for a frizz of ginger-colored hair sprouting from his crown. He has always reminded me of a gnome.

"I appreciate you seeing me. I hope I'm not keeping you here too late."

"No, no." He adjusts his gold wire frames. "Best time for me, after all the patients are gone. A quiet time when I can catch up on my paperwork before I go home to supper. Sit down." He waves to a chair by his desk. "So, you wanted to talk about April Brown's autopsy." He peers over his rims, small, beady eyes fixed on me. "That was a long time ago, but I got my protocols out of the files." He opens a folder and reads aloud. "Primary cause of death was a chest wound . . . evidence of aeroembolism." He glances up from the folder. "That's a sudden exit of air from the lungs," he explains, then returns to his notes. "A wound such as this is always fatal, and death is almost always instantaneous. Significant exsanguination." Holding his finger on his place in the file, he glances up again to explain. "Exsanguination is loss of blood or excessive bleeding from the wound."

I draw myself erect and clasp my hands together, squeezing hard. "Could a woman inflict such a wound?"

"What?" He looks at the wall, then focuses on me, still taken aback. "A woman? Well, I've learned to never say never, but in this particular case I'd say it's virtually impossible. It would have to be a big woman and a very strong one."

"How about a very mad one? What about adrenaline making someone super strong? I read about a woman who lifted a car up off her son who was trapped in a wreck."

"A great rush of adrenaline does have that effect on the human body. Still, in this case I believe the killer is a man, and if you're thinking otherwise, you're grasping at straws, Leona."

"Maybe I am on that subject, but my client is not the man who killed April Brown, and I have to find some way to prove it if I can't make any headway in the legal channels." I may risk appearing a fool, but I uncross my legs, place my feet solidly on the floor, and ask Dr. Hull the question I've come to ask.

He stares at me, shocked, unable to speak for a moment. His eyes then dart from object to object in the room, not settling on one thing long enough to take it in. "My goodness," he finally utters. "That is drastic. Truly drastic." He frowns, then clears his throat. "To answer your question. Yes, I believe it could be done. A famous Oriental coroner once said that a casket is a cold storage for evidence. And so it is. There are certain obstacles you'd have to overcome, though." He explains the ramifications, which as a lawyer, albeit a green one, I already know.

We discuss the subject thoroughly, including the length of time it might take to accomplish such a feat. Time is my enemy, and the frame in which I have to work is not encouraging.

I rise. "I won't take any more of your time. I appreciate your seeing me." I don't want to insult Dr. Hull, but I feel I must impress on him the importance of secrecy. I will not mention this to anyone until the time is right, not even to Tarsha or Ray Bell. Gossip is too cheap here. "Dr. Hull, you know as well as I that Grenola is a small town and talk gets around. I didn't come to you today as a patient, but I hope I assume correctly that this conversation is privileged."

Grasping the gravity of the situation, he obviously takes no offense. "Rely on it."

I leave with thoughts crowding my mind and drive to Ray Bell's. Bingo's had a fine time riding and has Band-Aids over the blisters to prove it. He holds up his hands. "I held the reins tight so the horse couldn't run too fast." The chocolate cake crumbs dusting his upper lip are a tribute to Wilma Ruth's cooking. We both thank them for their hospitality and head back to town. Bingo scrapes off the crumbs with a Kleenex. He rambles on about Ray Bell and Wilma Ruth, how much he likes them, funny things they've said, and that he's invited back anytime. "They're totally neat."

I honk when I pull up in front of Jack's house, rolling down the window. The evening has brought some relief from the heat, and the chirp of crickets fills the air. Bingo spots a lightning bug whizzing by and wishes for a jar to entrap him. He says that the movie he and Kit are going to see, some alien flick, has insects from outer space and wasn't I sorry to miss it for a dumb dinner at the club.

Kit and Jack come through the gate to the patio and hurry down the curving brick sidewalk to the car. Kit's in jeans and a flowered T-shirt, her curls pulled back with a bow almost the size of a small kite. Bingo groans, "Nobody can see around her in the movie." Jack wears a tan sports coat and a polka-dot bow tie, his loafers shined to a mirror finish. His hair just brushes his collar. He's central casting's idea of the hip professor. He's my idea of the perfect man, but without that certain dangerous air about him—the aura of a Jean-Paul Patel and even a Ray Bell Crosby that women should consider taboo but foolishly find irresistible. Jack is safe, steady, and deep in my heart I know those attributes are better for a relationship in the long run. Better to be a little bored than a lot brokenhearted.

They pile in, and I drive to the theater in the strip mall on the highway. Jack pulls out his battered wallet, a gift from his mother the Christmas before she died. He's always kept it, along with so many reminders of her. He's sentimental and easily moved, even to the point of tears over a sad movie or a beautiful poem. I've read the eulogy he wrote and delivered at his wife's funeral and had to swallow the lump in my throat. I sometimes think I'm undeserving of such a man's attentions.

I dig in my purse for money for Bingo, but Jack holds up his hand to stop me. He counts out bills for Bingo as well as Kit. He will always treat them equally. I watch Bingo's beaming expression as he receives his portion, unaccustomed as he is to a father's generosity that other kids take for granted. I can't help but feel sorry for the little guy.

Jack has looked up the movie schedule and tells the kids when we'll return. They race to the ticket booth, and I drive toward the club, suddenly aware of the tension in the car, Jack's rigid posture. I wrongly thought his demand for a dinner date stemmed simply from his desire to have me to himself for a change. Something's up. He glances out the window, composing what I'm not sure I want to hear.

To postpone the inevitable for a moment, I tell him about the Appellate Project and its offer of help.

I'm anxious for a reaction, but he doesn't meet my eyes, continues to stare in another direction.

"It's good you're not in the boat alone anymore. I've heard about them. Most are bright rebels who've turned down jobs with high-powered eastern law firms to go out and save the underdog." His tone is flat and without enthusiasm.

I wheel into the country club's driveway. "Wonder what your dad will think of that?"

"He's dealt with them before." He faces me with a look I don't like. "Why are you investigating Dad?"

I'm mortified. Here in the darkness of the car I'm suddenly so light-headed my world goes gray for an instant. My cheeks burn. "How do you know?"

The frown is etched between his eyes. "Ray Bell Crosby is not too subtle, Leona. Word gets around."

I'm overwhelmed by the urgent need to repair the rip in our relationship before it widens. I owe him an explanation. "Jack, please understand that I had to. You know how I wondered why Robert Weldon chose me. Well, when I went to see him, he said that I might come across some sensitive information that could hurt someone and only I would know how to handle it properly." I explain my rationale. "I figured it must have something to do with Mr. Jack and my link to the family. I just couldn't think of another reason why Weldon singled me out. Jack, I've prayed it didn't have anything to do with your dad, been so afraid I'd find something—"

"What?" He swings around on the seat, interrupting.

My breath is ragged, my voice shaky. "Weldon

wouldn't say what it was, only that he didn't want anyone hurt and I'd know what to do with the information, *if* I even came across it."

Jack is incredulous. "A death row inmate knows something to help his case, but won't tell his lawyer? Leona, I warned you about just such an instance. Those guys are desperate. He's conning you, and I can't figure out why. The very idea of pointing a finger at Dad—"

"He didn't point at Mr. Jack—it's the way I interpreted it."

"Dad's reputation is beyond reproach. You've known him forever, Leona."

"What else was I to think, Jack? Why did Weldon pick me?"

"Beats the hell out of me. I'm just sorry you took the bait."

"Weldon's innocent, and I'm going to prove it." Chill bumps rise on my arms. I open my door. "Let's go inside and have a drink, Jack."

We enter through the double front doors and settle at a table for two in the crowded dining room. Saturday night at the club is big in Grenola. We order Jack Daniel's old-fashioneds and continue our stilted conversation. Jack's words make me uneasy, but I don't waver in my belief that Weldon is innocent. Some static exists between us now, and we order dinner as we sip our drinks in relative silence. I don't like the turn in the evening. A hollowness grows inside me. I've lost something special if I've alienated Jack.

Halfway through my steak, I glance across the

crowd and spot Louella Fletcher and a darkly handsome man I assume is her husband, Ronnie, staring at
me. I spear some salad and try to ignore them. Out of
the corner of my eye I see them whisper to each
other, then glare at me, whisper more, then glare.
Ronnie crushes his napkin on the table and heads to
ours. The dinner crowd senses menace in the air, and
all eyes follow Ronnie Fletcher. I want to crawl under
the table and disappear. I look him straight in the eye
as he takes a stand by us. Even though I've had a
drink, I can smell alcohol on him. Jack glances up,
startled by the confrontation.

"Why, hello, Ronnie. That power mower I bought
from you runs great. Sure is good to cut my yard sitting down," he says cordially, trying to defuse the situation. "Oh, this is my friend, Leona Bingham."

Ronnie's eyebrows, bushy as two black caterpil-
lars, almost meet. "I don't give a shit about your yard,
and I know who she is."

Jack carefully places his napkin on the table.
"Hey, this is uncalled for. We're in a public place
here. No need for a scene. Why don't you just pull up
a chair and we'll talk quietly?"

Ronnie remains rooted in place. "This—this woman
here came over to my house, hintin' my wife mighta
had something to do with that nigger woman's murder."

I wince at the racial slur. A vision of the victim
flashes in my mind. "I wasn't hinting at anything," I
pipe up, ready to defend myself. "I was simply asking
questions, doing my job as Robert Weldon's lawyer.

Your wife certainly did know him, and it was only natural to talk to her."

He points his finger at me like a pistol. "You stay away from us, you hear?" He turns and stalks back to his table.

Jack and I look at each other without uttering a word. We've lost our appetites. "Let's get the check and go," I finally suggest.

Jack glances at his watch. "We have time for coffee and a brandy. We'll sit out the Fletchers, let them slink through the door first."

"I don't think Ronnie is into slinking." We both laugh nervously while others watch.

We linger over coffee and brandy, surreptitiously eyeing the Fletchers, who continue to drink. I smoke two cigarettes, feeling antsy. "Jack, they're not going to leave right away. I believe we've made our point, if there was one to make. Let's go. It's late."

Jack scribbles his signature on the check. "I'm sorry they ruined our evening."

"They didn't ruin it, just interrupted it. No big deal. Assholes are a dime a dozen."

Jack screws his mouth into a wicked smile and shakes his head. "Tell it like it is. We're outta here."

Just as we pull out of the parking lot, a dark car zooms around the corner of the building, seeming to come from nowhere, determined to get ahead of us, crowding us onto the shoulder. My headlights flash briefly on the occupants, the Fletchers. "The couple from hell," I comment.

The discovery of the investigation into Mr. Jack's background and the Fletcher encounter has taken a toll on one of our few evenings together. We pick up the kids at the movie, and I can tell immediately that Bingo isn't feeling well. His eyes look weak, as if it's an effort to hold them open. He's slightly sunburned from horseback riding and complains of a stomachache. He feels feverish to the touch.

"Well, you ate two chili hot dogs and popcorn," Kit reminds him.

"So did you," he snaps.

"Yeah, well, I'm not complaining about my stomach," she replies.

Jack and I listen to their banter. They're both tired and irritable. So are we, but we hide it.

After saying good-bye, Jack gives me one last, long look as they get out of the car. My heart is twisted in my chest. My only hope is the knowledge of how understanding Jack is. I drive home and Bingo nods all the way. I have to nudge him awake in our driveway.

"Come on, you're too big for me to carry, kiddo. Put one foot in front of the other, and we'll soon reach the door."

We climb the steps to the gallery, and I unlock the door. I usher Bingo upstairs. Modest as he is at this tender age, he undresses in the bathroom and dons his pajamas behind closed doors. When he comes out, I tuck him in bed, then get aspirin and a glass of water for him. I kiss him good night and go downstairs to turn off the lights.

Suddenly it dawns on me that Mister Marvel wasn't outside to greet us. Sometimes he wanders off in the woods surrounding our house, chasing rabbits and squirrels. Bingo was too zonked to ask about him. I flip on the outside lights in the kitchen and open the back door to call him. I step out on the landing and gasp at what confronts me. It's all I can do to keep from screaming.

9

MISTER MARVEL'S EYES ARE OPEN, HIS TEETH BARED, and his head is severed from his body. Vomit backs up in my throat like hot lava as I stare at the furry, bloody lumps. I want to scream, but through the maze of horror I realize I can't wake Bingo. Shaking, I glance from side to side, half expecting a fiend to leap out of the darkness and attack. I jump back into the kitchen before another grisly assault can occur, barely able to lock the kitchen door.

The phone rings, the sharp sound piercing my skull. The silent caller who's finally acted wants to savor my reaction. I grab the receiver, almost ripping the base off the wall. "You evil shit," I snarl, fury uncontrollable. "You filthy fucking piece of trash—"

"Leona, what in God's name has gotten into you?"

At the sound of Byars's voice I burst into tears. "Oh, Byars," I sob. "Somebody has cut off Mister

Marvel's head. There's blood everywhere. I thought you . . . I thought you were the caller . . ."

"What? What caller?"

"The one who keeps calling but won't say anything." I sink to the floor, my back supported by the wall.

"Julius said you called this afternoon. I've been trying to reach you . . . I'll be right there. Charles is here with me. Stay put."

I remain frozen, unable to think for a moment. I look up at the ceiling. Bingo's room is right above me. I want to check on him, but I'm afraid I'll wake him. I have to do something. What if he wakes and comes downstairs? I can't let him see the carnage, the butchery someone has inflicted on our poor dog. What will I tell him? Hot tears burn my cheeks. I feel hurt, violated, enraged.

I push up to a standing position. Mister Marvel has to be buried. The shovel is in the garage, and I'm afraid to go alone. Byars will be here soon, I tell myself. He'll help. In the meantime I'll get ready. I grab a plastic bucket from under the sink, turn on the hot water faucet, and pour in liquid detergent. I find a big brush. The back porch floor will have to be scrubbed clean. I suddenly spot the red smears on the kitchen floor. I've tracked in Mister Marvel's blood. I wrench off my shoes and throw them in the sink, submerging them in clear water that swiftly turns a sickly pink. I gag, on the verge of losing my dinner.

I fall to my knees with the bucket in hand, scouring in frenzied circles with the brush. The harder I scrub, the more pink foam bubbles I raise. I take out my rage on the floor, scrubbing until blisters rise on my fingers.

When I hear the car and see the flash of headlights through the dining room window, I jump up, slipping and sliding on the wet floor, making for the front door. I flick the lock and open the door. Byars and Charles climb the steps, both shocked to see me in such a state.

Byars envelops me in a bear hug. "Leona, it's okay. It's okay. I didn't say anything about this to Lily. It would upset her too much. Did Bingo see it?"

"He's asleep. I think he's sick."

Charles touches my shoulder. "Who in the world could have done such a thing? We should call the police." His voice is wooden, and he's tight with tension.

"Where's the dog?" Byars asks.

I rake my hands through my hair. "On the back porch."

We go inside, walking on the damp kitchen floor like we're crossing a frozen pond. Byars calls the police after he and Charles steal a quick look at Mister Marvel. "I don't think we should touch anything out there until Chief Lewis gets here. He could find something." Byars is bristling with pent-up anger.

"I'll make some coffee," Charles offers. "We could all use a cup."

I melt into a kitchen chair. "When Bingo gets up in the morning, he'll be looking for Mister Marvel . . ."

"Tell him he's run away," Byars suggests.

"I hate to lie, but I can't tell the truth." I press my

temples with my fingers. My head throbs and my pulse pounds. "If I tell him Mister Marvel's run away, he'll keep looking for him, expecting him to come home."

Charles eases into the chair next to mine. "Years ago when the kids were little, our dog got caught in a fox trap. When I found him, he'd almost chewed his leg off trying to get free. His hip and back were broken, and I had to shoot him to put him out of his misery. I didn't want the kids to see him like that, so I boxed him in a wood crate, told the kids he'd died in the night and we had a funeral, buried him out by that big old oak down by the bayou. The kids put flowers on his grave, and it was a sort of closure. That's the way we'll handle this."

I stare at Charles, truly amazed at the sensitivity I never knew existed. Maybe Estelle sees in him traits I never have. His perpetual frown has vanished, replaced by a wistful expression as he recalls the incident about his dog. Is he genuine, or is this a show for Byars? I hate myself for such a thought. "That's a good plan, Charles. Thank you for suggesting it."

Byars pours coffee for all three of us. His hand shakes as he sets down the cups. "This has something to do with the case, Leona. You know that, don't you? What about the caller you were talking about?"

I tell them about the calls I've received, recalling the sequence of events, the word scratched on my car and now this. The subterranean campaign against me is escalating, becoming more evident, more focused and, yes, it all began when I took on Robert Weldon's case. Someone doesn't want me digging into the past.

I had wanted Weldon to be innocent, tried to convince myself he was, and now I really know he is.

Byars sips his steaming coffee and winces from the heat. "Leona, like I said, this has to do with the case. You can't continue with it after this. It's too dangerous, just like I predicted it could be." He huffs. "God knows what might happen next."

"Robert Weldon is innocent."

Byars shakes his head. "He told you he's innocent. There's a big difference."

I reach for my cigarettes, take my time lighting one, and inhale slowly. "This proves Weldon's innocent, that I'm getting somewhere, rattling someone's cage."

"Could be you're just rattling some of the black people's cages," Charles says. "One of their own was murdered by a white man, and maybe they see you in the way of justice. The demonstration proves that. Maybe one of the protesters did this."

Maybe so. Maybe Ronnie Fletcher did it. "I have to go on, and I have help now." I tell them about the Mississippi Appellate Project. They absorb this news with interest. Byars might even be impressed. I decide to reveal why Weldon chose me to represent him, and my first suspicions that this information I might uncover had something to do with Jack Flannery Sr.

Byars pushes his coffee cup aside. "I've known Jack all my life. Sure, he's ambitious, but he'd never, ever do anything out of line just to win a case. Don't even think about accusing him on the say of some convict. What in hell's name is this Weldon talking about, information you just might uncover that only you would know how to handle?"

"I'm trying to find out." I glance at Charles. "Babaloo Brown knows something. Maybe now— with what all that's happened, especially to the dog— maybe he'll realize he *has* to tell me. And there's another strange aspect here," I say. "The fact that J. Clyde Perkins represented Robert Weldon pro bono . . . a low-profile case like this."

"I've wondered about that," Charles says, nodding, confirming to himself his curiosity had grounds. "Never heard anybody else say much about it. They were just so fascinated by Perkins's presence that they didn't question anything. People aren't particularly educated about lawyers doing pro bono work."

"Well, it's a cinch you and Bingo can't stay here alone, not after this," Byars says.

"It's not safe," Charles chimes in, underlining Byars's logic.

"You know you're always welcome. Our place is your home," Byars says, and exchanges a glance with Charles. Something has passed between them to which I'm not privy.

I drag on my cigarette, looking for a solution to my problem, and one jumps out at me. "Moving out would tip Bingo that something's in the air. I don't want that. These lawyers with the Appellate Project have to stay somewhere. I'm sure they don't have much spare money for expenses. The Inn is cheap." I look around. "But this place is even cheaper, like free. I don't know how many of them there are, but they can camp out here. Safety in numbers."

"Grenola's own commune," Byars says with sudden disapproval. He simply cannot get around his concern about what others might think, but as Lily said, he learned it at his mother's knee.

"You said the lawyer group, whatever they're called, can't get here until after next week. What'll you do till then?" Charles asks.

"Watch my back," I answer with false bravado.

"Not good enough," Byars states, casting a glance at Charles.

Charles clears his throat, folds his hands together, twirling his thumbs. He can't look me in the eye. He has something to say, but is obviously reluctant to part with whatever it is. His face flushes. Clearly he is in some kind of distress. "Uh, Estelle and I . . . well, we've had kind of a bad spat. She acts like she's lost her mind, ordered me out of the house." He finally meets my eyes. "My very own house. Been in the family for years."

So that's why he was at Byars and Lily's at this time of night. I hadn't thought about it until now, lost as I was in my own troubles. I don't know how I feel about the new development. "It's her house, too, Charles." The Bingham men believe all possessions to be solely theirs; even women and children are chattel. I'm about to expound on the subject, but before I can Byars quickly interjects:

"Well, that's beside the point. Charles was going to stay with us temporarily, just until all this gets worked out, and it most certainly will get worked out, but in the meantime it's none of anybody's business, and we certainly won't broadcast it."

No, we certainly don't want anyone to talk about the Bingham family, topic of Grenola's conversation as we already are. Suddenly I know what's coming next and don't like the prospect.

"Charles can stay here with you and Bingo instead of at our house. I'd feel better 'bout y'all if he did." Byars locks eyes with Charles.

My emotions are mangled from Mister Marvel's gruesome death, and I have no energy left to argue. I might get a better insight into Charles, observe him closely to either allay my suspicions or enlarge on them. A thought strikes me like a dagger. Will Bingo and I now be housed with a killer? Surely my imagination is working overtime. Surely.

"We can manage under the same roof, Leona." Charles produces a weak smile.

When I hear Chief Lewis's car, I hurry to the front door before his knock can wake Bingo. Flashlights in hand, he and his deputy enter, and although Byars briefly mentioned the crime when he telephoned, I explain in my own words what happened. "Nasty," the chief says, listening carefully.

Nodding at Byars and Charles in the kitchen, Chief Lewis and the deputy go outside while we wait. From the kitchen window I watch their beams darting around in the darkness, hoping they find a clue that will lead to the perpetrator of this senseless act.

I light another cigarette, focusing on Ronnie Fletcher's verbal assault earlier at the club and how, according to Ray Bell, Louella vented her anger on her neighbors. Did my visit and questions push two unstable personalities over the edge?

Chief Lewis and the deputy scrape the soles of their boots on the edge of the steps and come inside. "It's still pretty hot outside, so I can't rightly say how long the dog's been dead. You been upstairs?" Chief Lewis asks.

The question alerts me. "Just to Bingo's room. Why?"

"There's a trellis outside that's pulled away from the house and a few pieces of latticework are broken, like somebody was a climbing up the thing." He nods toward the deputy. "Godfrey and I better check it out up there."

I nailed the trellis securely into place. The weight of a human could have dislodged the nails and broken the crosspieces. A chill runs through me. Has someone slipped inside? Is Bingo up there where somebody is hiding? Panic takes me, and I run for the stairway. Chief Lewis is quick and grabs me on the first step, blocking my way. "You stay down here and let us do our job." He pulls out his gun. "If somebody's up there, we'll find 'em. We'll try not to wake the boy or scare him if he does wake up."

Byars and Charles usher me back to the kitchen. I'm frantic from worry. Maybe some ghoul already has Bingo. Maybe he . . . my mind explodes with horror when I picture Mister Marvel and what this monster is capable of inflicting. Staring at the ceiling, I pray no harm has come to Bingo. I put him in bed and left him all alone in a place where someone might be hiding, under a bed, in a closet, waiting.

My heart hammers as I listen to the overhead floorboards creak from the weight of the two men. At any moment I expect to hear gunshots, shouts, terrible noises. Byars and Charles talk, but their words are a blur.

I jump up and rocket to the hall when I hear the men descending the stairs. Byars and Charles follow. We all look up expectantly at Chief Lewis.

He's holding the blade of a bloody butcher knife with a handkerchief. "Bingo's fine. Sound asleep. I found this on your bed, Leona."

I gasp at the sight of the weapon, knowing how it's been used. I feel weak, my knees on the verge of collapse.

"Has to be the knife used to cut the dog's head off," Byars says. "Why in hell did whoever did it put it upstairs on Leona's bed instead of leaving it outside?"

Chief Lewis marches by us toward the kitchen. "Get me a plastic bag, Leona." He looks over his shoulder at Byars. "This message is way more subtle, Byars. 'See, I can get in your house anytime I want to.' Didn't want to break in downstairs so it'd be obvious when Leona got home. Nope. Climbed up the trellis, raised the guest room window, and went in. Wanted to scare her more by lettin' her come in, suspectin' nothing, then go upstairs and find this on the bed. Much scarier that way since she'd likely think someone was a-hidin' in the house. It downright chills even me."

He drops the knife into the baggie and seals it. "Godfrey's got a fingerprint kit out in the car. I want him to dust around the guest room window, but I don't expect to find prints other than Leona's. We're dealin' with somebody who's way too smart for that. Could be one of those demonstrators that were outside your office. Could be." He eyes the coffeepot. "Might have a cup while Godfrey's a-dustin'. Say, what you gon' do 'bout the dog out there?"

As I pour coffee for Chief Lewis, my hand shakes so hard the cup rattles in the saucer. Byars and Charles explain their plans about the dog.

"Godfrey'll hose off the back porch for you when he's done dustin', then we best get on back to town. I'll want to fingerprint you, Leona, just for comparison's sake."

We sit in silence, each with our own thoughts, until Godfrey returns from his chores upstairs. He takes my prints, then goes outside. I envision him dragging the carcass off the porch, wince with each bump down the steps. I hear him hook the hose to the faucet, and the blast of water is loud and powerful, washing away the last bloody remnants of Mister Marvel.

After they leave, Byars tells me to go upstairs, try to rest while he and Charles take charge of what has to be done. When they finish, Charles will lock the doors and spend the night. Charles asks for a big plastic garbage bag, Mister Marvel's shroud.

I check on Bingo, listen to his steady breathing, and touch his forehead. In repose his angelic face makes me want to weep. He'll wake tomorrow, a boy without his dog. He'll find a crude casket built by his grandfather and cousin and the grave they've dug for Mister Marvel's final resting place. We'll have a service and pick flowers from the yard to cover the fresh earth.

Staring at the window where someone intruded, I decide to put fresh linens on the guest room bed and hang towels in the bathroom. I move like a zombie to my room, strip off the bloody spread, undress, put on my old terry-cloth robe, and lie across my bed, closing my eyes. The steady tap of hammers from the garage breaks the silence of the night. I may never sleep again until this is over, but the incident tonight has infused me with a fierce determination to see that Robert Weldon is set free and the person responsible for all my grief is caught and punished.

By Thursday of the following week Ray Bell and I are on the highway to Parchman. I've worked relentlessly on the appeal, sleeping little and eating even less. Buoyed by nervous energy, I don't feel the effects of the strain, although the strange phone calls have continued to plague me. Bingo took Mister Marvel's death as any eight-year-old would, crying at first, moody and introspective after the tears dried and the burial was over. Wilma Ruth brought sandwiches, a cake, and cookies after our little ceremony as if it were a real funeral. Bingo is starting to mend as life pulls him back into its routine. Surprisingly, Charles has been a big help, cooked a few meals, taken Bingo fishing, and generally made himself handy. Apparently Estelle's dictum has caused him to take stock. I had always thought Estelle needed a spine donor, so I expected her to relent and allow him home, but she's standing firm after a lifetime of intimidation.

Only one thing gave me pause about Charles. As I headed to the kitchen for a late-night snack, I stopped short in the stairwell, appalled to see Charles rustling through my notes. When confronted, he covered his chagrin with a compliment on my work. There was nothing revealing or noteworthy in the material, but his act provided an opening to a question I burned to ask. "Charles, you knew Babaloo from way back." I steeled myself. "Did you know April?"

I expected shock or some attempt to hide an expression that might give him away, but he answered quickly and seemingly honestly. "Not personally, but I knew who she was after I asked around town about her. I was just curious. She could stop traffic and turn heads. All the men in Grenola knew who she was. Look but don't touch."

I want to believe him. If all the men in town were struck by her beauty, Ray Bell certainly wouldn't be immune to her charms. I glance at Ray Bell and I ask, "Did you know April Brown?"

"Me?" He whips his head around, startled, eyes on me. "Why do you ask such a question right out of the blue?"

Unlike Charles, he's unnerved by the question. "You were a policeman, got around town. I heard all the men in Grenola were aware of who she was."

"Well, there's a big difference between actually knowing her and just knowing who she was. You asked me if I knew her." His voice has an edge to it. "The answer to your question is no, I wasn't acquainted with her. I had seen her around and knew who she was."

He's defensive, has taken umbrage that I quizzed him like he might be a suspect. "I was just curious, is all. I asked Charles about her, and he said she stopped traffic."

Letting it ride, Ray Bell changes the subject as we near the penitentiary's entrance. "Lots of prisoners working in the fields today. Looks like a horde of locusts. They haven't had an escape attempt here since March of ninety-five. I believe I'd try it if I had to work in that blistering heat all day and then be cooped up in a six-by-nine-foot cell all night."

"You'd be dead before you got too far with those rifles trained on you."

"Those guards are taught to shoot to maim, not kill."

Ray Bell's law enforcement training is ever present in his mind. After the incident with Mister Marvel he began an intermittent nightly patrol around my house and grounds. His headlights beams comforted me. When I have paying clients, I hope to hire him.

"I sure appreciate Wilma Ruth picking up Bingo at school this afternoon."

"She'll keep him occupied until we get back. She's got a way with kids. Too bad we never had any." He glances out the window. "She's a good woman, been put through a lot in the past . . . the trial. You've never mentioned it to me—I mean, I appreciate you having some respect and trust for me after what I did. It like to broke my heart to see Wilma Ruth's expression when it all came out in court, my mistakes made so public and all. Lots of men have affairs, but they don't get aired like that."

"Everybody makes mistakes, Ray Bell. I don't call Bingo a mistake, but I know how it feels to be the

topic of conversation in Grenola." He speaks of
Wilma Ruth as a good woman, treats her with courtesy and respect, but shows little interest or real affection, which leads me to believe he doesn't really love
her, but feels obligated, duty-bound to her because
she stuck by him in adversity. Of those close to me, I
find no perfect marriages, Ray Bell and Wilma Ruth's,
Lily and Byars's, Charles and Estelle's, only compro-
mises, settling for less. In my mind I picture Jean-
Paul and his wife as the ideal couple, but in reality
that may not be the case. I will never know. I believe
Jack and I could have a strong and companionable
union, but is that enough?

I pull into the entrance and go through the routine with the guards, then proceed to John Dobbs's
office. From now on Weldon and I will meet in the
law library in Unit 32 of Maximum Security, not the
visiting area. When I made the appointment, Dobbs
said he would escort us and help us get organized.

I introduce my investigator to the prison lawyer,
and they shake hands. Ray Bell has worn a navy
sports coat and a navy-and-maroon-striped tie for the
occasion. He looks good, fresh and alert compared to
the lawyer's rumpled attire and weary demeanor. To
cover myself as much as possible from the leers of the
prisoners, I'm in a black cotton pantsuit, a yellow-
and-black-patterned scarf draped around my neck.
Ray Bell complimented me on the outfit.

John Dobbs addresses me. "I read the *Clarion-
Ledger* article. I guess I sicced that reporter on you.
He was in my office the day you decided to take on
Weldon's case."

"Well, something good came out of it." I tell him about the Appellate Group.

"You got lucky. They're a good bunch, but have to spread themselves around so thin, they can't help all those who need it."

"The part about Weldon having a lawsuit against the state if he's proven innocent bothered me."

"I wouldn't worry about anything but your case. You came off sounding pretty dedicated to it in the article. Some of the inmates' lawyers aren't, you know. Just go through the motions." Dobbs checks his old relic of a watch, the kind sold in drugstores years ago. "I'll ride over to the library at MSU with you if you don't mind making a stop first at Unit 17. We have a little time before Weldon will be brought down to the law library. I believe I told you that fifteen prisoners are allowed in there at a time and can use the place for four hours a day. We've got some pretty smart jailhouse lawyers researching their own cases."

"Unit 17 . . . isn't that where the gas chamber and lethal-injection room are located?" Ray Bell asks as we return to the car.

"Yes, it is." Dobbs hauls himself into the backseat. "And right next to those two rooms is a cell—the last stop, as I think of it—where an inmate is transferred twenty-four hours before the execution. The rest of the cells on down the hall are filled with the overflow of death row inmates that Section 32-C in MSU can't hold. We have fifty-four men at Parchman awaiting execution. Death row is death row, but these inmates here would all rather be over in 32-C.

Guess this place is just too close to death itself. Maybe you'd like to come in and see what environment your client lives in. He's in 32-C, but this is an exact duplicate of the layout over there, with the exception of the lethal-injection room and the gas chamber, of course."

Heretofore Weldon's daily life has been hazy in my imagination. With Dobbs's unexpected offer I now have a strange fascination with learning exactly how Weldon lives, yet I dread the emotions this might evoke. Uneasy about the experience, I follow John Dobbs's directions, take a side road off the main one, and pull to a stop in front of a one-story red-brick building surrounded, as is MSU, with a tall chain-link fence topped with heavy swirls of razor wire. Four guard towers are stationed at the corners of Unit 17. Locking the car, I join the men in front of the double gates. I drop the keys into the bucket that is lowered, and we enter the first gate, then the second.

A black female guard appears and gives us only a cursory search since we're accompanied by John Dobbs. She paws through my purse. The blue uniform is tight on her ill-proportioned body. Her thighs rub together as she walks and fan out like fenders on a car. Her face is her redeeming feature. Her eyes sparkle, and her smile is wide and toothy. I wonder how she can be so cheerful in such a depressing place.

"How you today, John?"

"Making it through. Sergeant Holloway, this is Ms. Leona Bingham, Robert Weldon's lawyer, and her investigator, Mr. Crosby."

"Oh, yeah? Robert's one of my favorites. Can't get too emotionally involved here, though. Most of these men are animals. Some of them are near 'bout crazy, been locked up so long, holler and yell stuff nobody can understand." We follow her to the door. I notice she doesn't wear a gun and ask about it.

"Well, see, if you had a gun you might relax your guard. You get so used to being in here. Then one of the inmates grabs it out of the holster and then we got a *situation*. We just have mace, is all."

I think about weapons and ask about eating utensils. "Sporks," she announces. "The prisoners eat with these plastic doodads that's a cross between a spoon and a fork. No knives." She fumbles through a heavy ring of keys and unlocks the door.

My breath catches in my chest. As I face the gas chamber, the sight of the big, ugly metal contraption sends a shiver through me. It reminds me of an extra-large diver's underwater chamber. The door is open, and I stare at the restraints by the seat inside, imagine being strapped in, the door closed and the lethal chemicals filling my nose. I sniff, realizing I actually smell an offensive chemical odor. Color drained from his face, Ray Bell stands before the chamber as if hypnotized, his eyes locked on the deadly piece of equipment.

"Makes you want to sneeze, don't it?" Sergeant Holloway makes a face. "They been practicing, make sure they get the right mix of chemicals, be ready when the time comes. Prisoners convicted before nineteen eighty-four get the chamber. Ones after that get lethal injection. Room's right over here. Supplies are kept in that closet." She opens both doors. Boxes and drums of supplies with skull and crossbones marked on the labels line the storage room. Syringes that look made for horse injections are covered in plastic. A gurney with straps centers the lethal-injection room and beyond, a glassed section for an audience to view an execution. I feel faint, my mind riddled with nightmarish scenarios. I can only begin to fathom how someone like Weldon feels, aware of what awaits. I have to keep him out of here.

"Sergeant, want to walk them down the row while I go back here and talk a minute with Warden Boone?" John Dobbs asks.

"Sure." She turns to me. "You gonna hear stuff you never wanted to hear. Burn your ears off, stuff they say. Don't pay any mind and keep away from the bars. They likely as not will reach out and try to grab you, throw somethin' at you."

This is the nightmare I at first envisioned. I'm tempted not to go down death row, but something compels me now that I'm here. "Ray Bell?" He tears his eyes away from the chamber, clearly shaken. The gruesome setting is enough to scare even the toughest of men.

Footsteps echoing, we follow Sergeant Holloway down a corridor that ends in iron gates. She speaks to the guard on the other side, and gates clang open. Most inmates rush to the front of their cells, holding the bars, looking out with desperate expectancy.

As we walk along death row, some yell and babble, one howls like a wolf. Others stare, wordless. The six-by-nine cells are clean, the paint fresh, not a dungeon with squalid conditions. Each has a stainless toilet and sink, a television. Some inmates are in red jumpsuits, a few wear only white underwear that looks new. One man tries to engage me in conversation. I say "Good morning" and move quickly along behind Sergeant Holloway, with Ray Bell tagging along at the rear. I hug the outer wall close enough to scrape off the paint. This is not an experience I'll soon forget.

We follow the sergeant down the last row, go out through the gates, and double back to the location of the gas chamber where John Dobbs waits. Ray Bell and I exchange nervous glances, both touched and frightened by the experience. My body is tensed, muscles knotted. I rotate my shoulders, trying to relieve the anxiety. Suddenly I realize that not one prisoner said anything vulgar or unpleasant.

"Quite an experience, huh?" Dobbs's sad, defeated eyes clamp onto mine. "All lawyers with a death row client should have the experience. Makes it easier to empathize with the client."

Work harder to save the client maybe, I think. Shake up the complacent or the lazy. I have a curious idea that Dobbs didn't actually have to stop here to see someone but brought us on purpose. His first impression of me was that of a lawyer who didn't much care about the client but reluctantly took the case. He was probably right, but things have changed. I look at John Dobbs in a new light and with growing admiration.

"You don't believe in the death penalty, do you, Mr. Dobbs?"

"No, I don't. I read in the article that you don't either."

We drive to MSU, go through the gates and routine search. Dobbs leads us to the far end of the doubled-tiered building and holds open a door. Entering the law library, I quickly survey the bookcases on all four walls, the computers on small desks, but my attention is quickly grabbed by fifteen convicts, leg chains hooked to an iron loop embedded in the floor, poring over law volumes at a long table in the center of the room. All activity stops and the men focus hard on us, staring with no reservations at our appearance in their midst. Most look intelligent, but hard eyes betray a streak of evil. We stand like statues until the inmates have satisfied their curiosity and return to their books, looking for loopholes to outwit their fates.

A guard ushers four more shackled inmates into the room, one of whom is Weldon. His eyes clamp onto me, and in his face I see his shame that he is before me in manacles. A second guard releases four prisoners to be removed from the library and attaches the men's leg irons to the loops in the floor, freeing their hands for work. Since Weldon is meeting with his lawyer, he is seated at the far end of the table for some modicum of privacy.

Talking to John Dobbs, Ray Bell has had his back to the men, but when he turns, Weldon is overcome with surprise. His mouth slightly agape, he blinks as if he can't believe what his eyes behold. He pulls out his wire-framed glasses and hooks them over his ears. We walk to where he's seated and take chairs on the other side of the table.

Weldon leans forward, clasping his hands together. "Ray Bell, I read in the *Clarion-Ledger* that you were Leona's investigator, but I never expected to see you here." His eyes cut to me. "Leona, that article quoting you gave me some hope."

Ray Bell seems anxious to talk, but I want to get business out of the way first. "Robert, I filed with the state court this morning." Opening my briefcase, I hand him a copy. He stares at it, lips moving as he reads. "I talked to the court clerk, and he felt the court will rule on it quickly." I don't want to use the word *execution* and plan my sentence carefully. "Since a date has been set, the state is required to answer right away. The attorney general's office is going to be hopping." I watch him carefully to see if mention of Jack Flannery brings any reaction. "If we're denied, I'll move it along to the federal court in Jackson."

Weldon looks up from reading and puts the papers aside. "What do you think our chances are?" Hope glimmers in his soulful eyes.

I'm afraid to let myself think I might get lucky with the first court and not have to move onto the next forum. I try to keep my mind in neutral so the possibility of disappointment won't crush me. "I don't know, Robert. There is one positive development." I explain about the Mississippi Appellate Project and their willingness to help.

This brings a ghost of a smile, that vague Mona Lisa expression. I suppose his desperate predicament won't allow much emotion. "That's a good thing. I'm glad you have help." He studies me closely, and I assume he's searching for any sign that I've uncovered the information he withholds. I glance at Ray Bell to signal he can have the floor.

"Robert," he begins, "we'd have a whole lot more help if you'd just tell us what you know—that information you told Leona she might come across."

Weldon quickly glances my way, then looks down at his leg chains. He remains silent.

Ray Bell lets it rip. "Man, don't just sit there holding back if you know something that can help you get out of this hellhole." He puts heat in his voice. "Let me tell you what's happened in Leona's life. Everybody's on her back about taking on your case—her family, the Flannerys, your old girlfriend and her husband, Louella and Ronnie Fletcher. She went out at night to talk to Babaloo Brown, and somebody scratched 'bitch' on her fender while she was in his juke joint. She thinks he knows something but won't come forward. A bunch of protesters demonstrated out in front of her office. Some nut has been calling her at all hours and won't say anything when she answers. Then, to top it all off, somebody cut off her son's dog's head, slipped in her house, and left the bloody knife on her bed."

"Oh, no." Weldon squeezes his eyes closed. He shakes his head, looking at me, tears ready to spill down his cheeks. "I'm so sorry for all the grief, Leona. I had no idea it would turn into this." His voice is low, laced with regret.

"Sorry enough to tell us what you know, Robert?" Ray Bell asks.

Weldon seems to draw into himself. It's obvious he's torn in all directions. I feel sorry for him. His situation is dire enough without an extra burden. Other convicts are now watching, aware of Weldon's discomfort.

Ray Bell starts again. "We're not getting anywhere with the investigation. Zip. Zilch. Up against a stone wall. Leona has nearly exhausted herself, working night and day, consumed as she is with the legal end of your case. She has no time for herself or her boy anymore. Her secretary and my wife have to take care of the little guy most of the time. Now, if you've got something to help her help you, you'd better come out with it. Maybe you just made all this up to get her interested in your case. Maybe you're faking. Maybe you are guilty." Ray Bell pushes the chair back roughly, as if he's ready to leave.

Hurt registers on Weldon's face but not anger. "I am not guilty of killing April Brown. I never saw her until that day. That's the truth." He looks away from Ray Bell and fastens onto me. "What I know has nothing to do with my guilt or innocence. It could help me, but I won't use it at the expense of others. It has to come from you, Leona. And you may never find it out, but I'll go to my grave before I tell anybody about it." He's gathering steam now. "I'm sorry about what's happened to you, Leona, but it shows you're getting somewhere whether you think you are or not. The killer is out there and getting nervous. You just may trip up whoever killed April Brown into revealing himself, or you may win in the courthouse. Either way, you'll crack this case if you just don't quit." He pauses for a beat, and I anticipate the next question before he asks. "You'll stay with it, won't you, Leona?"

I take a deep breath and catch a sidelong glance at Ray Bell. I feel like a gambler in a high-stakes game calling a poker hand. "I'm in."

10

I PARK IN MY USUAL SPOT AND HEAD TO MY OFFICE. A group of young black men loitering on the street corner eye me with open hostility. Several mutter to one another in low tones. They look as hard as some of the convicts at Parchman, only they don't wear stripes. One of them could have killed our dog.

Cupping my hands, I peer into the store vacated by the florist who relocated to the mall. Estelle has leased the space, and she and Lily have begun renovations on her decorator's shop. Our schedules are so conflicting I rarely see them. Estelle will stock fabrics, wallpaper, and a few antiques. She'll make a success of The Bingham Touch. Charles still holds me responsible for her newfound independence, but I've tried to drum into him an adage I pulled out of the air, the tighter the rein, the more the resistance, wives and children included. "Give them space and there's no need to run away." He looks at me as if to say, "What do you know?"

Although it's early, Tarsha's already at work, typing a will I've managed to draft. We have to maintain a few paying clients to cover her salary and our overhead. My purse strings as well as my nerves are frayed. "Morning. No calls?" I glance at the fax machine. I don't know when to expect a ruling from the state court on the appeal, but I live with agonizing anticipation as each minute passes.

Tarsha looks up from her typewriter. "Nothing. You look like warmed-over shit."

"Ditto." The strain she lives under, the pressure from her family and friends, shows in her face, but she doesn't mention it or appear depressed.

Tarsha catches the phone as it rings and turns to me, stunned, her hand over the mouthpiece. I'm immediately on alert. "Jesus! It's the death clerk from the United States Supreme Court. A Mr. Hodges."

My heart pounds, and as I reach for the phone I knock my purse off the desk, contents scattering across the floor. "Tell him just a minute. I need to get composed." I snare a cigarette and a lighter off the floor. I had expected the call, but not so soon. The death clerk monitors the final appeals of all death row inmates in the United States. Does this mean my appeal in the state court has been denied and the death clerk already knows? My lighter won't work. I flick and flick, then throw it and the cigarette on the floor.

"Good morning, sir, this is Leona Bingham," I say with false cheeriness, an "I've got the world by the tail" attitude.

"Good morning. Milton Hodges from the United

States Supreme Court. Death clerk." His somber tone matches his job. "I understand that this is your first execution."

What a way to put it. Sounds as if I'm about to be executed or hold the job of executioner. "Correct." I substitute a pencil for a cigarette. It shakes between my fingers. Tarsha comes to my desk to watch the conversation. Just hearing isn't enough.

"Do you have a copy of the court's rules?"

I'm tempted to lie so as not to sound naive. I can get a copy from Buchanan's firm. "No, sir, I don't."

"As soon as we're off the phone, I'll fax you a copy if you'll give me the number."

With my hand over the receiver, I get the number from Tarsha, relay it, and he continues. "These rules must be followed exactly." He explains precisely what the court expects from final appeals. "Every filing from now until the end, no matter in which court it is filed, must also be filed with us. We are, of course, inundated with claims and must have all motions and appeals in order to expedite matters coming before us. In that way we'll be able to rule quickly, grant an immediate relief or deny."

If my appeal in the state court is denied, the U.S. Supreme Court will be studying it as it passes through the federal court and then onto the Fifth Circuit Court before reaching the final forum, the Supreme Court. I pray I won't have to travel that far. I shudder at the possibility of going all the way to the Supreme Court and then being denied. No recourse left then but to fling myself at the governor and beg for clemency. And from what I hear, Danforth's anxious to execute. I'm anxious for the Mississippi Appellate Project group to arrive.

He continues. "This office is on call around the clock and has a checklist of every imaginable last-minute motion and appeal. If a lawyer happens to have missed an arguable issue, then we notify that attorney that he or she should pursue that point."

That's fair and more generous than I expected. "I'd like a copy of that list, too."

"As I said, we're on call around the clock, and I'll personally be by the phone for the twenty-four-hour period leading up to the execution."

His statement makes me queasy. It's couched for a losing situation. Is he this pessimistic with all cases, or does he just expect me to lose? "I certainly hope to find relief before we get within twenty-four hours of the execution. My first appeal of ineffectual counsel is now in the Mississippi State Supreme Court, as I guess you know. If I'm denied there, I'll certainly fax it to you and the federal court simultaneously. I'm also drafting a second appeal to follow my first through the courts."

"And what will that claim be?"

I don't have to tell him, but figure it won't hurt. "That execution by lethal injection is cruel and inhumane."

A period of silence develops before he speaks. "That's a first." A catch–22, something to tangle up the courts, something he doesn't like.

After we conclude, Tarsha returns to her desk and I stare at the fax machine across the room, waiting for the death clerk's correspondence. What an awful job title. I light a cigarette with a kitchen match I find in my drawer.

The light on the fax beeps red, and the machine hums to life. My eyes follow the sentences on the tongue of paper as they're printed. I squint. The fax is not from the U.S. Supreme Court. I stare in disbelief; some chemical in my brain cushions me from the shock. I rip the paper off the machine.

"My appeal of ineffectual counsel has been denied by the Mississippi Supreme Court. The ruling states that I failed to show that it was of such a nature that if Robert Weldon *had* testified, it would be unlikely that his testimony would have produced a different result. Shit!" I tear the paper, crumple it, and slam it in the wastebasket.

Resting my elbows on the desk, I cradle my head in my hands. Weldon is now one step closer to execution. I will have to tell him about the denial. Both J. Clyde Perkins and Jack Flannery Sr. will celebrate when the news breaks. Flannery probably already knows via the legal grapevine. And all I have to show for my efforts are a dead dog and a fear of being alone in my house at night.

"Here, have some coffee," Tarsha urges. "It's not the end of the war, just one battle. You can still win the next round or the next."

The fax beeps and starts to spill out the information from the U.S. Supreme Court. I understand that in death cases the courts watch each other carefully, appeals and rulings automatically passed along from lower courts to higher courts so they know what to expect. The denial of my appeal in state court will automatically be faxed to the federal district court in Jackson and assigned to a federal judge. I will now file with the federal court and fax a copy to the death clerk.

Finished with faxing, I sit erect at my desk, anger radiating inside me. I catch my breath and dial Babaloo Brown. After six rings a sleepy voice grunts a "Hello." I'm so surprised, so amazed to have him reached him personally that I'm momentarily silenced. I have one chance to make the right pitch, one shot to grab him.

"This is Leona Bingham. Somebody cut off my son's dog's head, slipped in my house, and put the bloody knife on my bed. And that's not all."

"What? What are you saying? You accusing me?" He's wide awake now.

"Certainly not. You want to hear the rest of it?" Tarsha's back at my desk.

"I reckon, now that I'm up."

"The night I came to your place somebody scratched the word 'bitch' on my car door—"

"Whoa, here. I'm not responsible for what happens in the parking lot."

"I didn't say you were. There was a demonstration outside my office."

"Heard about that." He sounds almost amused.

"Somebody has been calling me, and when I answer they won't say anything. My son and I can't stay alone at night, but I'm going on with the case because I believe all this proves that Robert Weldon is innocent and somebody wants to frighten me into dropping the case—the person who killed your sister.

The murderer is still out there, Babaloo, and I'm try-ing to catch him, but without some help I may not. I just lost my first appeal to save Robert Weldon, and that puts him a little closer to being executed for something he didn't do while the killer sits back and laughs. I'm losing, Weldon's losing, and you and your mother are losing because the murderer won't be punished. I know you know something that might help me get closer to the killer, some scrap of infor-mation you're holding back. You have to tell me. Time is running out. Please, please, tell me what you know."

Babaloo is silent, and I can almost feel him debat-ing with himself. I grip the receiver tighter, as if that will make him talk. Suddenly I worry that he's put down the phone. "Babaloo, you there?"

"Yeah, I'm here." He exhales loudly. "Okay, tell you what. I'll drop by your house tonight after I get things rollin' here, and we'll have us a talk. 'Bout eight o'clock."

I realize I'm holding my breath. "Thank you, Babaloo. Thank you."

I raise my fist in the air. "*Yes!*"

"So he really does know something, or says he does."

I look at Tarsha, puzzled by her tone. "What do you mean by that?"

"Well, while you were spouting off to him about all the things that have happened to you, I got to thinking. Babaloo Brown could have been behind every one of them. For instance"—she ticks off items on her fingers as she talks—"*he* could have scratched 'bitch' on your fender. If you remember, when we were at his place, he left the table for a while to take a phone call. He could have done it then. He could be making those phone calls to you. He could have organized that demonstration. He could have cut off the dog's head. He could be the very one who wants you to drop the case, wanting justice for his sister's killer, or I've got even another scenario of why he might try to harass you into dropping the case. If you'll recall from the trial transcripts, Ray Bell Crosby thought the man he saw running through the woods near where April Brown was killed was black. I know he said it was shadowy in there, but he *thought* the man was black. Maybe Babaloo killed his own sister."

Her theory puts me further on edge. "What's his motive for killing his own sister?"

Tarsha hikes her shoulders. "I don't know. Maybe because she had broken their mother's heart, pregnant by a white man, going to run off to California. And now Babaloo is coming to your house tonight. Maybe you just invited the fox into the hen house."

Her suspicions have merit in my book. I was so anxious to extract information from Babaloo that I didn't see the whole picture. That could have been his plan all along, play hard to get on the pretext of having some information; then when he does relent I'm too excited and overwhelmed to take precautions. Right now he could be saying, "Gotcha."

"If it was me, I'd have a little company around tonight when he shows up."

"Good thinking." Babaloo is comfortable with Charles. I dial Charles's house. Although he and

Estelle have come to terms and the relationship is healing, he still returns to my house after dinner to stay the night.

The housekeeper informs me that Charles is not home. I leave a message for him. I have a man about whom I'm now only slightly suspicious coming to intercede if another newly suspicious man poses a threat. Going in circles, I'm like a dog chasing his tail.

"Tyrone and I can come if Charles can't get over to your house in time," Tarsha offers. "Maybe you ought to get Ray Bell, too."

"Babaloo strikes me as the type that might get nervous around somebody who was connected with the police. I don't want to scare him off from talking with so many people around."

"Yeah, and maybe he's got nothing to say, either."

The phone jolts me. It's Jack, and he's heard about the state court denying my the appeal. Wondering if his father called with the news, I ask how he knows.

"It's all over the courthouse. Somebody heard it on the radio. It'll probably be on the noon television news."

"The appeal's on the way to federal court now. I've just filed. How long do you think it will be before it's assigned?" He knows procedure better than I.

"You've heard the saying that the wheels of justice turn slowly. Not when an execution date has been set. When every day counts, they get in gear. Right away, I'd say, depending which federal judge is free. Pray to get assigned to Judge Craig. He's the most reasonable, in my opinion. Judge Allen is the worst, hard, unyielding. Tough nut to crack, he is."

I tell Jack about my conversation with Babaloo Brown. Hands down I'd take Jack over Charles to be present when I talk to Babaloo, but it's improper to ask under the circumstances, and if it wasn't, the district attorney might scare Babaloo into silence—*if* he has actually withheld important information.

"This could be a break. So let me know how things go, Leona."

As I gather the material from the death clerk and begin studying, Ray Bell and Wilma Ruth arrive. He's been chasing the J. Clyde Perkins angle, and I'm anxious to hear if he's made progress.

"Come have a seat." One chair is close to my desk, and I drag over another. Tarsha offers coffee, but they decline. Wilma Ruth always brings something from her kitchen and hands Tarsha a brown paper bag full of muffins for the office, and a batch of chocolate chip cookies for Bingo.

"Ray Bell brought me in to town to do some grocery shopping." Wilma Ruth sighs as she sits. "Good to be sitting down." She reaches around and rubs her back. "The pasture's got to be cut, and our sitting power mower went out. Ray Bell didn't want to call that crazy Ronnie Fletcher about it, so I been bending over it all morning, trying to fix the motor. Finally got it going, but I like to have broken my back."

"Wilma Ruth can fix anything, and I have trouble changing a lightbulb."

"Go on." Waving him off, she smiles at the compliment. I don't think she hears many and savors the few she does. Her hands are chapped and cracked from hard work. The squint marks around her kindly eyes are now permanently etched. I'm sure men wouldn't agree, but the outdoorsy and weather-beaten quality shows character in my estimation, like a Georgia O'Keefe who wouldn't be the same with the smooth skin of a model. Wilma Ruth's only concession to youth is the glistening strawberry-blond braid that hangs past her shoulders. She wears her usual jeans and a blue button-down shirt. Her cowboy boots, like Ray Bell's, are shined to a mirror finish. I wonder who does the polishing, the Marlboro Man or the Good Country Wife?

Seated behind my desk, I finger the communiqué from the death clerk. "I've got good news and bad news. The bad is that the state court has rejected my appeal. I've already filed with the federal court."

A look of concern crosses his face. Ray Bell shakes his head. "That's too bad. Maybe you'll get some sympathetic federal judge. I hear they're a lot more lenient than the state judges."

"Some are, some aren't. Jack said I'd better hope the appeal isn't assigned to Judge Allen. The good news is that I called Babaloo Brown, and he agreed to come to my house tonight and talk. I always felt he was holding something back. Maybe this is the break we've been waiting for." I feel a rush that overrides the blow from the state court.

"That's great." The concerned expression evaporates, and Ray Bell's eyes light up with anticipation. "Want me there?"

"I think it's best just to have Charles. He and Babaloo go way back, and he'll feel comfortable enough around him to open up." I think of Charles's story of how he saved Babaloo from a beating. Surely Babaloo is only coming forward to repay an old debt and isn't dangerous, as Tarsha suggested.

"Well, I've got something for you. Something really big." Ray Bell pulls off his tie, folds it in his coat pocket, crosses one leg over the other, and rolls up his white shirt sleeves, taking his time to draw out the drama, savoring the moment. "Just pulled in from Memphis. It was kind of late when I finished last night and I was tired, so I stayed overnight. Anyhow, I called for an appointment at the Perkins firm and they said Perkins couldn't see me, but a Jeremy Ward could. I went on over there and talked to this Ward fellow, told him my brother down in Biloxi was being held for murder, needed a lawyer but didn't have any money to pay for one, that I wanted the best and heard the Perkins firm was tops, and could he defend him pro bono. Well, this fast-talking Mr. Jeremy Ward is suddenly very busy with too many commitments and can't handle it. Said the state of Mississippi would appoint a public defender. I ask if there wasn't *someone* in the firm that would do pro bono work, and he said not to his knowledge, that the Perkins firm doesn't do pro bono work. This guy doesn't know that I know better. So, now I figure something's not only rotten in Denmark, but in the Perkins firm, too."

I move to the edge of my chair, aware that some momentous piece of news is forthcoming. My mind races with possibilities. Ray Bell is bursting with pride, finally able to contribute to the investigation. Has he broken into the files after office hours? Was that the reason for the overnight stay? "Go on," I urge.

"When I was in the reception room, I had to wait awhile before I got to see this lawyer. I got to talking with this real tall woman there, J. Clyde Perkins's personal assistant." He glances at Wilma Ruth as if to say, "This was all in the line of duty."

"I met her, too, the day I was there. Tall is an understatement. Snooty, too," I add, hoping to diffuse any problems with Wilma Ruth.

"After I got nowhere with the lawyer and I was about to leave empty-handed . . . well, an idea struck me. It was late in the day, office about to close and all, so I went back to this lady's office. Her name's Olivia. I ask her to go have a drink with me at the Peabody Hotel bar, being as I was up there all by myself and always wanted to see the place. You know, real live ducks around the fountain in the lobby." His megawatt smile beaming, he glances at me, and we both know he's worked his magic on this woman. I have a sneaking suspicion he gathered some information between the sheets rather than over a cocktail table.

"We had a few pops, got friendly, and when she got a little loaded I said I'd heard J. Clyde Perkins defended somebody in Grenola pro bono and how come nobody in the firm would defend my brother pro bono. She gets this funny little look, like the cat that swallowed the canary, and tells me in all confidence that Perkins didn't defend Robert Weldon pro bono. That he was paid. One hundred and twenty-five thousand dollars."

I'm walloped by the bombshell he's dropped. I'm speechless. I struggle to assimilate the information. "Robert didn't have that kind of money. Who could have paid Perkins and why?" The answer to that question could crack the case wide open.

"Now that she didn't know. Perkins was paid with a cashier's check. Said he was always very careful, very secretive about it all."

"But doesn't a cashier's check have the remitter's name on it?" I ask, trying to recall having bought one.

"No, the name doesn't have to appear if the person who bought the check doesn't want it on there."

I get up and pace back and forth. Tarsha's heard Ray Bell's revelation and edges around the screen, stunned as I am. I glance from her to Ray Bell. Wilma Ruth is digging in her burlap satchel, seemingly unaware of the gigantic scoop.

"This goes deep," I say. "Lots more here than we first thought. Everything is taking on a different light. Weldon said Perkins just appeared at the jail, told him he was handling the case and not to worry about money, all pro bono. Perkins said Weldon was a congenital liar. Maybe this is what Weldon was talking about—information I might uncover and would know how to handle. But what? Who? We have to find out who paid Perkins, and I'll bet a dollar to a doughnut Weldon knows. Maybe the denial by the state court will scare him into telling me. I'll have inform him of the denial and that I've now filed in federal court." I plop down at my desk, head spinning. "Who in the world could have paid Weldon's legal tab, and why did they do it?"

The phone rings, and I grab it automatically without giving Tarsha a chance. "Leona Bingham."

"Ms. Bingham, this is Judge Andrew Allen with the federal court in Jackson. Your appeal has been assigned to me."

I squeeze my eyes shut. The wheels of justice are moving like those on a fast freight, and I've drawn the lemon of all judges. "Yes, sir." The words come out in a croak.

"Time is of the essence here, and to get on with matters I was hoping we could meet in my office in the federal courthouse on Capitol Street."

"Certainly, Your Honor. When?"

"This afternoon around two. That time is convenient with the governor and the attorney general."

I check my watch. This afternoon? And he's already talked to the others first. Are they all in cahoots? In league against me? "Two would be fine. I'll be there." Grenola is ninety miles from Jackson. I'll go to Parchman first, then floor-board it to Jackson to make the meeting. Glancing down at my clothes, I'm glad I've worn a suit instead of slacks or a warm-up. I can't imagine how long the meeting will last, but I must be home in time to meet Babaloo. Suddenly I feel harried, upset by snowballing events. Bingo has to be picked up at school and looked after until I return. Tarsha has mounds of work. Lily and Estelle are busy. My eyes fall on Wilma Ruth.

I explain my predicament, and Wilma Ruth quickly volunteers to see to Bingo without my asking. I grab my briefcase, stuff in my necessities, and leave for Parchman.

*　　*　　*

Seated across the table from Robert Weldon in the penitentiary's law library, I am uncomfortably aware of the contemptuous stares from the other inmates. Do I provoke those looks because I'm a lawyer or a person who is free? Could be it's because I'm a woman and that's where their troubles began? I try to ignore them.

Weldon's expectant eyes bore into me. "News?"

I nod. "The Mississippi State Supreme Court denied our claim of ineffectual counsel."

He tears off his glasses and wipes his eyes with the backs of his hands. "You'll file with the federal court now?" He puts the gold-wire frames back on and blinks.

"I've already done it. I'm on the way to Jackson after I leave here to meet with Judge Allen, who's been assigned the case. This is more bad luck. I hear he's the toughest, most narrow-minded judge on the bench. Governor Danforth and the attorney general will both be at the meeting." The thought of being in such powerful company rattles me to the core. I have to summon the strength to appear calm, conceal my nervousness with confidence.

Weldon takes a deep breath. "I guess nothing more has come of the investigation."

On the one hand, Weldon's situation bruises my heart. He's locked up here, impotent to fend for himself, and dependent upon one lone contact in the outside world to save him. The responsibility I've shouldered is more awesome that I thought possible. On the other hand, I'm angry and feel used that he won't

reveal what could help both of us. Now that I've discovered Perkins did not defend him pro bono but
was paid handsomely, I'm especially agitated and
confused. I believe Weldon has lied by omission and
I'm due some answers.

"There has been a development—two, actually.
Babaloo Brown has agreed to meet with me tonight. I
felt when I first talked to him that he might have been
holding back some piece of information that could
help us. Now I'm sure of it."

"That's a break, maybe." Weldon leans forward,
clasping his hands together. Again I wonder if those
hands held the knife that put the end to a life. Have I
gone off on some tangent, at great expense to myself,
trying to free a guilty man? Was Jack right about a
desperate man conning me? But what about Perkins's
fee? How does that fit? His eyes meet mine. "Leona,
is something wrong? You don't seem like yourself.
Has something else happened to you? Is there something you're not telling me?"

"Just the other way around, I'd say." I watch him
with laser intensity, waiting to gauge his reaction to
my next statement. "J. Clyde Perkins didn't defend
you pro bono. He was paid a hundred and twenty-
five thousand dollars for his services."

Either his shock is genuine or he's Academy
Award material. "I can't believe it."

"Believe it."

He glances around, as if looking for answers in the
air or on the walls, then settles on me. "Leona, I had
no idea. Just like I said, he walked into the jail after I
was arrested and said not to worry about money, that

he was going to defend me. You have to believe me."

"I don't know what to believe. Perkins told me you were a congenital liar. Maybe that was his excuse for losing the case." The case was lost because the evidence against Weldon was overwhelming. With such ego, Perkins thought he could sway the jury, or he wouldn't have taken a case that could spoil his record, no matter what the fee.

Weldon's face clouds. "I never lied to him or you. I know he thought I lied about my car needing fixing and about the jacket I left out by the lake, the knives, but everything I told him was true, absolutely."

Strangely, Weldon has not questioned the most important point here, a question anyone under the circumstances would have asked, and I wonder why he hasn't. "That brings me back to the big puzzle. Who paid Perkins's legal fees and why?"

For only an instant I catch a mysterious flicker in his eyes; then the glow is quickly extinguished. I stare at him, wondering if I've actually seen something or if I'm reading too much into his expression.

"How do you know this about the fees?" he asks.

"Ray Bell found out from somebody in Perkins's office." I draw a deep breath. "Robert, you haven't answered my question, one you should have asked if you don't already know the answer. Who paid Perkins and why?"

"I don't know." He blinks. "Does it affect my case in any way?"

"No, not legally." I know of no legal precedent concerning such a matter. I've considered bringing it to the attention of the powerhouses at the meeting this afternoon but decided against it. It's hearsay and could never be proved. Plus, of what is it proof? Another veil of mystery clouds the case. I may never find the answers to all the questions, but I won't stop looking, despite my growing frustration.

Checking my watch, I rise. "I have to get to Jackson. You'd better do some soul searching. You can count as well as I can and the days are flipping by, so if you're holding back anything that can help me get you a stay, you'd better speak up. I'm working in the dark here." I look toward the guard. "Guard, I'm ready to go."

The guard comes to escort him back to his cell, and I feel Weldon's eyes bore into my back as I leave. I was harsh and don't regret it.

I stop at the guard house while they perform the usual check, the floors of my car and the trunk. I nod like the veteran I'm fast becoming. Several trusties, leaning on hoes in the hot sun, watch the routine with envious eyes. I'm free to leave. Their turn is coming, unlike the inmates on death row.

I scorch down the Highway 82 and by 1:15 find my way to Capitol Street, the main thoroughfare through Jackson. Buildings and stores line the streets, but an entire city block is taken by the governor's mansion, a white antebellum home, surrounded by carefully tended grounds and towering magnolia trees. Fences with gates guard the area. I think of the power over life and death the occupant of that mansion possesses. Governor Robert Danforth can pardon an inmate or commute a death sentence to life imprisonment or remain steadfast on an execution.

I spot the federal court building. The domed capi-

tol building looms at the end of the street, a miniature of the Capitol building in Washington. I've read
that it was built with prison labor. A vacant parking
space yawns before the federal court building, and I
superstitiously take it as a good sign.

I enter the building, find Judge Andrew Allen's
office on the directory, and proceed down a long
marble hall. A gray-haired secretary and a twenty-
something man confer at her desk in Judge Allen's
reception area. My appearance stops their conversation, and they look as if they already know who I am.

"Leona Bingham, Robert Weldon's lawyer, here to
see Judge Allen about the appeal he's been assigned."

"George Van Cleve, Judge Allen's law clerk. I'll
show you to the conference room."

I follow the man with the buzz cut down another
hall. He opens a door, then stands aside. I stand in
the threshold, surveying a large paneled conference
room centered by a shining wood table. Seated in a
burgundy leather chair at the end of that table is a
small, paunchy man with narrow, beady eyes set too
close together and a dyed black wreath of hair
around a glistening pointed dome. He immediately
reminds me of J. Clyde Perkins. I assume he is the
Honorable Andrew Allen.

But the surprise is the presence on one side of the
table of the attorney general and his staff of five, and
on the other side the governor, whom I recognize
from the media, and his squadron of six. Stacks of
files and legal pads are before them. Crystal ashtrays,
filled to capacity with cigar and cigarette butts, line
the table. I glance at my watch: 1:40. A meeting has

been taking place before the appointed time. I don't like the feel of this. All eyes are on me. The men rise gallantly like southern escorts greeting a debutante.

Judge Allen comes around the table and introduces himself. "I believe you know the attorney general, Jack Flannery." I nod, and Mr. Jack produces a fleeting smile. "And Governor Robert Danforth."

A tall, imposing man, Governor Danforth smiles and shakes my hand vigorously. I'd guess he's in his sixties. "You had a long drive. All of us were close, so we got here early." I want to say that I'm also early. He has a high widow's peak, and his jet black hair is graying at the temples. He radiates charisma. His smoky gray eyes are alert, missing nothing, and bore into me as if his one desire in life is to see straight into my soul. I can see how he got elected. I detect a sense of fairness in him, a warmth and understanding for others. Reminding myself that he's strong on the death penalty, I won't be lulled into false security, but somehow feel I've found an ally in the hostile environment. He reminds me of someone, whose identity eludes me.

Governor Danforth introduces his staff and Mr. Jack introduces his, all attorneys from the criminal-appeals division who handle death-penalty cases. To say I'm outnumbered is an understatement. Judge Allen waddles back to his place and asks me to take a seat at the end of the table. He sticks on horn-rimmed glasses with lens thick as old Coke bottles.

"As I informed you, Miz Bingham, I have been assigned to your appeal in federal court." He fingers a file I assume contains my petition and addresses Mr.

Jack. "When's the earliest I can expect the state to respond?"

"Day after tomorrow," the attorney general replies, and those on his staff nod. "Of course, assuming the appeal is the same as the one filed in the state supreme court and raises the same issues."

"Identical," I answer, sensing they already know this. The staff members scrutinize me with looks that don't hide their opinion that I'm out of my league, floundering, with no idea of what I'm doing. They're not far off target.

"I'm glad we can move with all due speed, then." Judge Allen speaks like his mouth is full of sour mush and wants to spit it out as fast as possible. "I'll consider the appeal and response before the week is out and issue my ruling. Now, there's a possibility that I might decide to conduct a hearing, and I need to know how long it will take you people to get ready. How 'bout you, Miz Bingham? How long's it going to take you to prepare?"

I pray my face doesn't flush. I have no idea what he's asking. Maybe the appellate project people can help. "The Mississippi Appellate Project group will be assisting me." I glance around at the staff, wanting to say, "See I'm not such a rookie. They believe in my cause." I don't see any surprise or concern, only smirks. "I'd have to confer with them, but I'd say a week at most." I steal a look at Mr. Jack, wondering if the time I've specified sounds reasonable.

"A week suit you?" Judge Allen asks the attorney general, who nods in agreement.

Some wild streak in me decides to ruffle the steely-eyed arrogant staff and everyone else present. "Of course, something might change that hearing."

I couldn't draw more attention if I had come to the meeting naked. I give them a stingy smile and remain knowingly silent.

Judge Allen removes his glasses. "Well, what is it that could interfere with the hearing, if I see fit to conduct one?"

I've told Jack about the meeting with Babaloo Brown and know the confidence will be honored. "A witness in the trial is coming forth to talk to me. I can't say for sure, but I believe this witness might have some important information. So quite a bit hinges on what this witness has to say." I glance from Governor Robert Danforth to Attorney General Flannery. I've raised their eyebrows and erased the smug expressions from their staff.

"And just who is this witness?" Judge Allen asks.

"Your Honor, I think it's premature at this point to discuss the subject," I answer, feeling like a tough litigator. "If it is something of a nature that would bring cause for a new trial, I will let you know immediately." A witness who lied on the stand would be grounds for a new trial. I don't believe that is the case here, though.

Judge Allen stands. "Okay. I guess that's it for now. Meeting adjourned."

I scurry out of the courthouse without making further contact, although I would have liked to talk to Governor Danforth. I'm impressed with the man whose job Mr. Jack wants, and he may be my last resort.

I'm delayed in a traffic jam on the outskirts of Jackson, but finally reach the highway. I'm hot, thirsty, hungry, and need to use a rest room, but decide my wants can wait. I press down on the accelerator, and as I whiz down the road a jumble of thoughts and questions fog my mind.

By the time I hit Grenola, make it to Wilma Ruth and Ray Bell's, I'm drained. Wilma Ruth and Bingo are playing cards on the porch, a pitcher of lemonade beside them. Grabbing his backpack, Bingo runs out to greet me, and Wilma Ruth gives me a sign to wait while she goes inside.

"Where you been, Mom?" Bingo climbs into the Bronco. He's dirty and has that brassy smell of little boys who've been in the heat too long.

"Jackson on business." I kiss him on his cheek. He immediately wipes it away. "You have some fun today?"

"Yeah. Ray Bell mowed a pasture and I rode with him. Me and Wilma Ruth played some games."

"Wilma Ruth and I played some games," I correct.

"No, you didn't." He laughs, thinking he's made a funny.

Wilma Ruth comes out with a basket. "Knew you'd be gone all day, so I fried you some chicken for dinner. There's cornbread, some fresh field peas I cooked, potato salad, and a blackberry pie. Bingo, don't eat the pie first."

She's saved us from a fast-food junk dinner. "You are the greatest. I can't thank you enough. How can I ever repay you?"

She smiles, her eyes glowing. "Don't need to."

As we head home, I think how Wilma Ruth is a woman who's anxious to fill the needs of others. She needs to be needed. She'd be a lost soul without Ray Bell.

Bingo talks about school, tells me Kit has been elected junior cheerleader for next year's football season. I wonder if her popularity makes him feel insecure.

I make a sharp curve around the bayou, and Bingo swings to one side, even with the seat belt on. "Mom, why're you driving so fast?"

"I need to use the bathroom. Bad."

"Gross, Mom." He shakes his head, too old now for such intimate knowledge.

I pull into the driveway and rush to the front door, calling out for Bingo to unload the car, then shower and change. I hurry upstairs to the bathroom, peeling off clothes.

After a shower so cold I've raised goose bumps, I pull on a pair of jeans and a white T-shirt. Barefoot, I pad down to the kitchen and inspect the food basket. I place the potato salad in the refrigerator while tearing at a drumstick. I set the table with blue gingham mats and napkins, check to make sure all doors are locked, and settle down with a glass of much needed red wine and a cigarette.

Bingo comes down in fresh clothes, wet hair plastered to his scalp, and finishes his homework. The house seems empty without Mister Marvel, and Bingo has time on his hands. He finally wanders out to watch television. Though none can replace Mister

Marvel, I wonder about getting a new dog.

I'd like to drink the whole bottle of wine, but limit myself so I'll be ready for Babaloo. Every time I think of what information he might impart, my heart flops over an extra beat. So much depends on his words.

Keyed up, I smoke another cigarette and down one last glass of wine. I should be relaxed, but I feel as if wires are being tightened to a tensile strength inside me. I check my watch, willing the minutes to hurry and pass.

By the time Charles arrives, I've turned myself into a wreck. We discuss the possibilities of what Babaloo has to offer. I tell him about Perkins's fee for defending Weldon, and we chew on that subject. I pour him a glass of wine and barely listen as he launches into an account of how much money Estelle is spending on her shop. My comments are short and given without much thought. I'm sorry I'm not more sympathetic, but I'm centered on other matters.

I get supper on the table, and the three of us eat without much conversation. Charles tries his best with Bingo, but my son doesn't relate to him the way he does to Jack. A crazy thought strikes me. I've heard that dogs and kids have a weird inner antenna about which adults are good and which are bad. Maybe this is true in Bingo's case with Charles. His help has been invaluable and at his own personal expense, and I feel rotten when unpleasant thoughts about him pop into my head.

Bingo goes back to television, and Charles settles on the front porch with a cigar while I tidy the kitchen. To pass the time, I work on my briefs at the kitchen table, barely able to concentrate.

Eight o'clock comes and goes. By a quarter to nine I'm frantic. Has Babaloo changed his mind? I try to soothe myself with suggestions that he's been delayed at the club, gotten lost trying to find my house, had a flat on the way. At nine-thirty I can no longer contain myself. I dial his club. The smoky-voiced woman answers. I hear no background music or noise.

"This is Leona Bingham. I'd like to speak with Babaloo."

A long silence follows.

"Are you there?"

"Yes, 'um, but Babaloo ain't. He was shot right outside the club late this afternoon."

I feel like some giant hand has grabbed my guts and is squeezing hard. My hopes are punctured. "Is he . . ."

"He ain't dead, if that's what you're asking, but he's near 'bout. In intensive care at the hospital. Just hanging on, they say."

11

WE DROP BINGO AT THE BIG HOUSE WITH LILY AND Byars and dash to Grenola General. Walking down the hospital corridor with Charles at my side, I feel like a vulture. It's my fault that Babaloo has been shot, and still I've come to his deathbed on the slim chance of extracting what might be a critical piece of information that could save another's life.

Godfrey, Captain Lewis's deputy, stands guard by the ICU. The shooter could appear to finish the job that wasn't quite completed. "How bad is he?" I ask the officer.

He hitches up his pants over a bulging pot. "Bad off. Lost a lot of blood before the cook who was comin' to work found him slumped over in his car. Chief Lewis figures he was shot around six o'clock tonight. He's out there now talkin' to folks at Babaloo's place. Wild joint like that always has somethin' goin' on, shootin', stabbin'."

"Does Chief Lewis or anybody have any ideas about who might have shot Babaloo?" Charles asks.

Godfrey scratches his bulbous red nose. "Chief reckons it was some drug deal gone wrong. Babaloo was dealin'. We been suspectin' that for a long time, just couldn't get no proof on him."

"I don't believe that," Charles snaps, his voice laced with anger. "I've known him since he was a little boy. He's hardworking, always was just trying to make a buck."

"Yeah, a fast one," Godfrey snaps.

Dr. Hull rounds the corner from the ICU, white coat flapping behind him, and heads in the opposite direction. I catch up with him. "Dr. Hull?" He stops and whirls around.

"Leona, what are you doing here?"

"Babaloo Brown was coming to see me tonight . . . about the case I spoke with you about. He had something to tell me. I think that was why he was shot. How bad off is he?"

"Can he talk, is what you're asking."

I nod, feeling lower than a snake's belly.

"No, he's in a coma, and I don't believe he's going to regain consciousness."

We turn when Babaloo's mother comes out of the ICU. Though clad in worn clothes, stockings tied in a knot just below her knobby knees, Mrs. Brown moves down the hall with a sense of dignity and regal bearing possessed by few. She approaches Charles.

"I heard what you said about my son, Mr. Charles. Even if it ain't true, I 'preciate you saying it." Lifting her chin, she gives Godfrey a withering glance.

"I'm really sorry about Bobo, Mrs. Brown," Charles says.

"I believe you are. He always held you high, Mr. Charles."

I edge close to the pair, expecting a cold reception from Mrs. Brown. "I'm so sorry about your son, Mrs. Brown. Remember me? Leona Bingham."

She nods.

Charles pats his pocket, checking for his wallet. "Could we get you some coffee, a cold drink, something to eat? There's a snack bar down the hall."

"I'd just like to go outside for a little and breathe some fresh air, look at the stars, see if many are out tonight."

She has some superstitions that have to do with stars, I guess. We accompany her outside, and she perches on a ledge, wrapping her arms around her waist. She looks at the sky, her mouth moving. I don't know if she's praying or counting stars. I light a cigarette. Charles sits beside Mrs. Brown. The moon highlights her face.

"Your son was coming to see me tonight, Mrs. Brown. I feel responsible that he might have been shot because of it."

Her eyes slide toward me. "Bob ran with some bad peoples, he did. His gettin' shot wasn't no fault of yours. It's God's will." She seems more resigned to her fate than saddened by it. "Both my children come to a bad end, like I always said. If Bob don't make it, it'll be just me that's left."

Her words console me to a degree. Maybe it was only a coincidence that he was shot before he came to my house. I drag on my cigarette. This is a bad night, first and foremost, for the Brown family and also an unfortunate break for Robert Weldon's case. I will never know what Babaloo had to reveal.

Mrs. Brown removes the purse strap from her arms and digs in her bag. "I know Bob was coming to see you tonight, Miz Bingham. We talked 'bout it a whole lot."

A ray of hope suddenly blossoms inside me. "You know what he had to tell me?" Charles and I exchange quick glances. At that moment I wonder where Charles was around six o'clock. He was late arriving at my house. I'll make a subtle inquiry.

She nods, still plundering in her purse. "I do. See, Bob didn't do exactly right . . . back then when April was kilt. I don't guess I did, either. I was so tore up, but that ain't an excuse. I should have told the police right then, but Bob, he talked me out of it. Bob, he don't trust the law. Then after so much time passed, we was both a-scared we'd get in trouble." She pulls out a ring and presents it to me. "April's. This belonged to her."

I turn the gold band over in my hand. Centered in the middle is a medium-size diamond, maybe a carat, surrounded by smaller cut diamonds. A chance this could be traced to the purchaser is not unreasonable, with luck. I'm excited.

"Now, there's somethin' I gots to tell you about that ring. I don't know for sure that the white man April was goin' with give it her, and that was Bob's argument about us keeping it, 'cause it wouldn't do no good in the trial, no proof. And he said if we gave it to the police, they wouldn't give it back after the trial, would just keep it for theyselves. Bob said if the man what kilt April was the one who gave it to her, we ought to get somethin' for what he did since he was already caught and in jail." Mrs. Brown sighs, shaking her head. "Well, Bob went to sell it and guess what? It's one of them Hot Springs diamonds you get over in Arkansas out of them mines. Ain't worth hardly nothing, some kind of crystal that just looks like a diamond. Bob says that man what kilt April tricked all of us all the way 'round. Bob always wore it on a chain 'round his neck as a reminder to hisself to never be no fool again."

I remember he fingered something beneath his shirt that night, the ring on the chain. He was toying with telling me then. I wish he had. "I appreciate this, Mrs. Brown. It could help track down the person who really killed April." I want to leave her with a good feeling of having done something right. I'm not sanguine now about discovering who purchased the ring. Hot Springs diamonds are sold in a multitude of stores and even hawked on street corners in Arkansas. As she said, no proof exists that the killer gave April the ring. April worked in a beauty salon. Someone could have given her the ring as a present, or she could have bought it herself. To boot, this goes back more than six years. All I can do is put Ray Bell on it.

Tarsha and I go back and forth to the front windows, then return to our desks. We're like anxious children on Christmas Eve waiting for Santa Claus. The appellate group is due anytime. I try to put them from mind and concentrate on polishing and perfecting the appeal to the Fifth Circuit Court in case it's denied in federal court. The time draws near for Judge Allen's ruling, and I've drafted my oral arguments in case he calls a hearing.

Lost in a mountain of legal precedents, I glance up from the law books when I hear a commotion outside the office. Eyes shielded with hands, four people peer through the glass on the front doors.

"I think the cavalry has arrived." Tarsha's wide grin is contagious.

We both stand and move to greet the bright young group as they file through the door. "Hi, Karen Rice." Preceding the others, the woman I've spoken with on the phone is the obvious leader. She's tall, maybe close to six feet, black, skinny as an exotic model with hair cropped as closely as a man's. She wears jeans and a white short-sleeved cable-knit top that shows her ribs and a bust the size of two very small shoulder pads. From our conversation I know she's a Harvard graduate. And from Tarsha's expression I know Karen has already become her idol.

I introduce myself and Tarsha, then Karen takes the lead, presenting the others. Billy Boyer is short and wiry, radiating energy. He has Dustin Hoffman's nose, and his blond hair is a mass of coiled ringlets. He's from Stanford, and rather than in a courtroom I can picture him zipping over waves on a surfboard. He glances around, taking stock. "This must be the place. We'll make ourselves right at home."

Jim Webb is an athletic-looking black man in

wire-framed glasses. From the University of Chicago Law School, he has a cool demeanor, a brooding quality. He has little to say, Karen informs us with a smile. "But when he does talk, it's best to pay attention."

The last attorney is Samuel Zachariah from Yale Law. His jet black hair falls in wisps around his blue button-down collar. His onyx eyes warn that he is not one to mess with, unless you want to become a loser.

All in all, they look like a good group, not some scraggly misfits. "So, Karen, Billy, Jim, Samuel, I really appreciate your coming. I don't mind telling you that I've had a rough go and need your help."

"There's coffee over here." Tarsha points at the sideboard and mugs. She's not serving today, not to peers.

"Let's get set up first," Karen says. "We'll get our things from the van, then check in at The Inn. I've just two rooms reserved to save some pennies. The guys will stay together and see who draws the sleeping bag."

I hesitate. "That's something I need to talk to you about . . . living arrangements."

"In a minute," Karen says in a no-nonsense manner. "Let's unload."

They hurry outside and quickly return, time after time, with folding card tables and chairs, boxes and boxes of books, stacks of legal pads and supplies, an easel and poster boards, a computer and laser printer, and scores of legal documents. They remind me of industrious ants building their mound, with Karen as the queen in the hill.

When their individual stations are set up, books aligned just so, the computer and printer hooked in and the easel placed to the front, Karen calls a halt. "Okay. Let's go dump the clothes at The Inn."

"Wait a second," I say. "Let me just bring you up to date on what's happened here."

They turn their attention to me. "Incidentally, I have all the Weldon trial transcripts here for you so you can get caught up." I figure this is an efficient move on my part. We have no time to waste.

"We already have copies," Karen informs me. "Ordered them from the courthouse here when we decided to pitch in. We've all read them in our spare time off from the last case." She grins. "Such as it was."

They're way ahead of me. "That's good. Then, let me just start from the top, from the time I received Robert Weldon's letter, what made me go to Parchman in the first place, his reason for choosing me as his attorney, and why I decided to take the case, although I'm not a criminal lawyer." I pause. "I'm learning, though." That brings a chuckle from all but the serious Jim. "I hope you all are as good detectives as you are lawyers, because there's lots going on here that I can't figure out. Maybe you can shed some light."

They melt into their folding chairs, ready to listen. I begin at the beginning and take them through the series of events that have occurred, leaving out any of my own deductions or suspicions so as not to influence their opinions. I have their rapt attention.

"Babaloo Brown never regained consciousness

but Ray Bell is trying to track the ring. We don't have much hope." Silence ensues, but minds are at work. Especially mine. Charles wasn't with Byars late in the day when Babaloo was murdered. In response to my carefully couched question, Charles said he was riding around the plantation alone, trying to sort out the situation with Estelle.

I return to my spiel. "So that's why I need you to bunk at my house. It's free and I'm scared. Karen can take my guest room, and you guys can put the sleeping bags in my living room. All together that way, we can work longer hours. We can share kitchen duties. My son is a good kid and won't interfere with business."

Billy plucks at one of his curls, unwinding it. "Jeez! And somebody cut off his dog's head."

Jim pulls off his wire-framed glasses and in a studious motion polishes them on his shirttail. "The big puzzle to me is who paid J. Clyde Perkins and why that person wanted Robert Weldon acquitted so badly that the most renowned and expensive lawyer in the South was hired." He puts the glasses back on, and his eyes move slowly around the room, scanning the walls and floor as his thoughts take shape. He holds up a finger. "All this is assuming Robert Weldon is innocent. The real killer figures nobody will ever be arrested for April Brown's murder, but then an innocent man is locked up and headed for trial. The murderer in a warped way of thinking rationalizes that April Brown deserves what she got, but doesn't want another death on the slate, gets an attack of conscience, and hires Perkins in hopes of saving Weldon. If that scenario were so, the killer is somebody with plenty of money. Plenty."

Karen said Jim doesn't talk much, but when he does, it's best to listen. They do. I am in the presence of sharp minds with fresh angles. His speculation spins around in my head. A white man with money and status who had gotten April pregnant would certainly not want this to come to light in the community. Her threatening to expose him is motive enough for murder.

"Nah." Billy shrugs. "I don't buy it. Why pay Perkins to start with? The murderer would wait to see if a state-appointed lawyer could get Weldon off first; then the killer's not out the money. If Weldon was found guilty, then Perkins could be hired for the appeals. Nah, the whole thing won't swing. Take this: Weldon paid Perkins himself." He holds up his hand to stop the interruptions. "I know Weldon was a mechanic, and mechanics ordinarily don't have a hundred and twenty-five grand to throw around. Let's just suppose Weldon did, though. Maybe he acquired it in some way he shouldn't have, drug deal, blackmail, who knows? Weldon told Leona that Perkins just walked in the jail and said he was going to handle his case. Maybe Weldon just wanted it to look like he was being represented pro bono to keep it secret he had that kind of money. Maybe that's what he hints Leona might find out about—the source of the money. And remember, Perkins told Leona Weldon was a congenital liar."

"Perkins was paid with a cashier's check," I remind him. "How'd he do that from jail?"

"With somebody's help, maybe." Samuel holds up his hand. "Off that subject for a minute. So your investigator"—he hesitates, recalling the name— "Ray Bell Crosby, you don't think he'll have much luck with the ring? Maybe he should try the manufacturers before the hitting the outlets, and they could give him a list of the particular outlets that handle that design. Some manufacturers even have a mark embedded in the gold or metal setting where it can't be easily seen, maybe under where the stone is set, and that could narrow it down."

We all begin to bat around theories about every aspect of the case. Tarsha throws in her ideas. Karen stands. "Hey, hey. We're off the subject here. I know you all like being armchair detectives, but we're here to help with a death row inmate's representation in the courts whether he's actually guilty or not. So let's do it. We need to focus on the legal perspective, the appeals."

She moves to the easel and takes a marker to the poster board. "Just like always, we're going to diagram. We're going to list all the points made in the appeal, tear them apart, and see if we need to and can add some new arguments. Tune it up for the Fifth Circuit if Judge Allen denies in federal. We need to work on orals for Leona if Judge Allen calls for a hearing, anticipate the attorney general's arguments, and be primed and cocked to rebut them.

"We have to *assume*, just to be prepared"—Karen glances at me, then continues—"that the ineffectual-counsel appeal is denied all the way, including in the Supreme, and have the next appeal ready to start on

its way through the state even before the first reaches
the Supreme. So let's jaw on what claim we want to
use."

I speak up and explain my idea of a claim, the first
of its kind, that death by lethal injection is cruel and
inhumane, citing the cases on record I've found
where that method of death encountered difficulties
being carried out in Texas and Illinois.

They eye me with skepticism, but I've set their
minds in motion. My subject encompasses much
more than some of the frivolous last-ditch gangplank
appeals. Not easily rejected without some delibera-
tion, it could buy some much needed time. Suddenly
I can see in their expressions that my idea can be
molded into what could become a landmark. I think
I've scored a point with members of the Mississippi
Appellate Project.

I move over to the computer, admiring it, again
vowing to buy one when I have enough cash or can set
up an installment plan. Tarsha has been asking for one
for so long. "I've got to make a run up to Parchman to
tell Weldon about Babaloo's death. When I last talked
to him, I told him Babaloo was coming forth with
some information that might help, and I know he's
hanging in the wind about it. Also, I think knowing
that you folks are here to help and ready to go to work
during this crucial period will make him feel better.
You all know better than I, but I've seen the despera-
tion and fear in most of the inmates. Then they get a
glimmer of false hope from their lawyer or some legal
loophole they've researched themselves, and when it
doesn't pan out, as it usually doesn't, they get ground

down lower than they already were. It's happening to me, and I'm not locked up on death row, don't have what they do at stake. I get pumped up, then dropped, pumped up and dropped further down each time."

"That's emotional involvement," Karen says. "And we can't afford that. Neither can you. All we can do is the best job possible for the client within the legal system." Her eyes move over her partners. "We'll go to Parchman with you. I was going to suggest that. We always want to have at least one conference with the death row inmate before starting to assist the lawyer with the appeal."

Samuel takes the floor. "Not to hear the inmate's professions of innocence. Criminal lawyers never ask a client accused of a crime if they're innocent or guilty. Don't want to know. The answer might subconsciously affect their defense. But these inmates on death row are different. Twelve people thought they were guilty and convicted them. Even if they are guilty, we just want to help make sure their legal rights are respected under the laws. We had one inmate we were assisting and he said from the get-go he was guilty of murder, but his rights had been violated by the police when he was first arrested. And that was wrong. We got him a new trial, and by that time the state was tired of the case and the money it cost, memories had faded, and witnesses had died or were unavailable, so he got off. Some legal system, huh? But it's the only one we have. Sometimes it doesn't do much for the victim's family."

We leave my office, and Billy comments that the main street of Grenola looks like a used parking lot for Cadillacs. People on the sidewalk take notice of the group. Maybe news will travel to the black community that two of their own are working with me on the Weldon case. Tarsha will help spread the word that might ease racial tensions. Of course, Grenola's white contingent will have their set opinions of the mixed band of lawyers. We pile into my Bronco and head to Parchman.

On the way, I ask about the cases they've handled. They describe failures and successes, but no matter the outcome all take pride in their work. Job offers with good law firms have come their way, but for now they prefer free-wheeling it. Samuel tells me I have guts for taking on the Weldon case, and their final decision to assist with the case was based on that opinion. That, I figure, and the fact that they thought Weldon wouldn't receive proper representation from an inexperienced lawyer like me.

I look out the window in case I've blushed from the compliment. "Curiosity rather than guts is more like it. And the belief that Robert is innocent."

After the routine at the guard gate we proceed to John Dobbs's office. These members of the Mississippi Appellate Project are well acquainted with the prison attorney, and he seems genuinely glad that they're ready to battle for Robert Weldon's life. I believe John Dobbs would like to open the iron gates on death row, set all the innocent free, and have the guilty sentenced to life without parole.

I bring Dobbs up to date on the case. "Judge Allen should rule anytime now. I hope not to have to go through a hearing."

"Sometimes a hearing is a positive sign the judge is open-minded, not already set on a decision," Dobbs says, though he looked alarmed when I mentioned who had been assigned the case.

I have thought about my next question carefully, and the quartet of lawyers agree that we might uncover some important information, especially about who paid for Weldon's defense. "John, is a log kept of the inmate's visitors?"

"Yes, visitor records are on file in the administration building. You're asking to check Weldon's visitor list. I can do that for you and let you know."

Dobbs calls the law library in MSU, informs them that Weldon's lawyer will be accompanied by four others, and we head that way. The four colleagues have covered this ground many times before, and if it affects them as it does me, they don't show it. The pressure of representing a client on death row is excruciating, the attorney stuck on a knife edge of suppressed agony.

They recognize several inmates in the law library and pause to offer a good word. This unhinges me. Have those inmates been the recipients of help from the appellate project? The inmates are still here.

We settle at the end of the table under the stares of other inmates who are probably wondering why so many lawyers are in attendance and why such a battery is not there for them. Some inmates have that wild-horse look in their eyes. The stink of fear, as always, permeates the confines of this room. Watching the door through which Weldon will enter, I find myself strangely hoping that Weldon will impress the group, that they will think him innocent. This is important to me.

The guard ushers Weldon in, and his eyes clamp onto me, then travel to the four visitors. I snatch a look at them, trying to gauge first impressions. All faces remain stoic, without even the slightest hint of sympathy or judgment. They are present to carry out the law.

Weldon's shackles are removed, and he's chained to a loop in the floor. I move to the edge of my seat, my back as rigid as the straight chair in which I'm sitting. I wish for a cigarette, but smoking is not allowed in the law library. "Robert, these are members of the Mississippi Appellate Group I told you about. Karen, Billy, Jim, and Samuel."

He gives each his fair share of attention before speaking. "Thank you for coming to help Leona and me. You can't know how much it means to me."

The more affable of the group, Billy Boyer, smiles. The others nod. I gather from Weldon's body language, his momentary silence that their businesslike demeanor both frightens and pleases him. He seems unsure of how to react to these four strangers. He focuses on me, a familiar pillar upon which he hangs his life.

"Did you find out anything from Babaloo Brown?" He's learned from experience not to anticipate too much, but a note of expectancy rings clear in his question.

It seems I bring only disappointments to the table. I can't or don't dare imagine the thrill of coming here with uplifting news. "Robert, someone shot Babaloo

Brown before he came to see me. He never regained consciousness. Died two days later."

Breath catching in his chest, he bites his lower lip, the hope of what might have been wilting. "Did the police find out anything about the shooting?"

"They say it was a drug deal gone bad." The Grenola paper accorded little coverage to the death, and the police exerted even less effort to the investigation. Charles and I, along with Mrs. Brown and a few of Babaloo's employees, were the only ones present at the graveside services that were held a week ago. "Mrs. Brown did talk to me at the hospital before Babaloo died. She knew what he was coming to give me, a ring that belonged to April." I notice the four attorneys study Weldon carefully, wondering how that piece of information will strike him. Did he purchase that ring? Was he about to be trapped?

Weldon's eyebrows lift, a slight hope renewed in him. "Maybe it can be traced to the murderer."

"There's no proof that the man she was going with gave her the ring. She could have bought it herself, stolen it, found it, been given it by a customer." Again I deliver unpromising news as I explain about Hot Springs diamonds, but assure him that Ray Bell will investigate the matter.

"I don't think it was a coincidence that Brown was shot the very day he was coming to see you, do you?" Robert asks.

I glance around the table at the other lawyers. "No, Robert. I don't believe in coincidences. I think somebody wanted to keep Babaloo from talking to me. It was a terrible waste of a life because what he had to tell wasn't of much help, but someone didn't know that, didn't know what information he might have had about April, thought maybe she might have confided in him."

"Nothing obviously from my appeal in federal court?"

"Anytime now. I'll let you know as soon as I do."

Jim taps his fingers on the table as if playing the piano. "Mr. Weldon, we've all read the trial transcripts, and we're ready to do some research and assist with sharpening up the appeals. If there is *anything* you can tell us, any scrap no matter how small, to help us help you, now is the time for it."

Weldon averts his eyes from mine. "There's nothing I can tell you except that I'm innocent. I never thought an innocent person could be convicted of a crime they didn't commit."

"It happens," Karen says. "Unfortunately."

Samuel clears his throat and fastens his attention on Weldon. "If you didn't commit this crime and are somehow exonerated, you have one hell of a lawsuit against the state of Mississippi for wrongful imprisonment. I'm talking millions here. Leona's cut for handling that would make any lawyer salivate." He pauses to let the enormity of the possibilities sink in on Weldon. "So why in God's name don't you just tell us whatever this sensitive information is that Leona may or may not uncover and only she would be able to handle? That's pay dirt for her."

Weldon looks as if he's recovering from a hard slap across the face. He takes a deep breath. "It has to come from Leona, not me."

"Then tell her," Karen almost shouts, drawing attention from other prisoners. "Tell her now. It's privileged information. None of us could ever reveal what it is."

Apologetically, Weldon stares at me. "I can't."

Billy throws in his bit. "What if she never comes across this information?"

"I am innocent," Weldon contends. "I believe Leona will find a way to free me through the courts or by finding the real murderer even if she never discovers this information I mention."

Samuel frowns and, exasperated, jumps to his feet, almost upsetting his chair. "Well, buddy, we're getting down to the wire here. You didn't think you'd get convicted, and here you sit on death row. Now you say you don't think you're going to be executed because Leona is going to find some way out for you. We all came here to bust our butts to help Leona but mainly you." He glances at his colleagues. "And we weren't aware of the fact that you have some piece of information you won't give up. You know, there are plenty other death row inmates who need our help, and right now I'm feeling like we're wasting our time on you."

I freeze, feeling the wings of abandonment beating over me. Blessedly, Karen saves the moment. "Come on. This is counterproductive. We came to work. So let's get to it." She rises, and the others follow her out of the library.

With nothing left to say, I start for the door, then turn back and give a small wave to Weldon. Looking somehow smaller and forlorn in the red jumpsuit, he returns the gesture as the guard unhooks his leg from the loop and returns him to shackles. "Be careful, Leona," he calls to me before being ushered back to his cell. "The threat to you is still out there."

With his final words reverberating inside my head, I unlock the Bronco and everyone climbs inside, buckling their seat belts. John Dobbs pulls up in a state-owned truck and rolls down the window. "I checked on the visitors log. Weldon has had only one visitor in these six years. A Louella Waters. She came twice just after he was sent here."

"Thanks for checking." I turn to the others as Dobbs drives away. We bat around a few theories. Louella Waters, now Fletcher, has money. Did she pay for Weldon's defense? Maybe Weldon lied about knowing April Brown. Maybe Louella killed her in a jealous rage, trying to erase the competition, and paid for Weldon's defense when he was arrested for the crime, still trying to hold on to her lover. Maybe Ronnie Fletcher later discovered his wife paid for Weldon's defense, and that is what prompts his anger and rage at the mention of Weldon's name.

Leaving Parchman, we hit the highway home. I light a cigarette, not knowing or caring if it's offensive, and listen to the silence. Jim and Samuel weren't impressed with Weldon. I worry that their hearts won't be in their work.

On the outskirts of Grenola, Karen breaks the stilted atmosphere. "There's a grocery store in that mall. We'd better stop and stock up."

We go inside and fill carts full of food, each member adding his or her favorites. Jim throws cigars in with the groceries he's selected. Samuel adds two six-packs of beer to his. Karen stocks up on sweets, and Billy picks health foods and vegetables. My cart bulges with Bingo's choices—pizza, pasta, hamburger makings, and hot dogs. Junk food for a short period won't hurt him.

I pay for my items, and Karen takes the tab for the rest, carefully folding the bill in her expense book. We go back to their van parked in town, and they follow me to my house to unload. "Nice place," Billy comments. "Reminds me of some of the old Victorians in the California wine country."

I show them around the house, and they settle in with their things, appropriating the dining room table as their work station. Jim has brought little and stakes claim to a rocking chair on the gallery, smoking a cigar and scanning my appeal, while the others unpack.

From the living room window I see Byars's car around the curve in my driveway. He pulls to a stop, eyes glued on Jim. I fear a rude confrontation and go outside. Lily emerges from the car, fluttering close to Byars's side as they mount the stairs. Byars is dressed is his summer blue seersucker suit, and a red tie splits a snow-white shirt. Lily is adorned in a yellow organdy dress with ruffles around the skirt.

"Hi," I call. "Come on in. Jim, my parents, Lily and Byars Bingham." I'm uncomfortable, hemmed in an awkward situation.

Jim rises and offers his hand. Byars hesitates a beat, then shakes it. Jim senses this bigotry like a dirty smell and draws into himself.

"How do you do?" Lily greets Jim, extending her gloved hand. "You're here to help Leona?"

Jim nods. Beers in hand, the others saunter out to the gallery, and I introduce them. Byars glances from Karen to Jim and back again. These two bright people have done much more with their lives than Byars has with his.

Byars nervously jangles change in his pants pocket. "We just wanted to see how you are, Leona. Lily and I are fixing to go to Memphis to a party at the Claibornes'. We'll be back late."

"Is everything all right?" Lily glances uneasily at the front door as if trying to see inside the house, likely wondering where all these people are staying. "I just worry so."

I assure her everything is fine, although I don't know that is true. "We're about to settle in and go to work."

Lily fidgets with the safety catch on her gold and diamond bracelet that once belonged to my grandmother. "I hope y'all can help Leona, set that young man free. Do you think you can?"

I can see Karen wrestling with the type of vague question I'm accustomed to from Lily. "We're here to do what we can." She speaks with enough effort to burn calories. "Who knows how it'll all shake loose?"

"Oh, Lordy, I'd hate to see the young man executed for something he didn't do," Lily says. "Leona thinks he's innocent. She's always right about things like that." Lily floats down the stairs like a reluctant bride. I'm sure the group thinks they've bumped into the middle of a Tennessee Williams tale.

Byars opens the car door and looks back at me. Spears of sunlight pierce through the leaves of the towering oak tree, haloing Byars's entire body. For an instant he appears to be some deity. "You take care now, Leona."

Just as they depart, Wilma Ruth chugs into the driveway in her truck and kills the engine. She has picked up Bingo at school. He hauls out, dragging his backpack, eyes on the newcomers on the gallery. He wasn't thrilled by Charles's intrusion into our household, and now four strangers are camped here.

"Hi, Bingo." I bend to his level and give him a hug he doesn't return. He's stiff as a wooden toy soldier. "Come meet the lawyers who're here to help me with my case."

"Afternoon, Leona," Wilma Ruth says, sidling up to Bingo. She gives him a look and a prod toward the gallery. They've obviously discussed the home situation. "Ray Bell's not back from across the river. Those winding Arkansas roads sure slow you down. Don't reckon he'll be back till dark." She's speaking to me but watching the lawyers.

I introduce everyone, and Bingo goes inside for a snack. Wilma Ruth offers to do some baking since I have "company," as she puts it. I thank her, saying we've stocked the larder.

"Well, I best be getting on home to fix Ray Bell's supper. Nice seeing y'all. Let me know how I can help with Bingo."

After she leaves, I pop in to see to Bingo. Cookie in hand, he's prowling the house, checking out the group's gear strewn over the downstairs. Not an inch of space remains on the cluttered dining room table. The kitchen table is covered with bulging grocery sacks yet to be unpacked.

"Jeez! I'm like, where do I do my homework? You said you'd get me a desk for my room. I need one."

"Stop whining," I snap, and immediately regret it. "Come on, we'll go over to the Big House and get you a desk out of the attic. I know Lily has one."

I tell the others we'll be back shortly and to make themselves at home. Bingo and I race to the Bronco and drive to the house. Julius is off for the night, and I use my key to let us inside.

We climb the stairs to the musty attic, and to my surprise the cobwebs are gone, along with most of the old furniture Lily stored there for so many years. Suddenly it dawns on me that Estelle has probably confiscated the pieces for her new store.

In a far corner I spot four legs peeping from under a sheet. I walk over and jerk off the dust covering. "*Voilà*, Bingo. This is perfect." The small writing desk was in the guest room before Lily redecorated years ago. "Give me a hand. You get on one end, and I'll get on the other. It's not heavy, just unwieldy."

We bumble down the stairs, trying not to nick walls, and shove the desk in the Bronco. I go back, lock the front door, and drive home slowly so as not to topple the desk.

Jim leaves the gallery and helps with Bingo's new piece of furniture. A wall in Bingo's room is perfect, and an armchair from the dining room fits exactly. Bingo takes a seat, trying out the arrangement. He pulls on the small drawers.

"Hey, they're locked."

I run my hands under the desk, hoping a key is taped there. "No key. You don't really need the drawer space."

"Yes, I do," Bingo protests, irritable as an old curmudgeon.

"The locks don't look too sturdy. Maybe you can pick them," Jim suggests with a sly smile.

"Yeah." Bingo grins, liking the challenge. "Ray Bell could probably help me if I can't do it."

Karen calls from downstairs. "Leona, while you were gone, Tarsha telephoned. Judge Allen called your office and left his number. Wants you to call."

Little arrows of anxiety prickle my skin as I hurry downstairs. I feel hot and cold at the same time. Taking the number from Karen, I dial Judge Allen's office in Jackson. His secretary immediately puts me through to him. As I listen to his words, the quartet of lawyers gathers around me, anxious eyes searching my face for a clue.

I replace the phone with a shaking, clammy hand. "Bad news. Bad."

12

I DROP KAREN, TARSHA, AND BINGO AT THE TERMI-
nal and wheel around the concrete ramps at the Jackson Airport to the long-term parking. After driving
around in circles, I finally find a slot. Gathering my
carry-on luggage, I trudge back in the staggering heat
to the entrance. The sliding door opens, and I greet
the cool air with a welcome relief.

My group wants to buy magazines for the trip to
New Orleans, and I'll meet them at the departure
gate. Passengers are lined up in front of the airline
counters. There's an air of excitement and frustration
among the travelers. Porters push through the maze
with luggage piled high on carts. A harsh but almost
inaudible voice announces flights over the intercom. I
feel out of place amidst the hustle and bustle of the
airport, accustomed as I am to a place that drips with
the slowness of molasses. I realize what a small-town
person I've become.

I pass through security and settle in the crowded lounge area by the gate. Glancing around at the people waiting to board, I think about the awful telephone call that has brought me to this point.

Judge Allen's swift denial of Weldon's appeal, without calling for a hearing, made the front page of the *Clarion-Ledger*. A picture of Attorney General Flannery claiming another victory also appeared. I felt inadequate, defeated by the powers of justice and paranoid at the thought that Judge Andrew Allen, Governor Robert Danforth, and Attorney General Jack Flannery Sr. might be in cahoots.

The appellate group tried to relieve me of these notions with special assurance that I had done fine work with the appeal. The sympathetic but serious legal eagles, Karen and Jim, my staunchest supporters, are my favorites. Billy Boyer, witty and easygoing, wins Bingo's vote hands down. And if I was in deep trouble, Samuel Zachariah is the tough, unyielding lawyer I'd want on my side.

Judge Allen's clerk informed us that their office had faxed a copy of his order to the Fifth Circuit Court of Appeals in New Orleans. After some revisions and polishing, we faxed Weldon's appeal to that court and Fed-Exed the original, then filed with the U.S. Supreme Court death clerk.

The scene in my office two days later is as clear in my head as if it were happening now. The clerk of the Fifth Circuit of Appeals calls from New Orleans. All work in the room ceases immediately.

"Good morning, Leona Bingham here." I try to sound cheerful, crazily hoping that might have some effect on the court when I know I'm talking only to a clerk who has no influence on decisions whatsoever.

He identifies himself in a pleasant manner I take as a good omen, though I can't imagine why. "Your appeal has been received and is assigned to a panel of three circuit court judges. The judges have discussed the petition and want to hear oral arguments from both sides."

My heart flutters at the thought of standing before three strange judges, trying to defend my appeal while the attorney general looks on and waits to jump on his chance before the panel. Is this a good or bad sign? Have I finally caught the attention of sympathetic judges, or is this a formality? "That's certainly agreeable with me. When?"

"Day after tomorrow at two o'clock."

The time frame sends me into a mental spin. How will I ever be ready on such short notice? My hands start to sweat, and I hold the receiver tighter. "That's fine. I'll be there." I begin to make travel arrangements in my head. I'll fly. It's too far to drive and I need the time to prepare. I'll drive to Jackson and fly from there.

The clerk continues, "Ordinarily, the court doesn't hear oral arguments in the afternoon, but because of the time factor here in this case they decided to schedule a special hearing. I assume you have a copy of the Fifth Circuit's rules governing oral arguments."

Holding my hand over the receiver, I ask Karen if they have a copy of the court's rules. She nods and I return to the call. "Yes, sir, I do."

"Fine, then. Two o'clock sharp."

After the conversation the group and I jump into a discussion, all talking at once. Ray Bell's entrance breaks up the conference. He greets the group, with whom he's now become familiar. They tear their eyes away from the legal pads and the computer long enough to acknowledge him. Half-eaten sandwiches, doughnuts, and cups full of cold coffee litter the tables.

Settling into a chair, he makes his report after I explain what has transpired. "I'm getting nowhere fast with Hot Springs diamonds. They're just too common."

I air my new theories and suspicions of Louella and Ronnie Fletcher. "I know you've checked them out, but maybe there's something you missed about them." Driving down two lanes, legal and investigative, plays havoc with my concentration.

"Well, there's no way I could ever get a look at her bank records without a court order, and your suspicion that she might have paid for Weldon's defense certainly isn't grounds. What if she did pay J. Clyde Perkins? Weldon was her lover, and she was trying to help him. What does that prove?"

I'm on edge, and his words hit me wrong, irritate me like a fingernail on a chalkboard. "You're the detective. Tell me why the trouble was taken to keep the payments secret then, paying with a cashier's check without a remitter's name? Louella wasn't married to Ronnie Fletcher at the time."

"I'll do what I can with it, Leona."

I'm immediately sorry for being so brusque. He's working for free, and I'm behaving as if I have him on an expensive retainer. "I know you will. It's just that we can't seem to get any kind of break anywhere. Every new idea, every legal angle, runs us right into a brick wall."

My flight is called and I rise, wondering if I'm heading into another brick wall in New Orleans. I glance down the corridor, expecting to see Bingo, Tarsha, and Karen hurrying toward the departure gate. I experience a moment of panic when I don't spot them in the crowd. We cannot miss this flight. The next one will put us in New Orleans too late to make the hearing. Has something happened to them?

I have an urge to break into a run to the newsstand when I see them passing through security. I wave them forward angrily and we board the plane, settling into our seats.

The flight to New Orleans takes less than an hour. We drink bitter canned orange juice and nibble on stale sweet rolls. I've barely slept since the call from the court clerk and my eyes feel full of sand, but I'm as primed and ready as I will ever be to deliver my oral arguments.

Knowing the ropes, Karen has come along as support and to assist in any way possible, thanks to her public funding. Tarsha wanted to go so badly, I didn't have the heart to deny her a ticket, which I paid for out of my pocket. Although Wilma Ruth offered to keep Bingo, I felt I've worn out my welcome with her and was afraid to leave him behind with the three male lawyers who are busy on the next appeal in case this one brings no relief. I didn't want to impose on family, so I took Bingo out of school for a trip I think will be good for him.

He enjoys the bumpy plane ride, thinking of it as a first since he was too young to remember our transoceanic flight back home from Paris. The stewardess gives him a pin of wings from the pilot, and I attach it to his white dress shirt. He unbuckles his seat belt like a seasoned veteran as we pull into the gate.

We grab our carry-on luggage and scramble through the crowded airport to the taxi stands on the sidewalk. It has rained earlier, and the sun now turns the city into a sauna. We pile into a cab, and Tarsha and Bingo marvel at the lush palm and banana trees they've never before seen. As we pass the Superdome, Bingo is smashed against the window, trying to get a good view of the stadium he's seen on television on Super Bowl Sunday.

We cruise down Canal Street, the main thoroughfare, and turn into the French Quarter. Even at this hour we hear Dixieland and jazz coming from the bars. The driver stops in front of our quaint hotel, and we check into our rooms, Tarsha and Karen sharing, Bingo and I together. He wanted his own room, but I explained that we have to shave expenses, to say nothing of leaving an eight-year-old alone in a hotel in the Big Easy, sin capital of the South.

After freshening up—a change into an unwrinkled navy suit for me—we catch another cab to the building on Camp Street that houses the Fifth Circuit Court Appeals. Rows of steps, flanked by tall, impressive Greek columns, lead to the front entrance.

Clutching my briefcase, I tell my escorts, "I've heard people say they have butterflies in their stomachs. I think I have angry wasps and bees in mine."

"You can handle it," Karen assures me. "Try to relax. Remember the drills and rehearsals and all the preparations you've been through. Just get up there and dazzle them."

"Yes," Tarsha says, her eyes bright with excitement.

"Are you gonna get a grade on your work like in school?" Bingo questions.

"Not exactly, but performance counts," I answer.

We find the clerk's office on the first floor. Mr. Robertson is a courteous, diminutive man who reminds me of a strutting bantam rooster. He registers me as counsel and reviews the rules, then asks if we'd like a tour since we're early.

We follow him down the marble corridor to the courtrooms, passing the judges' offices and those of their staffs. The hall is lined with portraits of past justices, probably all now deceased.

"Maybe you'd like to see the En Banc courtroom," the clerk suggests. "The Fifth Circuit Court has fifteen judges, and sometimes the entire body sits en banc on a case, but usually the appeals are assigned to a three-judge panel, as yours is."

The huge room is both impressive and frightening. The judges' bench, fifteen chairs in a semicircle, is built high above the room and the podium where the lawyers plead their cases. Our voices echo in the vast area. Tremendous decisions have taken place here, I realize with awe. Bingo yells a time or two, enjoying the echo of his voice. I hush him, and we proceed to the courtroom where I will plead my case to the three-judge panel.

This courtroom is smaller but similar in layout.

The spectators' section, where Karen, Tarsha, and Bingo will sit and observe the action, is to the rear. We pass through the bar and to the podium where I will station myself after being called from the audience. I present my case first and have a time limit of twenty minutes. Twenty tiny, fleeting minutes in which to try to save Robert Weldon.

The clerk points at a doodad on the podium. "I'm sure you're aware that this is the timer. Twenty minutes," he says in an ominous tone. "When the green light goes on, you begin your presentation. The yellow comes on as a warning time is almost up, and when the red flashes, you must stop even if you're in the middle of a sentence and sit down."

"Which judges do we have today?" Karen asks.

"Magruder, Garrard, and Nabors." The clerk rubs his hands together as if washing without water. "I'll be in my office if you need me. We have a library here on the second floor if you need to use it, a waiting area with rest rooms down the hall." Shooting his cuffs, he checks his watch. "You don't have much time, but be sure you're in here by ten or five till two."

"I think we'll just sit down now and wait," I say. "Like you said, there's not much time left."

"Well, good luck to you," he says in parting.

We take seats on the hard benches, and Karen talks about the judges. "Magruder is a tough old bird but fair. Garrard is a screaming liberal, but we drew Nabors. She's a woman, a good one, and I believe she's secretly against the death penalty. If any one of them will lean toward our side it'll be Nabors." She brings me up to date on the judges' backgrounds.

Bored, Bingo kicks the bench in front of us, and Tarsha makes him stop. "Don't make noise in here. Don't you see it looks like a church, all these pews."

The double doors to the courtroom open, allowing harsh sunlight to spill into the room. Squinting, we turn to see the new arrivals. Attorney General Flannery and his staff of five enter like conquering heroes ready for another battle. Mr. Jack pauses by my bench to shake hands with me. We toss around a few banalities, and he joins his warriors on the first row behind the bar. I'm suddenly reminded of the school debate long ago when I reigned over his son while Mr. Jack looked on disappointedly. Now the father is my opponent in a debate much more crucial.

I take deep breaths, trying to relax. I feel the need to use the rest room, but it's too late now to leave. I keep reminding myself that this ordeal is only twenty minutes, that I can endure almost anything for that length of time. What can the judges do to me? Kill me right on the podium? Hit me with their gavels? Intimidate me? Yes! In front of everyone.

I take out my notes and review them. The words blur before my eyes. Can I remember the lines when I'm at the podium? Will my mind desert me like an Alzheimer's patient? I try to center on Weldon and imagine *his* anxiety at what is about to take place. He is getting the court's undivided attention for twenty whole minutes, and I have to make the best of it.

The back doors open again, and I turn around, shocked to the core. J. Clyde Perkins pauses in the entrance. The sight of him scares me beyond belief.

Why is *he* here? He parades down the aisle, giving me a sly smirk and an evil eye as he passes. I can smell his cologne in his wake.

"Is that a bad man?" Bingo asks. "He gave you a mean look."

I grab Tarsha's arm. "Know who that is? J. Clyde Perkins."

Tarsha's eyes almost pop from their sockets. "My God! What's he doing here? I can't believe I'm in the same room with him." She whirls around to Karen. "Know who that man is?"

Karen nods.

A rumble at the front of the room quickly draws my attention. The court crier materializes behind the bench. "Hear ye, hear ye. This court is now in session." I can hardly believe he actually said that, thought such language was abolished years ago.

Three somber judges in black robes enter, burdened with files, their faces masks of restraint. They settle in gigantic leather chairs high on the podium. Nabors, the woman, sweeps over courtroom with evaluating eyes. A few spectators slip into the benches, along with individuals I peg as reporters.

Weldon's case is called. I rise on weak knees and walk through the gate in the bar. Attorney General Flannery is right behind me. His assistants remain seated.

The presiding judge is the Honorable James Garrard from Louisiana. Judge Ida Nabors hails from Texas, and Judge Gordon Magruder is from Alabama. Judge Garrard dons horn-rims, pushes them up on his nose, and fastens his attention on me. "Miz Leona

Bingham representing Robert Weldon. Are you ready to proceed?"

"Yes, Your Honor."

"Step to the podium, then, please."

I walk with all the authority I can muster and take my place. The green light flashes on. For an instant I'm paralyzed, then regain control. I move directly into an attack on J. Clyde Perkins's ineffectual representation of Robert Weldon. I know he's behind me, eyes burning holes into my back. Making eye contact with each judge in order of the seating, I quickly cover the material submitted in my brief. They've read that, so I don't want to linger. Along the way I find my voice and continue in a strong, clear tone. I insist that because of J. Clyde Perkins's unfortunate and unwise advice my client unwillingly followed that proper justice was not rendered, that had my client been allowed a voice in court the verdict in all probability would have been different. I accuse J. Clyde Perkins of not giving adequate time and thought to Robert Weldon's case by advising him so recklessly not to testify in his own behalf. I contend that because Robert Weldon wasn't allowed to testify that he didn't receive a fair trial. This draws frowns from the judges, and I know to steer clear of the subject, as I am on the border of bleeding one claim into another. Ineffectual counsel and not receiving a fair trial do not go hand in hand.

"Robert Weldon was denied his day in court, and now at this belated hour I must become his voice . . . for twenty minutes." I put passion into the plea. "Robert Weldon was a mechanic, a good one, and had

he spoken for himself the jury would have heard in
his own words that the day of murder he was on his
way home to repair his car and happened on the
wrong place at the wrong time. He might have been
able to put doubt in the jurors' minds about the police
mechanic's testimony that nothing was wrong with
Weldon's car when he examined it. Maybe there was
nothing amiss with the car at that point. Maybe someone repaired the car in the interim to make Robert
Weldon a scapegoat." I suggest that if these words
and many others had come from Robert Weldon's
mouth in front of a jury, they would have reasonable
doubt about his guilt.

The judges are not only listening but paying rapt
attention. I almost believe Judge Nabors nods imperceptibly, but know she's far too experienced for such
a gesture. The yellow light flashes, and I'm almost
out of time with so much still unsaid. Again, I berate
J. Clyde Perkins's poor judgment and lack of proper
advice to his former client. If Perkins has been behind
a part of what has happened to me, made good on his
threat I'd be sorry if I claimed ineffectual counsel, he
will now probably kill me on the spot.

Knowing the red light will flash at any second and
not wanting to be caught in mid-sentence, I thank the
judges for their time and return to my seat. I feel on
the verge of collapse. This is behind me now. I did
the best I could, and it wasn't bad. I didn't falter. I
didn't lose my breakfast on the podium. I slapped
some facts at the judges. I take a deep breath. It's
Attorney General Flannery's turn.

With poise and authority Mr. Jack takes the podium.

He smiles with familiarity at the judges. Again my paranoia takes hold. Is this one great conspiracy here? Perkins is present. Is he a part of it? Are they going to bash an upstart for trying to tarnish an important power in legal circles?

My eyes are fastened onto Mr. Jack, his body language, his expression. I drink in every word that emanates from him. He is deliberate, unemotional and well prepared. With O. J. Simpson topping the list, he cites a long list of defendants who were accused of heinous crimes, advised by counsel not to take the stand, and were subsequently exonerated. The existing law is on his side and that of defense counsels. He touches on all the points in Weldon's case that provided the jury the evidence required to convict. From my vantage point I can't see the timer, but know his time is drawing to an end when he closes his file. "Thank you for your time and effort," he says, and saunters triumphantly back to his seat.

Judge Garrard emphasizes the urgency of the case and assures us that a ruling will be handed down soon. He bangs his gavel, and noise erupts in the courtroom.

Reporters rush to the attorney general and several surround me. "No comment at this time," I say, and head to the back of the room where my camp awaits. Before I can reach them, J. Clyde Perkins moves from his bench into the aisle, blocking my way. The urge to run around him is almost overpowering. He stands his ground. I halfway expect him to sock me on the jaw or worse, right here in the courtroom.

A twinkle of humor plays in his eyes. "So, we meet

again, L. Bingham. Disregarding the subject matter, I'd have to compliment you on your performance."

I'm staggered. "Thank you," I almost stammer. I start to leave, then turn back, gathering courage. I have just one shot at him. "Who paid you, Mr. Perkins?"

His eyebrows lift, but he's controlled. "Oh, first you think I'm ineffectual, and now you think me unethical. You know that's privileged information."

"Time is running out. I don't want an innocent man to die, and if I knew who paid you it might shed some light on the case."

"I thought you might know by now who paid me. You've obviously somehow uncovered the fact that I didn't take the case pro bono. That's pretty good detective work." He pauses. "Since you haven't discovered it yet, let me assure you that the identity of the person who paid my fee has no bearing whatsoever on Robert Weldon's guilt or innocence. It was simply an act of kindness."

I'm taken aback. He seems to have an art for this. "But why would someone pay for Weldon's defense? It has to be important."

He shrugs. "I believe your plate is full enough without wasting energy on that subject."

Again, I turn to leave. In his own way he's given me all I'm going to get. "Miz Bingham?"

"Yes?" I face him.

"If you ever decide not to bury your talents in Grenola, come and see me." He breaks into a sly smile. "You've got balls."

He's knocked the breath out of me. I want to yell

"Wow" and hear it echo in the courtroom. I want to call the attorney general over and have Perkins repeat what he's said. I actually laugh and say, "Thanks."

I'm walking taller as I cover the ground to the front door. Floating is more accurate.

"You were stone good," Tarsha exclaims. "What was Perkins saying to you? Threatening you again?"

"Mom, I was scared for you, but I didn't have to be. I didn't know you could do that, talk that way in front of so many people."

"You made an impression." Karen is not one for easy compliments, but she approves of my delivery.

Outside on the courthouse steps, I relay what Perkins said. We speculate about who paid his fee, at a complete loss as to the motivation of someone to fork over a fortune for Weldon's defense.

"You gonna take him up on his offer? Take me along if you are." Tarsha is all smiles.

We grab a cab back to the French Quarter. While we're here we've promised ourselves a miniature vacation of sorts. For the first time in weeks I feel safe, released from some dark threat. Along with masses of tourists, we stroll along the cobblestone streets of Royal, passing strip joints, antique shops, bars, and funky restaurants. Karen has seen it all, but Tarsha and Bingo gawk at the sights.

We pop into an oyster bar that opens onto a courtyard. We sit at a round iron table in the bright sun and order oysters on the half shell and Dixie beers. Bingo munches on a hamburger while we dip fat oysters in red cocktail sauce blended with horse-radish, Tabasco, and lemon juice. I haven't felt this serene in so long, and I savor the moment, knowing it can't last.

Tarsha's eyes dance with excitement. "I've never been here, and I want to cram everything in today. I've heard about Jackson Square, where the artists paint, and the Café du Monde, where they serve those square powdery doughnuts whose name I can't pronounce and chicory coffee."

"The River Walk is the place to see, all the shops, right on the Mississippi," Karen says.

Just listening makes me tired. "You guys go have at it. All I want to do is fall across the bed in the hotel until dinner."

"I don't want to go back to that ratty old hotel all afternoon," Bingo says. "I want to go with them and see stuff."

"I don't blame you, kiddo." Tarsha looks at me. "We'll take him along. Show him what's missing in Grenola."

I give Bingo money to sightsee and buy souvenirs, and we part company after lunch. I amble back to the hotel, enjoying the scenery, still savoring Perkins's words of praise, but savagely curious about who might have paid him and why. I pass through the small lobby and cross the lushly landscaped courtyard centered in the two-story building. Guests languish in the garden setting, some sipping pink concoctions in tall, curved glasses. Hurricanes, they're called. After a nap I'll come back for one before dinner.

I shower, slip into a blue silk robe I haven't worn for years, and slump on the bed like a person without bones. The unaccustomed beer at lunch works like a sleeping pill, or maybe it's exhaustion, but I know I'm drifting when a curl of drool slips onto my soft pillow.

Perkins is standing in the distance, and someone behind a curtain is handing him stacks of money. Perkins smiles and starts to chomp on the bills as if they were a bar of candy. I try to see around the curtain, but I'm unable to move close enough. My feet are stuck to the ground. I lean forward and my legs stretch like rubber, letting me come closer and closer to the person behind the curtain. Just as I'm about to peep around the edge of the curtain, the elasticity in my legs shreds and pops. From the force, I'm squashed into a ball and I roll off into infinity.

The phone breaks my dream, and I bolt up, dry-mouthed and disoriented. The slant of the sun through the curtains tells me it's late afternoon. I pick up the receiver.

"Hello."

The silence stabs me wide awake. "Hello," I bark again, supposing the hotel operator might have disconnected the party; then I hear someone breathing on the other end. "If you've bothered to call, why don't you say something?" I wait. Nothing. "Coward," I yell, and slam down the receiver.

I brush my teeth in the bathroom and throw water on my face. Hurrying back to the bedside table, I dial the operator. "This is Leona Bingham in Room 120. I just had a telephone call, but it didn't go through."

"Yeah?"

"They had to have asked for me. Can you tell me if it was a man or a woman?"

"Couldn't say with all the calls coming through. Sorry." She disconnects.

I light a cigarette and think about the call. Somebody has tracked me here, extending the harassment. I long for this to be over and come through in one piece. I'm determined not to let it ruin my one night away from home.

After applying makeup and taming my hair, I slip into a black linen dress with white buttons the size of coasters. I put on a pearl choker, matching earrings, black high-heeled patent leather shoes, and spray on perfume I've saved for a special occasion. I unload my business bag and stuff the contents into a square patent leather bag that matches my shoes. I look in the mirror and give myself an A in Chic 101. The Hurricane drink will quench my thirst.

Seated at a corner table in the courtyard where I can watch for Bingo and his two companions, I decide on a martini rather than the touristy Hurricane. It matches my mood, *très elegante*. My area of the courtyard is partially hidden from the crowd by surrounding tropical foliage, but the view of the patrons from this side is unobstructed.

I cross my legs, light a cigarette, and sip a frosty martini that seems to take the enamel off my teeth. I glance across the expanse of the courtyard, examining the faces of the customers. Most are in pairs, a few foursomes, several by themselves. My eyes suddenly grab on a lone man. I can't believe what I see. My face turns hot from a rush of adrenaline. I set my glass on the table, afraid my fingers may pop the stem. I lean back as far as I can in my chair, hoping the palm trees

will shade my face enough to make it indistinguish-
able. I want to slither away from the area, but there's
no escape without attracting attention. I stub out my
cigarette in the ashtray, ready to make some move.

He sees me. He glances away, then looks again,
recognition dawning. He isn't sure, considering if I
might only remind him of someone. Trying to disguise myself, I hold a hand to my forehead like
Rodin's sculpture of the man thinking. Out of my
periphery vision I see him stand, looking directly at
me. Hang on, Leona, I tell myself.

Jean-Paul Patel approaches like one would with a
strange dog. He cranes forward slightly, shielding his
sapphire blue eyes with a hand. He wears a dark
double-breasted suit with the smallest of pinstripes,
very expensive tailoring. His blue silk tie and matching foulard flowing from his pocket no doubt came
from Charvet in Paris, the Gucci loafers tooled in
Italy. "Leona? Is that you?" His accent is mellow as
honey.

I glance at him as if I don't recognize the face,
then decide to play it straight, cut the games. "Jean-
Paul. What a surprise."

Bending, he air-kisses me on both cheeks, Conti-
nental style. "This is marvelous. May I?" He waves a
palm at the chair.

"Of course, please sit." I'm glad I've dressed with
meticulous care.

He waves over a waiter. "Would you be so kind as
to bring my champagne from the other table?" He
glances at my drink. "I see you still drink martinis.
Another?"

"Yes, I'll have another. And no, I don't drink them often anymore."

I study him quickly as he settles in the chair across from me. My heart is in my throat. I'm actually facing the man who captured my soul. His curly dark hair is threaded with some gray. In a sitting position the bulge around his waist is obvious, hidden in a standing position by the expert cut of his coat. Slight pouches in the embryo stage semicircle his lower lids. Too much rich food and booze and too little exercise have taken their toll. He's still handsome, but his looks won't hold another decade.

He strikes a pose I remember, head tilted to the side, one finger touching the side of his patrician nose. "So what are you doing in New Orleans? Do you live here?"

I pray my voice won't crack when I speak. "No, I'm a lawyer. I'm representing a client in the Fifth Circuit Court here." I feel important, not at all the girl he rejected for a more suitable choice. "I remember that you have family here that you visit."

"Yes, I've come to see them." He raises his hands, palms up. "My, you're a lawyer. Fascinating, Leona. You must tell me all about yourself. You're married, of course, a beauty like you."

I consider lying. "No, I never married." I take a cigarette from the package on the table. He's quick with a gold lighter. "Oh, there's not much to tell." Oh, there's so much he'll never know. Bingo will bound through the front door at any time. I cringe at the thought that the two will come face-to-face, that Jean-Paul will figure out my son's heritage. "I got my degree from law school and practice in Grenola. Work pretty much all the time now on this certain case. And you?"

"Still with my father's brokerage house, but I do travel quite a bit. I've discovered Hong Kong." He sips his flute of champagne the waiter has brought. He's ordered a whole bottle of Dom Perignon, and it rests in a silver cooler on a stand by the table. He seems so extravagant, so self-indulgent. I can't believe I ever enjoyed the same kind of life.

I can't resist. "And Michelle?"

"My wife?" He asks as if he didn't have one. "Michelle." He flips his hand and grunts in that typical French way. "Michelle is . . . Michelle. She goes her own way. I go mine. I like it that way."

Jack would never say such a thing about me if we were married, not even to his closest friend, much less a stranger, which is what I am. I drag on my cigarette, thinking there's nothing like seeing an old flame in the flesh to extinguish the fire in the imagination. This man has been blocking my way to Jack. What a fool I am. I lost Jack once over this man and could have lost him a second time.

"All of a sudden you're very quiet, Leona, pensive. What are you thinking? Is it what I'm thinking? We're here alone. Ah, I have so many memories of the past, of you." He reaches over and takes my hand. "This is like a miracle. Let's be together again, capture what we had."

I slip my hand from his. "It's not possible. We didn't have anything." He has occupied so much space in my mind, and now I've deleted him just as

I've seen Karen erase a computer file with a keystroke.

"Mom!" I turn when I hear Bingo. Trust him to spot me here in the secluded space.

A look of amazement crosses Jean-Paul's face. "But I thought you said—"

"I never married, but I have a son."

Bingo bolts from Karen and Tarsha and crosses the patio to the table. "We had a great time. We bought like all these souvenirs." His eyes travel to Jean-Paul.

"Bingo, this is an old friend of mine, Mr. Patel. Jean-Paul, my son, Bingo." My son and his father will never know who they just met.

Jean-Paul offers his hand, and Bingo shakes it; then Jean-Paul stares at him with a strange curiosity, examining his face. I rummage in my purse and drop a ten-dollar bill on the table to cover my first drink. Jean-Paul can pick up the tab for my second.

I stand. "We have to go to dinner. It was nice to see you."

As Bingo turns to leave, Jean-Paul asks, "How old is your son?"

"Seven," I answer, and quickly move Bingo across the patio.

"Mom!" He grouses when we're safely out of earshot. "Why did you tell that man I was seven? You know I'm eight."

"I guess I forgot. You're growing so fast."

Tarsha and Karen have gone to freshen up for the evening, and I take Bingo to the room to do the same. While he's bathing, I dial Jack. He answers on the first ring.

"I just called to say I missed you."

"Well, thanks." He sounds surprised. "I miss you. I just got in from the office."

I can picture him loosening his tie, ready to settle into his favorite chair with a glass of wine or one of his famous margaritas. The scene feels good to me, warm and safe. And, above all, exciting. "Jack, I did okay today. I didn't flub up my lines or anything."

"Beat up on old Dad, huh?"

"I don't know about that, but I held my own."

"That makes me real proud."

"Jack, I'm coming back tomorrow."

"I know. What time do you think you'll get in?"

"You're missing the point. I'm coming back to you. Really coming back. We have something precious between us that I never want to let go of again."

13

WE ARRIVE IN GRENOLA BY MID-AFTERNOON AND
bring the guys up to date on the trip. Everyone is still
puzzling over who paid Perkins and why. The mystery is deeper, more meaningful now that the bene-
factor is obviously someone in Grenola, someone I
know. I almost physically ache from the urgency to
find that person's identity. Will it ever be revealed? If
I went to work in Perkins's office, I could snoop
through his files and satisfy my curiosity in the future,
but I need to know *now*.

We work on the new motion for the remainder of
the day. Bingo plays with the computer, his newfound
knowledge compliments of a few tricks from Karen.
The group plans to spend a few hours this evening on
another case in Clarksdale, sixty miles away, and Jack
and I have plans.

My mind is not totally on business. I'm relieved
that the specter of Jean-Paul no longer blankets my

life. On the way to dinner last night I spied him leaving the courtyard bar with an attractive woman much too young for a man of his age. The way she clung to him told me she was not one of his American cousins. I shake my head, repulsed, yet sorry for him. He is one of those men who will always need his ego stroked by increasingly younger women. I hope the genes I've passed down to Bingo will overpower the ones Jean-Paul has contributed.

I grab my purse. "Let's go, Bingo. See the rest of you later tonight."

"We're ready to head out now," Karen says, packing her briefcase. "I'll lock the office door."

"Hey, Bingo," Billy Boyer calls. "Speaking of locks. I finally picked the ones on your desk drawers for you while you were gone."

"Yeah?" Bingo grins. "What with? I thought we'd tried everything."

"Karen's metal fingernail file."

"Thanks for plundering in my stuff," she says with a mock frown. "What else caught your interest?"

Billy rotates his hands, purses his lips, and draws out his words, "Ohhhhh. Lots. A little round plastic container with all these pills encased in plastic, days of the week marked—"

"Cut it, voyeur boy."

Birth-control pills, I think with a smile. It's hard to picture the efficient Karen with time for a sex life. From their looks I'd say it's hard for the others to imagine, too.

Bingo and I walk down the sidewalk to Estelle's shop. Charles is taking her and their children to the club for dinner and has invited us. Bingo will join them while I steal the chance for some time with Jack.

We pass under the aqua-and-white-striped awning fronting her place and enter. A little bell tinkles, old-fashioned style, announcing an arrival. Her showroom is filled with furniture I recognize from Lily's attic. The pieces have been dusted, cleaned of cobwebs, and polished to a glowing sheen with beeswax. Some have even been refinished by Estelle. Swatches of material line the counter, and books with pictures of items that can be ordered are stacked in an armoire. In a tie and navy blue sports coat, Charles is seated in one of the cozy arrangements Estelle has on display.

He rises. "How was New Orleans?"

"I think it went well."

"Mom talked in front of all these people without hardly ever taking a breath, and I got some souvenirs," Bingo adds.

"You think you're going to get a favorable decision in the court down there?" His eyes search my face.

"I'm hoping. I think one of the judges was slanting toward me. Where's Estelle?"

"In the stock room in back. She'll be right out." He looks around the area. "She did a good job, didn't she? You know, she's got two contracts to decorate already. The Greshams' old plantation house and a client in Memphis. Got a referral for that one from a fabric place up there where she trades." Pride is seeping to the surface, but I believe he's still ambivalent about her success as she slips from under his control.

"Leona, Bingo, hi." Estelle's voice rings with enthusiasm as she rounds the corner. "Like it?"

No longer is she the well-coiffed, expertly made-up, exquisitely dressed specimen encased untouchably in cellophane. She's a real working woman in sensible low-heeled shoes, a tailored gray skirt with pleats that add substance to her thin frame, a creamy silk blouse, a ropy gold necklace, and plain gold ear studs. Her hair is loose and flowing, as if she might have stood before a fan. Her makeup is faint but dramatic, highlighting her chiseled features, not covering them as before. Estelle is finally herself, and I think I might have had a hand in helping her find that person.

"You bowl me over more. I thought I was the pretty one in the family. Damn if you haven't taken over." I laugh, feeling good, feeling anxious to get to Jack.

"You still hold the award for guts. I could never stand up before a bunch of judges. Tell me about New Orleans."

I'd like to tell them about Perkins offer if I decide to leave Grenola, but I don't want to infringe on her new success. I touch on the high points of the trip, and maybe someday in private I'll tell Estelle about Jean-Paul.

"Is your investigator, Ray Bell, getting anywhere with the ring?" Charles asks, pronouncing "investigator" like a dirty word.

"No."

"I hope this Weldon appreciates how much you've done for him."

"It's done a lot for me, too, Charles."

Estelle checks her watch. "We'd better get going. The kids are meeting us at the club. Charles Junior has been chauffeuring them around now that he's got his license, and it makes me nervous. I asked Lily and Byars, but Byars is playing poker at Parker Brumfield's and Lily wanted to stay in." Estelle and I exchange knowing glances. Lily jumps into the booze when Byars is out. "I'll call you when we leave the club to make sure you're home. Probably around nine."

"I should be there, but if I'm not, the lawyer group will be. One of them, Billy Boyer, is teaching Bingo chess." I turn to my son. "Be polite."

"Mom!" He rolls his eyes.

I drive to Jack's, a warm coil of excitement glowing inside me. Kit is spending the night with a friend, and he's let his housekeeper off for the evening. He comes to the patio gate when he hears my car door slam. He's shed his office clothes for a light yellow golf shirt and slacks.

An expectant smile wreaths his face, tiny laugh lines crinkling around his eyes. He moves forward tentatively, almost awkwardly, not yet fully knowing how to interpret our phone conversation from New Orleans. He will not push, so I'll lead the way.

I reach under his arms, encircle his back, and pull him close, feeling his warmth, the strength in his muscles. Opening my lips, I fasten onto his, kissing him hard and deep, urgent and probing. I trap his bottom lip with my teeth, pulling, almost biting. Holding my face in his hands, he responds with zeal, kissing my face, my neck, hungry for the taste of me.

Locked together, we edge away from the gate and out of sight of neighbors. We stay pressed together against the patio wall, neither of us wanting to end the moment. I feel him growing hard and urgent, matching the throb deep inside me.

"Let's go upstairs," he says, his mouth to my ear.

We lock hands and he leads me up the stairs, pausing halfway to kiss again. He grabs my butt and kneads the cheeks, separates them, pulling me forward into his erection. I'm not sure we'll make the bed.

On the landing, we melt to the floor, grasping each other, pulling and writhing out of our clothes. He moves on top of me as I spread my legs and arch my body to meet him. I am wet as liquid velvet. He strokes in and out, fast, then slow, almost withdrawing. I shiver with a passionate agony, feeling that a fast freight is racing through me on a crash course with another train. I wait for the explosion when the two trains hit head-on. They're coming, coming, closer and closer to collision. The crash erupts in a shock wave. Rockets of fire generate through me. I gasp as we both reach the moment where nothing in the world can intrude or stop the action of that instant.

I feel the burn of the carpet on my back, the after tingle of sex in my lower body. Jack holds onto to me like a dying man clinging to life. We roll over, still joined but slippery, and I am on top. I look at his face, stare deeply into his eyes, as he does into mine. Without a word we both know something has passed between us we cannot deny.

"You are truly back to me." Jack pushes my hair off my forehead.

"I never really left, Jack, just strayed."

He smiles. "Want to stray to the shower? I believe I have some melting margaritas on the patio."

Passing through his bedroom, I glance at the wide walnut bureau, wondering if he's kept his wife's pictures on display. Why wouldn't he? She was his partner in life and Kit's mother. A silver framed photo of the three of them is set on one of the end tables flanking the king-size bed. The beige silk padded headboard matches the spread of their marital bed. I feel an irrational pang of jealousy that I wasn't always a part of his life. I could have been.

Uplifted, we laugh and joke in the shower, then towel dry and dress. I take one last look at the bedroom before we go downstairs, wondering if I will inhabit it until the day I die. These walls might have heard and seen too much, the ghosts of the past still lingering.

The margaritas have melted into watery slush, and Jack makes another batch at the drink cart on the patio while I smoke a cigarette. I glance up at the sky. A scent of ozone infiltrates the air, a barometer of a coming storm. The weatherman on the radio predicted thundershowers and high winds. My nose picks up something else.

"Jack, I smell something burning."

"Oh, Lord!" He throws up his hands and rushes to the kitchen.

I follow. The water for pasta has boiled away and scorched the pot. Luckily, he has not turned on the heat under the pan with the sauce. He grabs the pot by the handle with a pot holder, carries it to the sink, and fills it with cold water. Steam rises and the hot metal hisses. I laugh at his culinary abilities and taste the sauce with a wooden spoon.

"Jack, this sauce is store-bought. I at least thought I'd be worth homemade sauce."

"It's the best I could do on quick notice. Don't complain. I had enough trouble getting the lid off the sauce jar. It's adult-proof."

Seated at the center island, I help him with the salad while the new pot of water boils. "Tell me about New Orleans. Dad said you did a credible job."

"Credible? Just credible?"

Jack shrugs and samples his margarita. "His word. You know Dad, and I know Byars. Neither of us would put things the way they do."

"I guess J. Clyde Perkins thought I was a bit better than Mr. Jack did."

"He was there?"

I flick my ash into a ceramic dish Kit made at camp. "Yep. And he told me to come to see him if I decided not to bury my talents in Grenola. His words."

I detect a tiny alarm going off in Jack. Maybe Charles heard that same bell when Estelle announced she wanted to open her shop. "You'd actually consider a move to Memphis to work for Perkins?"

"Well, it was flattering. Me as a rainmaker." I take a drag, exhale, and watch the smoke dissipate. "Jack, somebody paid Perkins to defend Robert Weldon. A hundred and twenty-five grand. He didn't do it pro bono."

He frowns, raking back a stray lock of hair with his fingers. "How do you know that?"

He doesn't think much of Ray Bell, and it's my chance to change his mind. "You know, I do have an investigator. Ray Bell found out." I don't say how.

His eyes bat rapidly. "Who paid him? Why?"

"Got me on both questions. I tried the 'who' out on everybody possible, even people walking down the street." I add the last part to be cute and to lead into my next statement. "How about your dad?"

He looks at me with an incredulous expression. "Dad pay Perkins to defend a man he's prosecuting?"

"Told you I've tried it out on everybody." I hold up a finger. "First, whoever paid Perkins has plenty of money. Your dad fits there. Second, who benefited from Perkins's defense of Weldon? Your dad fits there. Beating the master catapulted your dad into state prominence, then into the A.G. office. You know, candidates spend lots of their own money on their campaigns. A well-placed hundred and twenty-five G's could be most beneficial to a career."

Jack scoffs at the suggestion, and I can't blame him. "If Dad did hire Perkins, he'd have no assurance he was going to win over him."

I don't answer that because I don't know what assurances Mr. Jack had, if any. "I'm just sending up scenarios and shooting holes in them, is all."

"And you've got Swiss cheese." Jack gives me an affectionate quick kiss, shaking his head. "Leona, Leona."

I set the table in the kitchen's bay window and we put dinner together. I twirl a wad of spaghetti on my fork. "Jack, I saw Jean-Paul in New Orleans."

His fork stops midway to his mouth. He looks at

me, then completes the bite, trying to remain casual. "Oh, so you two . . . what, had dinner or something?" His voice has a strange ring to it.

"A drink."

He toys with his utensils. "You knew he was going to be there?"

I continue to twirl my spaghetti, winding it until the strands are so tight they unravel. "No. He has relatives there he visits now and then. I just happened to run into him in the hotel bar. I introduced Bingo to him."

Jack is taken aback, his face clouding with concern. "You told him about Bingo? Leona, he could cause you some legal problems if he wanted to, rights to visit—"

"Jack, he asked how old Bingo was, and I told him he was seven."

He laughs out loud. "You're something else."

"Jean-Paul is something else. An puffy old fart with nothing left but a sexy accent."

We both laugh and dive into dinner.

Out of necessity, not want, I'm home before nine. The legal eagles are back and relaxing in the living room with beers. Karen says that Estelle called and is on the way with Bingo. She looks at me a touch curiously, and I wonder if she detects the glow I feel inside.

Jim pats the vacant cushion next to him on the sofa. "Come sit. Let's talk a minute."

Samuel Zachariah perches on the edge of a companion chair to the sofa as if ready to spring forward, his feet splayed outward at a balancing angle. Indian-style, Boyer sits with his back braced against the wall. I'm suddenly alert that something has arisen.

"Anything wrong?" Uneasy, I sit by Jim, eyeing each member in turn.

His demeanor stern as usual, Samuel takes the lead. "We were discussing this on the way home from Clarksdale. It's time to begin preparations to schedule a clemency hearing with the governor. The clock never stops ticking, and we're getting closer to Weldon's execution date."

His tone and words frighten me. "You don't think I did well enough in the Fifth Circuit Court?"

His hard eyes bore into me. I'd hate to meet him on the witness stand. "It's not you, it's the issues. The U.S. Supreme Court is, as you know from the death clerk's call, watching your case. They were also watching the case we're on in Clarksdale. You know only he U.S. Supreme Court can overturn a ruling from the Fifth Circuit Court. The lawyer in Clarksdale got a favorable ruling for his client from the Fifth Circuit, and the U.S. Supreme turned right around and overruled the decision, essentially divesting the Circuit of its power. Now, that leaves the Clarksdale lawyer with little time to schedule his clemency hearing for his death row client. It'll be a rushed-up affair with scant planning and little time for the governor to consider his decision. The high court makes it an easy call for him, if nothing else just to save face and a lot of controversy. He won't grant clemency. So if you want to rescue *your* client from the jaws of death, you can plead in the clemency hearing for the governor to commute Weldon's sentence to life. Given enough time with what you've already presented about the ineffectual counsel, he just might commute the sentence."

"I don't want his sentence commuted to life. I want him pardoned or at least granted a new trial." My voice is so strident even I wince at the sound.

"And I want to head a hundred-man law firm on Park Avenue and then I want to become the U.S. attorney general. What you want and what you get are two different things."

Samuel is tough and I admire that, but I don't have to like him. "If the ineffectual counsel claim doesn't work, what about my other petition that lethal injection is cruel and inhumane?"

"It's a valid argument, but unprecedented." He sighs and shakes his head. "I don't know."

Billy Boyer unfolds from his position and stands. "Look, it boils down now to trying to save the client's life. Sure, we can go on through the courts with the new claim if the ineffectual counsel doesn't work, but it's time to get prepared and schedule with the governor."

"Governor Danforth is an advocate of the death penalty," I tell them, as if they didn't already know. "He's also bucking for the black vote in this state. If he commutes a sentence of a white man convicted of murdering a black woman, he won't get that vote. Besides, he knows if he commutes one inmate's death sentence to life, he'll have all the others and their lawyers on him. I don't think I stand a chance."

"He may be your only chance," Jim adds. "Karen says you were very impressive before the judges.

Maybe you can make a dent on him by reciting all that's happened to you since you took on the case. Impress on him that someone wants the case dropped. That could give him pause."

Lights flash through the windows, and I hear a car pull into the driveway. I go out on the gallery as Bingo hops out of the car. I wave to Estelle and Charles, thanking them. I watch their taillights disappear around my driveway. The sky is without stars, and dark, angry clouds gather on the horizon. The storm is coming. Luckily, their house is only a half mile down the road from mine, and they'll make it home before the sky unleashes its torrent.

"Have a good time, Bingo?"

He nods. "I had a shrimp cocktail first and a steak. Charlie had a beer in the locker room, and he's not supposed to drink yet. Just 'cause he got his license he thinks he's hot shit."

"Bingo!"

His cheeks redden from the slip. "Sorry. Is Billy Boyer here? I want to play chess."

"Right inside," I answer, opening the front door. "They might be busy tonight, so don't bother them if they are, okay?"

"Billy, want to play some chess?"

"Not tonight, partner, I'm kind of swamped with work. Maybe tomorrow. No, we've got to go back to Clarksdale late tomorrow. Next day." He reaches into his knapsack and produces his cellular phone. "Here. Now that I've showed you how to use it, you can call some of your friends and talk. No long-distance, buddy. And don't forget to put it back."

Bingo goes upstairs, and we continue our heated discussion. I don't want to face the possibility of losing Weldon to the needle. A break in the case doesn't seem likely. My glow is gone, and I feel tired and haggard. I escape to the kitchen to make a pot of coffee. Clad in pajamas, Bingo moseys in, carrying a slip of paper.

"There wasn't any treasure or even any coins in my desk drawers, just this old paper. Want me to throw it away?"

I take the yellow slip from Bingo and glance at it, then stare with the intensity of a laser. The words seem to fly off the paper and hit me in the eyes. My brain is numb, unable to assimilate what I see. I'm shocked beyond all comprehension.

"Mom?"

I hear him, but his voice sounds as if he's in a tunnel. I can't answer.

He moves closer. "Mom? You okay?"

I grab my purse and car keys. "I have to go somewhere."

I race through the living room. "Keep an eye on Bingo. I'll be back as soon as I can."

I get out of the house before any questions are asked and jump into the Bronco. My hands shake so that I can barely stab the key in the ignition. Gunning the engine, I wheel around the driveway, kicking up gravel, which sounds like grease popping in a hot skillet.

I dig in my purse for a cigarette, grab the pack, and scatter the contents over the floor. Reaching down, I almost run into a ditch. I right the car and take deep breaths, trying to control my emotions and regain my senses. Heart pounding, I shiver like a malaria victim.

Managing to retrieve a cigarette, I light it and try to put answers to questions I don't yet understand. I'm frightened to even explore the dark possibilities. Just hold on, I tell myself. Maybe it's not as bad as I think. But how can it be anything else? I've finally stumbled across the evidence I feared, possibly something worse.

I roar down the long drive to the Big House, under the dark shadows of the towering trees, and screech to a halt at the front entrance. I flick the cigarette as far as I can through the open window. Almost falling as I get out, I yank my purse off the seat, lope up the steps, taking two at a time, and stab the doorbell repeatedly. I grab the brass lion's head knocker and slam it against the door.

Tearing at a hangnail with my teeth, I wait. Filled with impatience, I ball my hand into a fist and bang on the door. "Open up," I yell. "It's me, Leona. Open the door."

Julius is gone at this hour, but I hear footsteps drawing near. "Who's there?" Lily calls at the barrier between us.

"It's me, Leona. I need to talk to you."

"Well, hold your horses, will you?" I hear her fumbling with the big locks and bolts.

The thick carved door opens. Devoid of makeup, Lily looks like a small ghost in a flowing white robe and gown. "Is something wrong, Leona?" Thankfully, her words are not slurred, but she's definitely been drinking.

"Yes, I believe so." I move inside. "I need to tell you something."

"Why don't we go back to the den?" Without expression she stares at me, then turns and drifts down the hall.

She slides onto a bar stool where a glass of amber liquid is waiting for her return. She reaches out for the glass, and for the first time I notice how old her hands are, little claws actually, liver-spotted and withered skin. The gloves she so often wears are not pretentious, just a disguise. I suddenly feel very sorry for her and what she's about to hear. I've judged her harshly in the past without consideration of what she might have had to endure, never once putting myself in her shoes. If she has any inkling, she's carried it off well by concealing it with vague behavior.

I lay the yellow slip before her. "Look at this."

She picks it up, stares blankly, and lays it aside. "I don't have my glasses."

She doesn't need glasses to read, only for distance. She's delaying. Picking up her drink, she takes a swallow, and I watch the extended tendons in her neck move.

I take a deep, halting breath. "Lily, this is the yellow customer duplicate of a cashier's check. Byars paid J. Clyde Perkins to defend Robert Weldon. Do you know what this means?" I've never felt as if I wanted to die, but now I do. My insides are twisted into knots.

Head held high, she swivels slowly on the stool to face me. Her chin quivers slightly. "No, Byars didn't pay J. Clyde Perkins. I did."

This information slaps me at full force. The pieces have just flown from the puzzle I've constructed in my mind. Everything is a blur now. "You? Why?" I can't even imagine the answer.

Lily blinks. "Because Robert Weldon was once like a son to me. I did something bad to him, and it has haunted me all these years. Paying for his defense was the least I could do to try to make it up to him."

I close my eyes and wonder if the floor has opened up and I've fallen through to another world where nothing makes sense. I'm shaking again. First I thought Charles could be a murderer, involved with April Brown, killed her when threatened with exposure, then Byars hired a fine attorney to defend an innocent man. Then I thought Byars might be the guilty one. Now my mother tells me my death row client was like a son to her. This is certainly the sensitive information Weldon said I might uncover and would know how to handle. I think of the far-reaching consequences of this discovery. Mountainous. I can't imagine that Byars knows about this.

I round the bar. "Maybe I'd better have a drink and let you tell me about this." No wonder I gained such easy access to J. Clyde Perkins that day in his office. Tarsha requested an appointment for an L. Bingham. Perkins and his assistant were shocked to see Leona Bingham instead of Lily Bingham.

"I hoped you wouldn't ever know about this, Leona."

"Why did you keep that copy of the check?"

Lily bites her bottom lip. "To look at sometimes, to remind myself that I did do something for Weldon."

I spill ice trying to make a drink, and cubes scatter across the marble-top bar. Something Weldon told me strikes a chord. He said that if I found out certain information, I would know how to use it to his advantage, that it had to come from me, not him. What could that be? Tonight is the night for earth-shattering surprises. No wonder Weldon chose me for his lawyer.

I finally manage to get a drink together and ease onto the stool behind the bar, facing Lily. I take a sip of my drink, not sure that it will go down. "I'm ready for the story, Lily."

Obviously planning her words, Lily opens her mouth, ready to talk, but nothing comes out. This is painful for her. Finally, she recovers her voice. "Robert is the illegitimate son of my best friend from childhood, Claire Craig. Claire and I were just young girls. The boy she was involved with didn't want to marry her. He had other plans for his life. She didn't know where to turn. It was much more of a disgrace back in those days. Impossible to get an abortion except by a backstreet butcher who would probably kill you in the process. So she had Robert and, poor as she and I were, I told her I'd help raise him while I worked keeping books at the lumber mill over in Starkville . . ."

"What are you saying? Poor? I was always told you came from a rich family out in the hill country. Starkville. Your parents died and left you money." This *is* a night for revelations.

"Just let me go in order. That part comes later. When Robert was five, Claire got sick, leukemia. She was so worried about Robert's future. She was on her deathbed when I promised I'd look after him and I did, for a time."

Eyes with a faraway look, Lily sips her drink, lost in times past. "Byars came to the lumber mill to buy wood for some projects down here on the plantation. Oh, he was a striking man then, full of life. Rich. I don't deny that appealed to me." She looks at me, pleading for understanding clear in her face. "You don't know how it feels to be dirt poor, to have to scrape through life, afraid you might not eat next week. It's frightening, Leona. You don't know."

She sighs and continues. "Byars was smitten with me right from the minute he came into that office. He took me out to dinner that night at some little place over there. Not anything fancy in the hill country like here in the Delta. Worlds apart. Anyhow, I was going to tell him about Robert, but when he started talking about his life on the plantation, his family and all . . . well, I just couldn't bring myself to tell him right then. I knew it was a big step for him to even take out somebody like me with no background, much less a girl trying to raise an illegitimate boy.

"Things between Byars and me got more serious, but I kept putting off telling him about Robert, and then too much time had passed before I could get up the courage. He asked me to come here and meet his mother. I didn't have any proper clothes for such a visit, so he bought me some. You know how Mother Bingham was. Byars, too. It matters to them what others think, and when I got here for the visit she told everyone I was from this wealthy lumber mill family. She had already started polishing my rough edges, but I didn't know it then." She glances around at her fine surroundings. "This place was like a mecca to me, as you can imagine. I knew telling about Robert would end it all. Byars wouldn't have me if Robert was included in the package. The Weldons were relatives of his and I knew they'd take good care of him, so I left him with them. Robert clung to my knees that day, crying, begging me not to leave him. I said I'd come back for him. I intended to, but I never did. You came along and I had my family. I thought about him so much over the years, but when he showed up here to see me one day, I was scared. I didn't really know him. I thought he'd come to blackmail me or something, but he said he just wanted to see me this once and wouldn't intrude in my life again." A tear rolls down her cheek, and she brushes it away with a finger and sniffs.

"Funny thing, when I first came here as a bride, Byars gave me money to open an account, wanting to impress the banker we had back then 'cause he spread the word over town about everybody's finances. Everybody in town would know that I actually was independently wealthy if I deposited a hundred thousand dollars in the Grenola Bank. That was a lot of money back then. That's the money plus interest I used to pay for Robert's defense."

"Lily, now that I know, are you going to tell Byars the truth?"

She actually shudders. "That there's a convict up at Parchman on death row that was like a son to me? That I abandoned him for a good life here? Oh,

Lord, no. You know how Byars is. He'd never be the same. Nothing would. Please, Leona, don't tell him now. I hate that you know what I did. You must think I'm terrible." Her words are flooded with remorse.

We sit in silence, each with our private thoughts. I'm about to ask a question when she speaks.

"Leona, save Robert. Don't let him die."

"I want to more than anything in the world, Lily. I'm trying as hard as I can."

"I don't know him, Leona. I don't know the child I raised for a while, really. You don't think there's a chance he killed that girl, do you?"

"No, I believe he's innocent." I pause, wanting to ask the question I planned to ask a minute ago.

"Lily, tell me about Robert's father. Who is he?"

"Robert asked me the same question. I told him and I'll tell you now."

She tells me. I can't believe what I've heard, but I now know what I have to do.

14

I FIX BREAKFAST FOR BINGO AND DROP HIM AT
school, then head to my office. I need privacy. Thankfully, the group is sacked out, having worked far into
the night. When I returned home from Lily's, I simply walked past them without a word and closed my
bedroom door. I feel as if I've not slept at all, but I
know I must have dozed, in and out of fitful thoughts
and dreams.

Is this whole situation a conflict of interest? Lily
will go to her grave without revealing her secret to
Byars, and I must do the same. A second mystery is
now the most puzzling. Who has gone to such
lengths to dissuade me from continuing with the
case? April Brown's killer or someone who's afraid of
what I might uncover? Byars is a clever man and
might be aware of more than Lily suspects. It would
not be beyond belief that he had her past investigated
before they married and has known all along about

Robert Weldon. Was he trying to protect me from discovering that my mother abandoned a boy she promised to raise? And what danger still exists for me if the actual murderer believes I'm moving close to the truth? I believe I have now found a way to diffuse the threat, but will remain on guard until the case is concluded.

As planned, I beat Tarsha to the office. I feel as if I exist in some alien world. Yesterday I knew the boundaries of my life, my family's; now everything has changed, every facet viewed in a new light.

Looking up numbers I need, I make the telephone calls I've rehearsed. My voice is firm, unwavering, projecting a false demeanor. I achieve my goal more easily than expected. The first step toward a clemency hearing has been taken.

I leave a sealed note for Tarsha, outlining my plans and asking her to pick up Bingo if I'm not back when school ends, though I fully expect to be here. I will call later and check with her. I don't know what plans the legal group has or if they will return to Clarksdale after office hours today.

Briefcase in hand, I hurry back to the Bronco and hit the highway to Parchman. The storm has not yet arrived but is gathering momentum, ready to unleash its force on the thirsty, dry land. The sky is dark gray and ragged clouds hover ominously. I light a cigarette and think about facing Weldon for the first time as someone whose past is linked to my mother's. My mind is still boggled by the revelation. This conflict of interest now intrudes on how I handle his case.

My next stop after Parchman is the critical leg in

the journey to save Weldon. I hope I'm up to the challenge. Every word I utter must strike home with mega-strength.

I pass through the ritual at the gate and park by the law library. After each stage of entry that takes me further into the bowels of the penitentiary, I finally wait at the table for the guard to bring Weldon. My palms sweat, and the start of a headache clusters at the base of my skull. I rub my neck to relieve the tension. The room is crowded with busy prisoners at work to save their lives through some magic they expect to find in dog-eared law books. Coming off their bodies like noxious gases, the stench of unwashed bodies mixed with the odor of fear seems more pronounced today.

I jump when the door opens and Weldon is ushered in by the guard. The sight of him in shackles has much more of an impact now. The guard releases the arm and leg irons and chains him to the loop embedded in the floor. As usual, he manages to maintain his dignity throughout the ordeal.

Leaning his strong forearms on the table, he claps his hands together. His fingers are long and graceful, like those of an artist. His fingernails are clean and cut short. He looks at me expectantly yet hesitantly, wanting to hear good news yet afraid to hope. "Leona, I read about Judge Allen's denial in federal court. What about the Fifth Circuit?"

"I've already been before them for oral arguments, a three-judge panel. They haven't handed down their ruling, but I felt my claims were well received, especially by Judge Nabors. J. Clyde Perkins was there to hear my claim of ineffectual counsel." I pause, swallowing the lump in my throat. "Robert, I know who paid him."

His cheeks color slightly, but he remains quiet, his eyes steady on me. He pulls the glasses from his pocket and carefully fits the wire frames behind his ears. This scene will be permanently etched into his mind, as it will be into mine. I think how divergent our lives have been, how a twist of fate has carried us in different directions.

"I had a long talk with my mother last night." My words sound so foreign, as if they come from a mouth other than mine.

"I didn't lie to you, Leona. I suspected she paid, but she never told me that. For all I knew, Perkins could have taken the case pro bono. Some lawyers do. I've had no contact with her since that day I went to see her right after I first moved to Grenola. I watched Mrs. Bingham for weeks before I ever approached her . . . that big house, the husband, family and all. I don't want to hurt her or cause her embarrassment. I just wanted to talk to her, just once. I loved her so when I was little. She's a pretty lady."

"Yes, I've always thought Lily was pretty." My voice quavers like an old woman's.

"Lily? You call her Lily?"

I nod with a smile. I feel awkward with him now. There are so many things he doesn't know about us. "I can understand now why you wouldn't tell me what I might uncover. As you said, I could have proceeded with the case and never have found out."

His eyes never leave mine. "How did you?"

I tell him about Bingo finding the duplicate of the cashier's check in the desk from Lily's attic. "I asked Lily why she kept it, and she said that she wanted a reminder that she'd done something for you in life." Hot tears well in my eyes, and I struggle to keep them from falling.

He reaches across the table and places his hand on mine. Alerted, a guard quickly takes notice. Prisoners are not allowed physical contact with visitors. Weldon withdraws his hand immediately. I want to hug him, and maybe one day I can.

"Robert, I can also now understand all the ramifications of what you said at our first meeting about how this information I might find must come from me, not you."

"I never wanted to hurt anyone." He blinks back tears.

"I know. At great risk to yourself you kept quiet. Not many people would do that. I admire you for it. Lily begged me not to let you die. I believe there's only one way to save you now." I tell him about my plan.

He stares at me, blood draining from his face.

"Now I just have to convince Governor Danforth. We're not getting any breaks in the investigation, and this is all that's left." I check my watch. "I'd better get moving. Wish me luck. Maybe we'll have a chance to get to know each other."

Tears fill his eyes now. He turns before I can witness a sob.

I cruise down Capitol Street toward the domed capitol building dead ahead. To my left is the governor's mansion, and I think about the imposing man who hopes to continue to occupy that residence despite the competition from the A.G. Governor Danforth has the power to perform miracles for death row inmates, and I intend to turn him into Houdini.

I park in the visitors lot adjacent to the capitol building. The wind whips my skirt, and I stabilize it with my briefcase to keep from being exposed outside the hallowed seat of government. I capture my hair with my other hand. It's wild enough without help. Forging up the many rows of steps, I pass beneath the columned entry and enter the cavernous marble lobby.

I find a rest room on the first floor and freshen up. I look at my image in the mirror. Early this morning I dressed for this moment of reckoning, linen suit the color of tobacco, shoes and bag to match, gold necklace and earrings to create an illusion of power. This is not a time for the fainthearted. "Go get 'em," I say to my reflection. A woman comes out of a stall, and I hurry through the door before she can catch a glimpse of someone who talks to herself.

The federal-style molding around the massive double doors is carved walnut, with the governor's name inscribed in gold. I turn a heavy brass knob the size of an artichoke and enter his sanctuary. A prim older woman with flashes of gray hair at her temples and half-lens reading glasses perched far down on her nose presides over the area from a gigantic mahogany desk, her command post. Two highway patrolmen sit stiffly in leather wingback chairs at the far end of the paneled room. The Mississippi state flag and the

American flag hang on stanchions flanking another door as massive and impressive as the front one; only this one bears an embossed gold seal of the state of Mississippi.

"Yes?" The woman looks over her glasses at me. For some reason this reminds me of the day I so naively went to J. Clyde Perkins's office. I was admitted there so easily because they expected another L. Bingham. I was granted an emergency appointment here because I represent a man who is shortly scheduled for execution.

"Leona Bingham, to see Governor Danforth."

"About scheduling the clemency hearing." She opens a huge wine-colored leather book the size of a pillow. "Governor Danforth's assistant will be right out." She punches a button under her desk. "After you talk with him and the governor, I can set up the date. Obviously it will have to be soon."

A young man in a navy blue suit with hair cut so closely, light bounces off his scalp materializes from around the corner. I recognize him from the last encounter with Governor Danforth at the federal court building in Judge Allen's office. He has a feral look, pointy teeth, and beady eyes. Old acne scars pepper his cheeks and neck.

"Max McLendon." He offers his small pink hand and gives me a bone-crushing shake he's probably perfected for campaign rallies. "If you'll follow me, we'll get a few things out of the way before you speak to Governor Danforth. He's going to be held up in conference for a while. Sends his apologies for making you wait."

I follow him to a small reception room filled with fake Sheraton furniture. The paintings of local scenes are genuine, but I'd discourage the artist from aspiring to a New York opening. We sit in a cozy grouping, knees almost touching. I cross my legs to avoid contact.

He takes a gold Mark Cross pen and a small memo pad from his breast pocket. "I understand that you've asked for a closed hearing rather than an open one."

I nod. A death row inmate, in most states, is entitled to a clemency hearing, but in Mississippi the matter is discretionary. No governor in his right mind would refuse to grant a clemency hearing. The power of the press is too great.

"How many witnesses do you anticipate bringing?"

"I'm not quite sure at this point." I glance around for an ashtray. "Am I allowed to smoke in here?"

"Oh, no, not in any state buildings, but I can ring for some coffee, Perrier, or a soft drink, if you'd like."

"No, thank you."

"Now, we understand the urgency for this hearing. So, when would you like to schedule it?"

"Actually, I'm not sure about that either, not until I've spoken with Governor Danforth privately."

"Well, someone for the state will, of course, testify. It's customary for the victim's family to be present for such a hearing. The crime will be discussed at length. You'd probably want someone from the prison to testify to what kind of prisoner your client has been." He hesitates. "I must remind you that a clemency hearing is an effort in futility on everyone's part if you do not have something new to add to your client's case."

"I understand."

"Any information you have to present must be overwhelmingly positive in your client's favor. If your additions to his case are thin, without substantial basis, or open to interpretation by the state, too many inmates and their lawyers would be on the governor's back asking why he can't grant clemency to their clients if he did for another. In other words, the governor must remain steadfast under the state laws that bind his decisions." He poises his pen over the pad. "Now, just what type of new material do you have to bring before the governor?"

I'm not duty bound to reveal anything yet and he knows it. He figures I'm like most lawyers who are bursting with newfound information to help their clients and can't wait to air it. "At this time I'm not prepared to discuss it."

He slaps the pad shut and puts away the pen. "Certainly, your prerogative." He stands and brushes imaginary lint on his suit. "Make yourself comfortable, and I'll come and get you when Governor Danforth is free." He glances at his gold watch. "Shouldn't be too long."

I wait nearly an hour, and the longer I sit the more nervous I grow. In anticipation of speaking with Governor Danforth, I willed an imaginary steel rod to run through my body and mind, but that mythical reinforcement is disintegrating by the second. How long is this going to take?

I go out to the prim lady at the front desk and ask if there's a phone I can use. She directs me to one down the hall on a small table and explains how to get an outside line. Sitting in a straight chair, I give the building's operator my office number and reverse the charges.

"Tarsha, did you get my note?"

"Yeah, so you're talking to the governor? What about?"

I glance around. "I'll tell you later. Is the group there?"

"Worked all morning. Went to Clarksdale a little while ago. They'll be back at your house sometime tonight."

"I'm running late. You can pick up Bingo for me?"

"Actually, Ray Bell's going to do it. I'm supposed to go to my niece's birthday party. He and Wilma Ruth dropped by earlier, and Ray Bell said he'll pick up Bingo and take him to a cattle auction he's going to over in Cleveland. He thought Bingo might enjoy it. Thing doesn't start until late afternoon after everybody quits work, so he won't have Bingo home till after supper."

"That's fine. The way things are going with the governor, the drive home in bad weather, I probably won't get back so early myself. Did Ray Bell have anything new? Anything about the Fletchers?"

"No, he didn't, but he's working on it. Listen, a woman called and insisted she had to talk to you, said it was urgent. I told her you were in Jackson at the governor's office. She said she lived in Jackson and would try to see you."

"Did she give a name?"

"Yeah, just a sec, got it written down here. Sybil Cooper."

The name vaguely rings a bell, then it dawns on me with full force. Sybil Cooper, I remember from the trial transcript, was the woman who took the stand and embarrassed Ray Bell by testifying she and he were in the backseat of his car and he couldn't have seen a man running through the woods right after April Brown's murder. Why is it urgent for her to speak with me? "Did she leave a number?"

"No, she didn't. Just said she'd try to get in touch."

A flash of apprehension hits me. "Were Ray Bell and Wilma Ruth there when she called?"

"Ah, let me think. Yeah, I believe so. No, wait. Ray Bell had already gone outside, but Wilma Ruth was unloading some gingerbread and brownies she made for the lawyer group. Should I have called Ray Bell in and let him talk to the woman?"

"Did Wilma Ruth know she called? I mean, did you say her name over the telephone?"

"Well . . . ah, yes. I asked how to spell Sybil. I might have repeated her last name as I wrote it. Why? Anything wrong?"

I have a strange, uneasy feeling. "Tarsha, remember from the trial transcripts? Sybil Cooper was Ray Bell's lover, the one who discredited his testimony."

"Oh, Lord. What could she want?"

"I don't know. Maybe she'll turn up here." I return the receiver to the base and try to sort out my thoughts.

"Oh, Miz Bingham?"

Max, the governor's assistant, scurries toward me. "Governor Danforth has a break now and can see you. Please follow me."

He leads me to Governor Danforth's office, opens the door with the gold seal of the state of Mississippi, and stands aside as I step into the spacious room. Governor Robert Danforth rises from behind a large partner's desk littered with papers and files.

"Please come in. Have a seat." He gestures to the green leather chairs scattered before his desk.

The gray plush carpet is so thick I feel as if I'm walking through water. The heavy gray linen draperies on the tall windows enhance the dark wood paneling. Floor-to-ceiling built-in book shelves occupy two walls. A seating arrangement—a gray leather couch, two club chairs, a coffee table, and end tables with brass lamps—occupy one end of the room. I suspect more casual meetings take place there. I am seated in the serious business section by his desk.

I focus on Governor Danforth's high widow's peak, his intense smoky gray eyes. He smiles, aware of my scrutiny, well aware of the effect of his charisma on his constituents. He sits erect in his chair, smartly attired in a dark suit and striped tie over a crisp white shirt, gold knotted cuff links peeking from under his coat sleeve.

He clasps his hands, forearms on the edge of the desk. "So, I understand you came to talk about a clemency hearing for your client, Robert Weldon."

I take a deep fortifying breath and hold his attention for a long moment. "Well, actually no. I just said that to get a private appointment with you."

His eyebrows lift and a look of slight alarm crosses his face. I wonder if he entertains calling in a security guard. "Beg pardon? I don't understand?"

"You will, sir. I'll make it perfectly clear. I did come here to discuss Robert Weldon."

He relaxes to a degree, but his expression is intense. "Well, continue."

"My death row client, Robert Weldon, is innocent, and I know a way to prove it with your authorization."

He's visibly irritated now that a rookie has come on false pretenses to waste his time. "Miz Bingham—"

I interrupt. "Governor Danforth, remember a young girl from your past . . . Claire Craig?"

His eyes turn to ice. "What in the world are you saying?"

"I'm asking if you remember Claire Craig."

He glances toward the door. "I don't recall anyone by that name."

Staring at him, I let the silence lengthen, let him suffer. "I think you do."

He grabs the armrests on his chair so hard his knuckles turn white. "If you've come here to blackmail me—"

"No, I haven't come for that. Nothing of the kind. That's why I asked for a private interview. Lily Lyon is my mother, Mrs. Byars Bingham. She was, as you'll recall, Claire's best friend. Claire's dead. Died when her son and yours was five. My mother promised she'd raise the child, but she didn't, left him with his relatives. So, I have no reason to go public with this."

Leaning back in his chair, he runs his hands over

his face, as if washing without water. "It was always in the back of my mind that this might surface one day. It's been so long I was beginning to feel safe."

I'm ready to deal the blow. "Governor Danforth, my client, Robert Weldon, is your son, and I've come to see that you help him."

"Robert Weldon? My son? God, my God! Oh, no." Knowing I now have the power to destroy him, he moans to himself and appears on the verge of tears. The stakes are high. If this becomes general knowledge, his reputation will be in shreds, public and personal life in ruin. Attorney General Flannery will surely become the next governor.

Stricken, he looks at me with those same smoky gray eyes of Robert's. "My son on death row. What irony."

"My mother secretly hired J. Clyde Perkins to defend Weldon. I found out only yesterday. I came across the duplicate of the cashier's check she paid Perkins, one hundred and twenty-five thousand dollars. My mother said she saved it as a reminder that she did something in life for the boy she abandoned."

He's pained, his face a mass of wrinkles. "I never knew that Claire died. She said she wanted to raise the child herself, and I moved away from Starkville. I never knew if the baby was a boy or a girl. I've always wondered about them."

"This has touched all of us." I tell him verbatim what Lily told me. I pull a cigarette from my purse and light it. I don't think he's going to tell me to put it out. "My mother and I will go to our graves with the secret—"

"But what about Robert Weldon . . . Robert?" He says the word as if tasting it for the first time.

"He could have told me from the start, but he didn't want to hurt anyone. You are his father, and I guess blood is thicker than you think. Besides, it would have paralyzed you from helping him. He was smart not to start talking. Think about it. How could you help him, play favoritism, if it came to light he was your son? Your hands would be tied, but now they aren't."

He sits erect, recovering to a degree now that he sees a way out of this tangled web. "Why do you think so strongly that he's innocent?"

I drag on my cigarette, and he produces an ashtray from his drawer. "You don't know about all of this, what's happened to me since I took on the case. All along somebody has been trying to get me to drop the case." I take him through the entire sequence of events in a slow, laborious manner, making sure every point sinks into his mind. Then I review the evidence in Weldon's trial, areas where he could have been framed, the discrepancy about his car, his coat, the knives.

When I finish, we look at each other in silence. He rises from the desk, goes to the window and, with his back to me, stares out at the rain pelting the city.

"I have very little space in which I can maneuver in this situation without arousing public interest." His shoulders slump. "What is it you want me to authorize?

I've got him. My heart kicks like a wild horse. "When Robert was arrested, DNA was in its infancy.

A test on the fetus and a blood test for Robert could have proven right away that he was not the father of April Brown's child. I've spoken with the doctor who did the autopsy. He said that a casket is a cold storage for evidence. That test can be done now, even at this late date, by exhuming her body with the victim's family's permission or by a court order. I think I could get April Brown's mother's consent, but I know you can get a court order and have arrangements made at Parchman for a blood test. After all these years they've just done a DNA test on blood left at the scene that posthumously cleared Dr. Sam Sheppard of his wife's murder—the doctor that the series *The Fugitive* was based on. Even a past president, Taylor, I believe, was exhumed to test if he was poisoned. You have the power to make it happen by simply stating that I've convinced you that the testing is warranted."

He turns from the window, a curious smile on his lips. "Yes, I believe you have."

I'm bursting with satisfaction. "Then you'll set the legal wheels in motion?"

"Immediately, but not without raising some political and legal smoke. Still, I'll work through that."

"Thank you, Governor Danforth. Like my mother, you'll always have a reminder that you did something in life for your son."

"Young lady, you've done the most for him . . . for Robert. I'll be in touch with you right away."

Leaving his office, I stop by the front desk and ask if someone has tried to reach me. I can't imagine why Sybil Cooper wants to talk to me.

"Yes," the prim lady answers. "As a matter of fact, a woman called and asked if you were here; then she came, said she'd wait outside for you."

I dash out the front door of the capitol building and spot a lone woman in a dark raincoat hovering close to a column. Her hair beneath a plastic cap is bleached a freaky shade of platinum, eyes exaggerated by too much mascara and black liner. The belted coat shows a voluptuous figure, and shiny black boots encase shapely legs. We lock eyes, and she steps forward.

"Leona Bingham? I recognize you from the papers." Her voice is husky but laced with tension. "I'm Sybil Cooper. I know you must know who I am. I need to talk to you." She glances around uneasily, clutching her purse.

"My car is in the parking lot." I motion with my head. "We can talk there."

Dashing through the rain and strong wind, we take refuge in the Bronco. The odor of wet clothes and her perfume permeates the close confines of the car. Apprehensive about what I'm about to hear, I light a cigarette. Sybil Cooper has busy hands, pushing her hair into place, brushing water off her face, smoothing her raincoat across her lap. She's as rattled as anyone I've ever seen. Whatever she has to tell is costing her.

"So, what is it you want to talk to me about?"

She twists her purse straps around her hand. "I know I have a bad reputation in Grenola. That's why I left town and moved here. So you may not believe what I have to say. It's just bothered me so much over the years. Then it kind of faded from my mind. After reading so much in the papers lately about you and Robert Weldon's case . . . well, I just have to get it off my chest. See, I figured back then he was probably guilty, so what I did didn't bother me so much, but now, reading your quotes and all about how he's innocent and how you're trying to save him from being executed, that Ray Bell Crosby is working for you—I just had to come forward, even if it means I'll be prosecuted and maybe face jail."

My pulse pounds in my temples, my body rigid with tension. "Go on."

She takes a deep breath and holds it, then explodes with the words: "I lied on the witness stand."

I'm stunned. Ideas ignite in my mind. Immediate legal grounds for a new trial. Overwhelming evidence to warrant Governor Danforth to authorize the DNA test without any political discomfort to him. When I finish with Sybil Cooper, I'll race back to his office with the news.

Her sad eyes implore me. "You must think I'm the worst slime on earth."

I want to shout, "That couldn't be further from the truth. You just put my world together with that confession." My jubilation is suddenly punctured with the realization of what her perjured testimony might concern. "What exactly did you lie about?"

She looks out the window at the raindrops creeping down the glass. "I wasn't with Ray Bell that afternoon, like I said I was."

Alarms clang in my head. All of a sudden I notice the ring she twists on her finger, a Hot Springs diamond, exactly like the one April Brown owned.

"I hadn't been with Ray Bell in a long time. He dumped me. Like to broke my heart. Dumped me for April Brown."

The words stab like arrows.

"Then when she was murdered, Ray Bell came to me, frantic somebody would find out he'd been going with April and accuse him of killing her. He begged me to get in touch with the D.A. and tell him I was with Ray Bell. I still cared about Ray Bell, and he can be so convincing. I did it, hoping we'd get back together, but that didn't happen. After the trial was over, he walked away from me. He knew he'd bought my silence with the threat of jail."

Ray Bell murdered April Brown. No wonder he was so defensive when I asked if he knew her. I should have caught it then, but I was too busy suspecting my own cousin. He's been behind all that's happened to me. Wilma Ruth knows Sybil Cooper called my office this morning, wanting to talk. I pray she didn't mention it to Ray Bell. But if she did, he knows both Sybil Cooper and I are in Jackson. *He has my son.* All of the life has been sucked from me. I have to regain control and gear for action. I hand her a piece of paper and pencil. She writes her address and phone number.

"Please, I have to go." I switch on the engine. "I have to get home. I'll be in touch."

I almost drive away before she exits the car. Swinging out of the parking lot, I gun the engine and maneuver around late-afternoon downtown traffic. I think about stopping at a service station to call someone to help. Who? Help how? Have Charles or Jack drive to a cattle auction somewhere in Cleveland and wrest Bingo from Ray Bell's clutches? That would alert him, back him into a corner, maybe cause a hostage situation. Call Chief Lewis and have Ray Bell arrested on the basis of what some woman in Jackson said? No way. I need her deposition or a direct confession to Chief Lewis for him to arrest Ray Bell. I have to think. I have to plan. How stupid I've been to hire a murderer as my investigator. He's clever. Insinuating himself into the case to have firsthand knowledge of the progress.

High winds and rain buffet my car as I speed down the highway. My arms ache from trying to right the swaying vehicle and hold it steady. I can't believe I've brought the case to the brink of success, only to have my son endangered because of that triumph. I have to make this work out right. I can't bear to think of the consequences if something goes wrong. My soul is bleeding. The only hope I have to cling to is that Wilma Ruth didn't mention the call to Ray Bell.

After an hour and a half of raw agony, I skid into my driveway. I race toward the dark house. Thunder roars like a battery of cannons, and lightning rips through the sky, for an instant turning night into day. My hand shakes as I fumble to unlock the door. Relocking it, I fly through the house, littered with sleeping bags, satchels, and the group's belongings, to the telephone in the kitchen, flicking on lights as I go. I'll call Jack and Charles and Byars. They'll know what to do, how to help. I wonder if I trust Wilma Ruth enough to warn her Ray Bell is a murderer and that she and Bingo could be in danger. She cares about Bingo and might be able to get him away from Ray Bell without suspicion. Nothing works, though, if Ray Bell suspects I've talked with Sybil Cooper.

Picking up the receiver, I start to punch in numbers when I realize the phone is dead. The storm has likely downed a tree on the lines. Thank God the electrical power is operating. I stare at the useless telephone, then jam it back into place. Pacing back and forth, I try to arrive at a quick decision. I can't leave on the off chance that Wilma Ruth didn't tell Ray Bell about the call and he will bring Bingo back here and find no one home. I need someone here if and when he comes, especially if he knows about the call. If he isn't aware of the call, Bingo will be out of danger and I can nail Ray Bell tomorrow.

A flash of headlights through the front windows and the slam of car doors grab my attention. My heart hammers hard. I pray the legal group has arrived. My legs are riveted to the floor, but I know I must move. It could be Ray Bell with Bingo. If he suspects Sybil Cooper was able to contact me in Jackson, or if he figures she didn't but will persist until she does, he'll kill Bingo and me while we're alone here and isolated from the world. I hear a key in the front door lock. The group has a key. Taking care of Bingo as much as they have, Wilma Ruth and Ray Bell have keys, thanks to my ignorance.

"Mom? Mom?" Bingo calls.

I glance around for some sort of a weapon, a knife, anything to save us, in case he knows. An aerosol can of hair spray Karen has left on the kitchen counter could sting his eyes painfully and throw him off guard, but only temporarily. Then what? Could I stab him? I eye my knives in the wooden holder. Just as I remove the top from the hairspray can, Bingo and Ray Bell enter the kitchen.

"Hi, Mom."

Ray Bell's smile is wide and friendly. "Howdy, Leona. We got back earlier than I thought."

I collect myself so as not to allow the panic to filter into my voice. "Hi. I thought you were my legal group." I look at my watch. "They'll be back any minute now." How I wish that were true.

Eyes on Ray Bell, I pull Bingo toward me and hug him close. "We had a good time. Ray Bell bought a heifer at the auction and let me raise my hand to up the bid. He would have bought some more, but all the lights went out in the place 'cause of the storm and we had to leave." He makes sounds like an auctioneer, and Ray Bell laughs.

"Old Bingo's a real pro now. He'll be wanting to start his own herd in your back pasture."

My heart is settling into normalcy. We are going to survive. Ray Bell doesn't know about Sybil Cooper's call. Or he's giving a good performance. I know from experience what an actor he is. I'll have to deliver an even better performance, but I can't let down my guard. We are in the room with a man capable of any kind of violence, including cutting off a dog's head.

"Have you eaten, Bingo? Maybe you'd like a snack."

He touches his stomach. "I'm about to bust. Ray Bell and I had hamburgers and fries and some barbecue, too."

"Well, then why don't you run on upstairs and do your homework so you can play a little chess with Billy Boyer when he gets here."

"I dropped my backpack in the living room." Bingo runs out of the room and bounds up the stairs.

"Anything new from Jackson? You really shot off fast down there today. What's up?" Ray Bell asks, leaning against the refrigerator.

I put defeat into my words. "The group thought it was the right thing to do. We talked long and hard about it last night. I'm preparing for a clemency hearing with the governor as a last resort. We might not prevail in the courts, and the investigation hasn't turned up anything. It might be the only way to save Weldon's life, but I don't think the governor is going to grant clemency. So, the situation ain't good." I edge toward the counter, within grabbing distance of my pitiful weapons. Lighting a cigarette as casually as I can, I will my hands not to shake. "I went to Parchman to tell Weldon, then drove straight to Jackson to the governor's office, talked to him, then hit the road home. My trip in a nutshell."

"That's too bad." His expression, the sympathetic spin on his words, are Oscar caliber. I can easily see how someone could fall under his spell. "You look tired, but keyed up, too." He pushes away from the wall. "I'd better get going and let you get some rest. On top of everything else you've had a long drive in bad weather. Maybe things will look better tomorrow." He gives me a two-finger salute and heads to the front door. "I'll lock up."

I stand in the kitchen until I hear the door close

and the lock click. Only when he drives away do I go check the lock. A terrible thought flashes through my mind. If he thinks Sybil Cooper and I haven't made contact, which I believe now he does, but knows she's called, anxious to talk, then he has to silence her before she reaches me. He could be heading to Jackson at this moment. I have to warn her, and we have to get out of the house for the night.

I race up the stairs and into Bingo's room. He's seated at his desk, reading a book. "Bingo, get some clothes together for school tomorrow. Pack your satchel with what you need. And hurry. We're going to Uncle Charles and Aunt Estelle's for the night." I hear the urgency, the near panic in my voice.

He jerks around, light from the lamp slashing across his face. "Is something wrong, Mom?"

"I'll tell you about it later. Just get ready."

I hurry to my room, grab a gown, robe, and throw a few toilet articles into an old paper shopping bag. As I descend the stairs a sense of foreboding grips me. I feel a presence in the house, a vague notion that all of the air has been sucked from the place and replaced with something evil. Has Ray Bell returned? Is he hiding, lying in wait? I try to discount my fears as an overactive imagination, born in so many rapidly developing events.

Setting my sack at the foot of the stairs, I go into the kitchen and stop dead in my tracks. Wilma Ruth is sitting at the kitchen table, one hand buried deep into her tote bag. For an instant I can't fathom what is happening here. Her eyes are so bright they appear to burn in her face. She radiates a sense of malice. So many shocks have buffeted me in the last twenty-four hours, but this almost fells me. "Wilma Ru—"

Before I can utter her name, she speaks in a hoarse, menacing voice. "You're trying to take Ray Bell away from me just like the others, and I won't let you."

"What are you saying?" Does she think I'm interested in him?

"Get him locked away for April Brown's murder. You talked to Sybil Cooper and you know."

"Sybil Cooper? No, no, I haven't talked to anyone by that name." I desperately try to imagine what kind of weapon she has in her bag. A knife or a gun?

"If you're not lying, you certainly will talk to her, and Ray Bell will be in trouble."

The view of the stairway is clear from the kitchen, and any moment Bingo will walk down and into the frightening situation. I have to reason with her. "Wilma Ruth, let's talk. You don't want to get yourself in trouble because of Ray Bell. The legal group will be coming in any minute."

She breaks into a crooked smile. Her teeth shine in the light, turning her into something satanic. "No, they won't. They're going to have car trouble on the way home. I fixed their van just like I repaired Robert Weldon's car to make him look guilty—framed him, took his coat, planted the kitchen knives, and took one."

"You?" She's gone to great lengths to protect a murderer and willing to go further. I'm fixed on the stairway, expecting Bingo's chubby legs to appear, pumping down the steps. Any moment now. The imminent danger we face sears my mind. Cold perspiration gathers under my arms and rolls down my skin.

Wilma Ruth's threatening tone continues: "Ray Bell and Bingo won't be back from that auction until later. And when they do get here, they'll find you dead."

She doesn't know Bingo is already here, but when he comes down she'll have to deal with him, too. My mind refuses to carry the thought to its awful conclusion. I'm standing rigid as a statue. I have to do something quick.

"I'll have to kill Sybil Cooper, too."

"I thought you cared about Bingo. You'd let him come home and find me?" Where is he? Why hasn't he come downstairs?

Her face almost softens. "I do care about him. Poor boy will be an orphan. None of your fancy folks would want him. Ray Bell and I, we'll take him. He'll be *our* son. We'll be a family. And nobody can take Ray Bell from me then." Her hands move deeper into her bag, gripping something. "At first I thought you and Ray Bell might hook up. He always had an eye for the women, first one, then another, Sybil Cooper included, but he always came back to me. April Brown was different, though. He fell for her. He was actually going to leave me and run off to California with her. Imagine that! Leave me for a pregnant nigger gal." Her expression hardens. "I listened to them talk and plan on the phone. Then, that day, I called the beauty shop where she worked and left a message for her to be at their meeting spot out by Four Mile Lake earlier than they'd planned."

I had thought she was only protecting Ray Bell.

The sudden realization that she, not Ray Bell, is the killer hits me with full force. Ray Bell was actually trying to find April Brown's murderer when he was looking at her every day.

I hear a noise, maybe only a creak of the house, but I'm afraid to look toward the hall, thinking absurdly that my eyes are holding Wilma Ruth in place and if I take them off her, she'll surge forward with a weapon. With as little motion as possible I ease toward the counter and the aerosol can.

"I got there before the nigger did, waited for her. When she came, I crept up that ravine to the tree where she was standing and stabbed her. It was me Robert Weldon and Ray Bell saw running through the woods."

I feel as if some giant fist has slammed down my esophagus, blocking my speech. "Weren't you afraid when Ray Bell came on the scene he'd be implicated?" I'm almost to the counter, and she hasn't noticed. Where is Bingo? I have to save us.

"No. Ray Bell was a policeman. Nobody knew about him and April, but Sybil Cooper and me. I knew she wouldn't tell, crazy as she still was about Ray Bell. She knew he wouldn't kill anybody." Her smile is maniacal. "My Ray Bell's clever. Got her to get up on the stand and lie." She laughs. "I didn't know he was going to do that. Surprised the hell out of me. Got to hand it to him."

"You killed April, framed Weldon, then killed Babaloo Brown. Three people . . ."

"I got afraid Babaloo might know something. I had to."

"And all the things you did to me."

"Had to. But I didn't kill the dog. I'd never do that. Probably Ronnie Fletcher or one of those demonstrators did such a bad thing."

I realize just how crazy she is. I edge closer to the counter.

"I thought it was all going away, but you just wouldn't stop on the case. Now see where it's got you." She makes a jerky move.

Startling both of us, a clap of thunder rattles the windows. Just as I grab the can, the lights go out. In pitch black I aim where I think her eyes are and press. She screams and I hear something thud on the floor. Her bag with the weapon. I have to get it before she can.

When the lights flash on, I blink, ready to lunge for the bag. My brain cannot accept the message my eyes send. I'm numb. Chief Lewis and his deputy, Godfrey, are standing in the kitchen, guns drawn and pointed at Wilma Ruth. Pained, she digs at her eyes, rubbing furiously, then shrinks into herself, suddenly aware of the officers. Picking up her bag, Godfrey slaps handcuffs on her. She screams, "I didn't kill the dog."

I'm torn in every direction, relieved yet wired from the ordeal and wilted from tension. "Where's Bingo? How did you know to come?"

"He's outside, waiting in our car."

"I still don't understand."

"Bingo heard you and Wilma Ruth from the stairwell. He knew he'd be seen if he came down the stairs, so he climbed down the trellis, slipped into the living room, and called nine-one-one. The sheriff picked it up and radioed us."

"How could he call? The lines are out."

"He knew Billy Boyer, one of your legal buddies, had a cellular in his duffel bag." He glances at Godfrey. "Go get the boy before we take the prisoner out to the car." He turns to me with a wide smile. "Well, Leona, looks like it's all over."

I shake my head. "No, Chief, it's just beginning."

CLARION-LEDGER
JACKSON, MISSISSIPPI

DEATH ROW INMATE FREED

Gary Marshall
STAFF WRITER

JACKSON—Regaining his freedom has been a long, hard battle, but Robert Weldon has finally traded his red prison jumpsuit for a coat and tie. Only weeks before his execution date Weldon was granted a full pardon by Governor Danforth, who greeted the former inmate with a handshake on the steps of the governor's mansion before a group of well-wishers, including Mississippi state Attorney General Jack Flannery Sr., members of the Mississippi Appellate Project, and Weldon's crusading attorney, Leona Bingham Flannery, now Attorney General Flannery's daughter-in-law.

Weldon was tried and convicted of first-degree murder in the stabbing death of April

Brown of Grenola six years ago. He was represented pro bono by the famed attorney J. Clyde Perkins. Subsequently, state-appointed attorneys handled Weldon's appeals to the higher courts. It was not until Leona Bingham Flannery came into the picture that the case took on another twist.

Wilma Ruth Crosby, wife of Leona Bingham Flannery's former investigator, has been charged with first-degree murder in the deaths of April Brown and her brother, Bob Brown. After her arrest Mrs. Crosby confessed to the slayings, and attorneys from the Buchanan firm in Grenola have entered a plea of insanity on her behalf.

Weldon was questioned about any animosity he might hold against the attorney general of Mississippi, the former district attorney who successfully prosecuted him in the trial. "No, he was just doing his job," Weldon answered. When asked if he intended to file a wrongful incarceration suit against the state Weldon was quoted as saying, "I'm not inclined to pursue it. I've had my fill of dealing with the legal system, but I will accede to my lawyer's wishes and advice."

Leona Bingham Flannery, who is currently in negotiations with several major Hollywood studios for the rights to Weldon's story, was asked about her intentions concerning a suit. "No comment," was her reply.